HEART AND HOME

Cathie Kinrade is all too used to hardship. Growing up on the Isle of Man in the 1930s, she sees her da set sail daily on dangerous seas while her mam struggles to put food on the table. Cathie has little hope for her own future, until a chance encounter changes her fortunes for ever. Fiercely determined, Cathie leaves for Liverpool, a bustling city full of possibility. With a lively job as a shop girl in a grand department store, and a firm friend in kind-hearted Julia, Cathie has found her niche. But the discovery of an explosive secret could put everything at risk. And when love comes calling, Cathie's new friends fear that she may be set to trust the wrong man with her heart...

HEART AND HOME

HEART AND HOME

by

Lyn Andrews

Magna Large Print Books
Long Preston, North Yorkshire,
BD23 4ND, England.

British Library Cataloguing in Publication Data.

Andrews, Lyn
   Heart and home.

   A catalogue record of this book is
   available from the British Library

   ISBN   978-0-7505-4309-5

First published in Great Britain in 2015 by
Headline Publishing Group

Copyright © Lyn Andrews 2015

Cover illustration © Ildiko Neer by arrangement with
Arcangel Images Ltd.

The right of Lyn Andrews to be identified as the author of this work
has been asserted by her in accordance with the Copyright, Designs
and Patents Act, 1988.

Published in Large Print 2016 by arrangement with
Headline Publishing Group Ltd.

Magna Large Print is an imprint of Library Magna Books Ltd.

Printed and bound in Great Britain by
T.J. (International) Ltd., Cornwall, PL28 8RW

Acknowledgements

For Rodger and Stephanie Corkhill and Michael Cleague, our wonderful accountants, who, with infinite patience, deal with our many queries and who have become more than just professional acquaintances. And for Ken and Sharon Devaney and the staff at the Harbour Bistro, Ramsey, who make our visits there so enjoyable.

My thanks also to Anne Williams, my agent, Marion Donaldson, my editor, and the entire staff of Headline Publishing Group who work so hard on my behalf.

Lyn Andrews
Ballaugh
2015

Chapter One

1933

'Mam, I won't do it! I *won't!*' As she faced her mother Cathie Kinrade's cheeks were flushed and her dark eyes flashed with mutinous determination. She was small and slight for her age – she had just turned fifteen – and the faded paisley print dress, being two years old now and too short for her, added to the illusion that she was still only a child. That was something Cathie herself would have realised was no longer true even if both her parents had not impressed upon her that, having left school, her childhood was behind her and from now on she must earn a living and contribute to the household.

Lizzie Kinrade sighed heavily and looked up from the kitchen table where she had just finished rolling out the pastry for the pie she was making for supper. She wiped her hands on her stained cotton apron and looked with annoyance at her eldest daughter. 'Cathie, don't start on that again! You have to get work, and what else is there here in Ramsey for the likes of us?' Her gaze strayed around her small kitchen, which, apart from the tiny scullery, was the only room on the ground floor of the stone cottage where she and Barney had lived all their married life. It opened directly on to the street and was both kitchen and living room. They had only the essentials in the way of furniture – which was just as well, she thought; when they were all at home you could barely move. Upstairs there were two small bedrooms; the minuscule yard at the back contained the ramshackle privy, a tin bath hanging on a nail in the wall and her washing tub. It was all they could afford and although with six children it was definitely overcrowded she considered herself fortunate that she had a good, hardworking husband, a roof over her head, food for the table, fuel for the fire and that she had not lost any of her children to hunger, disease, war or the sea as many women had on this small island.

Cathie clenched her hands tightly and pursed her lips, shaking her dark curly hair around her oval face; this was one battle she was determined to win no matter how much friction it caused. She had thought long and hard over this decision and was not going to give up on it.

'I *know* I've got to get work, Mam, and I *will*, but I'm not going to gut fish!' Inwardly she shuddered at the very thought of standing on the quay all day in all weathers, up to her elbows in the blood and guts of herrings, which would then go to be smoked or pickled, or mackerel or bass or cod or any other fish. All her life she'd witnessed the women and girls in their filthy, blood-stained aprons, wielding long sharp gutting knives as they worked by the Fish Steps in the Market Square beside Ramsey's outer harbour, which was where the fishing fleet tied up. They all looked hard and weather-beaten and they stank of fish. It was a pervasive odour that seemed to get into the very pores of your skin and no amount of washing, even with carbolic soap, could eliminate it. No, she'd decided that she wanted something better. Ever since she'd been a small child she'd been fascinated by the shops in Parliament Street, Ramsey's main thoroughfare, establishments that were far beyond the reach of her mother's very limited budget. She'd loved to stand and gaze at the displays of fashionable dresses, jackets and coats in rich fabrics and the magnificent hats and soft leather gloves and handbags. Of course she'd soon realised that she would never be able to afford to buy clothes like that. Indeed she'd come to understand that she'd never even be able to get work in such shops. Girls of her class and education could only expect to be employed in very menial jobs, but that didn't stop her dreaming and hoping that one day she might in fact achieve something better; something that would help to contribute to their standard of living, for her father and brothers worked very hard for little reward.

Lizzie sat down in her old, scarred, bentwood rocker and looked wearily at Cathie. In appearance the girl resembled her; with her dark hair and eyes and small but sturdy stature, she bore all the traits of her Celtic ancestors, like many people from the south of the island. However, in nature Cathie took after her father. Bernard – Barney – Kinrade was tall and well built, with blue eyes and fair hair – although now there was more silver in his hair than gold – attributes that harked back to the Viking heritage of the people of the north. He was a rather taciturn man and could be stubborn, but he didn't gamble or drink. Any man who went

13

out to sea with a belly full of ale was a fool, he often remarked. He was superstitious, but then all fishermen were, she conceded. His was a hard and dangerous life – the sea had claimed many lives – but he never complained.

'Cathie, we've argued this down to the bone and there's nothing more to be said. You've to work, and that's an end to it. Do you think Jack and Jacob *wanted* to go out on the boat with your da? Do you not think *they* wanted an easier, safer way of earning a living? Of course they did but what else is there for us? It's fishing or farming and we've no land to work. We're not fortunate enough to have a shop, a business or a house big and grand enough to take in paying summer visitors. The lads couldn't get an apprenticeship and for most other types of decent employment in this town you'd need a better education than any of you have had. I'll have a word with Madge Gelling tomorrow and see if you can start at the Fish Steps on Monday. There'll be no more arguments.'

Tears of anger and frustration pricked Cathie's eyes but before she had time to utter another word her younger sister Ella piped up.

'*I* won't mind working with Mrs Gelling and the others, Mam, when I leave school. I heard their Nora saying it's great getting your money at the end of a long week. It makes it all worthwhile.' From beneath her heavy fringe of dark hair she shot a surreptitious but triumphant glance at Cathie, who glared back at her. Ella shrugged. Cathie was just plain stupid if she thought she could get a good job.

'Oh, shut up, Ella! You just want to cause

14

trouble; it's all you ever do!' Cathie cried, knowing full well that her sibling delighted in goading her. Fenella – called 'Ella' by the family – was almost thirteen and had been a torment to her for as long as she could remember.

'Don't speak to your sister like that!' Lizzie snapped as she got to her feet, trying to head off a squabble. Those two fought like cat and dog and always had done. Her head had begun to ache and she still had a day of chores ahead of her before she could rest for a few hours by the fire after supper. Tomorrow was Sunday and they would all attend St Paul's Church in the Market Square, for Barney insisted they 'keep the Sabbath'. Tonight they would all take their weekly bath here in the kitchen, which meant hours of heating up water on the range. She would have to make sure that their clothes were clean and pressed and any rips or tears were neatly mended and their boots and shoes polished, ready for church in the morning.

'Ella, take little Hal and go and see if there's any sign of your da and the lads yet, while I put on the porridge – they'll be starving,' she instructed, and then turned to ten-year-old Meggie. 'You start to peg out the washing in the yard for me, girl. I'll come out as soon as I can to help and to make sure that there's not a wind getting up that may bring the rain.' Preoccupied by a seemingly endless list of tasks, she turned to five-year-old Harold – Hal – the baby of the family, and, despite his protests, bundled him into an old cut-down jacket of Jacob's to keep out the chill March wind.

While her mother was preoccupied Ella pulled a face at Cathie and hissed, 'You'll have to gut

15

fish and then you'll stink of them and no one will want to come near you!'

Snatching her cardigan from the back of a chair, Cathie slammed out before she too could be instructed to undertake some job. She wanted a bit of time on her own, away from her mam and Ella and Meggie and Hal, and before her da and her brothers came home and the kitchen filled to bursting. Then it would be hard to hear yourself speak, let alone think.

She shivered as she stepped out into Collins Lane and pulled her cardigan more closely around her. The narrow lane seemed to act like a funnel for the wind coming in off the harbour. Collins Lane ran between the West Quay and Parliament Street, Ramsey's main thoroughfare where all the best shops were located. But Collins Lane, at its widest point opposite the cottages, was barely three feet in width. It was so narrow and crooked that the sunlight hardly ever managed to penetrate to brighten or warm it. They lived in the middle of a block of three stone cottages which were over-looked by the wall of the warehouse on the oppo-site side. She stood for a few seconds debating which way to go; then she turned left and headed down towards the quay.

It didn't take her long to reach the end of the lane: ahead of her lay the harbour, divided by the swing bridge. In the outer harbour the fishing boats were already tying up, the boat her da and brothers worked on amongst them. They didn't own it; if they did they would be considerably better off. She shivered in the wind; she had no wish to see her da just yet – he'd only ask where she was going – nor had she any intention of heading towards the Market Square where the fish would already be being unloaded and the women gathered on the steps ready to start the gutting.

She crossed the harbour by the iron swing bridge which divided it into an 'inner' and 'outer' and could be 'swung' open to allow boats to pass through. She intended to head out towards the seafront along the promenade, away from the town, but she'd only gone a few yards when she heard her name being called and she turned to see her brother Jacob hastening across the bridge towards her, a grin on his face.

'Where are you off to, Cathie? What's the matter? Have you escaped Mam and the Saturday chores?' He fell into step beside her and despite her desire to be alone she couldn't help but grin up at him. They got on well and had always been close.

'I've come out to escape the lot of them! Our Ella's being a torment – as usual,' she replied.

Jacob tutted in mock disapproval. Like his father he was tall, well built and fair and at eighteen was considered by quite a few girls to be handsome. 'Squabbling again? What over now?'

'Oh, she was just being hateful, sucking up to Mam and saying *she* won't mind working with Mrs Gelling when she finishes school, and then taunting me that I'll stink of fish!'

Jacob frowned. He was aware of the arguments. He could understand Cathie wanting a better job but he also knew that for his sisters there wasn't much else on offer.

They walked in silence for a while until they reached the wide promenade that faced the sea and led out towards Mooragh Park, Jacob seemingly oblivious to the sharp edge to the wind, although Cathie now wished she'd put something warmer on. The sea looked choppy, its surface broken by white-topped wavelets. However, the sun was struggling to break through the clouds so she hoped it might get a bit warmer as the morning wore on. Overhead the gulls wheeled and dived, their strident cries grating on her nerves.

It was Jacob who broke the silence. 'So, you're still determined not to gut fish.' It was more a statement than a question.

Cathie nodded. 'There's *got* to be something else, Jacob. I worked hard at my lessons. I can read and write and do my sums well enough and Miss Costain said I have a "pleasant way" with folk and should look to "improve" myself. Surely I can do something better than gut fish?'

'All that's not enough, Cathie. I know it's hard but, well, you know we need every penny.'

She stared out across the wide sweep of the bay, her gaze settling on the half-mile-long Victoria Pier at the end of which a ferry boat was tied up. There were regular sailings to England, Scotland and Ireland, and in the summer months the ferries brought hundreds of visitors and day trippers to the island. Across the sea was England and ... Liverpool. Oh, she'd heard such tales of that city and its magnificent buildings, its huge ocean liners, its wide streets full of shops. Shops that were enormous compared to those here in Ramsey and even Douglas. She'd only ever visited the island's capital once and had never been off the island. 'There's a whole world out there, Jacob, full of chances and opportunities. Why shouldn't I go to Liverpool? I'd get a decent job there. Why shouldn't I make something of my life, "improve" myself, like Miss Costain said? I might even get a job in one of the big shops there, something I've always dreamed of! I have to try, Jacob!' Impatiently she pushed a few wisps of dark hair, tousled by the wind, away from her forehead. 'I don't want to be poor all my life. I don't want to be like Mam, always tired, always worried. Why can't I have hopes and dreams and a better life?'

He smiled down at her a little sadly. He was very fond of her and knew he was the only one she'd confide in. But she was still so young and didn't realise that for the likes of them hopes and dreams were a luxury which seldom became reality. You had to take whatever hand life dealt you; no use raging against it. 'Why can't you have hopes and dreams? Because for us, Cathie, they're like circles drawn in the sand. When the tide comes in it washes them away.' He paused. 'I ... I didn't want to follow Da into fishing but...' He shrugged. 'I got used to it and most of the time it's not too bad. We have to be grateful for what we've got; isn't that what Mam's always telling us?' If he'd had a choice he would have liked to have become a carpenter. He enjoyed working with his hands – he often fixed things around the house, and the boat too – but to have become a tradesman he would have had to serve an apprenticeship. His parents didn't have the money to pay for his indentures and so no one had been prepared to take him on.

Cathie bit her lip. It seemed as if there was no escape for her and yet she wanted so much more from life. But maybe Jacob was right. Maybe her wishes and dreams were simply circles in the sand.

'Come on, let's go home before we're chilled to the bone. I'm starving,' he urged more cheerfully.

Cathie didn't reply, still caught up in her thoughts. Her eye caught a young woman walking along the sandy beach. She was reading a book, apparently totally engrossed in it. Oh, wouldn't it be great to be like that, she thought enviously. Dressed in a warm, fashionable coat and a smart hat, so carefree that she could stroll along at this hour of the morning totally engrossed in a story or poem or whatever it was she was reading. *She* obviously didn't have any chores to do, or cares or worries either.

Jacob had seen her too and he frowned, his gaze going out to where the sea was washing against the harbour wall. The tide was coming in and the currents out there were strong; beyond the wall a wave, larger than the rest, was forming. 'What's she doing down there?' he asked, more to himself than his sister.

'It looks like she's reading something. That's a lovely tweed coat she's wearing. Wouldn't it be great to have all the time in the world to just walk and read. I bet she doesn't have to work at *anything*,' Cathie replied wistfully.

'If she doesn't get further up the beach she's going to get wet,' Jacob announced, pointing from their vantage point, which was higher than the beach where the wave was now increasing in size and gathering speed. He frowned; the young woman could possibly be in some danger.

Catching his meaning Cathie now realised the

young woman's predicament. 'Shout to her then! Warn her!'

They both yelled but the woman either didn't hear them or was ignoring them.

'She can't hear us! Come on, we'll have to go down on to the beach,' Cathie urged.

They both scrambled hastily down and over the stretch of pebbles towards the sand, still shouting. At last the woman looked up and then in response to their cries, turned and saw the white-crested wave crashing in towards her.

She uttered a shrill cry and tried to hurry across the sand but before they could reach her the wave caught her and swept her off her feet. She almost disappeared in the cold creamy foam. Only her head, now minus the hat, could be seen. Cathie screamed, 'Jacob, we've got to do something! She'll be dragged out!'

The lad raced forward and waded in, his legs working like pistons, until he reached her, followed by Cathie, ignoring the fact that neither she nor Jacob could swim. She gasped aloud as the icy cold water hit her.

'Can you catch hold of her?' she yelled, struggling on through the swirling water to reach her brother.

Jacob didn't reply but he at last managed to grab hold of the woman's arm as she thrashed helplessly in the sea. 'Hang on to me, miss! I'll pull you out!' he shouted.

Heedless of the cold water now surging around her Cathie at last reached Jacob's side and between them they managed to drag the woman out of the sea. 'You're safe now, miss! It's all right!

21

Just hang on to us!'

All three of them were soaked and shivering but the young woman was ashen with shock, her auburn hair plastered to her skull. 'Oh, thank you! I ... I ... didn't see it... I ... just didn't think...' she stammered through chattering teeth.

'It's a spring tide, higher than usual, and they come in so fast, miss. It's the currents, you see; that's why they're so dangerous. You'd have been pulled out into deeper water. But we'd better get you home now,' Jacob said grimly.

She dissolved into tears of shock. 'Into ... deeper water! I ... I ... can't swim! If ... if it hadn't been for you both...'

'Neither can we, miss,' Cathie informed her quietly. Many fisherman and their families were unable to swim; it wasn't unusual.

'I ... I'm so ... sorry!' Salt water was dripping from her hair and mingling with tears of remorse. 'I'm ... I'm ... Violet Christian. I ... I live just up there.' She pointed to the row of large Edwardian villas that lined one side of the promenade. Some were guest houses but many remained private homes.

Slowly the saturated little group made their way up towards the promenade, hampered by their wet clothes. As they drew near to the house Violet Christian tried to push her dripping hair back from her face; she was still shivering violently with cold and shock. 'Oh, it was so utterly ... stupid of me to ignore the incoming tide! I should have known better – and if it hadn't been for both of you and your ... assistance I might well have been pulled out and ... drowned! You must come in, you're soaked through too,' she urged as they helped her climb the four broad steps that led up to a heavy door topped by an ornate glass fanlight.

Cathie and her brother exchanged glances. To live in a house like this you had to be well off and they were certain that they wouldn't be welcomed in with open arms, even though they'd helped her. Soaked to the skin they must look like two urchins.

'No, miss, but thank you. Now that you're safe, we'll get off home. It's not far,' Cathie replied as Jacob pressed the brass doorbell. The sound echoed through the hall inside.

'But I ... I can't let you go without some ... reward. And I don't even know your names!' Violet exclaimed, looking perturbed.

The door was opened by a young girl in a maid's black dress, white cap and apron. She looked with horror at the dripping, dejected trio on the doorstep. 'Miss Violet! Oh, Lord! Whatever happened to you?'

'I ... I was foolish enough to get caught in a tide surge and these ... kind, brave people ... helped me.'

'Oh, miss! Come inside. You must get out of those wet things or you'll catch your death of cold!' She moved forward to escort her mistress inside but Violet turned again to Jacob and Cathie.

'Please tell me your names?'

'Well, it's Kinrade. Jacob and Cathie Kinrade,' Jacob replied.

'Jacob and Cathie, if there is anything ... *anything* at all that I can do for either of you, just ask.

You probably saved my life; there was no one else around. I really do mean that. Anything, anything at all I can do.'

Jacob nodded his thanks and took Cathie's arm and they both went awkwardly down the steps.

'She most likely means that now but she'll forget what she said later on, when the shock wears off. Come on, Cathie. It's going to be a long, cold walk home.'

Cathie nodded glumly; already she was so cold she could barely feel her feet. Had Miss Violet Christian really meant what she said? The name was familiar – the Christians were a well-known family in this town. Suddenly a thought struck her. Could Violet help her realise her dreams? The notion sustained her as she trudged along beside Jacob.

Chapter Two

Their appearance when they walked into the kitchen was met first with shocked silence and then with cries and exclamations.

It was Lizzie who recovered her composure first, rushing to fuss over them both. 'What in the name of heaven have the pair of you been doing? Come over here to the fire! Get those wet things off before you catch a chill! Ella, go upstairs and find some dry things for your sister. Jack, get up and let your brother sit in that chair!'

Barney Kinrade finished his tea and got to his

feet, taking in the sight of the dripping, shivering pair of miscreants and suspecting some form of trouble was behind their appearance. It usually was. 'So, lad, just *what* have you been up to? Where did you go sneaking off to?' he demanded grimly, annoyed that Jacob hadn't stayed to help them unload the catch.

'I didn't "sneak", Da. I shouted to our Jack that I was going after Cathie. She looked upset and I wondered why,' Jacob replied quietly. Lizzie handed him a towel and he started to dry his hair, still trembling in his wet clothes although the heat from the range was slowly beginning to dissipate some of the chill.

Jack, the eldest at nearly twenty, nodded his agreement, although he hadn't passed that piece of information on to his father: he'd been aware that it would have been viewed as "shirking", but had reckoned that his brother would no doubt explain the reason for his disappearance later.

As dry clothes were brought and more towels handed out and hot mugs of strong tea dispensed, between them Cathie and Jacob informed their parents and siblings of the events of the morning.

When they'd finished Lizzie shook her head and tutted reprovingly. 'If you hadn't gone running off like that, Cathie, then neither of you would have got a soaking, and you left your sisters with your share of the chores. Not a thought in your head but what *you* wanted to do.' She sighed. 'Still, if you hadn't been there then that young woman would have been in serious trouble.'

Barney fixed his son with a disapproving glare. Jacob was old enough to know better. The boy had been foolhardy – in fact they both had. So, Miss Violet Christian couldn't swim, but neither could they. 'You young fools, you'd all have been in trouble if the current had dragged you out. They'd have had to send out the lifeboat and then there would have been an almighty fuss!'

'We couldn't have just left her, not done anything to help, Da!' Cathie protested, though she was now beginning to realise the danger they'd put themselves in.

'Neither of you should even have been there. What's got into the pair of you? Taking a walk along the Mooragh Promenade when you both had work to do.'

'We're sorry, Da, but surely you'll admit it was fortunate we were,' Jacob apologised, aware what terrible heartache they would have caused their parents had tragedy befallen them both.

'And she was so grateful, Da! She really was!' Cathie enthused. 'She wanted us to go into the house – well, we wouldn't do *that* – and she said if there was anything at all she could do to help us...'

Barney frowned. For hundreds of years the Christian family had been the most powerful on the island, living in a grand mansion on the Milntown Estate, until recently waited on by a small army of servants. The Great War had changed all that. Although the descendants of the illustrious and revered Sir William Christian, or 'Illiam Dhone' as he was known in the Manx tongue, had died out there were still minor branches of the family and many were wealthy. 'Take no notice of what she said, Cathie. She's a Christian. Why would the likes of them go out of their way to help one of us?'

'She might, Da. She said she meant it,' Cathie persisted, unwilling to give up on this one hope of evading the hated gutting.

Barney's frown deepened. 'Forget what she said, Cathie.'

'But, Da...'

'Don't argue with your father, Cathie! Haven't there been enough arguments in this house lately? And wasn't one of them at the root of this morning's ... episode?' Lizzie reprimanded her sharply.

Jacob tried to catch his sister's eye but she wasn't taking any notice. He'd tried to warn her not to put too much faith in Violet Christian's promise.

'What have they done for us so far, Cathie? Who do you think has the largest share in the *Girl Violet* and half a dozen other boats? And who takes the biggest share of the catch?' Jack asked grimly, referring to the boat he, Jacob and his da worked on. His views were with his da on this matter.

Cathie looked puzzled. 'You mean she ... they...' she faltered. 'It's named after *her?*'

Barney nodded. 'It is. Violet Christian's father owns the largest share in it. So, we'll hear no more of her doing anything to help any of us. Put the experience behind you, but mind you learn from it.'

Lizzie nodded her agreement and became brisk. 'Ella, Meggie, you can come with me. I've some shopping to do and your da and the lads all need a rest. They were out all night, they're tired. Cathie, when you've warmed up, bring the washing in and fold it. Then you can tidy up this kitchen. Oh, and keep an eye on Hal too, he's playing in the lane with Tommy Corkish from next door.'

'Are we going to Parliament Street, Mam?' Ella asked, thinking of the better-class shops and feeling rather smug that Cathie was to remain at home.

Cathie bit her lip, disappointed, for she liked going to Parliament Street even if they couldn't afford to buy anything there; she loved watching all the fashionably dressed women and girls who could.

'We are not! I'm going first to Kermeen's in Peel Street to see what I can afford for dinner tomorrow and then into old Ramsey for the rest of my shopping,' Lizzie replied firmly, referring to the butcher's and the small, cheaper shops in the narrow streets behind St Paul's Church.

Cathie got to her feet as her mother shepherded her sisters out. Any hope that Violet Christian might help her were fading fast. There was nothing she could do now except turn up at the Fish Steps on Monday morning.

It was on the Tuesday morning, a grey, damp and chilly day, that she trudged reluctantly down towards the quay. The boats hadn't gone out on Sunday so there'd been no fish on Monday, although she'd accompanied her mother to the home of Madge Gelling that day and it had been arranged that she should start this morning. Madge had explained that it was 'piecework' and she would be paid according to the amount of fish she gutted, so the faster she worked, the more money she'd get at the end of the week. She was bound to be slower than the others to start with but she'd soon catch up.

Now her hair was tied back and covered by a cotton kerchief, she wore her oldest clothes and under her arm was tucked a heavy coarse calico apron that would almost envelop her but would hopefully protect her clothes from the worst of the mess. On her feet she wore a pair of short rubber boots and knew that in a few hours her feet would be freezing cold.

The Market Square was always crowded with people. A group of men, all wearing suits and hats, had assembled outside the Union Hotel, and she realised that these were the buyers who had come from the outlying small towns and villages. Townsfolk mingled with fishermen and chatted and women gossiped with the market stallholders and there was the usual sprinkling of boys playing truant from school in the hope of earning a penny or two running errands. In the far corner by the stone steps that led up from the wall of the quayside the women and girls were already waiting for the barrels of fish to be manhandled across to them. They were all similarly dressed; some of the girls were laughing and joking, but the older women seemed more preoccupied and rubbed chilled hands together. Cathie's heart sank still further as her nostrils were assailed by the strong odour of fish as she approached them.

'So, you're here to start work, Cathie,' Madge Gelling greeted her. She was a big buxom woman whom Cathie judged to be around her mam's age. Her greying hair was snatched back in a tight bun and her face lined and wrinkled from years spent working in the open air.

'I am, Mrs Gelling.' Cathie tried to sound enthusiastic but knew she wasn't very convincing.

Madge became brisk and businesslike. 'Right then. Put on that apron and here's your knife. See you take care of it and hand it back to me when the work's finished.' She held out the bone-handled knife by the tip of its long, thin, razor-sharp blade.

Gingerly Cathie took it from her by its worn bone handle; she'd been told that she would be expected to purchase a knife of her own when she'd earned a week's wage.

'Come on with me. Our Nora will show you the ropes,' Madge instructed and Cathie followed her towards a group of four girls who had already begun to work.

'Nora, girl, show Cathie here what to do,' she instructed her eighteen-year-old daughter, who was as big-boned as herself, before turning away and heading back towards the group of older women who were quickly yanking fish from the barrels beside them.

'You don't look as if you'll last the morning, Cathie Kinrade,' Nora stated flatly as she slapped four herrings down on the scrubbed and knife-scarred wooden bench in front of Cathie.

'I will,' Cathie muttered sullenly. She didn't like Nora Gelling very much. She'd often seen her around the town and thought she was loud, rough and ill mannered.

Nora winked at one of her companions. 'Right, first it's off with the head, tail and fins, then you slice it along the belly ... like this.' She wielded the knife deftly while Cathie tried to follow the

30

swift movements. She was beginning to be affected by the stench that surrounded her.

Nora grinned as she took in the younger girl's increasing pallor. 'Be careful though, it's easy for the knife to slip and if it does you'll lose a finger and have to be carted off to the Cottage Hospital! Mind you, it might not be so bad at that, there're some decent-looking fellers there – porters, of course, but you might get lucky!'

One of the other girls laughed. 'She probably wouldn't know what to do with a feller even if she got lucky!'

'But I bet you would, Elsie!' Nora shot back.

'And you too, Nora Gelling. I saw you up Post Office Lane with that lad from the boatyard on Saturday night!'

Nora shot a surreptitious glance at her mother. 'Shurrup, Elsie, or I'll never hear the end of it,' she hissed.

Cathie clenched her teeth at the thought of a severed finger but managed to nod. Gripping the knife tightly she proceeded to attack one of the fish. She quickly realised it was not as easy as Nora had made it look but, although she was considerably slower than the others, who seemed to be able to work and keep up a conversation, she persevered.

It was not long before she felt her stomach begin to heave with the stench from the horrible, slimy mess that covered her hands and the front of her apron. The blade and handle of the knife were red and had become increasingly slippery and she couldn't help remembering what Nora had said about it slipping. Her nausea increased

31

and her movements became slower and slower as she fought down the bile rising in her throat; at last she could stand it no longer and, dropping the knife, she turned away and staggered to the edge of the wall and vomited.

'I said she'd not last long! Look at her, sick as a pig and she's only done four!' Nora mocked but a couple of the other girls looked sympathetic as they caught sight of Cathie's brother making his way towards them. Jacob Kinrade was considered a good-looking lad by most of them and it wouldn't hurt to show a bit of concern for his sister.

As her stomach heaved again at Nora's words Cathie felt terrible. Oh, she hated Nora Gelling and she just wanted to run away. To get as far away as she could from all ... *this!* She leaned against the wall feeling weak, sick, dizzy and utterly humiliated.

'Take no notice, Cathie. Here, have a few sips of this, you'll feel better.'

Looking up and wiping her mouth with a fairly clean corner of her apron, Cathie saw Jacob looking down at her, his blue eyes full of concern, a tin mug in his hand.

'Go on. It's only water. I went into the Commercial House Hotel and asked Ben Quirk for a drop. I was coming across to see how you were getting on and ... well, I could see you were already looking a bit green...'

Cathie thankfully took a sip. 'I can't do it, Jacob! I ... *can't*. It's horrible!'

Before he could reply Madge was beside them. 'Hey, boy! What's the matter with her?'

'She's just feeling a bit sick, Mrs Gelling,' Jacob informed her.

Madge nodded. She'd seen it often enough. 'You'll get used to it, Cathie. Everyone does. By the end of the week you won't be turning a hair. You'll be chatting and laughing with the rest of them. Take a few more mouthfuls of that water and some good deep breaths of fresh air and you'll be fine. Then go back and pick up that knife. It'll get easier as the day goes on, lass. Think of your wages at the end of the week and how pleased your mam will be. That'll see you through.' Madge moved away.

Cathie closed her eyes. She didn't want to go back. She didn't care about her wages.

Jacob put his arm around her. 'Do as she said, Cathie. Take some deep breaths –you'll begin to feel better. And she's right. You'll get used to it. I was dog sick myself on my first trip out, but now it doesn't bother me.'

Slowly Cathie nodded; she was beginning to feel a bit better and knew she had no choice but to go back and try to stick it out. 'I'm all right now, Jacob.'

He smiled at her. 'Good lass. I'd better get back to Da or I'll get the rough side of his tongue for shirking. I'll see you later, when you've finished.'

She felt desolate as she watched him stride away but then she squared her slim shoulders and walked slowly back towards Nora and the others.

She hadn't vomited again but she'd gagged a few times. She'd worked on grimly, ignoring the other girls, her back aching, her feet and fingers cold, which made wielding the knife more hazardous. When at last they'd all finished she realised she'd only done a fraction compared to the others. That would affect how much she'd be paid but at this precise moment she couldn't care less. All she wanted to do was go home and scrub her skin until it no longer felt contaminated by the blood, scales and guts of innumerable dead fish.

Wearily she took off her apron and bundled it up, making sure the stained side was to the inside, handed the knife back to Madge and smiled weakly when the woman said cheerfully, 'Now, that wasn't too bad, lass, was it?'

Threading her way through the diminishing crowd of people she reached the black and white timbered Commercial House Hotel on the corner of the quayside and leaned against the wall facing the harbour, thankful for the feel of the fresh salt breeze on her cheeks. She breathed in deeply, trying to expel the stench of fish from her nostrils. They'd all want to know how her first day had gone, she thought tiredly. She knew Jacob wouldn't reveal that she'd been publicly sick but Mam would no doubt hear about it from someone. Oh, she had hated every single minute of the day so far! She hated Nora and the other girls who had laughed at her and she hated feeling so ghastly. How could she do it all again tomorrow and the day after and the day after that? She couldn't! She *wouldn't!* She didn't care how much she would be paid. Twenty golden guineas a week wouldn't be enough to make her spend the weeks and months and even years ahead gutting fish.

She straightened up and began to walk slowly

along in the direction of home. She didn't care what her da said, she was going to go to see Miss Violet Christian and remind her of her promise. Ask her to help her get to Liverpool and find a better job – a better life. She wasn't going to give up on her dreams. Yes, she was only fifteen but if she could survive a day gutting fish with her stomach revolting, she could surely survive in Liverpool?

Chapter Three

She'd said little about the events of the day and tactfully Lizzie hadn't questioned her too closely, knowing she hadn't wanted to go. Only Ella had asked probing questions.

'So, what's it really like? How many do you have to gut each day? How much will you earn?' she'd demanded.

Cathie had shrugged. 'I don't know how much I'll earn, I'm only learning at the moment – and it's ... grim!'

'Well, what did you expect?' Ella had shot back.

Again Cathie had shrugged.

'You certainly smell like the rest of them,' Ella had taunted, wrinkling her nose.

'Ella, that's enough!' Lizzie had snapped, sensing Cathie's disillusionment and knowing that Ella's persistence would end in an argument. She had curtly dispatched Ella on an errand, defusing the situation.

Somehow Cathie had got through the next three days although her distaste increased both towards her work and her companions. She seldom spoke to Nora and the other girls and they in turn ignored her.

She'd made up her mind that on Saturday she'd go to see Miss Christian. She hoped they would finish early – they usually did, according to Nora, and so she'd be able to go home to get washed and changed for she certainly couldn't go to that house looking and smelling like this. She thought a great deal about what she should say, how best to ask for Violet Christian's help, and decided that she would just be honest about how she felt. Truthful about what she wanted from the future. It was useless to try to skirt around it all using fancy words – even if she knew enough of them, which she didn't. No, plain speaking would be best. She would tell Violet Christian about her dream to work in a big classy shop and that she hoped that perhaps Miss Christian could suggest somewhere where she might stay. She wasn't going to ask for money – she felt that wouldn't be right at all. She just needed some help and she hoped the young woman could suggest something.

Thankfully they did finish early on Saturday and she was grateful for the money she was paid, even though she knew it was only half of what the others had earned. Still, she didn't really care as she had to hand it over to her mam; she'd never had money of her own. For the first time that week she felt her spirits rise as she walked briskly home, her soiled apron under her arm, the weak spring sun feeling warm on her cheeks.

'Well, that's your first week over, Cathie,' Lizzie remarked as she walked into the kitchen and handed over her meagre wages.

She nodded. 'I'm sorry there's not more money, Mam. I'm still slow. I'll put this apron in the scullery.'

'Put it in the bucket to soak, I'll scrub it later and hang it out in the yard,' Lizzie instructed as she continued to peel the potatoes. 'Oh, and Cathie, lass, don't worry about the money,' she added.

As she returned to the kitchen Cathie broached the subject tentatively. 'Mam, I ... I was thinking I might go for a bit of a walk, after I've got myself cleaned up, that is. It's a fairly nice day and–'

'I thought we'd go and have a look around the market stalls for something as a bit of a treat for you, Cathie. Maybe buy a bit of nice ribbon for your hair or one of those coloured plastic slides,' Lizzie interrupted. The girl had worked hard all week, hadn't complained and had handed over her wages without being asked. And she'd heard how sick she'd been that first morning, something her daughter hadn't mentioned.

Cathie shrugged but smiled. 'It's all right, Mam. I really don't need anything and I'd prefer some time to myself. I've had to listen to Nora Gelling and that lot going on all morning about what they are going to do tonight and tomorrow.'

Lizzie nodded; she could understand that. Then she frowned: they tended to be a rather loud lot, something Cathie really wasn't, and none of them were ever seen in church on a Sunday. 'All right, lass. You have a bit of time to yourself. You deserve it.'

Cathie scrubbed herself until her skin was red and then ate a couple of slices of bread spread with dripping before getting changed. She wished she had something a bit better than the faded blue rayon blouse and grey skirt to wear but the only decent dress she had was already pressed, ready for church tomorrow, and she knew Mam would suspect something if she insisted on wearing it today. But she brushed her hair vigorously and it fell in curls around her ears. She hoped she looked fairly respectable as she inspected her image in the small mirror that hung above the scullery sink.

'Don't be back too late, Cathie. I've a few things I want you to help me with,' Lizzie called as Cathie pulled on her jacket and prepared to leave.

'I won't, Mam,' she promised before closing the door and stepping out into the lane.

She walked quickly along the quay and across the bridge, hoping she wouldn't meet anyone she knew. As she reached the promenade her heart began to beat a bit faster and she felt butterflies fluttering in her stomach. What if Miss Christian wasn't in? 'What if she wouldn't see her? What if she had in fact forgotten all about her drenching in the sea last week? She tried to push the doubts from her mind. This was her only chance; she couldn't give up now.

Reaching the house she stopped outside and looked up at the front door, thinking that she hadn't spotted before that the name 'Claremont' was painted in gold lettering on the glass fan-light, but then they'd all been too cold and wet then to notice anything. She took a deep breath, went up the steps and pressed the doorbell. It seemed an age before the door was opened and the maid stood there.

'I'd like to see Miss Christian ... please? We ... my brother and I helped her last Saturday – do you remember us? We all were soaking wet. I'm Cathie ... Cathie Kinrade.'

The girl nodded. 'If you'll just step inside I'll go and see if Miss Violet will see you. Wipe your feet,' she instructed curtly.

She disappeared down the hallway, leaving Cathie staring around curiously. She'd never been in a house like this before and was taken aback by the size and grandeur of the hall. It was bigger than the whole ground floor of their cottage, she thought. The floor and stairs here were carpeted; they only had handmade rag rugs on the floor at home. The walls were covered with striped wallpaper in two shades of pale green and adorned with paintings, and some lovely, delicate china ornaments were displayed on the top of a small highly polished table. She wondered what the rest of the rooms were like but her deliberations were interrupted by the girl's return.

'You're to come with me,' she stated.

Cathie breathed a sigh of relief as she followed her down the hall to a door. She squared her shoulders, determined not to be distracted no matter how fine the furnishings in this new room. It would be rude to gawp around and besides she needed to concentrate entirely on what she'd come to ask.

Violet Christian had been surprised to learn of the visit but she rose smiling from the chair where she'd been sitting. 'It's Cathie, isn't it?'

Cathie nodded. The older girl looked far better than when she'd last seen her. She wore a brown and cream checked wool skirt and a fine pale cream jumper, a gold locket suspended from a chain hung around her neck and her short thick auburn hair shone. Cathie felt very dowdy but the young woman's smile gave her some confidence.

'Please sit down. I hope you didn't catch a chill? You must have been frozen by the time you got home. Did you have far to go?' Violet asked, thinking that despite her rather drab and shabby clothes Cathie Kinrade was quite a pretty girl.

Cathie sat gingerly on the edge of the up-holstered brocade armchair Violet indicated. 'No, we live in Collins Lane and I'm fine, miss, really. Were you ... all right, afterwards?'

Violet nodded, smiling a little ruefully. 'Thankfully I was, although I received a ticking-off from my father, I can tell you, as well as managing to ruin my new coat and lose an expensive hat. He said I should have had more sense than to put myself and others in jeopardy and of course he was right. I hope you didn't get into trouble.'

'No, miss,' Cathie replied quickly, pushing her da's remarks about the Christians from her mind.

'Well, is there something I can do for you, Cathie? I presume that's why you're here?'

Cathie nodded slowly. It was now or never. 'I came because ... I'm hoping you can help me, miss. You see I started work this week and ... and I hate it! Oh, it's not the fact that I have to work that I'm complaining about, just the job itself,' she added hastily lest the young woman thought she was lazy or work-shy.

40

Violet looked at her curiously, wondering what was so awful about this job. 'Why is that?'

Cathie twisted her hands together in her lap awkwardly. She hated even admitting it. 'It's ... gutting fish in the Market Square. It's horrible! Really, really *horrible!*'

Violet shuddered involuntarily. She'd seen the women and girls at work but usually she kept far enough away from them so she wouldn't see clearly what the process involved, although you couldn't help but smell it. Of course her father owned large shares in half a dozen fishing boats – one of his many enterprises – and fishing provided a livelihood for so many as well as being a much needed staple food, but she sympathised with the girl. If Cathie Kinrade said it was utterly horrible, then she believed her. 'Do you have to do it, Cathie? Can't you find something else?'

'I do, miss. At least that's what my mam and da say, that there's nothing else for the likes of us and they ... we need the money. There are six of us, you see, as well as Mam and Da. He's a fisherman, miss.' She didn't add that her da worked on one of her father's boats. 'But it's always been my dream to work in one of the grand shops they have in Liverpool, miss,' she confided.

Violet was trying to remember if there were actually any houses in Collins Lane: it was very narrow but there were warehouses, she knew that. On occasion she'd used it as a shortcut but she couldn't remember seeing any houses, yet there must be for the girl said she lived there. 'How old are you, Cathie?' she enquired.

'Fifteen, miss, and I did well at my lessons. We

41

did Maths and English Grammar and Geography, History and Religious Education. I ... I liked school, but I had to leave. I came to ask you, miss, if you could help me get a better job?'

Violet was wondering what she could do to help. 'Is there something you had in mind, Cathie?' she asked. She had promised, after all, and at least the girl wasn't asking for money.

Cathie clenched her hands more tightly and looked at her earnestly. 'As I said, I'd really like to go to Liverpool, Miss Christian. I've thought about it a lot and I really would love to get a job in one of the big shops. My teacher, Miss Costain, said I should aim to "improve" myself and I know I'd do well if I got a chance. I'd work hard and it would be a way for me to have a much better life and ... and I could send some money home and it would be ... wonderful not to have to even look at another fish! You've no idea how messy, smelly and dirty the work is. I'm ashamed to say, miss, that I was actually sick the first morning.'

Violet looked slightly shocked but then nodded sympathetically. The poor girl; she must really find it abhorrent. She could fully understand Cathie's desire to better herself and why shouldn't she? She might be poor but she came from a hard-working family and her ambition was admirable; however, she was very young to go across to Liverpool alone. 'What about your parents? Would they let you go? You're still quite young.'

'I know I am, miss, but I'd be all right. I think I'm quite sensible for my age. Please, Miss Christian, it's my only chance to better myself. I ... I don't want to be poor all my life. I don't want

42

to be gutting fish forever!' Cathie begged.

Slowly Violet nodded. 'Let me write some letters, Cathie. We have ... contacts in Liverpool but I can't promise anything. I'll do my best for you though – I did make you a promise. Will you come back in a couple of weeks? I might have some news then.'

Cathie nodded, getting to her feet and trying not to jump up and down with relief and excitement. She really liked Violet Christian and was so very thankful that she seemed to want to help her. 'Of course, miss. Oh, thank you. I'm very grateful! Really I am.'

Violet too rose. 'Don't build up your hopes too much. I think that perhaps you'd better discuss it all with your parents. I'd hate them to think I was encouraging you to leave home, although I realise that many people do have to leave the island to find work.'

'I will, miss,' Cathie replied, wondering about the wisdom of this. Her da wouldn't exactly be delighted to learn that she'd defied him and come here to ask for help, but the excitement she felt at perhaps being given the chance to see that great city and realise her dream pushed the thought away.

She thanked Violet Christian again and also the maid who showed her out, informing the girl that she'd be coming to see her mistress again in a fortnight.

'Indeed,' the girl replied rather frostily.

Cathie didn't care that she obviously disapproved of her and as she went down the steps she felt considerably happier. Of course Miss Violet

43

had said she couldn't promise anything but they had 'contacts' so surely something would come of it? As she walked briskly back home she tried not to feel too excited but it wasn't easy. Then she remembered she would have to go on working with Nora and the others for the next two weeks, at least. That did put a damper on her spirits, as did the fact that she'd have to keep silent about this afternoon's visit. She hoped that no one she knew had seen her either entering or leaving Claremont – such an unusual occurrence would definitely be reported to her parents.

When she reached home her mother and sisters were out and for that she was thankful, but her da and her brothers were in.

'Where've you been, Cathie?' Jacob asked, for his mother had only said Cathie had gone for a walk.

She shrugged. 'Just for a walk for a bit of peace and quiet. I'm sick of listening to Nora Gelling and the ... rubbish ... she talks.'

Barney nodded; he disapproved of Nora and her friends. In his opinion they were far too loud and forward for young girls.

Jacob wasn't taken in; he knew Cathie too well. He'd press her on the matter later if an opportunity arose although that wasn't guaranteed, not when his mam and sisters returned and there were eight of them in the kitchen.

It was little Hal who presented him with the opportunity half an hour later when he came into the kitchen clutching his cheek and sobbing.

'Oh, what's the matter, luv? What's happened to you?' Cathie cried, bending down and gently removing the child's hand from his face, revealing a long, jagged, bleeding scratch.

'I fell ... off! It hurts, Cathie!' he sobbed.

Jacob picked him up and carried him into the scullery, followed by Cathie, for he'd disturbed Barney, who'd been dozing by the fire.

'Let's get it cleaned up, Hal, then it won't hurt as much,' Cathie soothed.

Jacob sat the child on the wooden draining board. 'Hush now and let Cathie bathe your face, like a good lad. You fell off what?' he asked.

'The wall. Jimmy dared me to climb up and walk along the top,' the child replied, his sobs diminishing.

'You fell off the top of the yard wall! It's six feet high!' Cathie cried. 'Oh, honestly, Hal, you're lucky all you've done is scrape your cheek – you could have broken your arm or leg. You take too much notice of that Jimmy Corkish,' she remonstrated as she dabbed at his cheek gently with a damp piece of clean rag.

'Cathie's right, Hal, and you'd better not let Mam or Da find out you climbed up there or you'll be in big trouble,' Jacob advised.

The little boy nodded, realising that what his older brother said was true. 'I'm not going to play with Jimmy no more,' he said sullenly.

Cathie ruffled his hair. 'Yes you will; he's your best friend. Just don't let him dare you to do anything else. And if he does – ignore him.'

Jacob lifted him down. 'Go into the kitchen and sit by the fire. You've had a bit of a shock.'

He turned to Cathie when the child had gone. 'So, where did you walk to, Cathie? Mooragh Promenade?'

45

Cathie glanced quickly at the kitchen door and then nodded. 'Promise you won't say anything, Jacob? You know how much I hate that job. I ... I went to see Miss Christian.'

Jacob shook his head; he'd suspected as much. 'And?'

'She was very nice. She said she would write some letters. They have what she called "contacts" in Liverpool.'

Jacob's eyes widened. *'Liverpool!* You really meant it about going?'

'I did. Why not?'

Jacob too glanced towards the door from behind which he could hear Jack talking to his little brother. 'I don't think they'll let you go, Cathie. They'll think it's too big and dangerous a city for a fifteen-year-old girl to be alone in.'

'Lots of folk have to go across to find work. I know I'm young but I'll manage. Anyway, nothing is certain yet. And if I *do* get something on her recommendation, surely they can't refuse?'

Jacob shook his head. She was taking all this chasing her dreams too far and he could only see disappointment ahead for her.

Chapter Four

When the appointed Saturday finally arrived she could scarcely believe it. The wait had seemed endless. Once work was finished she collected her wages and walked quickly home to get washed and changed. She'd kept up her hour's walk at the end of the working week so now there were no questions or comments from either her mother or sisters. Jacob had given no indication that he knew she was desperately waiting for news but sometimes he wasn't at home on Saturday afternoons: either off fishing or down at the harbour helping to mend nets. There was always some kind of work to be done on the boat. The weeks had seemed to drag and she'd prayed there would be good news. She'd turned up for work each day and even though the gutting didn't affect her as much she still hated it. But she had become quicker at the task and had earned more and she'd even felt that she could put up with Nora; after all she had the chance of a better life than Nora did.

'I'm off, Mam. I won't be long,' Cathie called to her mother, who was in the scullery.

Lizzie smiled to herself. She was a good lass; she'd stopped complaining about her work and she was never longer than an hour on a Saturday afternoon. She willingly helped with the chores when she got back and her wages had increased these last couple of weeks, although she'd evaded buying her own gutting knife so far. She couldn't go on using one of Madge's, so this week she'd have to go to the chandler's where they sold knives and kitchen utensils, small tools and the like, Lizzie mused as she scrubbed at the stains on her daughter's apron.

If Cathie had felt nervous the first time she'd come to this house she was even more so now, she thought as she rang the doorbell at Claremont.

'She's been expecting you all afternoon. Come in,' the Christians' maid greeted her bluntly upon opening the door.

Cathie didn't reply but dutifully wiped her feet before she could be instructed to. Her stomach beginning to churn in nervous anticipation, she followed the girl down the hallway and into the same room.

'Cathie, come and sit down,' Violet greeted her. There were two envelopes on the table beside her and she was pleased that she had good news to impart. She had realised when writing the two original letters that the girl would be bitterly disappointed if the responses to her requests weren't favourable.

'Thank you, miss. Is there–?'

'There is, Cathie,' Violet interrupted. 'I thought hard about what I could do and decided to write to a cousin of my mother's who lives in Liverpool. Sadly, my poor mother passed away nine years ago, when I was twelve.'

'Oh, I'm sorry, miss,' Cathie said politely although she wasn't surprised; she'd heard from Jacob that Mrs Christian was long dead and that it was Violet who kept house for her father. She had an older brother but he was away in India, apparently, with the British Army.

'Thank you. Now, I've had a reply from her and I'm delighted to tell you she's willing to take you in – in return for you doing some light housework. She says she is getting old and has developed arthritis and so would welcome some help. She was rather older than my mother; her name is Mrs Ethel Johnston. I haven't seen her

48

for some time but I remember that she's a decent, kindly enough person. Mr Johnston still works at the Cotton Exchange I believe, although he must be near retirement age. Their only son was killed in the Great War; it was a huge loss for them both to bear.'

Cathie nodded, trying to digest all this information. 'And she ... she's happy to let me lodge with them? Will I have to pay her for my keep, miss?'

Violet smiled. 'No, Cathie. I explained in my letter that you're only young, have very little money and probably won't be paid a great deal, which is why she's mentioned some "light housework" in return.' Violet had also explained that being so young, coming from a simple but hard-working and decent family and only being used to living on a small and mainly rural island, Cathie would need someone to keep an eye on her. She was certain the well-mannered girl would cause no offence or trouble though.

Cathie was so relieved. She'd expected to have to find herself lodgings and pay for them. It seemed too good to be true that a complete stranger was prepared to give her a place to stay; she wouldn't mind doing some housework at all. It must have been a very persuasive letter Miss Christian had written.

Violet reached for the other letter and Cathie noticed that the address was not handwritten, like the one on Violet's lap, but had been done on a typewriter. 'And there is more good news, Cathie. When you arrive in Liverpool, if you present your-self to Miss Edgerton at Lewis's department store, she will interview and hopefully find you a position there, although doing what exactly she doesn't say.' She smiled again. 'She was a childhood friend of my mother's and they kept in touch. My mother was originally from Liverpool and although, unlike her, Miss Edgerton didn't marry she has done very well in her career; she's been at Lewis's for a long time. I don't suppose the wages will be very much, Cathie, to start with but I'm sure there will be opportunities for advancement.'

Cathie was so happy that tears of sheer gratitude pricked her eyes. Miss Violet had done far more than she had ever expected her to. A place to stay and the possibility of a job in a big department store: it was everything she had ever dreamed of but never really expected to happen. 'Oh, Miss Christian, thank you! Thank you so much. It's ... it's ... *wonderful!* You've been so kind! I'll work hard, I promise, both for Mrs Johnston and at Lewis's – if they give me a job. I don't mind what kind of a job it is, I'll do *anything!*'

Violet smiled at her unconcealed delight. 'Well, I did promise I'd try to help you, Cathie. You and your brother probably saved my life, and at the risk of your own.'

Cathie could only nod; there was a lump in her throat. She felt like hugging Violet Christian but was aware that wouldn't be at all the proper thing to do.

'Did you speak to your parents about it?' Violet asked as she handed Cathie the letter from Avril Edgerton.

Some of Cathie's excitement drained away. 'I ... haven't, miss. I ... I didn't want them to be wondering about it all in case nothing came of it. I did tell Jacob though – my brother who was with me the day we pulled you out of the sea.'

Violet looked concerned; she really had no wish cause the girl's parents any worry or grief or to alienate them by dividing the family. It wouldn't be right, for one thing, and for another it would greatly displease her father. 'Then I think it's imperative you discuss it with them as soon as possible, Cathie. Here, take both letters and show them to your parents and tell them what I've told you about both ladies, and impress upon them that I really was only trying to help you, not cause trouble,' she urged seriously.

Cathie took the letters and nodded. 'I'll tell them the very minute I get home, miss. I promise,' she replied. How could they possibly refuse to let her go when she had a respectable place to stay and the hope of a good job?

'Then I wish you good luck, Cathie, and a happy and ... successful future,' Violet said as Cathie prepared to leave.

Cathie smiled at her, happiness shining from her dark eyes. 'Thank you, Miss Christian. I'll never forget how kind you've been and I won't let you down, you can be sure of that.' She meant it. She'd been given the opportunity of a lifetime, one she'd never expected, and she intended to make the most of it. She would improve herself, just as Miss Costain had urged her to.

To her surprise she found Jacob waiting for her, leaning on the sea wall a little further down the promenade, his hands in his pockets.

'I knew it was today you were to come back

here. What did she say?' he asked, falling into step beside her.

She gazed up at him, her eyes shining with excitement. She held out the two letters. 'Oh, she's been so kind, Jacob, so ... good! She wrote to a cousin of her mother's and an old friend too and ... I've got a place to stay and an interview at Lewis's department store!'

Jacob whistled through his teeth. This certainly was a turn-up for the books, something he hadn't expected. It just showed what money and influence could do.

'She gave me their letters to show Mam and Da, so they'll know I'll be all right. It's got the address of the Johnstons' house and Miss Edgerton's promise of an interview.'

He nodded. 'That'll be useful, Cathie, because I'm still not at all sure they'll let you go.'

Cathie frowned at his words, feeling anxious now. 'Jacob, will you help me tell them? Sort of ... back me up? You know what Da said about me asking *her* for help.'

Jacob was torn. He really didn't want her to go; it all sounded great but he was afraid something would happen to her. On the other hand how could he not help her try to achieve her dreams? She'd set her heart on going to Liverpool and it looked as if those dreams were actually going to be within her grasp. At last he nodded. 'All right, I'll back you up if you need me to. But seeing as you've got the proof she's gone to such lengths to help you, you might not need my help.'

Greatly relieved at his words and tucking her arm through his, she smiled. 'Come on then, let's go home and tell them. Oh, just think, Jacob. No more smelly fish! No more having to listen to Nora Gelling and no more being tormented by our Ella!'

Jacob smiled down at her. And no more Jack, Hal, Meggie, Mam and Da and of course himself, he thought. He'd miss her and wondered if she would miss them all too. She'd never been away from home even for a night. How would she cope in such a huge, impersonal city as Liverpool?

When they arrived home Cathie was relieved that the kitchen seemed relatively quiet. Her father was dozing in the chair by the fire, both her sisters and little Hal were out, Jack was engrossed in the *Courier* and her mother was sitting darning a pair of the thick socks her brothers wore under their sea boots.

'It's all very peaceful in here, Mam,' Jacob commented.

Lizzie smiled at him and nodded.

Cathie took a deep breath. 'Which is just as well, Mam, because I've got some really great news and I wouldn't want to have to listen to our Ella's catty remarks about it.'

Lizzie looked puzzled. 'What news? What have you been up to, Cathie?'

Barney sat up, alerted by Lizzie's questions.

'I know you told me not to, but ... but a couple of weeks ago I went to see Miss Christian—'

'Oh, Cathie, you didn't! After what your da said?' Lizzie cried.

'What's all this about, Cathie?' Barney demanded.

'Da, I've got some really great news,' Cathie said, although some of her excitement had faded and she looked at Jacob for support.

'Barney, she's been to see that Miss Violet Christian,' Lizzie informed him.

'Mam, before anything more is said, hear Cathie out,' Jacob urged quietly.

Cathie shot him a grateful glance. 'You know I never wanted a job gutting fish. I know I have to work but it ... it's always been my dream to go to Liverpool and get a job in one of the big expensive shops there.' Seeing the look on her parents' faces, she paused.

Both her parents were shaking their heads but it was her father who spoke. 'Ah, Cathie, lass, we all have dreams but life is hard; dreams don't pay the rent or put food on the table,' he said not unkindly.

'I know that, Da, but I ... I won't give up on mine!'

Barney frowned. 'Cathie, you'll have to!'

'No, Da! Miss Christian has been very kind to me. She promised to help me and she has. She's got me a job interview at Lewis's department store in Liverpool and ... and she's found me a place to stay too.' She held out the letters to her father. 'See, it's all here! And I really, really do want to go!'

Barney scowled up at her. 'So, you defied me, Cathie. You went asking her for help after I told you to forget what she said.'

This wasn't the way Cathie had wanted the conversation to go. 'I'm sorry about that but oh, Da, I wanted so much more than ... gutting fish!

I *hate* it! I really hate it! I was actually sick the first day. I *had* to do something about improving myself and she ... she ... she's been so helpful,' she faltered.

'Cathie, you're fifteen. You've only just left school and now you want to go and leave the island!' Lizzie cried. She was shocked, hardly knowing what to think about this news.

Barney nodded his agreement. 'Your mam's right, Cathie. You're far too young, lass, to be going off to work in Liverpool. It's a huge city, a huge port; you'd not cope with it all. You'd be right out of your depth.' His voice was firm, that of a man used to being listened to.

Tears started in Cathie's eyes. She hadn't expected him to refuse to let her go. He hadn't even read the letters. 'Please, Da! Please, just read the letters?' she begged.

'Won't you read them, Da, please?' Jacob urged, coming to her aid.

Stubbornly Barney shook his head. 'No. I've said you're too young and there's an end to it. I can understand you wanting a better job, Cathie, but I can't understand you wanting to leave your home and your family to go miles across the sea to live with ... strangers!'

Cathie burst into tears of bitter disappointment as she saw all her dreams being snatched from her. Without another word she ran from the room, through the scullery and into the yard where she perched on the edge of the washtub and cried as though her heart was breaking. She wasn't too young! Oh, after all Miss Christian had done – the trouble she'd gone to! It wasn't fair. It just wasn't fair. She wanted to go so much! She wanted a chance in life! She wasn't going back into that house to face them all, not even if she had to stay out here all night. Her sisters would be in soon and Ella would demand to know what was the matter, why she was crying, and would be hateful about it as usual. She couldn't stand that on top of everything else.

They'd all just stared as she'd fled, Lizzie shaking her head in confusion, Jacob feeling upset for Cathie and Jack, the newspaper now forgotten, wondering how his sister had managed to persuade Violet Christian to go to such lengths. Still sitting in his chair, Barney felt both angry and uncomfortable that he'd disappointed and upset his daughter.

Jacob sat down at the table and looked at his mother with some sympathy; he could see she was worried and upset. 'Mam, won't you and Da just think about it? She's set her heart on going. She wants to make something of herself. Is that so bad?'

'I know she does but ... but she should have asked us first, Jacob, it would have saved all this upset,' Lizzie replied, shaking her head sadly.

He nodded and turned his attention to his father. 'Da, I know she's young but is it right to deny her this opportunity? She *does* hate her job. And she's not at all keen on the girls she works with – I don't blame her for that. What has she to look forward to here? Nothing very much.'

Barney looked steadily at his son. 'And what about you, boy? Did you not think to ask Violet

Christian to get you something better? An apprenticeship, maybe?'

Jacob shook his head. 'No. I ... I never even considered it.'

'Well, why not? You're just as deserving as Cathie for pulling that one from the sea; why shouldn't she try to help you too?'

Jacob shrugged. 'I didn't think about it because I suppose I really didn't think she meant what she said. But she's surprised me, Da. She kept her promise and she's gone to a lot of trouble for our Cathie. If Cathie doesn't go she'll think us at best ... ungrateful. Will you just think about it, please?' He was trying his best for his sister.

Lizzie bit her lip and looked from her husband to her son. Maybe Jacob had a point. It would seem as if they were very ungrateful. And were they being fair in denying Cathie this chance? Oh, she didn't want her to go, she'd be worried out of her mind about her, but she knew there were many other mothers in this town who were in that situation: lots of young ones left seeking work and a better life.

Barney sighed heavily. 'I'll read the letters and then I'll think on it. That's all I'm promising.'

Lizzie looked uncertainly at Barney. 'If ... if we decide not to let her go, perhaps I should go and see Miss Christian and try to explain why, but...' She didn't finish. What she wanted to say was that she didn't know the right words to use and would feel humiliated by the lack.

Barney understood. Neither of them had had very much of an education; people like them didn't. He'd spent more time fishing with his own da and brothers than he had at school and Lizzie had had to go scrubbing floors in one of the hotels down at Port Erin at the age of twelve. Cathie was bright, she had ambitions, she wanted more than life here in Ramsey could offer: was it fair to deny her a chance of that? But she'd be mixing with all kinds of people across there. What if she got into bad company? What if she didn't get this job, or this place to stay? What would she do then? He sighed again. Well, he'd read these letters; he might be able to judge from their tone what kind of a future Cathie might have if she went and then he'd try to decide.

Jacob got to his feet. 'I'll go and see if she's all right,' he said, receiving a grateful look from his mother.

When he'd gone Lizzie looked at her husband anxiously. 'What'll we do? She does hate her work and it is a good opportunity for her – something neither of us ever had, nor the rest of them either.'

Jack picked up the newspaper again. Cathie wasn't his responsibility: the decision was his father's; but if he was truthful he knew if he'd been given such a chance he'd have taken it and he considered Jacob a fool for not asking Violet Christian to use her influence on his behalf too.

Barney looked thoughtful as he drew the sheets of notepaper from one of the envelopes. It wasn't going to be an easy decision to make.

Cathie was still crying, racked with disappointment, utterly miserable and dejected.

'Cathie, lass, wipe your eyes,' Jacob urged gently.

Cathie rubbed the cuff of her blouse across her

face. 'Oh, it's not fair, Jacob! I'm not too young!'

'Hush now. Da's promised to read the letters and think on it. He might change his mind.'

Cathie looked up hopefully. 'Do you really think he will?'

Jacob shrugged. 'It might help if you come back into the house and apologise for running out. Oh, I know how disappointed you are, but if you can tell him that you're sorry and hope he'll think about it, it will show him you're being ... sensible. That might help, Cathie.'

Reluctantly Cathie nodded. She would try anything if it would help her da change his mind; she could hardly bear to think about what she would do if he didn't.

Chapter Five

Barney had read both letters twice over and spent hours thinking about their contents. Mrs Johnston sounded a decent if rather straight-laced person, which he'd thought was no bad thing. They were, he gathered, comfortably off but not exactly wealthy and she obviously wasn't going to treat Cathie like a drudge. Miss Edgerton he thought sounded sincere in her statement that she'd give Cathie an interview and if that proved satisfactory she would find a position for her, although she did not say in what capacity or indicate what kind of a wage she'd earn. But he was still beset with anxiety as he weighed these matters and tried to come to a decision on Cathie's future. It was possibly the hardest decision he'd had to make for many years, he admitted to himself. Lizzie hadn't said much to sway him one way or the other, apart from wondering if they were being fair but admitting that she'd be worried about their daughter if she were to go. She'd said she knew that ultimately it was his decision and that she'd be happy to abide by it but he still hadn't made up his mind.

Standing in the lee of the wheelhouse he frowned as he peered through the curtain of rain. The mild spring-like weather of the past few days had turned back to the cold wind and rain of winter, but conditions changed rapidly on the island and more so out at sea. The small fishing boat shuddered slightly as it climbed out of the trough of a wave and cold salt spray stung his cheeks. The wind had risen considerably once they'd left the harbour and the traditional 'nickie', as this type of boat was called, was now struggling against the gusts and a heavy sea. Damn! They'd not be home until evening at this rate and it would be hard and heavy work bringing in the nets. Through the rain and spray he could see Jack, Jacob and young Tom Kermeen, who was a year younger than Jacob, struggling grimly with the sheets while trying to keep their footing on the wet, heaving deck and being systematically drenched by the spray constantly washing over the gunwales of the boat. What the hell kind of life was this for young lads? he thought grimly. It was the only life he'd ever known but he'd always secretly hoped for something better for his sons.

Cold water dripped from the brim of his sou'wester and trickled down the back of his neck. His feet, despite the thick socks and heavy sea boots, were numb and he knew there were hours more of this weather to endure, both for himself and the lads. His thoughts turned again to Cathie. How could he deny her the chance to go to Liverpool? To live in what sounded like a comfortable place with respectable people to keep an eye on her. To work in pleasant surroundings, out of the rain, wind, cold and in summer the scorching sun – not in the Market Square gutting fish. To experience life in a big, bustling city, to make new friends. She'd mix with different classes of people and maybe meet and marry someone with a good job who'd provide a decent home for her. In time she might even be able to do something to help Ella and Meggie get good jobs, although neither he nor Lizzie wished to see their daughters leave the island. To deny Cathie all that would be selfish and cruel.

He squared his shoulders and braced himself as the bow dipped and the boat dropped into the next trough. He'd reached his decision. Cathie would have her chance. He wouldn't deny her it and condemn her to the drudgery of work dependent on the fickle elements. His own and that of his sons was and that was enough. Cathie would have her chance to 'improve' herself.

Cathie was soaked through by the time she got home, but what was worse was that she felt sick with apprehension. This waiting for her da's decision was taking its toll. She'd gone back into the house that night and apologised and nothing more had been said and these past days she'd tried her best to carry on as normal, not to complain or badger her mam, or ask when her da would make up his mind, but it had been so hard.

'Cathie, lass, get out of those wet things!' Lizzie urged as her daughter came into the room. The girl looked so cold and miserable that her heart went out to her.

'It's that drizzly rain now, Mam, it seeps into everything. But at least the wind's dropped,' Cathie answered, thankfully stripping off her wet things. Lizzie handed her a towel and a warm dry jumper she'd had airing on the rack above the range and then took Cathie's stained apron and wet clothes and dumped them in the scullery.

Cathie sat down in the chair beside the range and held out her hands to the warmth of the fire as her mother bustled back in.

'I wonder will your da and the lads be home any time soon? It's not the best of weather to be at sea,' Lizzie stated.

Cathie nodded. 'Charlie Crennell's nickie was coming into the outer harbour when I left the Market Square and I know he went out with Da.'

Lizzie looked relieved. 'Well, I'd better heat up some of that oxtail soup; they'll be hungry and tired as well as cold and wet, but at least there'll be work for you girls tomorrow.'

Cathie curled her toes in appreciation of the warmth now seeping back into them. They would indeed be all the things her mam had described but how she wished her da had come to some decision; not knowing was agony.

Their faces pinched with cold and fatigue and crusted with dried salt water, their heavy oilskins glistening and dripping with rainwater, Barney, Jack and Jacob arrived at the cottage.

'Thank God you're all home safe,' Lizzie exclaimed as she always did on their return from sea.

'It's not a bit like spring out there, Mam. More like the middle of winter,' Jack remarked drily.

'The lad's right, but at least the catch was a good enough one,' Barney added as Lizzie, Cathie and the girls helped them out of their outer clothes.

Barney sat in the chair Cathie had vacated and began to pull off his boots, and Ella bent to help him whilst Cathie assisted Jacob.

'Cathie, lass, I've something to say to you,' Barney informed her, while smiling at his wife.

Lizzie smiled back although a little sadly. It was obvious that he was going to let Cathie go. She wasn't surprised; she'd thought he would give Cathie this chance but, oh, she'd miss her and worry about her too.

Cathie turned towards him, biting her lip, her dark eyes wide, her nerves as taut as piano wires. She prayed he was going to relent but she just couldn't be sure.

Barney sighed heavily, more from weariness than anything else. 'Well, I've decided to let you have your wish. It wouldn't be right or fair to keep you here, not when you've the chance of a good job across there.'

Cathie uttered a little shriek of delight and relief and, jumping up, flung her arms around

63

him. 'Oh, Da! Thank you. Thank you! I ... I'm so ... relieved. I'll work hard, I'll really try to make something of myself, I promise!'

Lizzie nodded at her husband. She didn't want to lose Cathie but it had been so upsetting to witness the girl's utter dejection and now the decision had been made she felt more content about the whole business.

Jacob was grinning and wishing Cathie 'good luck'; even Jack, who seldom showed his feelings, looked happy.

'What job? Across where?' Ella demanded sharply, annoyed that there was obviously some secret between them she hadn't been a party to.

'I went to see Miss Violet Christian and she's got me an interview at Lewis's department store in Liverpool, and a place for me to stay, but Da wasn't sure about letting me go ... until now,' Cathie said triumphantly. It hadn't been easy to keep all this from her sister for Ella had a way of wheedling things out of people.

Ella stared at her sister. '*You* ... you're going to Liverpool and to a job like ... that!' she cried; this was the last thing she had expected.

'I am,' Cathie said firmly.

Ella's dark eyes filled with jealousy. 'Isn't she lucky to have friends like *her!*'

'She's not a *friend,* she's more a ... a benefactor,' Cathie replied, 'someone who is kind and helps other people,' she added for the benefit of her mother, who was looking puzzled by the word.

'I *know* what it means and *I* wouldn't have gone whining to her about hating my job, even if I had dragged her out of the sea,' Ella shot back, having worked out that this what Cathie must have done. Now she knew why her sister had gone off by herself on those Saturday afternoons.

Cathie was about to retort that Ella was just being spiteful but her father forestalled her.

'That's enough of that, Ella! Who knows, if your sister does well in the future she might be able to do something to help you and Meggie.'

Ella's expression changed; she hadn't thought of that. Despite what she'd said to her mam she certainly didn't want to gut fish either.

Cathie stared at her father, taken aback by his words. She hadn't thought about that as Ella still had another two years at school ahead of her.

Lizzie became brisk and businesslike. 'Right then, now that that's settled, I've some hot oxtail soup and fresh bread,' she informed her husband and sons. 'And, Cathie, I think you'd better write to that Mrs Johnston and Miss Edgerton and tell them that you're delighted and that you'll let them know when you'll be arriving. That's only right and proper,' she instructed before turning to Ella and Meggie. 'Girls, take all these oilskins and boots into the scullery, hang up the coats and put the boots on pieces of old newspaper.'

As Barney and his sons went to the table and helped themselves gratefully to chunks of fresh crusty bread to dip into the thick, meaty soup, Cathie went and got the small, cheap writing pad from the dresser drawer and settled at the other end of the table. She felt so happy and excited that she could hardly settle her mind to think of the right words to use. Soon, very soon, she'd be walking down the length of the Victoria Pier towards the ferry which would take her across to a new life. Oh, she could hardly believe it! It was *so* exciting!

After she'd helped her mother to clear away and wash up, both she and Lizzie sat down at the table.

'Right, we'd better start and make some plans for you, Cathie, lass,' Barney said. 'We'll pay your fare and I think it would be best if you go on the morning ferry on Sunday. I know the times of the sailings.'

Cathie nodded her agreement. Meggie and Hal seemed to have lost interest and Ella was sitting by the range pretending she wasn't in the least bit interested in the conversation but Cathie knew she was sulking.

'You know, lass, that we haven't got much money but we can spare you a few shillings to tide you over. I'll not have you going to Liverpool penniless,' Barney added.

Cathie smiled at him. 'Thanks, Da, that's really generous of you.'

'And you'll have to have a hat, Cathie. No respectable girl is seen without one and this Mrs Johnston will certainly expect you to be wearing one. I'll go to Quale's and see what I can get,' Lizzie said firmly.

Again Cathie smiled. She'd feel really grown up wearing a hat although it wouldn't be new: Quale's was a second-hand shop situated in one of the narrow streets that ran behind St Paul's Church.

Lizzie continued: 'I'll wash and iron all your clothes, luv, so they'll be ready for you to take – not that there's many of them.'

'Thanks, Mam.' Cathie reached and took her hand and gave it a quick squeeze.

'Jack and I will chip in to help with your fare,' Jacob offered and Jack nodded his agreement.

'Oh, that's really good of you both,' Cathie enthused. She'd not expected this as neither of them earned a great deal.

'And if I were you, Cathie, I'd ask this Mrs Johnston for directions from the Pier Head where the ferry will berth to their house in this Clivenden Street.'

'I will, Jacob. That's a good idea.'

Lizzie got to her feet. 'Right then, now all that's settled I'll put the kettle on.'

Cathie got up to help her wondering how she was to get to sleep tonight; she had so much to think about and was bursting with excitement.

She walked down the quay next morning with a spring in her step. Before she started work she was going to post the letters she'd spent hours composing. She'd tell Madge Gelling that she wouldn't be here next week and the reason why – and she intended to make sure that Nora and the others heard her.

After posting the letters, she walked happily down to the Fish Steps where Madge was gossiping with Agnes Crennell and where, as usual, Nora and her cronies were laughing loudly at the recollection of some incident or other.

Cathie stood and waited politely until Madge turned to her. 'Is there something you want to say to me, Cathie?' Madge asked a little impatiently; she was well aware that the girl hadn't really settled into the work and didn't seem to want to mix with the other girls.

'Yes – that I'll be leaving, Mrs Gelling, on Saturday. I'm going across to Liverpool on the Sunday-morning ferry,' she said clearly, noting that the girls had fallen silent.

Madge was taken aback. 'What for?'

'To work. I've an interview at Lewis's … it's a big department store.'

'I've heard of it. Quite an expensive one too,' Agnes Crennell said, nodding.

'Aren't you a bit young to be going across?' Madge enquired. She'd seen Lizzie Kinrade a few times in the last couple of days and she'd not mentioned this.

'I suppose I am but I've got somewhere to stay, so Mam and Da are letting me go. I'm lodging with a Mr and Mrs Johnston.'

'How did you manage to get an interview *and* a place to lodge?' Nora demanded, openly envious. She'd give her right arm to go to work in a big shop in Liverpool.

Cathie had anticipated this. 'Through someone I know who has contacts there. It's no one you know, Nora. No one from Ramsey,' she added. She was reluctant for them all to know that her good fortune was due to Violet Christian – it would be bandied all over town and she didn't want people gossiping about either Miss Violet or herself.

'Well, that's a turn-up for the books, I have to say, Cathie. But you've not really settled into gutting, have you?' Madge said, still surprised.

Cathie shook her head. 'No, I haven't, Mrs

Gelling, but I'm grateful you gave me a chance to work at it,' she replied. Her mam had urged her to thank Madge politely. 'Actually, I ... I hate it,' she added, unable to stop herself and excited by the thought that after Saturday she would never have to handle another fish.

'Oh, *actually I hate it!*' Nora repeated her words loudly, at which the other girls laughed.

Madge took the situation in hand, though she was a little annoyed by Cathie's words, for she knew how jealous Nora really was. She didn't want any scenes. 'Right, that's enough. There's work to do for all of you,' she instructed as she handed Cathie the gutting knife, realising now that that was why Cathie Kinrade hadn't bought a knife of her own. Well, she was a fair-minded woman, she thought, she wished the girl well in her new life. You had to take whatever opportunities arose.

Despite having to work, the days just flew by now for Cathie and indeed Lizzie too. She'd bought her daughter a small black felt hat decorated with a white band of ribbon around the crown and she'd pressed and brushed her one good jacket, wishing that funds would stretch to a new one for Cathie. She wanted her to go off looking smart. She'd shed a few tears when she'd been on her own washing the remainder of her eldest daughter's things. Still, she comforted herself with the fact that Cathie had had a nice letter from Mrs Johnston by return post, giving her instructions how to get to Clivenden Street and saying she would have the room ready for her. It would be quite a luxury for Cathie to have a room and a bed to herself; she'd always had to share. Lizzie had made her promise she'd write and tell them all about the city, the house, her job ... everything. Cathie was good with words and Lizzie knew she'd never get the opportunity to go to Liverpool herself. She would be able to see everything through Cathie's eyes, she told herself.

As she vigorously scrubbed the kitchen table a thought suddenly occurred to her. Saturday night's supper would be the last one Cathie would share with them all. Shouldn't she try to make it special? She'd get a nice bit of meat from Kermeen's Butcher's. What did it matter that they would have to make do with fish pie for the next couple of Sundays? She'd talk about it with Barney when he got home and maybe Meggie and Hal could make a card at school for their sister. It would be no use asking Ella to do anything, she knew that. Yes, it was something of a special occasion, Cathie being the first of the family to leave her home on the island. Lizzie wanted her to take the memory of a happy family meal with her.

Barney agreed it was a good idea when she mentioned it to him that evening after supper.

'You won't mind us not having our usual Sunday dinner for a couple of weeks? What with buying the hat, giving Cathie a few shillings to take with her and paying her fare, there's not much left in the housekeeping,' she reminded him.

'You know that won't bother me, Lizzie. I'd sooner we made the most of the last meal we'll share as a complete family.'

Lizzie smiled at him. 'And Meggie and Hal are going to make a "Going Away" card for her at school,' she added.

He nodded, filling his pipe with tobacco from the little tin box that was kept on the mantel above the range. It was the one luxury Barney allowed himself, a pipe of tobacco after a long, hard day.

Jacob took a paper spill from the jar, held it to the fire until it caught and passed it to his father to light his pipe. He'd noted that no mention had been made of Ella. He and Jack were going to contribute something but he wanted to give his sister something else, something just from him, something that would remind her of home. He'd scour the small junk shops in old Ramsey to see what he could find, he mused. He'd miss Cathie; he knew they all would. Even Ella would miss the squabbles. He didn't know why those two didn't get on. They were both fine with Jack, himself, Meggie and Hal, but they just seemed to rub one another up the wrong way and always had done. He often thought that Ella resented Cathie just for being older – he couldn't put it down to anything else, for Mam and Da had always treated them all equally fairly. They had no favourites. Da did rely on Jack a lot more these days but then Jack was the oldest. As he stared into the flames of the fire, Jacob supposed there were a lot of brothers and sisters who just didn't get on: Cathie and Ella weren't unusual. Still, in a matter of days Cathie would be gone and he really would miss her. Life was strange. If Cathie hadn't gone off that Saturday morning she would never have come into contact with Violet Christian and her dreams would have remained just that – dreams.

71

Chapter Six

When Cathie had gutted the last herring on Saturday afternoon she wiped her hands and the knife on her stained apron, took it off and bundled it up and gave Madge back the knife.

'Thank you, Mrs Gelling, for the use of it, it was very kind of you,' she said politely.

Madge nodded. 'Here're your wages, Cathie. Your mam will miss your money now, I expect,' she remarked, knowing how tight funds always were for folk like them.

'I intend to send money home as soon as I can, Mrs Gelling. I don't want Mam to lose the benefit of my wages; it's hard enough for her to manage now,' Cathie replied.

Madge smiled her approval. 'You're a good lass, Cathie. Well, good luck in Liverpool but don't you go forgetting where you come from,' she instructed.

Cathie smiled back at her. 'I won't. Ramsey will always be home for me.' She felt so happy that before she walked away she raised her hand and waved to Nora and the others. She really felt that from this moment her life was changing.

'That's me finished with gutting fish forever, Mam!' she announced with satisfaction as, from habit, she shoved her apron into the bucket of water to soak. She'd never have to wear it again.

Lizzie smiled at her. 'You did well to stick at it,

Cathie, and now we've a bit of a treat. We're all going to have our "Sunday" dinner tonight. There'll only be time for a bit of breakfast in the morning, what with the ferry leaving at half past nine. We'll all see you off and then we'll go on to St Paul's for Sunday service as usual. After you've had a good wash go on upstairs: I've laid everything out on the bed for you. You can fold your things later tonight and I've found a big hemp bag to put them in.' They didn't own a suitcase or even a Gladstone bag: they'd not needed one for none of them had ever travelled anywhere before; but the strong hemp bag would do as well.

'Thanks, Mam,' Cathie replied, giving her a quick hug.

In the small bedroom she shared with her sisters and her mother she found her few clothes and underclothes laid out neatly on the bed. Her jacket was hanging on the back of the door, her hat placed on top of the chest of drawers, on the floor beside which was the woven hemp bag with its two strong carrying handles. Suddenly it hit home that in the morning she would really be leaving here. This cottage where she'd been born and had lived all her life; her parents, her brothers and sisters; this small town where she'd grown up; this island with its hills, moors, glens and wide sandy beaches. For the first time she felt a frisson of doubt run through her. What if she was homesick? What if she didn't like Mr and Mrs Johnston? What if she didn't come up to Miss Edgerton's expectations and didn't get the job in Lewis's? Resolutely she pushed the thoughts away. No, everything would be fine.

This was what she had set her heart on. There was no turning back now.

'I don't know why everyone is making such a fuss over you leaving,' Ella announced pettishly as she came into the room. 'And I hope you're not going to leave all that stuff on the bed all night,' she added tartly.

'I'll fold it and pack it later on. Don't worry, Ella, it'll all be done before you and Meggie go to bed,' Cathie replied just as tartly. 'And I didn't ask anyone to make a "fuss". Mam wanted my last night at home to be a bit special, that's all.'

Ella frowned. 'Well, at least after tomorrow I won't have you looking down your nose at everything I do or say.'

Cathie sighed; her sister was spoiling for an argument as usual but this time she would be disappointed. She wasn't going to rise to the bait. 'Ella, why do you always have to be so nasty?'

'I'm not!' Ella shot back.

'Well ... argumentative then? I'm *not* always looking down my nose at you and I'd try to help you more if you weren't always so ... prickly.'

Ella narrowed her eyes. 'You always get what you want, Cathie. Mam even let you go off for "walks" by yourself when you should have been helping with the chores and that wasn't fair! And it's not fair that you're going off to Liverpool.' She picked up the hat Lizzie had bought for Cathie, her resentment deepening. 'Still, what if you don't get this job? What if they don't think you're good enough to serve in a posh shop at all? Or any kind of shop.' She twirled the hat around on her fingers. 'All this will have been for nothing. A total

74

waste of money! What'll you do then, Cathie? You'll just have to come back home with your tail between your legs and then Nora Gelling and that lot will all laugh at you and your fancy ideas. Everyone will laugh at you, Cathie, and I'll be the one laughing the loudest!'

Cathie glared at her. She was hurt by her sister's words, and shaken – what if they came true? But she was determined not to show it. 'I'm not even going to bother to reply to that, Ella. I'm going down to help Mam,' she said firmly before she left the room, leaving Ella sitting on the edge of the bed looking mutinous.

She found Lizzie and Meggie setting the table and immediately went to the dresser to fetch more dishes to help. There was a delicious smell of roast lamb coming from the oven and she wrinkled her nose appreciatively. 'You're a great cook, Mam,' she complimented her mother and received a warm smile in return.

Before long her father and brothers arrived home; the weather had been mild and spring-like again today and so they were early.

'Something smells good, Mam,' Jack remarked, winking at Jacob.

'Well, get your things off and get washed,' Lizzie instructed. 'By then I'll have the vegetables and potatoes ready to serve,' she added as she bustled about checking the pans boiling on the range.

The kitchen and scullery became a hive of activity and noise and Lizzie smiled to herself, relishing the sounds of her family gathered happily together at the end of a working day to share a good meal. As she placed the small joint of lamb she'd bought on a plate, ready for Barney to carve, and drained the potatoes, she urged them all to sit at the table, which, with some good-natured banter, they did.

'Where's Ella?' she asked, turning to place the joint on the table and noting that the girl's place was empty.

'I left her upstairs, Mam,' Cathie informed her.

'Jack, go and call her to come down at once,' Lizzie instructed, determined that she would stand no nonsense out of Ella this evening.

Ella at last appeared and took her place, shooting a sullen glance at Cathie.

'Well, isn't this a great meal your mam's cooked?' Barney said jovially, brandishing the carving knife and fork.

'It seems a bit strange for a Saturday evening, but it is Cathie's "farewell" dinner,' Jacob remarked, smiling across at his sister.

'Don't let it go cold after all my hard work,' Lizzie urged and after that there was little conversation as they all ate.

When they'd finished, Cathie rose, ready to start to clear away, but Lizzie waved her back into the chair. 'Leave them, Cathie. I'll do them later and Ella and Meggie can help me.' She got up and took something from the mantel above the range and handed it to Cathie. 'There're the few shillings we promised you, Cathie. I've made a little bag to keep them in. Hang it around your neck, under your blouse; it'll be safe there.'

Cathie smiled her thanks; Mam was always practical.

'Jack and I chipped in, Cathie,' Jacob said

quietly and Jack nodded. Cathie smiled gratefully at them both.

Meggie passed her a card, a piece of stiffened paper on which the little girl had drawn a lake surrounded by shrubs and trees and flowers. 'I made this for you, Cathie, for good luck. It's supposed to be the lake in Mooragh Park.'

'And I did this for you too.' Hal passed over another card, depicting a rather lopsided-looking boat with a big yellow sun shining in the sky above it. 'It's the ferry,' he added in case there was any doubt.

'They're both lovely. I'll keep them safe, I promise.'

Barney and Lizzie exchanged glances, both feeling the stirrings of sadness that their daughter was leaving home.

'I wanted to give you something too, Cathie,' Jacob said, delving into the pocket of his trousers.

'But you've already given me money,' Cathie protested, knowing how little there was left for himself after he'd handed his 'keep' over to Mam.

'Oh, it didn't cost much. I ... I thought it would always remind you of home,' he replied a little awkwardly as he passed over the small gift.

'Oh, Jacob, it's ... beautiful!' Cathie exclaimed. It was a little base-metal brooch depicting the three Legs of Man, which had been enamelled in red, yellow and black. She'd never owned a single piece of jewellery before and was touched that her brother had gone to so much trouble to find and buy this for her. Carefully she pinned it on the lapel of her blouse.

'So, now you're all set, Cathie,' Lizzie said,

getting to her feet. She'd not missed the envious and resentful looks Ella had given her sister or the girl's pursed lips. She shook her head resignedly. Still, after tomorrow Ella would be the oldest girl at home, so maybe she'd be a bit happier with her lot. 'Girls, let's get these dishes stacked. I'll wash, Ella you can dry and Meggie you can put them away. Let's leave your da to his pipe.'

Cathie too got to her feet; she hadn't expected to receive gifts: the little purse Mam had made for her, the cards, money from Jack and Jacob and this beautiful little brooch. She was deeply touched by it all. 'I'll go up and fold and pack my things, Mam,' she said.

Jacob grinned at her. 'I don't suppose you'll get much sleep tonight, Cathie, you'll be too excited.'

'Excited and ... a bit nervous,' she admitted. It was a huge step she was taking, facing an unknown city where she knew no one and an unknown future, but she felt confident she'd manage.

To her surprise she slept well but she woke early to find the sunlight streaming into the room through the small curtainless window. When she went downstairs she found that both her parents were already up, washed and dressed.

'Sit down, Cathie, and have this bowl of porridge,' Lizzie instructed. 'And I've made you some sandwiches to eat on the boat. You'll need them for it'll be after midday by the time you arrive and you won't know when you'll be getting anything else to eat,' she added, indicating the small packet wrapped in greaseproof paper on the top of the dresser.

'Thanks, Mam. I hadn't thought of that,' she said, tucking into her breakfast.

One by one her brothers and sisters came down and suddenly it was time for her to leave.

'Now, lass, let me look at you.' Lizzie placed her hands on Cathie's shoulders as she inspected her daughter's appearance. She tilted the hat a little to one side and then nodded. 'You look smart enough.'

Cathie thought she detected the brightness of tears in her mam's eyes but she didn't say anything. She picked up the sandwiches and placed them on top of the bag.

Her father cleared his throat. 'I think we'll all say our goodbyes here; then we'll not be providing a spectacle for those on the pier,' he announced. He wasn't given to public displays of emotion; he didn't think them 'seemly'.

Lizzie nodded as she hugged her daughter for the last time. 'Take care of yourself, Cathie. Remember to be well mannered to everyone and work hard. And don't forget to write and tell us all about everything.'

'I'll do all that, Mam, I promise,' Cathie replied, a lump in her throat. Her tears were not far away now.

Barney then gave her a quick, rather awkward hug. 'Good luck, lass. Like your mam said, work hard and mind your manners.'

Jack gave her a quick peck on the cheek and added his 'Good luck' and then Jacob hugged her.

'Take care, Cathie. We'll all miss you, but you go and make those dreams come true.'

She smiled up at him. 'I will, Jacob. They're not

like circles in the sand now – they won't be washed away by the tide.'

Both Meggie and little Hal hugged her shyly and then Cathie turned to Ella.

Her sister embraced her stiffly. 'I suppose I'd better wish you good luck too,' she said ungraciously.

'Thanks,' Cathie replied, wondering if she would ever see her sister again. Would she see any of them again? She fervently hoped so – it wasn't a long journey by sea and the ferries were regular.

The little group set off for the East Quay which led out to the Queen's Promenade. It was a fine, sunny, spring morning and many people were taking advantage of the weather but there was no time to stop and chat to acquaintances, except to wish them 'Good morning', for the family would have to walk all the way back to attend church in the Market Square.

When they at last reached the entrance to the pier flanked by the large houses of Stanley Mount East, they could see that the ferry *Peveril* was tied up at the seaward end.

'You've a fine day for it, Cathie,' Barney announced. 'It'll be a fairly calm crossing.'

"Which is just as well seeing as she's never been on a boat before,' Jack remarked succinctly, winking at his sister.

'Now, you've got your ticket and your money's safe?' Lizzie fussed, suddenly feeling very anxious now that the moment had arrived.

'I have, Mam, and I've got Mrs Johnston's instructions for when I arrive,' Cathie said, smiling.

'Well, off you go, lass. It's a fair walk but there's

a "shelter house" at the other end if you have to wait to board,' Barney said rather gruffly, trying to hide his emotions.

There was a little train that ran down the length of the pier but Cathie wasn't going to waste any money paying to ride on that. It was a fine day and she didn't mind the walk, and other people were making their way towards the ferry too. 'I'll write in a couple of days, I promise,' she said as she strode away from them, turning to wave after a few yards. Her heart was beating rapidly; this was *it!* She was going to follow her dreams! It was the start of a big adventure.

As the others turned away Jacob stood staring after her for a few more seconds, a small, slight figure in a dark jacket and a black and white hat that drew further and further away. He didn't think he'd ever known anyone with as much hope, determination and courage as his sister. Fifteen years old and going to Liverpool to follow her dreams with a packet of sandwiches, a hemp bag and seven shillings. He sighed as he turned away. 'Good luck, Cathie, lass,' he muttered to himself. 'You deserve it.'

Chapter Seven

When the heather- and bracken-covered slopes of North Barrule at last became just a faint blur on the horizon Cathie turned away from the ship's rail and the final sight of her island home. As

81

they'd pulled away from the pier there had been many other people on the deck of the *Peveril* but most had gone below now and she decided that she too would go and explore the rest of the ferry.

In the main saloon people were settling themselves for the journey. As she looked around she thought it looked comfortable enough with portholes and rows of padded benches, tables and even some prints of other Steam Packet ferries attached to the bulkheads, softening its otherwise practical appearance. At the far end of the saloon there was a staircase and she decided she'd see where it led to. To her surprise she found it descended into another saloon, a smaller but very much grander one. Here there were chairs and sofas covered in cut brocade and small polished side tables with brass rails around their tops bolted to the deck, which was covered in black and white checked linoleum made to resemble tiles. In the centre of the saloon was a large arrangement of ferns around which was a circular, deeply upholstered seat. At the far end of the room stood a set of glass doors; as everywhere was deserted she decided to have a look what lay beyond them.

She peered through into a dining room, the like of which she'd never seen before. The tables were set with pristine white damask cloths and napkins, silver cutlery, fine china and in the centre of each table was a small china vase containing flowers. It all looked so ... elegant, she thought, realising also that she couldn't feel the movement of the boat much down there.

'Can I help you? We're not open yet, I'm afraid. Have you booked, miss?'

Cathie turned, startled by the voice, and found a man in a white jacket standing looking enquiringly at her. 'Oh, sorry! Er ... no. Am I not supposed to be down here? It's all very ... grand,' she stammered.

He smiled kindly at her. 'It's the first-class lounge, miss, and through there is the restaurant. You have to book a table in advance.'

Cathie smiled back, relieved she wasn't going to be admonished for being in here. 'Oh, I see. I've never been on the ferry before and I was just ... having a look around.'

'You get a very good meal here – the best of everything,' he informed her good naturedly.

'How much does a meal cost?' she asked tentatively, although she had no intention of eating here.

'Two and six, but it's excellent value for three courses. Plus coffee or tea,' he replied.

She was shocked at such a high price for a meal. 'Oh, I can't afford to pay anything like that and, besides, Mam made me some sandwiches to eat.'

'Are you going across to work, miss?' he enquired.

Cathie nodded. 'I'm hoping to get a job in Lewis's. I've never been to Liverpool before.'

'Then I hope you do well for yourself. If you do, who knows? One day you might be able to come home – first class. Good luck, miss. If I were you I'd go back up and find somewhere comfortable to eat your sandwiches before other people have the same idea,' he urged, for the restaurant would be opening shortly. 'You can get a cup of tea in the public saloon too,' he added.

Cathie smiled at him again and turned to retrace her steps. She didn't linger in the public saloon, however, but went back out on deck. The weather was warm and sunny and there were benches set at intervals out here, bolted to the deck like the tables she'd seen downstairs. She'd eat out here, she decided.

She found a seat on an empty bench near the bow and sat staring out to sea where in the distance she could see a couple of small fishing boats. They reminded her of her da and brothers and for the first time since she'd boarded she felt a bit lonely. The sea seemed to stretch ahead endlessly; she couldn't see any land at all and she wondered how much longer the journey would take. Carefully she unwrapped her sandwiches and ate slowly, speculating about what kind of food you'd get for half a crown. It would have to be marvellous for such an extortionate sum. When she'd finished she folded the greaseproof paper and tucked it back into her bag, then she got to her feet and walked a bit further along the deck. Surely they must be nearing land now? She seemed to have been on board for hours.

As she leaned on the rail, gazing down at the grey-green waters of the Irish Sea, in places topped with white foam from the bow wave, she became aware that they seemed to be slowing down. She was puzzled as to why and, turning, she saw an elderly gentleman leaning on the rail a little further down. 'Sir, are we slowing down, do you think?' she called to him.

He nodded and moved closer to her so as not to have to shout. 'We are indeed slowing down. Captain Teare always does when we reach this point.'

Cathie assumed that he was a frequent traveller if he knew this to be a fact. 'Why is that, sir? Where is "this point"?'

'I take it you're Manx so I know you'll have heard of the *Ellan Vannin?*'

'Oh, I have. There's a plaque near the harbour steps in Ramsey and there's a church service every December for those who were lost.'

'This is where they think she went down. Captain Teare's grandfather – Captain James Teare – was the master of that ship, so it's his way of paying his respects.'

Cathie nodded slowly as understanding dawned. On the night of 3 December 1909 the little ferry boat had left Ramsey in the teeth of a storm with thirty-five crew and passengers. They'd almost reached the bar light at the entrance to the Mersey when they were struck by a gigantic wave and the ferry had sunk with the loss of everyone on board. It was one of the worst tragedies the island had experienced and since then no other ferry had born the name *Ellan Vannin*. She shivered, mindful that her da and brothers faced the dangers of the sea nearly every day of their lives. 'Have we got much further to go now, sir?' she asked, thankful that they had begun to pick up speed again.

'No, we'll be in the Mersey in about half an hour,' he supplied before raising his hat politely and strolling away down the deck, his hands clasped behind his back.

She stood peering intently ahead and at last she saw the outline of the banks of the river on either side of the ship. It wouldn't be long now, she thought, before she got her first sight of the city that was to be her home. Slowly the lighthouse, then the fort at Perch Rock and the tower at New Brighton became visible and she marvelled how wide the river was here, compared to the Sulby River which flowed into Ramsey harbour. And many other ships were either sailing out or lying at anchor: dredgers, cargo ships and the ferries ploughing their way across the river between Liverpool, Birkenhead, Wallasey and New Brighton. Finally the spire of St Nicholas's Church became clear and then the outline of the three magnificent buildings on the waterfront at the Pier Head: the Royal Liver, the Cunard and the Docks & Harbour Board buildings. She'd heard they were called the 'Three Graces' and had seen pictures of them at school. Her excitement began to mount again as she realised they'd almost arrived, and she clutched the rail tightly.

As they drew closer to the Landing Stage she was amazed to see an enormous ship tied up there. It completely dwarfed the ferry boat, she thought. Many other people had now come up on deck and as they drew alongside she craned her neck to look up at it. The black-painted hull towered above her and the four red and black funnels emitted wisps of grey smoke; her gaze took in the white lettering on the side. *'Aquitania'*, she read. It was a Cunard liner, one of the famed, fast 'floating palaces' that regularly crossed the Atlantic to America. Well, it certainly was a great sight and she'd put that in her first letter home; her da and the lads would find it interesting.

It wasn't long before they'd tied up and people

began to make their way towards the gangway. Clutching Mrs Johnston's directions in her hand she joined the crowd. It must be high tide for it wasn't too steep, she thought as she walked up the floating roadway towards the Pier Head, which was crowded and not only with passengers disembarking from the *Peveril*. There were passengers and crew from the *Aquitania* too, which she realised was almost ready to depart. There were Cunard officials and clerks, porters manhandling luggage, people still emerging from the Riverside Station and those who had just come to witness the spectacle. She stood for a few seconds unsure whether to turn right or left; everyone else seemed to know where they were going and it was all a bit daunting. Catching a glimpse of some trams, she squared her shoulders and negotiated her way determinedly through the crowds towards the tram terminus where a line of green and cream trams waited. She soon found the one Mrs Johnston had told her to get and prepared to climb aboard.

'How much does it cost, please?' she asked the conductor.

'Depends where you're going, luv,' he replied laconically, fiddling with his ticket machine.

'Clivenden Street,' she read from the letter.

'It'll be tuppence then.'

She took two pennies from her pocket, for she'd anticipated she'd need the tram fare before she disembarked from the ferry, and handed them over. 'Can you please put me off at the nearest stop to there? I don't know where it is, you see.'

He grinned at her as he handed her ticket. 'I'll

give you a shout, don't worry, girl.'

'Does the tram go past Lewis's?' she asked hopefully, thinking she'd love to actually see the department store where she would be going for her interview on Tuesday morning.

'I'm afraid not, luv. We go along Chapel Street and Tithebarn Street and out of the city centre that way. Lewis's is in Ranelagh Street.'

Feeling a little disappointed, she settled down on the seat. She was slightly self-conscious about her hemp bag and second-hand hat but she soon noticed that many of the other passengers were quite plainly dressed. As the vehicle trundled slowly away from the Pier Head she stared around her in amazement at the wide streets, the magnificent buildings, and what seemed to her crowds of people thronging the pavements. Many were very fashionably dressed but as they reached Scotland Road she noticed that many more were very poorly dressed indeed – she even saw children without boots or shoes and wearing what her mam would have termed 'rags'. As the tram progressed the streets became narrower and more and more filthy, the houses alarmingly dilapidated. In all her dreams she'd never imagined that there would be such poverty in so grand a city: it was a sobering thought.

True to his word the conductor eventually roared, 'Here's your stop for Clivenden Street, girl!' down the length of the tram and with a start she made her way towards the platform, nodding her thanks to him.

'It's the second road on the left, you can't miss it,' he instructed.

The sun was warm on her back as she walked along the road, which even on a Sunday was busy with traffic. She felt optimistic although a little nervous, wondering what the house in Clivenden Street and its occupants would be like. As she turned the corner she noticed that the houses were tall terraced villas and looked well cared for – this must be a more affluent area, she deduced. They all had tiny front gardens enclosed by a wall and two steps leading up to the front door beside which was a bay window. She also noted with relief that all the curtains were clean, the paint-work unchipped and the brasses gleamed.

She stopped in front of number twelve. The two rose bushes in the garden were just beginning to come into leaf; the paintwork on the door and windows was a rich brown colour. So, this was to be her new home, she marvelled: even from the outside it was so different from and clearly much bigger than the cottage in Collins Lane. She went up the steps and knocked, her heart in her mouth. She sincerely hoped she'd like Mrs John-ston. It was all a bit daunting.

An older woman opened the door with a polite smile. 'You must be Cathie Kinrade. We've been expecting you,' she greeted her.

Cathie relaxed a little. Ethel Johnston was a small woman with grey hair set in the rigid marcel waves fashionable ten years ago, and she wore a black wool dress also of that era. She wasn't much taller than herself but she was three times as wide, Cathie noted. Still, she looked pleasant. 'It is, Mrs Johnston. Your directions were very helpful.'

'Well, come inside, you've had a long journey,'

she instructed.

Cathie followed her down a narrow lobby that boasted a striped runner on the floor and a couple of framed prints on the walls. She was led into a very neat kitchen that was large enough for a table and chairs, as well as a gas cooker and an earthenware sink and wooden draining board. The walls were lined with shelves covered in patterned oilcloth on which the pans and crockery were displayed. It was a very modern kitchen, Cathie thought, with no range to be seen and two taps over the sink. There would be no need to heat up water here.

'Put your bag down, Cathie, and take off your jacket and hat. I'll make a pot of tea then I'll introduce you to Mr Johnston and show you your room.'

Cathie did as she was told, wondering if she should have offered to make the tea.

'We have a light supper at about seven,' the older woman informed her as she placed two china cups and saucers on the table and poured the boiling water from the kettle into a brown glazed pot.

'I had some sandwiches on the boat. Mam made them for me,' she supplied.

'Very sensible,' Ethel Johnston replied approvingly. 'Now, Violet has told me that you are fifteen, one of six children, that your father is a fisherman – as are two of your brothers – and that you did her a very great service. Is that all correct?'

Cathie nodded her assent.

'Violet thinks highly of you but you do realise

that agreeing to take you in is something of a ... risk for us? I am assuming that you are completely trustworthy, honest and have high ... morals?'

'Oh, I am, Mrs Johnston!'

The woman nodded, relieved. The girl seemed to be polite and well brought up and was quite pretty too. 'Good. Violet assures me you're a well-mannered girl from a God-fearing family.'

'We attended Sunday service each week, Mrs Johnston,' Cathie assured her, sipping her tea, thinking that although the kitchen was bright and modern it didn't seem to have the same atmosphere as her mam's. The house was very quiet, something she wasn't really used to, but then there were only two people living in this house while at home there were eight – or there had been.

The 'light housework' duties were outlined in detail while she drank her tea. She would be expected to make her bed and keep her room tidy and dusted; she would get her own breakfast and wash up each morning; and she would do her own laundry. When she returned from work she would help prepare and cook the evening meal and if she couldn't bake a decent pie her landlady would teach her.

'My mam taught me to bake when I was ten and I know how to make soups and stews,' Cathie replied, not wishing Mrs Johnston to think her unable to cook.

The older woman nodded. 'You will then help with the washing up and on your day off you will help me to clean and polish the hall, parlour and kitchen. I don't expect you to do it all by yourself.'

It didn't sound like a great deal of work, Cathie

91

thought. Although the house was much bigger than she'd been used to, she'd always helped her mother. 'I'm very grateful, Mrs Johnston, and I'll be happy to do the chores. I've helped Mam since I was quite small.'

'Yes, Violet said she assumed you were quite used to helping out at home. I should tell you we keep ourselves to ourselves. I don't gossip with the neighbours and I don't expect you to either. You'll find people here are friendly but quite often that disguises a certain nosiness. Keep your own counsel, Cathie. And there is just one other thing. I'm sure you will soon make new friends but ... but ... I'm afraid it won't be possible for you to bring them here – especially ... er ... gentlemen friends. It's too much of a responsibility for us and also Mr Johnston doesn't like his evenings to be disturbed.' She stood up. 'Now, I'll take you through into the parlour to meet my husband. It's his habit to read his newspapers in there on a Sunday.'

Cathie followed her out into the lobby. She'd not even thought about bringing friends here but obviously Mrs Johnston had. Well, she had made her feelings quite clear. The parlour was a rather gloomy room: the heavy draw curtains and thick cotton lace ones seemed to shut out the light; the furniture was dark and cumbersome, although it looked comfortable enough; and there were ornaments and photos in silver frames dotted about. Her mam would have given her right arm for a parlour with furniture and ornaments like this, she thought.

Mr Johnston was a thin man with grey hair that had receded from his forehead, a clipped moustache and pale blue eyes that regarded her from behind spectacles. Cathie thought he looked rather dour.

'So, you are Cathie Kinrade,' he remarked as she shook his hand.

'I am, Mr Johnston, and I'd like to thank you for allowing me to stay here.'

He nodded briefly. 'Ethel persuaded me after Violet's recommendation. I hope you will settle in; we are not exacting people.'

'I'm sure I will,' Cathie replied and he then returned to his newspaper, leaving his wife to usher her out and up the stairs. Cathie realised that she had never met people quite like this before. They were a bit reserved; there didn't seem to be any of the easy friendliness she'd always encountered before and she had an inkling that they would prove to be quite strict.

She was utterly delighted with the room she was shown. At the back of the house, it overlooked the small and very tidy yard. There were blue and white flowered curtains at the window and a blue and white cotton counterpane on the single bed. The lino on the floor was clean and well polished and a small rug was set beside the bed. A wardrobe, a chest of drawers and a small bookcase holding a few books completed the furnishings. 'Oh, it's lovely, really it is! I didn't expect anything as ... nice as this,' she enthused.

Mrs Johnston smiled, gratified by her obvious pleasure. 'Across the landing is a bathroom and two more bedrooms, neither of which you must enter. I must stress that emphatically, although of course you will be quite free to use the bathroom and I trust you will clean it after you've used it.'

'Of course, but will I not be expected to help clean the other bedrooms?' Cathie asked, thinking it quite reasonable that she shouldn't go into what was obviously her landlady's bedroom. But what about the other one?

'No! I'll do that myself. Those rooms are no concern of yours,' came the quite curt reply.

Cathie nodded, a little taken aback by the sudden change in the woman's demeanour. But then the smile and the softer tone were back. 'I almost forgot, Cathie. This arrived for you.' She handed over an envelope which Cathie was surprised to see bore a Manx stamp.

'It's from Violet, I assume, or maybe your parents?' Ethel Johnston inferred.

Cathie shook her head. 'No, it's definitely not from Mam or Da. I only left this morning.'

'Well, I'll leave you to open it and get unpacked. Come down when you're ready, and you can tell me what plans you have for tomorrow.'

When she'd gone Cathie sat down on the bed and looked around, the letter in her lap. A room of her very own and a bathroom! That was an unexpected luxury. No more washing in the scullery or taking the weekly bath in the tin tub in the kitchen or having to go out into the yard to the privy.

She opened the letter. It was indeed from Violet Christian, a short note saying she hoped Cathie would settle in with the Johnstons and do well at her new job. She had also enclosed two one-pound notes which she wanted Cathie to have as an 'emergency fund', so that should any kind of problem arise and she needed to come home she would at least have her fare. Tears pricked Cathie's eyes as she folded the notes and tucked them into the little bag with the rest of her money. She was so grateful! She'd never expected this! Miss Violet was so thoughtful. Suddenly she realised that she had never had so much money in her life before. What would she do with two pounds seven shillings? Of course she'd put enough away for her fare home in case she ever needed it, but now for the first time she could afford to spend some on herself. Oh, she was so fortunate, she thought. She had this lovely room, a bright modern kitchen to use and of course the bathroom – it was all so unexpected. So Mr and Mrs Johnston were un-demonstrative and clearly rather set in their ways, but they were old and she hadn't really expected them to greet her like a long-lost daughter. She was after all a stranger – a lodger who would do housework for her bed and board.

She got to her feet: she'd unpack her things and then she'd go down and tell Mrs Johnston that her interview was on Tuesday morning. She would have tomorrow to settle in. Oh, what an eventful day it had been; she had so much to tell them all at home. First thing tomorrow she'd purchase a writing pad and envelopes, she decided. She'd write to Miss Violet too to thank her for her generosity. Mrs Johnston would be able to tell her where the local newsagent's and post office were and how to get to Ranelagh Street on Tuesday. She'd feel at home here in no time, she told herself. She'd soon be able to find her way around the city – even though it was so big – and if she got the job ... well, she would be quite well off by her standards and she'd soon be able to send some money home. She had so much to look forward to now, she thought happily as she hung up her good dress in the wardrobe, her mind buzzing with plans and excitement.

Chapter Eight

The following morning, after she'd completed her chores and Mrs Johnston had given her the directions, she walked to the local shops to make her small purchases. Anfield wasn't too far from the city centre at all, the woman in the newsagent's informed her chattily after she'd explained that she was newly arrived from the Isle of Man.

'Yes, I thought I hadn't seen you around here before. It's not far, really only about four or five stops on the tram, luv. I bet you're a bit confused by all the streets and the traffic, coming from a small place like that. Not that I've ever been, mind you.'

Cathie smiled. 'I'm getting used to it. It's all rather ... exciting actually,' she confided.

'I suppose you've come over to work. Where are you staying? Somewhere local?'

'Yes, just a couple of streets away,' she replied before she remembered her landlady's instructions to keep her own counsel. 'How much do I owe you, please?'

'Just sixpence, queen.'

Cathie handed over the coins thinking that Liverpudlians were indeed friendly. They seemed to have a variety of terms of endearment which they happily used to strangers. Now she'd make her way to the post office for stamps and then she'd explore more of the local area before returning to Clivenden Street. It would be useful to get her bearings.

On Tuesday morning as she walked through the ornate doors into Lewis's department store Cathie stood still for a few seconds, her eyes wide with astonishment and wonder. She'd never imagined a shop could be like this! It was enormous, brightly lit by chandeliers no less, suspended from the high ceiling. There were endless counters that seemed to stock every conceivable luxury. When she'd alighted from the tram in Ranelagh Street where Mrs Johnston had told her the main entrance was (although the building stretched around the corner into Renshaw Street), she'd begun to realise that it was unlike any shop she had ever known. For a start it was five storeys high. The ground-floor windows were huge and above them rose ornate stonework; on the very top floor above the doorway was a large clock whose hands had pointed to ten minutes to ten.

Now she looked around in some confusion, wondering how she was going to find Miss Edgerton's office in a building as big as this. She decided she'd better ask someone, so she headed for the nearest counter, which seemed to stock perfumes and other toiletries displayed in fancy coloured-glass bottles.

'Can I help you, miss?' the assistant asked

97

politely but a bit distantly.

Cathie informed her she had an interview with Miss Edgerton.

'Really? Then go up to the fourth floor in the lift, it's over there.' The girl pointed across the sales floor. 'Tell the attendant which floor you need and good luck,' she finished, smiling.

Cathie thanked her; how the girl's attitude had changed when she realised she might be working here!

This was another new experience for her, she mused as she stepped into the lift. She'd never been in one before. The attendant closed the doors and there was a humming sound and it only seemed like seconds before the lift stopped and the doors were opened. They'd arrived, she marvelled, wondering how much longer it would have taken to walk up all those flights of stairs. Off the main sales floor, which appeared to be displaying furniture and soft furnishings, there was a long corridor with many doors leading off it, the floor and the walls of which were of polished wood. Clutching the letter in one hand she knocked on the door which bore the legend 'Miss A. Edgerton – Personnel'.

When she went inside she found a young woman sitting at a desk typing. 'Miss Edgerton?' she enquired a little nervously.

'No, I'm her secretary. I assume you're Miss Kinrade? If you'll sit down I'll tell her you're here.'

Cathie handed her the letter and sat down in the chair indicated, clasping her hands tightly in her lap. Oh, so much depended on the next few minutes, she thought. She prayed that Miss Edgerton would find her satisfactory. If she didn't get this job she didn't know what she would do. She'd set her heart on working here. She remembered Ella's hurtful words and prayed they wouldn't come true.

She didn't have to wait long before she was ushered into another office, a larger room but sparsely furnished with a desk, chairs and rows of metal cabinets.

'Miss Kinrade? Miss Catherine – Cathie – Kinrade? Please take a seat,' Avril Edgerton instructed, thinking the girl looked quite young and was obviously very apprehensive.

'Thank you, Miss Edgerton,' Cathie replied politely. Miss Edgerton was much older than she had imagined she would be; she'd been picturing her around Violet Christian's age although now she remembered that this woman had been a friend of Violet's own mother. She was tall and slim with light brown hair cut and set in fashionable soft waves; she wore a tailored suit in a pale grey material under which was a plain white blouse pinned at the neck with a brooch.

Avril Edgerton took in the neat but well-worn clothes and the rather unfashionable hat and the fact that the girl carried neither a handbag nor gloves. She was aware, however, of Cathie Kinrade's background and circumstances. 'Well, Miss Christian speaks very highly of you. But you have no experience in working in a shop, I believe?'

Cathie shook her head. 'No, I'm afraid I haven't, Miss Edgerton. In fact I haven't much experience of work at all; I've not long left school. But I did

99

well there and I enjoyed it,' she said not wanting Miss Edgerton to think she was uneducated. 'I'm good at reading and writing–'

'What about arithmetic?' Avril Edgerton interrupted; she could see the girl was very eager.

Cathie nodded. 'I always did well at that too. I know all my times tables and I can add up in my head ... up to a point,' she conceded, not wanting to appear to be boasting.

The woman nodded. Violet had written that the girl was well mannered, willing and eager for an opportunity to improve herself and that if Avril could possibly find a position for Cathie she would be most grateful. 'And how do you get on with people? A pleasant and helpful manner is essential and sometimes a great deal of patience is required in dealing with customers.' She'd noted that the girl spoke quite well and her accent was more Lancashire than Liverpool.

'I was taught to be polite, miss, and to try to be ... as helpful as I can, and I always got on very well with my fellow pupils and teachers at school,' Cathie replied earnestly.

'And hardworking, honest and punctual?'

'Oh, yes, Miss Edgerton.'

The woman smiled. She seemed on the surface to be quite suitable but only time would tell. 'Good. Well, there's a position for a junior assistant in ladies' millinery and I'm willing to give you a six months' trial. You'll be under the supervision of Miss Vickers and will obviously work the same hours as everyone else, Monday to Saturday. Your starting salary will be thirty shillings a week, which after the six-month trial period will increase to thirty-five shillings, if you prove to be satisfactory. It will increase by increments as you get older and rise in seniority. You will of course have to work a week "in hand".'

Cathie didn't know what 'increments' and 'a week in hand' were but she didn't care. She was being offered a job! In the millinery department and at thirty shillings a week – far, far more than she'd ever earned before and she loved hats. She wouldn't even have minded had it been a job sweeping the floors. 'Oh, thank you, Miss Edgerton! I'll work hard, I promise,' she said, beaming happily.

The woman got to her feet. 'Right then, I'll take you to meet Miss Vickers. Will you be able to start work on Thursday? I realise it's rather irregular but the weekends are always our busiest time, apart from Christmas and the January sales that is.'

'Yes. Oh, yes indeed,' Cathie replied.

'You will of course be paid for the three days of this week. It will be included in your first wage packet,' she was informed.

As she accompanied Miss Edgerton down the corridor and into the lift she felt like shouting aloud for joy. But it did feel a bit unreal. On Thursday she would actually be starting work in this wonderful place and be paid a good wage. Miss Edgerton told her that the ladies' millinery department was on the second floor, which also housed ladies' fashions and children's clothing, but she didn't have time to stop to admire the clothes on display as she followed Miss Edgerton across the shop floor towards the millinery counter and its adjacent displays.

'Miss Vickers, this is Miss Kinrade. She'll be joining you on Thursday as a junior assistant. Perhaps I can leave her with you now so that you can enlighten her on her duties and so forth?' Avril Edgerton was brisk and businesslike in her introduction.

Cathie smiled shyly at the girl who was to be her co-worker and supervisor. She had thick fair hair that seemed to wave naturally and blue eyes and Cathie guessed she was probably in her twenties. 'I'm Cathie and I'm really, really pleased that I'm coming to work here.'

Miss Vickers smiled back. 'And I'm Julia. How old are you, Cathie? Have you worked in a shop before?'

'I'm fifteen and I've no experience of shop work but I'm very willing to learn.' She didn't want to divulge that her previous job had been gutting fish; it would be too demeaning in these palatial surroundings.

'I'm sure you'll take to it like a duck to water. We start at eight o'clock – we don't open until nine but there are always things to do like fetching stock or rearranging the displays, dusting, tidying trimmings, checking the till roll and the float. We close at six so are usually out by six fifteen, half past at the latest. We all have Sundays off of course and have a week's holiday in the summer and the usual Bank Holidays. Holidays are staggered so the store doesn't have to close. You'll be expected to buy your work dresses but you can pay for them in instalments if you like – we get paid on a Friday. There's a staff canteen where you can get a meal at a reasonable price – again if you wish, or you can go out and buy a sandwich. And we get a discount on any purchases we make in the store.'

Cathie nodded, trying to take everything in. 'Can I ask what "a week in hand" means? I ... I didn't like to ask Miss Edgerton. I've not heard of it before – I'm from the Isle of Man, you see.'

Julia smiled at her. She liked the look of this pretty girl with her dark curly hair and large brown eyes – she was a long way from home so everything must seem strange. 'It means you have to work your first week sort of for free; you won't get paid until after your second week, but you will get that week's money back if you decide to leave for another job. Will that be difficult for you, Cathie? Will you be able to manage for two weeks?' It was standard practice but for someone like Cathie it might cause real hardship as she wasn't living at home.

Cathie frowned but then remembered she did have money. 'I've got some money ... er ... Julia. So I'll manage.'

'Have you got relatives in Liverpool? Are you staying with them?'

Cathie shook her head. 'No, I don't know anyone here but I've got lodgings in Clivenden Street. Anfield, I think the area is called. I'm to do housework in return for bed and board. Mr and Mrs Johnston are quite elderly, you see.' She paused. 'Can I ask how much my work dresses will cost?' She'd noticed that everyone wore the same type of dress, plain black with long sleeves but with a small white Peter Pan collar. They looked quite smart, she thought.

'Five shillings each, it's a reduced price

especially for staff, and they're decent material too. The collars are detachable so you might be able to make do with just one dress to start with. You can just wash the collar; you get two with each dress and if you wish you can pay for them weekly; the cost will be deducted from your wages. Now, let me show you some of our stock and I'll tell you which styles are most popular, show you the different trimmings we can provide, then how the till works. After that you can go and see Mrs Evans about your dresses.'

Cathie had never seen such smart hats and there were so many different styles and colours. They were mostly small with curled or tilted brims, adorned with a variety of trimmings from ribbons in velvet, satin and grosgrain to feathers and artificial flowers and net veiling. They ranged in price from three shillings to twenty-two shillings, which she considered very expensive, although Julia informed her that in the likes of the Bon Marché and Cripps you would have to pay upwards of two guineas for a hat. From Julia she learned that not only did Lewis's sell clothing for men, women and children but also furniture, soft furnishings, lightshades and household goods, dress materials, paper patterns and haberdashery. There were shoes, handbags, gloves, scarves and hosiery; a large food hall was on the ground floor where not only groceries could be bought but also exotic fruit and vegetables. There was even a bank open to the customers six days a week, a service most high street banks didn't offer. There was a café for tea and coffee and pastries and cakes, a restaurant for fine dining and even a hairdressing salon. Train and theatre tickets could be purchased here and at Christmas there was a grotto for children which, Julia said, was quite spectacular – and on the very top floor of the building there was even a menagerie, something that was unique to Lewis's.

'You mean there are wild animals up on the roof?' Cathie asked in amazement.

Julia laughed. 'Oh, nothing really dangerous, Cathie! Just monkeys, exotic birds – things like that. They're all in cages or enclosures and have special staff to look after them.'

Cathie shook her head in wonder; she'd never expected anything like that in a shop.

'The firm was started by David Lewis back in the last century,' Julia informed her dutifully, 'and now there are stores in Manchester, Glasgow, Leicester, Leeds – in fact all over the place. Our motto's "The store for thrifty people". I think that means we price things midway, not too expensive, not too cheap.'

Cathie smiled; she liked the sound of that. 'I know I'm going to enjoy working here, Julia.' She looked down a little shyly. 'You see, it's been my dream.'

Julia smiled back; she'd really taken a liking to Cathie. She was clearly a bit over-awed by everything but she had a pleasant, friendly, open manner. 'Then it's a dream come true and I'm sure we're going to get on like a house on fire. Now, off you go and see Mrs Evans – her office is in the basement – and I'll see you at eight sharp on Thursday.' Julia turned away as a customer approached.

After she'd found Mrs Evans's office in the basement and her first work dress had been carefully parcelled up with her name and address marked down in a ledger, she spent the next couple of hours wandering through the store. There was so much to see, she marvelled. The food hall, permeated by delicious odours, had fruits the like of which she'd never seen before, let alone tasted – it seemed they had every possible type of food. The choice of shoes, handbags, gloves and scarves was so extensive that even if she had had a fortune to spend she just wouldn't know what to pick. There were cosmetic counters with all kinds of creams, lotions, make-up and nail varnishes as well as counters selling perfumed soaps and bath products – luxuries she'd never encountered before.

The café looked very smart and she decided to venture in and have a cup of tea. As she sipped her tea she wondered if she could afford to buy a handbag and a purse. She didn't have either and she would definitely need something to keep her money, a handkerchief and a comb in. Perhaps before she left she'd have a look, but then she thought maybe it would be best to leave it until she could get her discount. At length she decided she would go and have a look at the menagerie – Julia had made it sound extraordinary.

When she got out of the lift she found herself on the roof where there were cages of all sizes surrounded by ferns and other types of greenery with pathways between them and there was a wonderful view of the city. She wandered amongst the cages, peering at their labels which gave information about the occupants and where they came from. There were strange-looking birds with

106

colourful, exotic plumage; their cries were nothing like anything she'd heard before, mainly harsh and raucous – definitely not 'singing', she decided. There were monkeys, too, of all sizes and types with bright intelligent eyes and grasping little hands, some lizards and snakes, and some rather odd furry creatures which looked like oversized rats; she wasn't very keen on them at all. She couldn't believe that all these creatures lived up here, on top of a shop, in the middle of this great city.

At length she realised that she was hungry and so decided that she'd try to find somewhere where a pie or a sandwich wouldn't cost too much, and after that she'd have a wander around the city centre and see what other shops there were, before she returned to Clivenden Street. Once back there she would hang up her work dress and write a very long and detailed letter home for she had so much to tell them. Then she'd help Mrs Johnston with the 'supper', as her landlady called it, and start on the chores.

As she strolled back into Ranelagh Street she realised that from now on her days would be very busy, with both her work in her lodgings and her job. There wouldn't be much time left over for anything else, but she didn't mind. Maybe tomorrow she'd come back into the city centre and have a closer look around the other shops, which so far she had just seen from the outside.

Chapter Nine

Mrs Johnston had seemed rather relieved, Cathie thought, when she'd returned and imparted the news of her new job to her landlady. After hanging up her work dress, she'd peeled the potatoes and the carrots and left them in bowls of cold water; there were lamb cutlets to go with them but they wouldn't need to be cooked yet.

'Is there anything else, Mrs Johnston?' she'd asked.

'Not for the moment, Cathie, but you can set the table for supper just before my husband arrives home.'

'Then I think I'll make a start on my letter home. I'll finish it later tonight then I can post it tomorrow.'

Mrs Johnston nodded her agreement. 'Yes, your mother will be most anxious to hear from you, I assume.'

'Then I thought I might go out for a while to sort of get used to the area? Find my way around.'

The old lady frowned at her words and shook her head. 'No, Cathie. I don't think that's a very good idea at all. It will be dark by then and it's not ... wise for a young girl to be wandering the streets unaccompanied. Not the kind of thing a respectable girl would do at all. I'd suggest you stay in and perhaps read? I've put some books in your room.'

Reluctantly Cathie nodded her agreement. No

one had ever forbidden her to go out after dark alone in Ramsey and she was fifteen. But maybe it really wasn't safe to go out in Liverpool? 'Then will it be all right if I go back into town tomorrow afternoon, after I've helped you with the cleaning?' she asked tentatively.

Mrs Johnston had nodded her approval to that and so she'd started what she knew would be a rather long letter to her mam.

That evening she sat in the kitchen at the table while Mr and Mrs Johnston sat in the parlour. When she'd at last finished her letter she went upstairs and selected *Jane Eyre* from the book-case and took it down to the kitchen to read. Again, it struck her how quiet the house was. She supposed she'd get used to it, she thought as she opened the book, but she did feel a little lonely.

The following afternoon she walked to the tram stop after posting her letter. She'd brought some of her precious money with her for she was acutely aware that she needed a purse and a handbag. She was beginning to recognise the different streets now, she thought as the tram trundled towards the city centre. She'd remembered one shop in particular from yesterday afternoon – Blackler's in Great Charlotte Street; she'd seen it advertised in a copy of the *Echo* too. She'd go and have a look in there first.

It wasn't as big as Lewis's, which was just around the corner, but in its own way it was just as astonishing, she thought as she stood in the foyer and gazed upwards. A cage was suspended from the high ceiling and in it was a large parrot with red, yellow and bright blue plumage. It seemed to be a popular thing to have birds in shops, she mused, or maybe it was something peculiar to Liverpool. As she wandered through the departments she realised that things here were not nearly as expensive as in Lewis's and even without a staff discount she could get what she needed more cheaply.

She bought a purse and then what she considered to be a smart black handbag. Beside all the fashionable clothes her own looked very dowdy and dated and after she'd tried on a black and white checked jacket that was trimmed with black braid she decided to buy it, for it was at a bargain price. It would look good over her black work dress, she thought, and go with her only hat and her new bag. With her purchases in their distinctive carrier bags she felt she had spent wisely as she walked down towards Church Street where the Bon Marché, Henderson's and George Henry Lee were situated. Of course she couldn't afford to shop there but she could look and there were many other shops in Church Street too. Marks & Spencer, Woolworth's, C&A Modes, Cooper's and on the corner was Bunney's, another department store. There was certainly plenty to see, she thought happily, Mam would love it and Ella would be so envious. The shops in Parliament Street just couldn't compete.

Mrs Johnston suggested that after supper it would be best for Cathie if she had an early night so she would be fresh and at her best to start her new job. Cathie had agreed and after putting out everything she would need for the following morning decided she would continue with *Jane*

Eyre for an hour or two because it was unlikely that she'd be able to sleep so early.

On Thursday morning she was up in plenty of time and did her chores before she let herself out of the house. It was a fine morning but a little chilly, she thought as she joined the other people in the queue at the tram stop, but she felt pleased with her appearance. The new jacket looked smart, as did her bag, but she determined her next purchase, after she was paid, would be a new hat. Hers seemed very dull and old-fashioned compared to the ones she could see on the other girls in the queue. She was surprised at the number of people who were on the streets already and the tram was very crowded so she had to stand all the way, but she didn't mind for today she was actually going to start her dream job. As the tram journeyed on she thought back to her first day's work in the Market Square. There was just no comparison.

When she arrived at the store she made her way straight to the second floor, thinking how quiet it seemed for there were as yet no customers, only staff. Julia Vickers was already at the millinery counter checking the till. 'Cathie. You're very prompt, but why didn't you leave your things in the cloakroom?'

'I didn't know I had to,' Cathie replied, a little perturbed.

'Come on, I'll show you where it is and find you a locker for your bag and hat,' Julia offered, wondering why Miss Edgerton hadn't mentioned this to Cathie but then thinking she herself should have done so.

Cathie looked quickly around the large room full of girls and women hanging up coats and jackets and chatting. Julia found her a peg for her jacket and then an empty locker.

'Put your things in there, Cathie, then lock it and keep the key with you. You can put it on an elastic band and attach it to the belt of your dress until you can get a little chain.' She indicated a similar small key that hung from a chain attached to her own belt. 'You can't be too careful with your valuables – that's why we're not allowed to wear jewellery, except a wristwatch of course, if you have one.'

Cathie thought of her little brooch pinned to her jacket and decided to remove it and put it in her purse. She certainly didn't want to lose Jacob's precious gift.

When they were back at the millinery counter she helped Julia as they dusted the display cabinets and tidied the trimmings drawers. 'What happened to the other junior assistant, Julia? The one whose job I've got now,' she asked.

Julia frowned. 'I'm afraid she was dismissed, Cathie. Alice Stockdale's timekeeping was terrible – the worst I've ever known – and she had one day off sick – allegedly – too often.'

'Wasn't she sick at all?' Cathie enquired.

Julia shook her head. 'I doubt it. I've never known any illness where you are completely laid low one day and fine the next. No, I think she was just lazy. It was nearly always a Monday that she failed to turn up.'

'Well, you won't have that way of going on from me, Julia,' Cathie assured her.

The older girl smiled. 'No, I don't think I will.' Julia gave the counter a last quick inspection to check everything was neat and tidy. 'Right, we're all set now and there's Mr Moorfield, the floor walker, so they must have opened the doors downstairs.'

In the hour after they opened Cathie actually found that the time seemed to drag a bit because they were not very busy at first, Julia being easily able to deal with all the customers; Julia confided to her that it was quite often like this but that as the morning wore on it would become busier and indeed this proved to be true.

Her first customer was a young woman in her late twenties who wanted something smart but, she said, bright and cheerful, and Cathie had carefully selected three hats. The woman finally chose a small red felt with a tilted brim and a black artificial flower attached to the crown, and Cathie assured her it really did suit her and was both smart and bright. The woman was delighted and as Cathie placed the hat in the box, surrounding it carefully with tissue paper, and the woman paid for it, she felt a real sense of achievement. As she watched her first customer walk away, pleased with her purchase, she noticed a rather formidable-looking middle-aged woman approaching the counter. She was dressed in a very well-cut beige costume, underneath which she wore a coffee coloured crêpe-de-Chine blouse; a fox fur – complete with head, tail and legs – was draped around her shoulders. Over her iron-grey hair she wore a coffee and cream hat which boasted a curled feather around the brim.

'Good morning, Miss Vickers,' the woman greeted Julia affably and Cathie realised she must be a regular customer.

'Good morning, Mrs Fleetwood-Hayes. I take it the Captain has sailed?' Julia replied.

The woman nodded. 'Indeed he has, yesterday. So, I've been to pay my usual visit to the menagerie.'

'And what was it this time, may I ask?' Julia enquired with a knowing smile.

Cathie looked on bemused.

Mrs Fleetwood-Hayes raised her eyes to the ceiling. 'Birds! Little green and yellow things, with very sharp beaks, which constantly managed to escape from their cage. Every pair of lace curtains in the house is totally ruined! They've stuck their beaks into the holes in the patterns, wretched creatures. I've just been and ordered a complete new set in the soft-furnishing department and now I've come to treat myself to a new hat.' Her gaze settled on Cathie. 'You have a new assistant, I see?'

Julia nodded. 'Yes, this is Miss Kinrade. She started this morning, didn't you, Cathie?'

Cathie nodded, rather in awe of the obviously quite well-off Mrs Fleetwood-Hayes.

'And how are you finding working at Lewis's, Miss Kinrade?'

'Oh, I ... I like it very much, madam. It's my first job in a shop, you see.'

'Indeed. Then it's to be hoped you prove to be an improvement on the last assistant.'

'I'm sure she will be. She's from the Isle of Man, so she's a long way from home,' Julia informed her customer.

'Really? I went there once with the Captain and the girls for a holiday. Quite a pretty place if I remember rightly, but a terrible crossing. Of course it didn't bother the Captain at all but myself and the girls were dreadfully sick and I swore I'd not go again. Now, Miss Vickers – Julia – I thought I'd like something to go with my new pale green linen suit. I've an event coming up shortly.'

Julia became businesslike and Cathie busied herself tidying the ribbons – again – until she was distracted by another customer.

When Cathie had served her customer and Mrs Fleetwood-Hayes had also left, happily carrying a hat box, Cathie's curiosity got the better of her. 'Julia, why did she take birds up to the menagerie?'

Julia laughed. 'Her husband's a sea captain. He's away for long periods, goes to South America I believe, and each time he comes home he brings some kind of exotic creature, which drives her mad, so as soon as he's gone she donates whatever it is to the menagerie. This time it was obviously a pair of some type of small parrot.'

'But when he comes back doesn't he wonder where they are?' Cathie asked, still bemused.

Julia shook her head. 'She tells him they've either died from the cold and damp of the climate or they've escaped. She's quite a character, Cathie, I can assure you, but she's a very good customer. She has two daughters – Monica and Eileen – who she admits herself are "a pair of spoiled brats" – and she always brings them in for their clothes, shoes and hats. She's well liked. You'll get used to her; she can be a bit ... formidable though.' Julia

115

hesitated. 'And I'm distantly related to her – very distantly by marriage on my dad's side. I don't think my mother likes her so we don't have anything to do with the family – socially.'

Cathie nodded. Mrs Fleetwood-Hayes certainly did appear to be an unusual woman.

By the time she'd finished work on Saturday Cathie felt she'd settled in quite well, at least that's what Julia had told her. Julia had confided that she always treated herself to a cup of tea and a toasted teacake in Lyons Corner House before she went home on a Saturday and asked Cathie if she would like to join her. Cathie had been delighted and so they'd gone to the nearest Corner House and settled down at a table in the window. There were tea rooms in Ramsey of course but she'd never been in one and now she wrinkled her nose appreciatively at the mixed odours of tea, coffee and freshly made cakes and buns.

'It's nice to sit and relax and watch the crowds rushing for the trams and buses. By the time I'm ready to leave the shop at least I can usually get a seat,' Julia remarked as they ordered.

'Thank you for inviting me, Julia,' Cathie said politely.

'You've done very well these past three days, Cathie. You've got a good eye for colour and shape and a pleasant way with the customers.'

Cathie beamed at her. 'I've been trying very hard and I enjoy reading about all the latest fashions.'

Julia nodded her agreement. 'So do I. I always like to see what the Queen is wearing, and the Society women too, in newspapers and maga-

zines. I always think it helps in our line of work.'
Julia stirred her tea thoughtfully. 'So, what will
you do on your day off, Cathie?'

'Work, I expect. Housework, I mean,' she stated
flatly although she really had no idea what would
be expected of her. 'I don't mind though, I've got
a really nice room,' she added.

Julia nodded as she cut her teacake in half. 'I
expect you find everything very different from
home?'

It was Cathie's turn to nod. 'I do. Ramsey's a
small town and where I live now, in Clivenden
Street, it's very quiet and not as overcrowded.
You see at home we ... we live in a small stone
cottage and it's a bit cramped to say the least. I've
got three brothers and two sisters and then
there's Mam and Da. So there was always quite a
bit of noise, always something going on.'

'I often wish there was a bit more noise in our
house,' Julia replied.

'Do you live at home? Cathie enquired.

'I do. There's just myself and my mother and her
health isn't ... good, so I have quite a bit of
housework to do too, and I often think the place is
too big for just the two of us. We live on the ground
floor of a house at the bottom of Everton Valley.
They're big houses and when my father was alive
we used to live in all of it, but then my mother
found it difficult to manage – financially. I was
only seven when he died, you see, so she rented
out the rest of the house, but we have a sitting
room, a dining room, a kitchen, three bedrooms
and a bathroom.'

Cathie nodded. Mrs Johnston's house was

similar, though without the dining room.

'Do you get on all right with Mr and Mrs Johnston?'

Cathie frowned thoughtfully. 'I suppose I do. I've not been there long and I've not seen much of Mr Johnston, he's at work all day. They are quite old; their only son Henry was killed in the war – which is sad for them. I suppose I'll get used to them in time.'

They drank their tea and Cathie confided to Julia how Violet Christian had helped her to come to Liverpool and get her job and told her of the circumstances that had led up to her leaving home.

'Well, I think that was quite brave of you, Cathie, and you clearly did the right thing by taking her up on her offer of help,' Julia stated. She went on to tell Cathie a little of her own childhood which Cathie thought seemed to have been quite a lonely one. She couldn't imagine not having any brothers or sisters. Julia, it turned out, had gone to a private school, just further up the road from where she lived – a convent – until her father had died and her mother couldn't afford the fees. She discovered that Julia had only just turned twenty-one and Cathie was quite pleased that there wasn't too much of an age gap between them.

All too soon it was time to leave and Julia stood up, gathering up her bag and gloves. 'Well, I suppose we'd better get off home,' she said, pulling her coat around her. 'Have a good weekend, Cathie, what's left of it, and I'll see you on Monday morning.'

'Thanks. You ... enjoy Sunday too,' Cathie replied, wondering how she would spend this evening and the following day. She certainly intended to indulge in the luxury of having a bath and she'd wash her hair, regardless of anything else.

When she arrived back in Clivenden Street it was to find that her landlady was rather put out by the fact that it was well after the time she usually got home.

'Where on earth have you been, Cathie? I was getting quite worried, thinking something had happened to you.'

Cathie looked abashed. 'Oh, I'm really sorry, Mrs Johnston. Julia Vickers invited me to go with her to Lyons Corner House and I ... I just didn't think. She goes every Saturday after work as a bit of a treat, and I thought...'

Mrs Johnston tutted impatiently. 'Really, Cathie! Did it not enter your head that I might wonder where you were? And I hope you haven't spoiled your appetite. I've had to prepare supper by myself and Mr Johnston is already home.'

'I really am sorry, Mrs Johnston,' Cathie said contritely as she began to hastily set the table although she did feel a little irritated by her landlady's attitude. Was she to be allowed no time to herself at all? she wondered.

'I take it you will be making it a regular occurrence on Saturdays, if this Miss Vickers does so?'

'If you don't mind?' Cathie replied.

'Just as long as I *know* about it in advance, Cathie,' was the rather curt reply.

Cathie nodded. She supposed it was only right that she tell her landlady about any outings ahead of time. It wasn't really fair to worry the

119

woman, and it showed the old lady was thinking about her welfare.

She marvelled that it was only a week since she'd arrived in Liverpool as she travelled to work on Monday morning. Sunday had been the quietest she'd ever known and possibly one of the most boring. She'd been used to going to church with her family and afterwards they would stand and chat to friends and maybe window shop in Parliament Street before returning home where her mam always tried to put a good meal on the table for lunch. In the afternoon if the weather was fine she would go for a walk with her brothers and usually Ella either along the promenade or up to the Albert Tower from where you got a spectacular view across the whole of Ramsey Bay and beyond. Yesterday there had been no attendance at church – the Johnstons were not regular churchgoers – she'd spent the morning cleaning and then preparing and cooking the vegetables for lunch which had been eaten almost in silence. After she'd washed up there had been no walk in the afternoon; she'd spent that doing some ironing. Then she'd finished her book, had a bath and washed her hair and put out her things for this morning. In fact she had begun to feel a bit homesick. Still, she was determined not to let the sombre atmosphere of the house in Clivenden Street get her down. She was looking forward to the working week: the other assistants on her floor were all friendly and chatted to her, Mr Moorcroft the floor walker had told her that she seemed to be fitting in very well, and of course there was the visit to Lyons with Julia on Saturday to look forward to. She just wished she had a bit more time to herself and could please herself without having to ask permission. In that way it was worse than being at home. But it wasn't much of a price to pay for free bed and board, she told herself firmly. She would be well paid and able to send money home to Mam, as well as have something over to spend on herself – providing she saved for things, and she couldn't do that if she was paying for her lodgings. She was sure, too, that she wouldn't find anywhere else as clean and comfortable. She was fortunate; she shouldn't feel resentful at all.

But as the weeks passed she did begin to feel more and more aggrieved about the restrictions placed upon her for after she returned home from work it was assumed that she would not venture out again but would remain in the house either reading or writing her letters home. There were times when she felt increasingly homesick, missing her parents and siblings – even Ella – and the noisy but light-hearted atmosphere of Collins Lane. She also missed being able to go out for a walk in the evenings; at home she would either go down to the harbour where she would stand and enjoy the view and any activities that were going on or she would stroll around the town where she always met someone she knew and could stop and chat to them. Now her evenings were solitary, something she wasn't used to. Yes, she could understand that the Johnstons had suffered grief and loss in their lives but surely it shouldn't have eaten away at them for all these years, making their outlook on life so ... dour, she thought.

And then there was the mystery of the locked bedroom next door to hers. It intrigued her and she'd tried the door once or twice just to see if it was indeed locked. It had been. Then two nights ago after she'd finished reading, switched off the light and settled down to sleep she'd heard someone come upstairs and unlock that door. She'd sat up in bed, wondering whether or not to turn on the light. She'd decided against it as she heard the door being quietly closed and had thought little more about the incident until the following night when she'd been woken by the sound of someone crying and it was coming from the room next door. It had made her shiver involuntarily; it reminded her forcefully of the woman in the attic in *Jane Eyre*.

From then on her curiosity had grown until a couple of months later it finally got the better of her. Both Mr and Mrs Johnston were downstairs in the parlour listening to the news on the wireless; she had informed them that she would finish her weekly letter home and then go up to bed.

On the landing she hesitated but then, with one eye on the staircase, she slowly turned the door handle, her heart beating a little more rapidly. Of course it was locked. She stood for a few seconds just staring at the door, wondering if she should just forget the idea, then she reached up and felt along the ledge above it and found what she was searching for: a key.

Inserting it into the lock she turned it, hoping it wouldn't make a noise, and then pushed the door open. The room was in darkness but she felt along the wall until she found the light switch.

122

She was totally unprepared for the sight that met her eyes. The curtains were drawn across the window but the bed was made up; there were books and toys placed on the shelves, high up and pushed towards the back but still visible, and clothes laid out on the bed. Even a pair of slippers had been placed at the foot of the bed. It was as if the room had not been touched since Henry Johnston had left it all those years ago to go off to war. She shivered. It was ... unnatural, she thought. It was years since he'd been killed.

As silently as she could she crossed to the wardrobe and opened it. Inside there were more clothes: suits, jackets, trousers and an overcoat. She closed the door and turned towards the chest of drawers, carefully easing open the top drawer. Just as she had expected there were socks of various colours but mainly grey and black. She shivered again but the corner of an envelope sticking out from beneath the socks caught her eye. Tentatively she pulled it out to discover that it was one of a bundle of letters, tied with a black ribbon and all addressed to the Johnstons.

She sat down on the edge of the bed and stared at them. Mrs Johnston had obviously kept all the letters her son had written from the trenches. Suddenly she felt guilty. What on earth was she doing? It wasn't like her to snoop and it wasn't right that she should read them; that would be prying into the very private moments of what were actually his last days. She stood up and turned the bundle over in her hands. The last envelope was very different to the rest; it was an official-looking brownish-buff colour and stamped 'H. M. War Of-

123

fice'. She sat down again and, her curiosity overcoming her scruples, opened it, withdrawing a single typed sheet, thinking it was probably the official notification of his death. It wasn't. A cold shiver swept over her as she read the terrible, stark fact that Private Henry Arthur Johnston of the King's Lancashire Regiment had been tried for cowardice and desertion, found guilty and shot on 15 December 1917. Her hands were shaking as she tried to push the single sheet back into the envelope. Oh, how terrible! How tragic! How devastated the Johnstons must have been! She felt even guiltier now.

'Just what are you doing in here?'

Startled, Cathie jumped to her feet, uttering a cry, her hand going to her mouth as she saw Mr Johnston standing in the doorway. Quickly she tried to hide the letters behind her back. 'Oh, I... I'm so ... sorry! I...' she stammered, her cheeks flaming. What could she say? There were no words – she had no defence.

He glared at her from behind his spectacles as he closed the door behind him.

'Give me whatever it is you are hiding, girl!' he demanded. Hesitantly, she handed him the envelope and the other letters.

He glanced at them and then back at her. 'So, you now know about ... Henry,' he stated flatly.

Cathie nodded, dumbstruck. There was such bitterness and anger in his tone that she suddenly felt afraid.

Standing erect, making no move, he spoke again, almost spitting out the words. 'His mother was of course ... distraught. She never got over it.

124

This...' He paused and with a sweep of his hand indicated the books, toys and clothes. 'This seems to ... help her but... You can have no idea just how ... appalled I was and still am at his conduct.'

Flinching at his harsh words, Cathie still had no idea what to say.

He pushed past her and returned the letters to the drawer, closing it firmly. 'It will never be known beyond these walls that a son of mine died a ... coward and a traitor to his country! *Never.* Do you understand that? So you will never breathe a word of what you know.' He turned to her, his eyes cold and hard. 'Is that entirely clear? I will know if you do, because not another soul here in Anfield is aware of the truth. I will not have you bringing shame and humiliation down on us.'

Cathie nodded, wilting beneath his glower. But he had not finished.

'But you can no longer remain in this house, Cathie Kinrade. I won't allow it, not after what you have done. You have openly flouted the trust we placed in you. You have a week to find new lodgings and you will not mention any of ... this to my wife. I won't have her upset! You will inform her that you have found lodgings elsewhere.'

Cathie gasped in shock and horror. 'But ... but, Mr Johnston, where will I go?' she stammered.

'That is not my concern. Now, you will leave this room which you never should have entered in the first place.'

Cathie fled past him and back into her own room. She leaned against the door, her heart pounding, and heard him close and lock the door and then go back downstairs. She sat down on the bed and found she was trembling. She knew Henry Johnston hadn't been the only one who had reached the point where he couldn't stand the horror of the trenches and the constant fear of mutilation or death any longer. People now called it 'shell shock' and slowly public opinion was changing about those who had been executed. That Henry Johnston had been one of them was awful – clearly a terrible tragedy for his parents – but it seemed even worse to her that his own father still viewed it as cowardice and was ashamed of his son, unable to find pity in his heart for him. She was ashamed of herself too. She should never have let her curiosity get the better of her. And now it had been her undoing: she was being thrown out. Where could she go? How would she find somewhere else to live in a week? She would have to pay rent – what if she couldn't afford to? She loved her job; she loved being in this busy, vibrant city. How could she bear to have to leave and return to Ramsey in disgrace – a failure? Oh, Ella would be delighted. She couldn't do it. She couldn't go!

She didn't sleep much that night, tossing and turning as she considered all her options. She couldn't afford to pay very much in the way of rent and therefore she was certain that all she would be able to afford would be a room in a hovel in the slums and the thought both appalled and terrified her. What kind of furniture would somewhere like that contain? Very little, she assumed, and she shuddered as she thought of the bugs and vermin that would no doubt inhabit it too. There would be no electricity, no piped water, no heating in winter. There certainly wouldn't be a bathroom either and she would be forced to share a privy with heaven alone knew how many other people – all strangers. How could she keep herself and her clothes clean and tidy, her appearance up to the standard that was required for her work? It just didn't bear thinking about. Oh, she'd found the atmosphere in this house cold and a little ... morbid, and she'd resented her lack of freedom, but it was clean and comfortable and she'd become used to the modern amenities. There were far worse places to live and far worse people to have to share a roof with. For the first time since she'd left home she felt afraid and very uncertain about her future. There had to be something she could say to him to make him relent? Surely what she had done hadn't been *that* bad? She was becoming desperate, she realised.

She'd gone over everything in her mind for hours and at last, as the first streaks of dawn penetrated the curtains, she concluded all she could do was to try to speak to him when his anger had subsided a little. She would plead with him, beg him to reconsider, impress upon him that she was terribly sorry, she hadn't meant to pry and she would swear not to say a word to anyone. Surely he would relent when he saw her contrition was genuine?

She said nothing until after supper the following evening, sitting in the kitchen awaiting an opportune moment and rereading with despair the list of houses and rooms to rent in the copy of the *Echo* she'd bought as she'd left work. She'd said nothing to Julia about what had happened although her friend had sensed something was wrong; she'd passed it off, saying she felt tired as she hadn't slept well last night.

At last Mrs Johnston rose from the table and announced that she was going upstairs to fetch her spectacles and needlework. After a few seconds Cathie followed her out and went and knocked quietly on the door of the parlour. When she entered Mr Johnston was sitting reading his newspaper.

He looked up at her, frowning. 'What do you want?'

Cathie clasped her hands tightly together. 'I ... I've come to beg you to reconsider, Mr Johnston. I meant no harm and I'm very, very sorry. I know that I should not have defied your instructions and ... and intruded into that room and I apologise. Obviously I had no idea about ... about your son and I ... will never say a single word. I promise – truly. Your secret will be safe with me, I swear. Please, please, I beg you to reconsider?'

He stared at her but said nothing and she felt her heart sink. It wasn't going to work; he wasn't going to change his mind.

At last he slowly shook his head. 'No, I'm afraid–'

'But I have nowhere else to go!' she interrupted, desperate now. 'I have no family here in Liverpool and I don't earn enough to find somewhere as ... respectable as this. I'd be alone in one of the slum areas near the docks, having to live in ... squalor. I'm so ... afraid – I can only imagine what such places are like. Please don't condemn me to that...'

He got to his feet, his expression grim. There

was a long silence and Cathie's hopes faded further. But then he spoke.

'Very well, you may stay. I cannot in all conscience risk a young girl's safety in the slums of this city. But you will keep your promise. I will not have my poor wife subjected to any more upset. I will not allow her – either of us – to become the butt of vile gossip and speculation and ... scorn!' She shrank back at the coldness in his eyes. 'But let me tell you, Cathie Kinrade, that I despise you for the way you behaved. You may stay but do not think your life here will become easier. And as for myself, I will not speak to you unless it is absolutely necessary. Now, get out of my sight!'

Cathie felt tears pricking her eyes. She didn't blame him for despising her; she despised herself. She had overstepped the mark. Idle curiosity was one thing, but prying into another person's private correspondence – their private grief – was quite another. She had almost sabotaged all her hopes and dreams because of her snooping and she truly was very sorry. She left the room quietly and quickly climbed the stairs, seeking the privacy and sanctuary of her own room. She was very, very relieved that she wouldn't have to leave but she knew that from now on life in this house would never be easy. Well, it would be a tribulation that she would just have to bear. She had learned her lesson.

Chapter Ten

1934

Cathie stood staring longingly at the dress displayed in the centre of Blackler's ladieswear department. It was the most gorgeous garment she'd ever seen: pale green taffeta shot with lilac so that in one light it looked green and in another lilac. It had a full skirt with a sash at the waist, short cape-like sleeves and what was called a 'sweetheart' neckline. It was obviously a dress to go dancing in. She would feel so elegant and grown up in a dress like that, the colours would suit her and it was also reasonably priced at ten shillings and sixpence. She could afford it; she'd been saving up for a while now. She sighed heavily as she turned away. Where would she wear a dress like that? She didn't go dancing, she didn't even go out, didn't have what people called a 'social life'. Oh, Mavis and Dorothy, the young assistants on ladies' dresses at Lewis's, had asked her to go with them to the Grafton and the Locarno Ballrooms but she'd never been able to. Mrs Johnston, quite forcefully backed by her husband, thought they were 'dens of iniquity' and definitely not suitable for a young girl like her. Only 'fast' young women frequented places like that, she said. Cathie's only form of entertainment was her weekly trip to Lyons with Julia, the rest of her 'spare' time she spent doing household chores. As Mr Johnston had predicted her life in Clivenden Street hadn't improved and now she really hated going back to that silent house.

She glanced at the large ornate clock on the far wall and realised her lunch break was nearly over and she'd better be getting back. As she made her way towards the staircase she felt very downhearted. All the shops were magnificently decorated for Christmas, which was fast approaching, but she wasn't really looking forward to the festive season.

Last year it had all been so new. She'd been completely overawed by the grotto Lewis's featured every year – she'd never seen anything like it before. It was decorated to look like a scene from a storybook, and with real people dressed as the characters from *Sleeping Beauty*, plus elves and fairies to help out. Parents brought their children to see it and they often had to queue for hours to marvel at the tableaux, then for the children to wait to sit on Santa's knee and tell him what gifts they'd like him to bring them and then were given a small toy. Of course it cost the parents money, but it was such a special occasion for the excited children, Cathie thought it was well worth it. She'd written long letters home describing it and all the decorations and the special goods on display.

This year she'd enjoyed watching all the preparations for the grotto, but there were other things on her mind. Oh, she loved every minute she was at work even though the nearer the holiday drew the more hectic things became – that was all part and parcel of the season. But back in Clivenden

Street she knew there would be no decorations, no bustle, no sense of it being a happy time of year. Last year, apart from a few sprigs of holly stuck behind the pictures in the hall and the mirror in the parlour, there'd been very little to mark the season and she could now understand why. The Johnstons had little to celebrate; for them it was a time of grief, loss and shame. As she reached the main doors of Lewis's, she turned and glanced around. Yes, everything looked splendid, but it didn't do much to lift her spirits.

She walked out into the bitterly cold December afternoon, thinking that in a few hours darkness would fall and then the strings of coloured lamps which decorated the outsides of the shops would bring an added sense of festive cheer. Last year Mrs Johnston had explained that they really didn't go in much for 'celebrating' Christmas and hadn't done since poor Henry had been killed. There didn't seem much point to it any more, she'd said by way of an explanation. Again Cathie felt that sense of unease: now she understood fully, but the woman just didn't seem able to accept the circumstances of her son's death. Cathie shoved her hands deeper into the pockets of her coat as she walked towards the corner of Ranelagh Street. This December would mark seventeen years since Henry Johnston had been shot.

She crossed the road and made her way to the staff entrance of Lewis's, thinking how cheerless Christmas Day last year had been. There had been no exchange of presents, a very meagre lunch, little conversation – Mr Johnston had barely acknowledged her, let alone wished her 'Seasons greetings'. In fact it had been dreadful and she had wished with all her heart that she'd been home in the overcrowded kitchen in Collins Lane. At least everyone there would be enjoying Christmas Day. She had spent that evening in her room in tears, she had been so homesick. The cheerful colours, the glittering baubles that decorated the sales floor did little to lighten her mood and as she made her way back to her own department she noticed that Julia didn't look her usual happy self either.

'It's freezing outside. There'll be frost on the pavements by the time we're going home,' Cathie remarked.

Julia nodded, half-heartedly rearranging the black veil, spotted with red dots, on a small black-velvet pillbox hat. 'Cathie, would you go and bring a couple more display units down? There's some new stock due in and I've nowhere to put it,' she asked.

Cathie nodded her assent and as she walked towards the lift which would take her to the stockroom she wondered what was wrong with Julia. It was unusual for her to be so glum. They'd become firm friends in the year and a half they'd been working together; they'd not once had a disagreement never mind an argument and she'd learned so much from the older girl. She was aware that she was now far more confident, that she'd gained valuable experience both in dealing with customers, in the hats they sold and in her personal dress sense. Also her wages had increased, first to thirty-five shillings a week, then to two pounds when she'd turned sixteen and then to two pounds five shillings when she'd completed her first year of service. When she was seventeen she would be earning two pounds ten shillings a week. She regularly sent home as much as she could spare and after her fares and lunches, she'd saved up for the clothes she had bought. They consisted mainly of skirts and jumpers and blouses, although her first big purchase last year had been a good warm winter coat in the very fashionable shade of 'Marina Green', so called after the new Duchess of Kent – Princess Marina of Greece. She didn't go anywhere to warrant buying flowery summer dresses and picture hats which would shade her face from the sun or smart costumes and equally smart hats for spring and autumn or matching shoes and bags. Her thoughts turned back to the gorgeous taffeta dress and the fact that her life outside work was so ... dull and depressing. In three months' time she would be seventeen years old and she wanted to have some fun, some enjoyment, some excitement in her life.

Dutifully she collected the painted wooden 'heads' on which the new hats would be displayed and went back down to her sales floor.

Julia had just finished serving a customer. 'Oh, some people would try the patience of Job!' she muttered wearily.

'An awkward one?' Cathie concluded aloud. She paused. 'Julia, is there something wrong? You're not your usual self at all.'

Julia sighed as she placed a hat on one of the units Cathie had fetched down. 'It's Mother. Sometimes ... sometimes, Cathie, I really do wonder if she is as ... frail and unwell as she says she is. I was really looking forward to seeing Fred Astaire and Ginger Rogers in *The Gay Divorcee,* there was a matinee on Sunday afternoon at the Trocadero Cinema, but I couldn't go. She took one of her "turns".'

Cathie looked concerned. She'd often asked Julia just what was wrong with Mrs Vickers but Julia had said it was hard to know, even the doctor who seemed to be a regular visitor was perplexed by her mother's many ailments. 'Can't you go one evening after work? Surely it's still on this week as well?' She too would have dearly loved to have seen the film, Mavis had been in raptures over the dancing and the elegance of the evening gowns, but she'd not even contemplated it, knowing Mrs Johnston's views on the modern cinema and the fact that the word 'divorce' was featured in the film's title.

Julia shook her head. 'No, it was finishing on Sunday and besides, Cathie, you know I never go out in the evening. She doesn't like being left alone in the house after dark.'

Cathie refrained from saying that Mrs Vickers wasn't alone in the house; there were two couples living upstairs.

Julia sighed heavily again. 'And I'm not looking forward to Christmas much either.'

Cathie nodded her agreement. 'Neither am I. It was really awful – downright miserable in fact – last year. I've still got some holiday left and I was wondering about going home, but it would only be for a couple of days as we're open again the day after Boxing Day and at this time of year the weather is bad and the crossing could be terrible.

During the winter, I've seen ambulances waiting for the ferry to arrive in Ramsey, people have been so badly injured on the crossing.'

Julia shuddered. 'Then I definitely wouldn't risk it, Cathie. It would be a bit of a waste of money too,' she added.

'I know. I saw a gorgeous dress in Blackler's but ... but I'd get no wear out of it. I never go anywhere, let alone to a dance.'

'We're like a pair of Cinderellas, Cathie,' Julia remarked gloomily.

Cathie nodded. 'Oh, Julia, I really do hate living with the Johnstons. I ... I'm wondering if I can stand it for much longer – especially with Christmas so near.' She couldn't keep the despair and loneliness from her voice and tears sparkled on her lashes.

Julia looked concerned. 'Oh, Cathie, I didn't realise it was so bad!'

Cathie bit her lip. 'I wish ... I really wish I could afford to find somewhere else. But I'd end up in a room in a slum house!'

Julia looked horrified for a moment but then her expression became thoughtful. 'Cathie, would you consider ... coming to live with us – Mother and me? There's enough room...'

Cathie's eyes widened in surprise. 'Do you really mean that, Julia?'

Julia nodded firmly. 'Of course I'll have to speak to Mother but–'

'Oh, Julia, thank you! Thank you! I ... I'd be absolutely delighted!' Relief flooded through Cathie. She hardly dared to think how her life would change.

Before they had time to discuss it further they saw Mrs Fleetwood-Hayes approaching, smartly dressed as usual in a full-length musquash fur coat and a chestnut velvet hat trimmed with feathers. She was accompanied by a girl of about Cathie's age with short wavy brown hair and blue eyes.

'What has the pair of you looking so delighted with yourselves?'

'Oh, Mrs Fleetwood-Hayes, we were just discussing Cathie coming to live with me and Mother.'

'Really? This is a surprise. Have you spoken to your mother about this, Julia?'

Julia shook her head. 'Well, not yet, but I intend to.'

Elinor Fleetwood-Hayes nodded, wondering what the outcome of that conversation would be. She had never liked Maud Vickers, who had married a second cousin of the Captain. The woman had ideas far above her station in life and was full of totally unnecessary airs and graces – or she had been until she'd been widowed. It hadn't been a happy marriage. Also, she treated Julia disgracefully. The girl was twenty-two and she had had no opportunities to make friends – let alone gentleman friends – and so no opportunity of 'walking out' as courting used to be called. She knew that in Maud Vickers's opinion all men were completely untrustworthy, a fact she had impressed upon her daughter. She considered Julia's mother a domineering malingerer who used her feigned illnesses to keep her daughter dancing attendance upon her.

'You see, Cathie was telling me how miserable

137

she is in her lodgings and I was telling her that Mother took one of her turns on Sunday afternoon when I'd planned to go to the cinema. I wanted to see *The Gay Divorcee*,' Julia explained.

'I saw it and it was just *wonderful!* Fred Astaire is so handsome and his dancing is ... sublime,' the girl with Mrs Fleetwood-Hayes enthused.

She must be one of the Captain's daughters, Cathie surmised.

'You'd have your head turned by anyone in an evening suit, Monica,' her mother said sharply but not without humour. 'So, that put paid to your afternoon's entertainment then, Julia?'

Julia nodded.

'And what's the matter with you, Cathie Kinrade?' the older woman asked.

Cathie bit her lip. She didn't want to sound as if she were complaining about her lot in life.

'She's not looking forward to Christmas, are you, Cathie?' Julia answered for her.

'No, not much,' Cathie answered, trying not to feel envious of Monica Fleetwood-Hayes's emerald-green coat and matching hat. She knew they were expensive – they were the height of fashion.

'I suppose you miss your family; that's only natural, Cathie.'

'I do but ... but, well, you see the Johnstons – the people I lodge with – really don't do much in the way of celebrating Christmas,' Cathie informed her.

'You mean no decorations? No tree? No festive fare? No cards or presents? Is it all against their religious beliefs?'

Cathie shook her head. 'No. You see, madam,

their only son was ... killed just before Christmas in nineteen seventeen.'

The woman shook her head. She could understand how that must have grieved them, she herself had lost two brothers in that conflict, but it was seventeen years ago.

'And you see Cathie isn't allowed to go anywhere in her free time. Mrs Johnston considers dance halls and ballrooms and even the cinema to be places a young girl like Cathie shouldn't visit. Her only outing is tea with me at Lyons on a Saturday after work,' Julia added, thinking it was usually her only outing too.

'Good heavens! How awful for you, Cathie.'

'So what do you do in the evenings and at the weekends?' Miss Fleetwood-Hayes asked, looking appalled.

'When I've done what chores need to be done, I ... read or I write home,' Cathie replied.

'Oh, how dreadfully dull for you,' the girl said, although her tone was rather sneering.

Elinor glared at her daughter. 'Maybe now you and your sister will realise how fortunate you are,' she snapped before turning back to the two sales assistants. 'It's no wonder you're homesick, Cathie.'

'I ... I really am not very happy living there, madam, and it's getting me down, but they don't charge me for lodgings. I do housework in return,' she confessed.

'Well, I think Julia's suggestion is excellent. It will benefit both of you. Julia, yours is a large house and it would be livelier and far less restrictive for Cathie, and younger company for you, Julia.' She also thought that perhaps it might help put a stop to Maud's selfish demands upon her daughter. 'You seem to get on well together,' she added.

Both girls nodded.

'Oh, we do, we're really good friends, but I don't know what ... Mother will say.'

'Don't ask her, Julia, *inform* her. Don't give her the opportunity to object or cause an almighty fuss. Just tell her that your friend from work is unhappy where she is and that you've asked her to come and live with you.'

Julia nodded slowly. 'You think that's the best way to go about it?'

'I most certainly do! It will prove to be the best thing for you both, take my word for it.' The matter sorted, she turned her attention to their merchandise. 'Now, Monica is starting work in the Income Tax Office after Christmas, and they are quite ... formal, so none of the hats she possesses will be suitable. She needs something smart but not too bright or ... ostentatious. Something in black or navy, I think.'

Julia focused on the task in hand while Cathie turned to serve another customer. Monica Fleetwood-Hayes didn't look very happy about her mother's choice of colours. But, given that working in the Income Tax Office was sure to be a really good job with a matching salary and *she* seemed able to go to the cinema whenever she liked, she felt it hard to feel much sympathy for the girl.

All afternoon Cathie had found it hard to concentrate on her work, even though they'd been busy.

She couldn't stop herself from thinking how different her life would be if she went to live with Julia.

'It's as if *everyone* wants a new hat for Christmas! I'm quite worn out,' Julia exclaimed when the store finally closed.

'I could murder a cup of tea,' Cathie added.

'So could I. Let's go to Lyons and we'll discuss your moving.'

Cathie nodded. 'I could hardly concentrate all afternoon,' she confided.

When they'd walked the short distance and managed to find a table in the rather crowded tea rooms, Julia looked enquiringly at Cathie. 'Well, are you happy at the idea of coming to live with us?'

'Oh, Julia, I'm delighted. I can't tell you how thrilled I am. I'd be able to help you in the house and of course I would give you a few shillings for rent—'

'I don't want you to pay anything!' Julia interposed.

'Well, if you're sure ... I really hate living in Clivenden Street. It's so dull and miserable and I've been feeling very ... depressed.'

'I can't guarantee that things will be any livelier in our house, Cathie. My mother isn't the ... easiest or the happiest person at times and she is always warning me about men. She insists that none of them are to be trusted. I don't know why as I seem to remember that she and my father got on well enough together before he died.'

'I won't mind all that, Julia. We're out all day and we'll have each other to chat to in the evenings and maybe we can take it in turns to go out? That way your mam won't be left on her own in the evening,' she suggested.

Julia smiled at her. She'd enjoy having Cathie to live with them and maybe, as Cathie said, they could both have a bit of a social life. 'We could even travel to and from work together,' she said.

'I'd be able to help with the shopping too and I really wouldn't mind paying something towards the household expenses. Oh, Julia, it'll be great!'

Julia nodded. 'Right, that's settled. I'll tell Mother as soon as I get home and if she makes a fuss – too bad! I'll say I've already told you you're welcome so I can't go back on my word. When can you move in?'

'As soon as possible, if that will be all right? I haven't got much to pack, just my clothes, although I've nothing to put them in.' She now had far more than when she'd arrived in Liverpool and the hemp bag wouldn't be big enough.

'I'll bring a suitcase in with me tomorrow, then you can pack tomorrow night and move in the day after, is that all right?'

'It's ... perfect! Oh, I'm looking forward to it so much, Julia. Christmas won't be nearly as miserable for me this year,' Cathie replied happily.

'We'll have a great Christmas, Cathie, see if we don't!' Julia enthused, catching Cathie's excitement. She raised her cup, smiling. 'Here's to us, Cathie!'

Cathie laughed as they clinked the cups together. 'I'll tell them as soon as I get back and then I'll write and let Mam know I'm moving,' she replied, thinking it didn't matter now that she'd be late home. In two days she would be leaving Mr and Mrs Johnstons' depressing house and the ghost of poor Henry Johnston too.

Chapter Eleven

Cathie waited until supper was over before she broke the news to the Johnstons. 'I have something to tell you both,' she started and her landlady looked at her curiously.

'What is it?'

'I'm leaving here. My friend at work, Julia Vickers, has asked me to go and live with her and her mother in Everton Valley. I'll be going the day after tomorrow.'

Mr Johnston got to his feet and, nodding curtly, left the room.

'Good heavens! That's a very surprising and, I might add, sudden decision, Cathie.'

'She only asked me today and I agreed.'

Mrs Johnston frowned. 'Are you not happy here?'

'I ... I'd much sooner lodge with Julia; we get on so well together,' Cathie replied, too polite to say how unhappy she was here.

'And has her mother agreed to these arrangements?' Mrs Johnston asked, her tone becoming much colder.

'She's a widow and not in good health but Julia knows she will agree. I can help Julia out with the housework.'

Ethel Johnston pursed her lips in disapproval. 'I think you are being rather ungrateful, Cathie, to spring this decision on us so suddenly. We took you in – a complete stranger – only because dear Violet asked us to.'

'I know and I'm really grateful,' Cathie tried to explain. 'But ... but I think I'll be happier living with someone my own age.'

'Well, I hope this Mrs Vickers has your welfare in mind, Cathie, something we have always been very aware of. I hope your mother approves of this move. I take it you haven't yet informed her of this decision?'

'No, not yet. But I know Mam won't mind.'

'That remains to be seen! And I think you should write to Violet too – I certainly shall,' her landlady snapped.

Cathie didn't reply but she felt annoyed by the woman's attitude. She wasn't her legal guardian or anything; she couldn't forbid her to go to live with Julia. Yes, she'd taken her in but she, Cathie, had worked hard and she'd never given the Johnstons any cause for concern apart from that terrible episode over her finding out how Henry Johnston had died, and Mrs Johnston didn't even know about that. 'I'd better go up and start my packing,' she said, relieved that she would only have to spend two more nights under the Johnstons' roof. The woman was clearly very angry.

As Cathie carried the heavy suitcase into the staff cloakroom she was greeted with a few enquiring and some openly curious looks.

'You going on your holidays then, Cathie?'

Mavis asked, laughing. She didn't expect an answer as she already knew Cathie was moving in with Julia and her mother. 'Perhaps now you might get to come with us when we go to the Grafton next?' she added.

'I hope so, Mavis,' Cathie replied, feeling far happier than she'd done for months.

'Did she cut up when you left this morning?' Julia asked as they made their way down to the sales floor.

Cathie shook her head. 'Thankfully, no.' In fact, no more had been said on the matter. Mrs Johnston had hardly spoken to her the following evening and this morning had just said, 'Goodbye, Cathie,' as she'd carried her case into the lobby. 'She was very offhand but I didn't expect her to be all smiles or wish me good luck. Not after the other evening.'

Julia nodded, thinking that Mrs Johnston must be annoyed at losing her unpaid cleaner. 'Well, I suppose that's a blessing,' she stated. Mrs Johnston might have made a scene, which would have been awful. 'In my lunch break I want to go down to Woolworth's and buy some tinsel and decorations for the tree. I rooted out the box we keep the Christmas stuff in last night and the ones we've got we've had for years and are looking decidedly tatty!'

'I'll buy some too, Julia. And some crêpe paper to make chains. I used to do it at home for Mam. Our Ella and Meggie were supposed to help me. Meggie did, but Ella always managed to be doing something else.'

'You really don't get on with your sister, do

you?' Julia commented. She'd often heard Cathie make disparaging remarks about Ella.

Cathie shrugged. 'Not really. Of course she might have changed; she'll be fifteen next year.'

She didn't sound too convinced about it, Julia thought as they reached the millinery department. She'd never had a sister so she had no experience of these matters but having Cathie to live with them would be like having a younger sister, she surmised, and they *would* get on.

As they both got off the tram at the bottom of Everton Valley, Cathie was surprised to see just how large the houses were, set back off the road with quite long paths leading up to them. They reminded her of the Edwardian villas on the Mooragh Promenade where Violet Christian lived. There were four stone steps up to the front door which also boasted a glass fanlight above it, with wide bay windows like those on the promenade, but these houses were all soot-blackened, like every building in the city.

'When your father was alive did just the three of you live in the entire house?' she asked.

Julia nodded as she produced the front-door key. 'Yes, you see they wanted more children, but ... well, it never happened.'

Cathie left her case in the large square hallway, off which led quite a grand-looking staircase, and followed Julia into the living room.

It was comfortably furnished if a bit old-fashioned, Cathie thought, but it was warm.

'Mother, this is Cathie Kinrade. I've told you all about her,' Julia informed her mother, giving her a peck on the cheek.

Cathie was surprised by Mrs Vickers. She wasn't at all how she had imagined her to be. From what her friend had told her she'd presumed that the woman would be small, thin, pale and frail-looking. In fact she was quite plump with fair hair and blue eyes like Julia but with a rather ruddy complexion. In fact she looked the picture of health. 'I'm very pleased to meet you, Mrs Vickers, and so grateful that Julia asked me to come and live here.'

'Come over here and let me look at you more closely, Cathie. I have some difficulty getting up out of my chair.'

Cathie duly did as she was bid while Julia removed her outdoor clothes.

'You're an attractive girl, Cathie. And you're nearly ... seventeen?' Maud pronounced.

'Yes, and Julia has taught me a lot about fashion and colours...' Cathie replied, smiling across at her friend.

Maud Vickers also looked across at her daughter. 'Yes, well. Now, you'd better get unpacked.'

'I'll do that later, if that's all right? I told Julia I'd help with ... things.'

Mrs Vickers nodded. 'Good. Then Julia will show you the kitchen and dining room. I expect you are both hungry. I know I feel quite peckish myself, even though I don't eat much. Certain things tend to upset my digestion, I'm afraid.'

Cathie smiled sympathetically as she followed Julia out of the room. She didn't quite know what to make of Mrs Vickers and wondered how she would get on with the woman. Still, this was now her home and she was certain it would be an

147

improvement on the last one. After she'd unpacked she intended to write to her mam before she heard the news of her change of address from Violet Christian for she was certain Mrs Johnston would have been quick to inform her cousin.

She was delighted with the bedroom Julia showed her. 'Oh, it's lovely, Julia, and I hadn't expected it to be so big!'

Julia smiled. 'All the rooms are quite large, Cathie. I suppose we're lucky in that respect.'

Cathie nodded. It was twice the size of the room she'd had at the Johnstons'. There was a double bed, made up with a pale pink bedspread and eiderdown. There were pink curtains at the window, which was large and looked out over the side of the house. The walls were covered in white wallpaper sprigged with clusters of apple blossom although in parts it was discoloured with age. There were two large wardrobes and two chests of drawers and a dressing table complete with a stool. The floor was covered mostly by a large rug but the lino surround was well polished.

'I'll leave you to get unpacked, Cathie,' Julia announced.

'Well, there's certainly plenty of space for my clothes – too much, I think. I haven't got that many!' Cathie laughed.

'Neither have I but for these big rooms you need lots of large pieces of furniture otherwise they look sort of ... half empty, half furnished!'

Cathie smiled at her as she opened the suitcase. 'I just know I'm going to love living here, Julia.'

'Good, well, when you've finished come back into the sitting room and you can have a proper chat to Mother.'

Cathie drew out a jacket and went to hang it in a wardrobe, wondering if Mrs Vickers really did have something wrong with her. Perhaps after she'd spoken to Julia's mother at more length she might find out.

The time just seemed to fly by, Cathie thought as they entered the last few days before the holiday. She had settled quickly into the routine of the house in Everton Valley and Julia had confided that it was such a boon to have someone to help. Cathie hadn't made up her mind as to whether there was anything seriously wrong with Maud Vickers. She did get a little breathless at times but her appetite was good and she privately thought that the woman would benefit from taking more exercise, although she didn't say anything to Julia. She had found the best thing was not to ask Mrs Vickers how she was feeling – although it did seem a little impolite – for she complained enough without being given any encouragement. She'd found that out one afternoon when she'd sat with the older woman while Julia had gone out to the library to change her mother's books.

'How have you been today, Mrs Vickers? Are you looking forward to Christmas?' she'd asked as she cut red and green crêpe paper into strips.

Maud had sighed heavily. 'I'm never at my best at this time of year, Cathie. It's partly due to the weather and partly due to certain ... memories.'

'Oh,' Cathie had replied, wondering whether she should ask about the 'memories'.

'I hate the dark, cold winter days, they don't

149

help my arthritis and I find them depressing. They remind me too much of all the time I spent alone when Julia was younger.'

Cathie had nodded. 'It must have been hard for you then, Mrs Vickers,' she'd said sympathetically, thinking the woman was recalling the early days of her widowhood.

'You have no idea how hard, Cathie, and even before Ralph died I was often ... on my own. But that's all in the past now,' she'd finished briskly.

'Julia and I are both really looking forward to the holiday; it's going to be great.'

The woman had nodded. 'Oh, what it is to be young and carefree! I expect you'll both be wanting to go off to dances and the like, but I should warn you, Cathie, just as I am always impressing upon Julia, that men can't be trusted! Not even the best of them. They will charm you with compliments, presents and promises but don't believe their lies. In my experience it will only lead to grief. Take my advice, Cathie, have nothing to do with any of them.'

Cathie had nodded but had begun to wonder just what had happened in the past to make Maud Vickers so bitter towards men. Her da and her older brothers were the most trustworthy people she knew and she hoped that in the future she'd meet someone special, be courted and eventually married with a family of her own.

Maud Vickers nodded knowingly. 'I'm old now and much wiser, Cathie, so heed my advice. And of course I'm not a well woman and sometimes I wonder if I've much longer on this earth...'

'Oh, don't say that, Mrs Vickers!' Cathie had

cried in horror. 'You're not *that* old! I think you're probably about my mam's age and that's not old at all. And what would Julia do without you? We're both so fond of you and want you to have a really wonderful Christmas.'

Maud had finally smiled. 'Thank you, Cathie, that's very kind of you. You're a good girl – as is Julia.'

Cathie had smiled back but had determined not to bring up the subjects of either Mrs Vickers's health or her mistrust of men ever again.

They had both bought decorations from Woolworth's and spent a very enjoyable evening decorating the tree. They hung the paper chains Cathie had made across the ceiling in the living room and dining room and Julia had bought some holly, which they used to decorate the hallway. Julia had said that she was going to go down to the food hall to purchase some of the more exotic foods as this year she was determined they were going to have 'all the trimmings'. Cathie had soon learned that groceries, milk, bread, meat and greengroceries were delivered to the house, Mrs Vickers apparently being unable to go out to do the shopping. She'd thought how much more time her mam would have had had she been able to have things delivered but then she knew her mam preferred to make her own purchases. Lizzie considered shopping to be part and parcel of her household routine.

Cathie had already posted off the cards and the small gifts she'd bought. Of course she did feel a little sad that she would miss another Christmas

151

with her family, but then she reminded herself that this year she would at least have Julia and her mother for company. She wouldn't spend most of the day alone in her room.

The day before Christmas Eve, Mavis and Dorothy said they were going to a Christmas Eve dance at the Grafton and invited Cathie to go with them.

'Go on, you'll enjoy it! You could even buy that dress you liked so much – they'll have had more than one in stock,' Julia urged.

Cathie was unsure. It would mean leaving her friend on her own for the evening with all the preparations for the meal the following day, and she couldn't see when she would get time to go across to Blackler's – and she doubted they would still have one of the taffeta dresses anyway.

'Thanks for asking me, Mavis, but I'll give it a miss this time if you don't mind. We'll both be exhausted by the end of the day; you know what it'll be like – everyone rushing around at the last minute buying things they've forgotten to get. We've both got lots to do at home too and I haven't got anything decent to wear and no time to buy something. And, well, my dancing isn't great,' she explained.

Mavis had smiled and shrugged. 'I just thought I'd ask.'

'But I'd like to go with you at some time in the future,' Cathie added eagerly before Mavis turned away.

'Why didn't you say you'd go?' Julia enquired.

'For all the reasons I gave Mavis and besides ... I really *can't* dance. I never learned how to and

I'd make a complete fool of myself.'

Julia smiled at her. 'Well, we can soon remedy that. I'll teach you the waltz and the foxtrot. We've got a gramophone and we'll have the holiday to practise in. We'll soon have you gliding around the dance floor like Ginger Rogers.'

Cathie laughed. 'I doubt that but ... but I would like to learn. I'd like to go with Mavis and Dorothy in the future. I'd have gone if you had been coming too,' she confided.

Julia shrugged and smiled ruefully. 'I couldn't possibly leave Mother on Christmas Eve.'

'I know that and I couldn't possibly leave you to do all the preparations for Christmas lunch by yourself, it wouldn't be fair,' Cathie replied firmly. She frowned in thought. 'But maybe in a few months when the evenings start to get lighter we could both go to a dance or the cinema – together?' she suggested. 'After all, she won't be in the house on her own; there are the Hardcastles and the Butlers upstairs.' Cathie had met both couples and they had seemed nice, amiable people, albeit more Julia's mother's age than her own.

Julia too looked thoughtful. 'Perhaps we could, Cathie. We'll see.'

'Julia, can I ask you something?'

Julia smiled. 'Of course you can.'

'Why is your mother so set against men?'

Julia smiled ruefully. 'I see she's been advising you against trusting them?'

Cathie nodded.

Julia sighed. 'I really don't know but once or twice when she's been warning me against accepting invitations she's said, "Your father was no saint, believe me," so it must have something to do with him. But don't take too much notice of her, Cathie, she's old and set in her ways – and of course she's not well,' she added before turning away to serve a customer.

Leaving work on Christmas Eve both Cathie and Julia felt a sense of excitement rising in them. They were really looking forward to tomorrow.

'Let me take one of those bags, Julia. You seem to have bought an awful lot of stuff from the food hall,' Cathie remarked as her friend handed over a brown paper carrier bag.

'Only some fruit but I did manage to get the very last pineapple. I thought we'd have some of it after tea, this evening. Start the festivities off, sort of.'

'I hope you know how to cut it up or whatever you have to do with it. I certainly don't!' Cathie laughed.

'And I bought some shortbread biscuits and sweets and Turkish delight for Mother – she's very partial to it,' Julia informed Cathie as they boarded the crowded tram.

When they arrived home they found that the vegetables, groceries and the capon had been delivered that afternoon and after supper they began to prepare for next day.

As Cathie peeled the carrots, parsnips and potatoes, which would then be placed in bowls of cold water, Julia started on the capon: the large chicken Mrs Vickers had ordered. It had to be plucked and drawn and then washed before it would be left to stand on the marble slab in the larder all night.

'What did you have at home for Christmas dinner, Cathie?' Julia asked.

'Usually a goose. Mam always went to one of the farmer's wives at the end of November and chose one. A lot of people do that on the island although you can get them from the butcher's. She always asked for a price so she knew how much she had to save,' Cathie replied, making a start on the parsnips.

'Mother said it was not really economical for us to have a goose just for the two of us, there would be too much wasted. So, we've had a capon for as long as I can remember. It usually makes two meals and then soup.'

'That makes sense,' Cathie agreed. 'Mam always started on the pudding very early too; she said it tasted better if it was left to "stand" for a while after it was cooked.' She smiled. 'It would be boiling away on top of the range for hours and hours, wrapped in muslin, and the smell filled the kitchen. That smell always made us realise that Christmas was coming. I loved it.'

Julia nodded, brushing away a stray feather that had settled on her nose. Christmas in Collins Lane seemed to have been anticipated with more excitement than she'd been used to, but tomorrow would be different, she was certain.

On Christmas morning they all sat beside the fire in the living room and opened the gifts they'd bought for each other. Even Mrs Vickers had seemed far brighter.

'Oh, Julia, this is lovely!' Cathie exclaimed as she

opened her small parcel. She was truly delighted with the necklace. It wasn't gold or silver but it was pretty, consisting of small silver-coloured filigree flowers linked together and set with coloured stones. 'It'll go with any colour,' she enthused.

'That's what I thought, Cathie,' Julia replied. 'Oh, what a pretty scarf! What gorgeous colours!' The silk scarf that was Cathie's gift was in shades of blue and green, colours which suited her.

'It's not real silk; but it took my eye when I saw it downstairs on the ground floor,' Cathie confided.

Julia was impressed. 'You bought it at work?' As Cathie nodded she felt a bit guilty that she'd bought the necklace in Woolworth's.

'It's the thought that counts, Julia,' Mrs Vickers reminded her as she carefully unwrapped the soft pink bed jacket Julia had bought for her and then the box of lace-edged handkerchiefs from Cathie. 'What lovely and useful presents,' she commented happily.

They'd had a truly magnificent lunch, and despite Mrs Vickers's 'delicate' stomach she had managed two helpings of pudding followed by some Turkish delight from the food hall. After that she had announced that she'd really eaten far too much and needed to go for a rest. They'd cleared away and washed up and then they'd rolled up the carpet and the dancing lessons had begun. They'd spent hours laughing and giggling as Cathie had repeatedly tripped up but by evening she had managed to master a passable waltz and Julia insisted that she was doing really well.

'I'll go with them to a dance next time, Julia,'

Cathie announced as she finally flopped down on the sofa. 'After all, why waste all your hard work and patience? And I'll have plenty of time to buy a decent dress,' she added.

Julia nodded, her cheeks flushed with her exertions and the heat of the fire. 'You should be able to get something in the sales, Cathie. Why don't you ask Mavis to keep her eye out for something suitable? She's in the right department and you'll get it at a good price with your discount off as well.'

Cathie hadn't thought of that. She was glad now she hadn't bought that dress in Blackler's for she'd get something of a far better quality in Lewis's sale, she thought, marvelling that for the first time in her life she would be able to afford a really classy dress to wear to a proper dance. Yes, she'd definitely made the right decision to leave the Johnstons' house.

Chapter Twelve

1935

As she gazed at her reflection in the long mirror on the outside of the wardrobe door Cathie felt that for the first time in her life she looked really elegant – glamorous even – and she wished her mam could see her now. She had changed so much from the dowdy little fifteen-year-old she'd been when she first arrived in Liverpool.

The dress was perfect and the colour suited her. Mavis had picked it out from the sale stock. 'It was an expensive dress but it's been greatly reduced. If you ask me this colour doesn't suit everyone – probably why it hasn't sold at full price – but it will look great on you, Cathie. It could have been made for you!' she'd enthused.

'Thanks, Mavis, it was very thoughtful of you,' she'd replied, thinking it was really gorgeous. The full skirt was of silk organza and the bodice was lace, in a shade of magenta that really did suit her dark colouring. It had a square neckline and small cap sleeves and an artificial flower in a darker shade was attached to the narrow belt at the waist.

Around her neck she wore the necklace Julia had given her for Christmas and she had bought a pair of black high-heeled shoes and a small black evening bag, both of which had been in the sale. She felt excited and nervous at the same time as this was the first time she was going to a real ballroom. It was a St Valentine's Day dance and Mavis had said the ballroom was usually decorated with red balloons and scarlet heart-shaped bunting.

She turned away from the mirror and, picking up her bag and her coat, went through into the living room.

'Oh, Cathie, you look gorgeous!' Julia enthused, looking up from the magazine she'd been leafing through. 'Mother, doesn't she look elegant? And so grown up!'

'I *feel* elegant and grown up.' Cathie smiled. 'In a few weeks I'll be seventeen.'

Mrs Vickers nodded her agreement but she was thankful that Julia wasn't going with Cathie this evening. 'Lovely, Cathie. It's a pity Julia can't go with you but I really don't feel well and I think I'll be having an early night. And don't forget what I said about men – they're fickle!'

Julia raised her eyebrows. Sometimes her mother harped on too much about men and their faults – real or imagined. 'Well, I'm going to wait up for you, Cathie. I want to hear every single detail,' she said. She couldn't help feeling a little resentful although they had agreed that as it was February and the evenings still dark, they wouldn't both go. She had said there would be plenty of other occasions in spring and summer and that for Cathie's first dance she should go with the girls from Lewis's who were her own age.

'I won't be late, Julia, after all we've both got work in the morning,' she promised as she prepared to leave.

She met Mavis and Dorothy at the tram stop outside the ballroom; there seemed to be crowds of people going into the building. 'It's such a shame I had to wear a coat over the dress. It's so much nicer than all my other clothes, Mavis,' she said as she greeted the girls.

'As soon as I saw it I knew that colour would look great on you, Cathie,' Mavis replied. 'And it really does,' she added, smiling.

They went inside and made their way towards the cloakroom where they handed in their coats and received a ticket in return. Cathie carefully tucked hers into her bag; then they went to check their hair and lipstick in the large mirror where other girls were jostling to do exactly the same thing.

'I'm not at all sure about the colour of this lipstick but Joan Meakin on the make-up counter said it was the very latest shade: "Crimson Fire",' Dorothy mused, peering intently at her reflection. 'What do you think, Mavis?'

Mavis studied her friend's reflection and then nodded. 'I think it's fine but if you're not really sure, wipe a bit off,' she advised.

Cathie thought the shade actually seemed to drain the colour from her friend's face for Dorothy was naturally pale, but didn't say so as her opinion hadn't been sought.

Mavis fiddled with her fringe, frowning. 'Oh, it's a mess. Lend me your brush, Dot, will you, please? I'll have to brush it out.'

Before Dorothy handed over the hairbrush Cathie shook her head. 'Give it to me; I'll do it. All it needs, Mavis, is just a tweak here and there,' she advised and with a few deft strokes had Mavis's hair looking immaculate again.

Mavis smiled. 'Thanks, Cathie! You're a real pal.'

As they entered the ballroom Cathie was completely mesmerised. It seemed huge and a balcony ran all around it where there were tables and chairs where you could sit and watch the people below on the dance floor. Suspended from the ceiling was a big silver-coloured glitterball which revolved slowly, casting beams of light on the dancers, and the floor was already crowded. Mavis had been right, she thought, the place was full of red heart-shaped bunting and balloons. At the far end of the room was a raised dais where the band was installed, playing 'Red Sails in the

Sunset', a favourite of both herself and Julia.

They managed to find seats at a table not too far back from the edge of the dance floor. 'It's not worth going to the trouble and expense of getting all dressed up to the nines if we just sit at the back of the room where no one can see us,' Mavis commented.

When Cathie was asked to dance by quite a good-looking lad she felt a frisson of excitement run through her – now she could put all the hours practising to good use. She could dance as well as anyone else on the floor and she'd quickly realised that her dress was much more elegant and expensive-looking than many others. It felt a little strange to be held in a boy's arms, but pleasurable, she thought, as he expertly guided her around and she smiled a little shyly at him.

'That's a gorgeous dress; it makes you stand out. What's your name?' her partner asked.

'Cathie Kinrade. What's yours?'

'Ben Thompson. You're a great dancer too, Cathie!'

She smiled, blushing a little; she was very grateful for Julia's patience now, she thought.

They were all frequently asked up to dance but Cathie hardly seemed to be off the floor. She was very flattered by all the attention she was receiving, and thoroughly enjoying herself. One young man, who introduced himself as 'Freddie Chambers', had asked her up three times and had even offered to buy all three of them a drink although Cathie had refused the offer as graciously as she could for she felt it would be giving him ideas and she didn't like him well enough for that.

All too soon they announced that it was time for the 'last waltz' and Cathie felt a little relieved that the lad called Ben Thompson got to her before Freddie Chambers did.

'I've not seen you here before, Cathie, but you've been in great demand,' he said as he guided her around the floor.

'No, it's the first time I've been but it definitely won't be the last,' she replied happily. 'I've really enjoyed myself.'

'Then I'll probably see you here again some-time,' he said hopefully.

'You probably will,' she replied, smiling up at him.

There was rather a crush at the cloakroom and they had to queue to redeem their coats.

'I wish they'd get a move on. I'll miss my tram at this rate,' Mavis said impatiently, tapping her foot.

'Is it that late?' Cathie asked, a little alarmed, thinking of Julia waiting up for her.

'Not really, we'll be all right. It's well before midnight and we're not Cinderellas,' said Dorothy, grinning, to allay Cathie's anxiety. They'd all had a great evening and she was glad as it was Cathie's first dance. Hopefully it wouldn't be her last.

As they all lived in different areas of the city, once outside they said their goodbyes and went for their respective trams. The tram was crowded and Cathie had to stand and now she realised that her feet were aching. She was unused to wearing such high heels, she thought ruefully, but it was a small price to pay for such a good time.

The tram stop was a short distance from the

162

bottom of Everton Valley so when she alighted she decided to take off her shoes, which were pinching unbearably. Gasping as her feet came into contact with the cold pavement, she hurried her steps.

When she had nearly reached the house she realised that there was a car parked outside. She frowned: it was Dr Clarke's car; she'd seen it often enough before in the time she'd lived here. Oh, poor Julia, she thought; had Mrs Vickers had one of her inexplicable 'turns'?

Lights blazed from all the downstairs rooms and a few upstairs too, which was unusual at this hour, and as she went into the hall she saw the door to the sitting room stood wide open. Julia was sitting on the sofa while the doctor seemed to be passing her something. Suddenly a feeling of dread crept over her. It was after midnight. What had happened that the doctor was here so late?

'Julia? What's ... wrong?' she asked tentatively as she went into the room.

Dr Clarke turned towards her, his expression grave. 'Miss Kinrade – Cathie, I'm afraid I have some bad news. I'm sorry to say that Mrs Vickers has died. From a heart attack, I suspect, although I won't know for sure until after the post-mortem. Naturally it has been a terrible shock for Julia...'

Cathie's eyes widened in horror. 'Oh, Julia, no!' she cried, barely able to take in the fact that her friend's mother, who had seemed reasonably well when she'd left, was ... *dead*. Julia looked stunned, she thought as she went and sat beside her and took her hand. 'Oh, I'm so ... so sorry!'

'I've given her something to make her sleep and I'll stay until the ambulance arrives,' Dr Clarke

163

said quietly.

'Ambulance?' Cathie was puzzled as she looked up at him.

'To take Mrs Vickers to the city mortuary,' he replied gently. They were both so young to have to cope with something like this, he thought as he went back into the hall to wait for the ambulance.

'Julia, what happened?' Cathie just couldn't believe it and she felt guilty for having left her friend.

Julia shook her head, her face deathly pale. 'She ... she said she didn't feel well but ... but, oh, Cathie, I really didn't believe her and now...'

'Hush, Julia! Don't think like that! Don't blame yourself. We ... we both know – thought' – she quickly amended – 'she wasn't suffering from anything so ... so serious.'

Julia nodded. 'She went to bed quite early and about an hour ago I thought ... I thought I heard her call out so I went to see what she wanted. She ... she wasn't breathing, Cathie! I didn't know what to do so I ran upstairs to ask Mr Hardcastle and he ... he told me to call the doctor!' Julia broke down into racking sobs and Cathie gathered her into her arms and tried to soothe her. Everything felt so unreal.

The ambulance arrived and the two girls remained sitting huddled together as Mrs Vickers was taken from the house. The doctor advised them both to take a dose of the sedative and go to bed. He promised to call the following morning to help Julia with the formalities.

Cathie went into the kitchen and put the kettle on, then got a glass of water and went back to Julia. 'I'm making us some tea. Meanwhile, you

164

should do as Dr Clarke instructed and take some of this medicine. I'm not having any,' she added, thinking that she'd have to go into work in the morning and inform them what had happened so there was no point in her taking a sedative; besides, she felt she didn't really need it.

Obediently Julia did so, thinking that it couldn't make her feel any more dazed than she already was. She couldn't seem to think straight at all.

As Cathie returned to the kitchen she noticed that the door to Mrs Vickers's bedroom had been left wide open. She automatically went to close it and noticed the pale pink bed jacket Julia had given her mother at Christmas lying on the floor. She went and picked it up and placed it on the bed. If she was truthful, she thought sadly, she'd never believed that there was anything wrong with the poor woman. As she closed the door she felt guilty. She'd thought it was all an act to gain attention. Oh, how wrong she'd been. Maud Vickers had obviously had a weak heart which to-night, while she'd been out enjoying herself, had given out. All she could do now was help Julia to get through these next few terrible days. She uttered a silent prayer as she thought of her own mother, who was the same age as the dead woman. What would she do, how would she feel if anything as tragic happened to Mam? She would never forget this St Valentine's Day, but for all the wrong reasons.

Before they both went to bed Mr and Mrs Hardcastle called.

'I know it's late but we were both worried about you girls,' Mr Hardcastle informed them. He was a small, dapper man in his late fifties who had been polite and cheerful whenever Cathie had seen him. His wife was also small and slim, but rather more reserved.

'We saw the ambulance arrive and then leave. We are both so sorry, Julia. If there is anything either of us can do to help...' Mrs Hardcastle offered.

'That's very kind of you both, but the doctor has given Julia a sedative and we were just on our way to bed.'

'Of course. Best thing for you two now is to try and get some sleep. Things always seem to look a bit better in the morning,' Mr Hardcastle agreed. 'But, remember, you only have to ask. We'll do whatever we can in this ... difficult time.' He took his wife's arm. 'Come along, Hilda, let these girls get some rest.'

'We really are very, very sorry. Of course we'll let Mr and Mrs Butler on the top floor know about your poor mother; there's no need for you to go through the ordeal of explaining. Good-night to you both.'

Cathie thanked them and showed them out. 'They really are a nice couple.'

Julia nodded, thankful that she wouldn't have to try to explain to any of the lodgers what had happened. She could barely believe it herself.

Next morning, after making sure that Julia was reasonably all right given the circumstances, Cathie left for work. Upon arriving she went straight to Miss Edgerton's office and informed her what had happened.

'I really hated to leave her this morning, Miss

Edgerton ... but ... Dr Clarke was coming round.'

Avril Edgerton nodded. 'Of course, that's totally understandable and I hope you will pass my condolences on to Miss Vickers.'

Cathie nodded.

The older woman frowned. 'Of course, we can't leave an important department totally unstaffed. Will you be able to manage, Miss Kinrade? Until arrangements can be made for you to have some assistance while Miss Vickers is unable to return to work?'

Cathie bit her lip. She'd expected as much but she really didn't want Julia to be on her own all day. 'Of course, Miss Edgerton.'

When she reached the millinery department she was quite thankful that, as the sales were over, business at this time of year was rather slack. But the spring stock had arrived so that would at least give her something to keep her busy, she thought.

She began to unpack the latest fashions in spring hats while waiting for the new display units Julia had ordered to be brought down to her. It made a nice change to see the pastel colours, she thought, although neither she nor Julia would be wearing any of them, at least not for a while yet. She had carefully unpacked half a dozen when she looked up to see the familiar figure of Mrs Fleetwood-Hayes approaching.

She could have cried out aloud with relief. 'Oh, madam, I'm so pleased to see you!'

'Thank you, Cathie. Such a pleasant greeting.' She looked more closely at the girl. 'What's wrong? Where's Julia?'

Cathie told her of the events of the previous

night and the woman's eyes widened in shock.

'Good God! So she really *was* ill. I take back everything I said to the contrary. Poor Julia! Such a terrible shock for her – such an ordeal.'

Cathie nodded. 'I didn't want to leave her this morning but I had to come in to tell them ... and there's to be a postmortem...'

'Of course. Now, I did come in to have a look at your new stock but I think I'd better go and see how Julia is coping. She has no close relatives, you see, and she's so young to have to contend with all this. There will be formalities to complete and she'll be in no fit state...'

Cathie nodded. 'It's very hard for her. She said this morning she just feels numb and can't even think straight. Mr and Mrs Hardcastle from upstairs kindly offered to try to help but...' she replied, thankful that someone as utterly capable as Mrs Fleetwood-Hayes had decided it was her duty to aid Julia in her hour of need.

'...but they're only neighbours, tenants really. No, it's best that I go,' the woman said firmly.

Cathie had returned to her task when she was interrupted by a young man in the brown overall coat of a warehouseman.

'I was told to bring these down to you. Are you Miss Vickers?' he asked cheerfully.

Cathie shook her head. 'No, she ... she's not in today. I'm Miss Kinrade – Cathie. I'm her assistant.'

He grinned. 'Pleased to meet you, Cathie. I'm Charlie Banks, I've only been here a week. Now, where do you want these, luv?'

Cathie looked at him without much pleasure.

His cheerfulness irritated her but then she realised he was only trying to be friendly. 'Just put
them on that counter over there, please.'

'I'll take the packaging off them and take it
back to the yard with me. Have you worked here
long, Cathie?' he asked, thinking she was the
most attractive girl he'd seen so far in the store.

'Almost two years,' she replied rather curtly, her
mind still on Julia.

'Has anyone ever told you that you're a real
stunner?' he asked, standing back and gazing at
her with a cheeky grin.

Cathie stopped what she was doing and stared
at him. She judged him to be about nineteen; he
was tall, well built with dark wavy hair and brown
eyes and she supposed he was quite handsome.
But he was also cocky and full of himself, she
thought. 'No, and if you don't mind I'm not in
any mood to be listening to flattery, there's been
a bereavement in the family. Shouldn't you be
getting back to the stockroom?'

He instantly became contrite. 'Oh, I didn't
know that. Sorry. I didn't mean to offend you,
Cathie. Er ... my condolences,' he added.

She just nodded and as she looked at him she
thought that he didn't sound entirely sincere but
she pushed the thought away. She had more
important things on her mind than to be paying
much attention to Charlie Banks.

After he'd gone Mavis came across to her. 'What
was he saying, Cathie? You didn't look very
pleased.'

'Nothing much, Mavis. He's new and clearly
full of his own importance – though I don't know

169

why – and I'm just not in the mood for such ... nonsense this morning.'

Mavis nodded sympathetically. 'No, you won't be, Cathie. I bet you'll be glad when we close. Do tell poor Julia that we're all very sorry and that we're thinking of her; at least she won't need to come in to work for a bit, although she'll not get paid for the time off. Dorothy and I are going to start a collection for flowers for poor Mrs Vickers,' she added.

Cathie managed a smile. 'That's good of you but ... but we don't know when the funeral will be yet.'

'That's all right, we'll at least have the money for a wreath when it's all arranged,' Mavis replied.

When at last Cathie arrived home late that afternoon it was to find Mrs Fleetwood-Hayes still with Julia. 'How is she?' she asked tentatively.

'Still very dazed and upset but at least I've made her have something to eat. I've spoken to the doctor who has promised that, as soon as a cause of death has been established, he'll sign the certificate and bring it round and then we can contact the funeral directors. You know, Cathie, she'll feel a bit better after it's all over and she's back at work. Now, are you sure you'll be able to manage?'

'I'm sure. I'll have to go into work though; Miss Edgerton has promised me some help until Julia returns.'

The woman nodded. 'Right then, I'll be going but I'll come back tomorrow; those two girls of mine are old enough to see to themselves for a few days. She really shouldn't be on her own just yet.'

'Is the Captain not home?' Cathie enquired.

'Not for another two weeks,' Mrs Fleetwood-Hayes replied, pulling on her gloves. 'Oh, and, Cathie, I don't think she should go on taking that stuff the doctor left; it won't help in the long run. Grieving is a natural process...' She left the sentence unfinished.

'I'll see what she says,' Cathie replied. She knew that the woman had known grief in her life and so, she thought, had Julia, although she'd only been a child at the time of her father's death. It was the first time she herself had experienced it at such close quarters and it was very upsetting.

Chapter Thirteen

Cathie worked on alone till the end of Saturday, having been promised some help for the following Monday. When she returned home it was to find Julia a bit better and seemingly a little more able to try to come to terms with her loss. Mrs Vickers's death had now definitely been attributed to a severe heart attack and Mrs Fleetwood-Hayes had in her usual capable manner gone to instruct the funeral directors. Cathie found her no-nonsense attitude very reassuring as she listened to her discussing with Julia the wording of the announcement for the newspaper, the flowers and the hymns for the service. At least

171

Julia was starting to make decisions, she thought, no matter how painful they were.

'And I take it you'll forgo the usual funeral tea,' Mrs Fleetwood-Hayes gently pressed Julia.

Julia nodded. 'There's only Cathie and yourself who'd come; there isn't anyone else. We ... we really weren't well acquainted with the Hardcastles or the Butlers upstairs, although they are friendly enough. Mother ... always said it was best to keep ourselves to ourselves,' Julia replied sadly. Her mother had always maintained it didn't do to mix too freely with people who were just tenants but Julia had felt it was as if they were living in a house occupied by strangers – albeit pleasant ones – they knew so little about them.

Mrs Fleetwood-Hayes nodded; that sounded like Maud. 'Then afterwards why don't the three of us go for a meal in one of the hotels in town – my contribution to the occasion. I'll arrange it.'

Cathie thought how generous it was of her as she was only a distant relative of Julia's, and she admitted to herself that they couldn't have managed without her help.

'And then, Julia, I think the best thing for you would be to return to work. It won't help if you spend too much time here. Oh, I know there are things to be done still, and going through ... belongings isn't a pleasant experience but I'm sure Cathie will help you. You could do a little each night,' she suggested.

'Yes, I'll help,' Cathie promised, thinking it wasn't the greatest way of spending an evening. But which of her mother's things Julia wanted to keep had to be decided before she could try to pick up the threads of her life again. Once the funeral was over she was hopeful that Julia would be able to look at her life in a different light.

The funeral had been a very quiet affair, Cathie thought the morning Julia returned to work; she and Julia were walking to the tram stop. Of course it had been very sad but also very dignified. Julia had worn full mourning, Cathie had worn her good coat with a black armband and a black hat, Mrs Fleetwood-Hayes had been elegant in a black wool coat with an astrakhan collar and cuffs and a black velvet hat. Cathie had, as usual, described everything in her weekly letter to Lizzie.

'I suppose you're thinking that things feel rather ... strange this morning?' she said to Julia.

Julia nodded. 'Everything still seems unreal, Cathie, but I'm sure that I'll feel more like my old self once I'm back behind the counter. I'll have plenty of things to occupy me.'

'And I'm delighted you're back. Honestly, that Tilly Hopworth they sent me from Accessories was little better than useless. She had to be told to do *everything!* She was useless at thinking for herself.'

Julia managed a smile. 'Well, things will get back to normal now.'

Cathie nodded. She'd already had a quiet word with some of the other girls on their sales floor and they'd all promised not to harp on too much about Julia's bereavement, but as Mavis had said, 'We'll have to at least say how sorry we are, Cathie, otherwise she'll think we're completely heartless.'

Julia had coped with everything quite well so far,

Cathie mused as they both busied themselves displaying the new season's millinery to best advantage. There was a lovely pale blue straw hat trimmed with marabou feathers dyed the same shade curled around the small brim that she'd taken quite a fancy to, although she couldn't wear it just yet – that wouldn't be at all seemly, but she comforted herself with the thought that until March was out the weather probably wouldn't be suitable anyway. It was more expensive than the hats she'd bought previously but she would buy it as a birthday treat.

'You sent up for more boxes and tissue paper, Cathie. Well, here they are!'

She looked up to find Charlie Banks grinning at her. She nodded before turning to her friend. 'We were getting a bit low on both, Julia.'

'So you're Miss Vickers?' Charlie surmised aloud.

Cathie sighed a little impatiently. 'This is Charlie Banks; he's a new assistant in the stockroom.'

'Nice to meet you, Charlie,' Julia said politely before turning away to check the items he'd brought.

Charlie looked at Cathie hopefully and leaned across the counter towards her. 'Er, I ... I was wondering if you'd like to go to the cinema one evening, Cathie?'

Her eyes widened in surprise. She barely knew him, she thought. She'd only spoken to him once before and now he was asking her out. 'Isn't that a bit ... forward of you?' she said quite bluntly.

He winked at her. 'The early bird catches the worm and all that...'

She wasn't very happy about being referred to in that manner. 'I'm afraid I'll have to say "no thanks", Charlie.'

He didn't appear to find her refusal discouraging at all, instead he grinned. 'I told you the first time I met you, Cathie, you're a stunner, so you can't blame me for asking. And I don't intend to give up,' he promised as he walked away, whistling cheerfully.

'He ... he's ... so full of himself!' Cathie stated hotly.

'He's certainly very confident and he seems to like you, Cathie. And you have to admit he is quite handsome,' Julia replied.

Cathie pursed her lips, not quite knowing what to say. She hadn't given him another thought since their first meeting, but she supposed Julia was right. He was handsome and quite personable. Did she feel flattered? she wondered. She'd wait and see and if he did ask her out again, then she might ... just *might* consider it.

The following week they both reluctantly started the task of sorting through Mrs Vickers's possessions; as Cathie reminded Julia, it was painful but necessary.

'It being necessary doesn't make it any easier,' Julia replied as they started on the shelves in the wardrobe.

'Let's get everything out and make a start on the handbags,' Cathie suggested.

They both sat on the floor, half a dozen bags of various sizes and colours between them.

One by one they were examined but Julia made the final decision as to what was to be kept. 'If there's one you particularly like or think might be of some use to you, Cathie, then take it. Although I have to say they are all rather old-fashioned.'

'Do you think I might be able to use this one for work?' Cathie asked, holding up a navy blue leather satchel-type bag.

Julia nodded. 'Possibly. It will certainly hold all the things we need to cart around with us every day.'

Cathie handed the bag over, not wanting to pry. 'You'd better have a look inside in case there's anything been left in it.'

Julia smiled wryly. 'Maybe a five-pound note? Some hope!'

Cathie smiled back as she picked up the next bag and started to examine it but a sharp intake of breath from her friend made her look up. 'What's wrong?'

Julia was holding an envelope and looking puzzled. 'I found this. It's a letter Mother wrote to my father. It's addressed to him at a place in Scotland but she obviously never posted it, even though it's got a stamp on.'

'Scotland?' Cathie repeated, surprised.

Julia nodded. 'He travelled a lot with his job. He was often away for days at a time, occasionally even a whole week.' She sat back on her heels. 'Should I read it?'

Cathie shrugged, wondering why Mrs Vickers hadn't posted it. Maybe she'd just forgotten about it or maybe it had been overlooked when she'd changed handbags? It had obviously been in the bag for years as the stamp was an outdated one.

Julia felt slightly guilty that she was prying into

176

her mother's past as she drew out the folded sheets of paper, but she was curious to know what the letter contained and why it had never been posted. As she read the words in her mother's familiar handwriting she grew increasingly horrified.

'Julia, what's wrong?' Cathie asked, startled, for the colour had drained from her friend's face.

Julia shook her head and bit her lip in disbelief as she handed the letter over to Cathie. 'Read it, Cathie! I'm ... so shocked!'

Cathie read it slowly, trying to digest the words: Julia's mother had written that she was going to leave her husband. She was going to take the child – Julia – and go, she didn't know where to but she expected him to support them both, it was the least he could do, for she was sick of his infidelities.

The letter went on to describe his affairs, the pain and humiliation they had caused and the letter ended with some very frank comments on his character.

'Oh, Julia! I ... I don't know what to say,' she said sympathetically as she folded the letter and returned it to the envelope.

'Neither do I, Cathie. It's unbelievable – completely at odds with the memories I have of my father.'

Cathie bit her lip. 'It's only to be expected ... only right that your memories are good ones, Julia.'

'I ... I never knew, never even suspected any of ... this! It's ... horrible! But it must be true and that makes it all even more of a shock!'

Cathie nodded. 'I suppose it must be. Oh, how awful it must have been for your poor mother.'

'But ... but they must at least have tried to patch things up before he died because none of this was ever mentioned,' Julia added, still dazed.

'What will you do with it?' Cathie asked tentatively.

Julia put the letter on the floor beside her. 'I'll burn it. I don't want it in the house. I wish now I'd never set eyes on it!'

Cathie nodded. 'I think that would be the best thing.'

'It will take me some time, Cathie, to ... to get used to it all. It's very distressing to realise that my father seems to have led a double life. Now I know what my mother meant when she said he was no saint – maybe she was right about not trusting men.' Whoever would have thought that the quiet and seemingly family-loving Ralph Vickers had been constantly unfaithful? And what lies must he have told to conceal the fact? It was indeed very shocking and she resolved that she would take her mother's advice seriously now. She would have to be absolutely certain about any man before she would trust her heart to him – or maybe she would just concentrate on her career. Be like Miss Edgerton, independent and self-reliant. She already had a comfortable home and maybe in time she might become a millinery buyer instead of just the senior assistant in the millinery department.

Cathie got to her feet. 'Let's leave all this for tonight. I'll put the kettle on and I think, Julia – under the circumstances – we should get rid of that bag too,' she urged. She certainly didn't want it now. She couldn't possibly use it. It would be a constant reminder to Julia of her father's lies and deceit.

Charlie Banks often managed to find some excuse to be 'just passing through' their department, Cathie noticed with a mixture of amusement, irritation and a small inkling of pleasure. Sometimes he stopped to chat; sometimes he didn't, particularly if Mr Moorcroft the floor walker was in the vicinity.

'He's quite persistent, Cathie. You have to admit that,' Julia said with a wry smile after he'd stopped to inform them that a new system was to be introduced into the stockroom which would ultimately affect all departments. 'He didn't need to come to tell us that, he knew there'd be a memo about it sent to every department. He just wanted to see you.'

Cathie nodded thoughtfully. 'I know; it was just an excuse.'

'Well, if he asks you again, will you go?'

Cathie shrugged. 'I don't know, Julia.'

'Do you like him? He seems a pleasant enough lad,' Julia asked.

'I have to say I'm getting more used to him,' Cathie replied. 'Now I'd better see just what that young woman is looking for. She's picked up three hats so far,' she added to change the subject. However, it was true, she mused. She didn't seem to find him so overbearing in his manner now and Mavis had remarked a little enviously that he seemed very taken with Cathie. Wasn't she the lucky one, had been her words – all the girls thought he was very handsome. And it was true, she admitted. He looked rather like Clark

Gable but without the moustache.

A week later, Mrs Fleetwood-Hayes, who'd just been up to the menagerie, came into the store to see how both girls were getting on.

'Two monkeys this time, tiny little things. I told the Captain they'd not survive a month but he never listens. The girls were quite taken with them but I certainly wasn't. Now, how are you getting on? You look far brighter, Julia.'

Julia managed a smile. 'You were right; the best thing for me is to come to work. It does take my mind off things.'

'And we've done quite a lot of the "sorting out",' Cathie added, thinking of the evenings when she'd bolster Julia's spirits as her friend tried to decide which of her mother's things to keep and which to get rid of. 'And we've settled into a sort of routine now. Things are beginning to feel more normal.'

The woman nodded, thinking they were both still very young to be living without an older person's guidance, something Maud Vickers's solicitor had remarked upon. She'd informed him quite firmly that Julia was well able to run the house and collect the rents and that she was prepared to keep an eye on them both. But now at least the girl had a much less restricted future to look forward to.

Cathie turned away to leave Julia to attend to Mrs Fleetwood-Hayes and found Charlie Banks hovering around the end of the counter. 'What is it this time, Charlie?' she asked but without any note of irritation in her voice.

He grinned at her. 'You wouldn't believe me if I told you – so I won't! But I can't hang around for long. What's your favourite song, Cathie?' he asked conversationally.

She frowned, trying to think. 'I do like "Isle of Capri" – it makes me think of exotic foreign places.' Then she smiled, glancing at Julia and her customer. 'But I wouldn't say that to *that* lady, she's just donated some creatures from an "exotic foreign place" to the menagerie.'

Charlie nodded. Everyone in the store knew about the Captain's redoubtable wife. 'Mine is "I Only Have Eyes for You."'

Cathie found herself blushing. 'Oh, stop it, Charlie Banks!'

'I mean it, Cathie,' he said seriously.

Before she could reply Julia interrupted, smiling. 'Hello, Charlie. Cathie, I was just telling Mrs Fleetwood-Hayes that it's your birthday in a week's time.'

Mrs Fleetwood-Hayes was studying Charlie intently. 'And who are you, young man? I haven't seen you before.'

'I'm Charles – Charlie – Banks, madam. I work in the stockroom and I think I'd better be getting back there,' he replied respectfully. But he intended to come back later in the day. Now he had the perfect excuse to ask Cathie out – as a birthday treat.

'I think you have an admirer, Cathie,' Mrs Fleetwood-Hayes remarked jovially.

'He's already asked Cathie out once but she refused,' Julia informed her.

'But now he knows it's my birthday next week, I've a feeling he's going to ask again,' Cathie said.

Mrs Fleetwood-Hayes nodded. 'Well, he seemed

181

a pleasant enough young man and quite hand-some too and you should do *something* to celebrate a birthday.'

'You think ... I should agree to go?'

The woman smiled at her. 'It's entirely your decision, Cathie, but you never know, you might enjoy yourself.'

When she'd gone Julia turned to Cathie. 'Will you? If he asks, that is?'

Cathie looked undecided. 'Won't you mind me not celebrating my birthday with you?'

'Of course not! You can do what takes your fancy. Neither of us has anyone to say we can't do this or can't go there now. I hope in a couple of months I'll feel like going out too. No, Cathie, you have your own life to lead,' Julia urged, feeling now wasn't the time to warn Cathie to be careful about trusting Charlie. The fact was she'd heard a few comments about him and they hadn't been favourable but she didn't want Cathie to think she was disapproving or, worse, envious.

Cathie smiled back at her. It seemed as if everyone was encouraging her.

Charlie didn't reappear but when the store closed she found him waiting for her by the doors to the staff entrance. Julia walked on ahead.

'I'll walk you to the tram stop,' he said, falling into step beside her.

She smiled her thanks at him.

'I said I wouldn't give up, Cathie, and as it's your birthday next week, will you come to the Grafton with me on Saturday night?'

She nodded. 'Yes, I'd like that. I enjoy dancing,' she replied, thinking she could wear the magenta

182

dress again. She doubted Julia would mind her not wearing black.

He beamed at her. 'That's great! Will I call for you or meet you outside?'

She wasn't sure if Julia would like him calling. 'I'll meet you outside. I know where it is, I've been before.'

'Then I'll be there at half past seven on the dot. You won't stand me up, will you?'

'Of course not, Charlie! I've agreed to go so I'll be there. Why wouldn't I be?'

He shrugged. 'Changed your mind. Some girls do that and just leave the fellow standing around in the cold, looking like a fool.'

'Well, I won't change my mind. I'm not the type of girl to go back on a promise. I'll be there by seven thirty,' Cathie replied firmly, and she meant it.

As she alighted from the tram and made to cross the road she spotted him waiting for her outside the ballroom. He looked quite different out of the brown shop coat he wore at work and she noticed that he was wearing a double-breasted lounge suit, the very latest fashion for men. He was indeed handsome, she thought, feeling excitement rising in her. She was looking forward to the evening ahead.

'Right on the dot, Charlie, as I promised,' she greeted him.

He smiled at her as he took her arm and they went inside. 'I'll wait here for you,' he said as she went towards the cloakroom.

This time she hastily checked her appearance

in the mirror and then went back into the foyer.

'Cathie, you look ... gorgeous!' he said, thinking how stunning she was in that colour. It set her apart from the crowd – and she was his 'girl' for the evening, he thought with pride.

'Thanks,' she said a little shyly.

They found a table and then he handed over a nicely wrapped box. 'For your birthday.'

Cathie was very surprised. 'Oh, Charlie, I didn't expect you to buy me anything – you've brought me here!'

He shrugged. 'Go on, open it,' he urged.

It contained a small bottle of perfume, something she'd never had before; it was 'Evening in Paris' in its distinctive dark blue bottle, which was very popular. 'How did you know it's something I've been meaning to buy myself?' she asked, delighted.

He leaned across the table and took her hand. 'I didn't but I thought it was a perfume you'd like. Maybe one day we'll have an "evening in Paris" together, but for now an evening at the Grafton will have to do. Shall we take a turn around the floor?' He was pleased by the look of genuine delight on her face and he was anxious to show her off – he'd already noticed a few envious looks cast in his direction.

She felt a little light-headed as he held her in his arms and spun her around the floor. 'You're a good dancer, Cathie,' he said, smiling down at her.

'So are you, Charlie, and I love dancing.'

'Then we have that in common as well as working together. I have the feeling that we'll be coming here quite often from now on.'

She smiled happily. 'Will we really?'

'You bet. You're my favourite girl now, Cathie,' he replied, winking as his arms tightened around her.

Cathie blushed. He must be taken with her to say that and she felt secretly delighted. She really did like him a lot... Was she falling in love? she wondered as the dance ended and he guided her back to their seats, his arm still around her waist.

At the end of the evening he walked her to the tram stop. She had thoroughly enjoyed herself, she thought, and she'd learned quite a lot about him too. He was nearly twenty; he lived in Walton with his parents and one younger brother, who was still at school, and two sisters, one of whom was older, the other younger. His father worked as a guard on the railway, a secure and quite well-paid job so naturally his mother didn't need to go out to work. He'd started his working life in Frost's, a small department store on County Road, had progressed to T. J. Hughes in London Road, a bigger store, and now to Lewis's.

'And where will you go next? Henderson's?' she'd asked, naming one of Liverpool's most prestigious stores and thinking he did seem to be ambitious.

He'd shrugged. 'Maybe, but for now I'm quite happy where I am. I like the company and especially a certain assistant in millinery,' he'd replied with his infectious grin.

As they reached the tram stop she smiled up at him. 'Thanks, Charlie, for a really great evening. I've enjoyed it. And thanks again too for the perfume.'

'Will you come out with me again, Cathie? Maybe next Saturday we could go to the cinema?'

She nodded. 'I'd like that.'

'Here's your tram. I'll see you in work on Monday,' he replied, giving her a quick peck on the cheek

He stood and waved as the vehicle lumbered off and she settled into her seat. She'd not expected him to kiss her, nor had she expected him to buy her a birthday gift. He really must like her, she thought. Was this the start of her very first 'romance'? she wondered, feeling a frisson of excitement and pleasure run through her. She supposed only time would tell. He did seem *different* out of work, she thought. She was already looking forward to going out with him next week.

Chapter Fourteen

Their outings had become a regular thing and by the end of April Cathie felt maybe she *was* falling in love with Charlie; by the end of May she was certain. They got on so well together; he made her laugh and he made her feel very special. At first she had always met him outside the ballroom, dance hall or cinema as Julia hadn't been too sure about how it would look if young men came calling to the house as she was still officially in mourning for her mother. Although cautious, by the beginning of May Julia had relented and now Charlie called for her when they were going

186

out, and when they didn't go out but stayed in playing gramophone records or listening to the wireless or playing cards, Julia always allowed them some time on their own. She just loved being with him, Cathie told herself. He was such fun, such good company and even when she was tired or a little down in spirits – for there were still times when she was homesick – he always managed to make her feel better. And of course he was handsome too.

The first weekend in June the weather was glorious, the first day of what could be termed 'summer', and so he'd suggested they go across to New Brighton on Sunday.

'I've never been there, Charlie. I saw the place from the deck of the ferry when I arrived in Liverpool, of course,' she confided, thinking how long ago that now seemed.

'It's a great place, Cathie! There's so much to do. There's the beach – if the tide's out you can walk to the fort. Then there's the promenade with shops and cafés and amusements, and there's the ballroom and the tower and the pier. You'll love it!'

Cathie nodded, although it sounded a bit like Ramsey – except for the tower and fort. But she was looking forward to seeing it all with him, whatever it was like.

The ferry was crowded as the sun beat down from a cloudless blue sky. People were intent on enjoying the weather, full of high spirits and laughter. The waters of the river were flat calm and spangled with gold from the sun's rays as the ferry chugged its way along. At least there was a bit of a breeze up here, she thought as she followed

Charlie up to the open top deck where they managed to find space to sit at the end of a bench seat.

She wore a summer dress in bright yellow rayon with white polka dots and a short bolero with puffed sleeves. A large white hat with a yellow ribbon around the crown shielded her face from the sun. Charlie had said she looked wonderful – outshining the sun even – and that she'd turned quite a few heads already. She'd laughed but had secretly been flattered by the compliment.

The beach, when they arrived, was already very crowded with people sitting in striped deckchairs and children of all ages digging in the sand, making castles, running about or paddling at the water's edge.

'We're not going to get much peace to sit and relax down there, not with all those kids,' Charlie commented when they reached the seafront. 'Let's go for a stroll along the promenade instead,' he suggested.

He held her hand tightly as they walked almost to the far end and although it was nearly noon and now very hot she was enjoying herself. They went into a little café that didn't seem quite as crowded as the rest and he ordered a pot of tea and some sandwiches.

'All the world and its wife seem to be out here today! Well, at least most of Liverpool,' Charlie commented.

Cathie laughed. 'It's the same at home in the summer. There are so many beaches around the island but people always head for the main ones,' she informed him, thinking of the wide sweeps of Ramsey and Douglas Bay, Peel with its two beaches and the castle on St Patrick's Isle, and the sandy expanses of Port Erin and Port St Mary in the south: all crowded on a day such as this with holidaymakers and those who could afford the time to relax and soak up the sun.

He looked at her puzzled for a second and then he laughed. 'I suppose this is something of a busman's holiday for you, Cathie? I'd forgotten you come from a seaside town.'

She shook her head. 'No, I'm enjoying it, Charlie, and Ramsey's a working port too. On a Sunday at home after church and then lunch, we'd go for a walk in the afternoon. Sometimes along the pier or the promenade – it's much quieter than this one – or up to the Albert Tower. But we didn't go in for sitting on the beach or paddling in the sea.'

'Not even as kids?'

She shook her head. 'There wasn't time. There were always chores to do and Da and the lads were usually out fishing – and not for pleasure. Sunday was the only day we got to ... relax together a bit.'

He thought that Sundays in their house in Ramsey sounded exceptionally dull, especially the bit about church. He couldn't remember the last time he'd been in one. 'So I can't tempt you to have a paddle?'

She shook her head, smiling. 'No. That water will be freezing, despite the weather,' she replied, thinking of how cold she'd been the day she and Jacob had pulled Violet Christian out of the sea. 'And I can't swim,' she added.

He grinned. 'I wouldn't recommend anyone to go swimming here. It's still the Mersey and the

189

Lord alone knows what you'd catch!'

She finished her tea. 'So, what will we do next? We've hours ahead of us yet.'

'Let's see if there's anything going on at the ballroom – it might be a bit cooler in there,' he suggested.

They spent the afternoon at a tea dance which they both enjoyed and then wandered back along the promenade and had fish and chips out of a newspaper, which Cathie declared tasted far better than on a plate. It had become much cooler and people were now beginning to make their way back to where the ferries docked and so they too joined the crowds. She felt a little chilly once the boat pulled out into mid-river and Charlie took off his jacket, put it around her shoulders and pulled her closer to him.

'Is that better?' he asked.

She nodded, gazing up at him. 'Oh, Charlie, I've had a wonderful day and I really love being with you!'

He kissed her lightly on the forehead. 'And I love being with you, Cathie. You're a delight, truly. And you do know that I love you?'

She felt a glow of happiness sweep over her. He felt the same way about her. It was the first time he'd said that.

'Do you think Julia will be back by the time we get to Everton Valley?' he asked. She'd told him that Julia had been invited to Mrs Fleetwood-Hayes's house in Aintree for afternoon tea and had agreed to go, although she still didn't think she should be going out to dances or the cinema yet.

'I don't know. They're only distantly related

190

and I don't know how well she gets on with Mrs Fleetwood-Hayes's daughters. One's about my age, I think, and the other one's a bit younger so she might not have much in common with them. And of course they've got far more money than Julia has so they've had a better education.'

'*You* get on very well with Julia even though she's years older than you,' he reminded her, hoping that Julia would stay out later and so give him time alone with Cathie. She was so *desirable*, he thought, feeling her body so close to his.

'I do but we work together too. We're shop assistants – one of those girls works in the Income Tax Office: that's the sort of difference I mean,' she informed him.

He kissed her forehead again. 'Oh, give me "shop girls" over "office wallahs" any day,' he murmured. 'And I bet she's not half as gorgeous as you, Cathie Kinrade,' he added.

When they arrived back Cathie was surprised Julia wasn't already in. 'She must be getting on well with them all,' she commented as she took off her hat.

As he sank down on the sofa Charlie hoped Julia would remain with her relatives for the rest of the evening as he was sure she didn't really like him, although she was always amiable towards him. 'Why don't you put some music on, Cathie,' he suggested. 'It'll be more romantic.'

She smiled at him. It would be the perfect end to a perfect day to spend some time alone with him. She put on one of her favourites, 'Red Sails in the Sunset', thinking it was very appropriate as well as romantic.

Charlie pulled her down beside him and took her in his arms. 'I've enjoyed today but I'm glad we're alone now,' he murmured, seeking her lips.

She fastened her arms around his neck and gave herself up to the happiness and rising excitement that were flowing through her. Oh, she thought, he was so wonderful and she loved him so much. His kisses became more and more passionate and she felt she was being swept away in a tide of love and desire and it was such a heady feeling that she didn't want it to end.

She was suddenly aware that his fingers were caressing her breast and she was very tempted to let herself be carried along but reluctantly she pulled herself together. 'Charlie! No!'

'Why not, Cathie? It's only natural that I want to ... love you.'

Part of her really wanted to agree, for they were in love, but reluctantly she drew away from him. 'I ... I can't. It wouldn't be ... right.'

He looked at her solemnly. 'I thought you loved me, Cathie?'

'I do! Oh, I *do*, Charlie,' she cried, stricken by his hurt expression.

'And I love you, so it's not wrong. As I said, it's natural.'

She was confused. 'But I didn't think... I thought it was something you did ... when you got married.' It was what her mam had impressed upon her emphatically: she must save herself for her husband and not allow anyone to take liberties, that would be cheapening herself and she certainly wouldn't be respected for it. Now she wished she had taken more notice of what Nora

Gelling and the others had hinted and joked about; maybe if she had she wouldn't feel so ... confused now. And what if he tried to force her? That sudden thought frightened her but she tried to push it from her mind. He wouldn't do anything like that: he loved her.

'If you really do love me, Cathie, you won't make me wait *that* long. That would be very cruel; it's hard for a man to control his ... feelings. I'm not a monk, you know.'

She bit her lip for she detected a bitter note in his voice. 'Oh, Charlie, I don't mean to excite those ... feelings, but ... I just *can't*. I really do love you though, you've got to believe that!'

He was about to tell her that there were names for girls like her but Julia's arrival home put an end to the conversation and he stood up hastily.

Cathie sat up straight and patted her hair into place. She was very thankful for her friend's timely arrival – the situation felt as if it was getting out of control.

'Did you have a good day?' Julia enquired, sensing there'd been some kind of argument, judging by Cathie's flushed cheeks and the expression in her eyes.

'Yes, it was great. How did you get on?' Cathie asked while Charlie busied himself turning the gramophone off.

'Very pleasant indeed. It's a beautiful house in a lovely quiet road and the food was delicious; but she really does spoil those two girls – they have the most fashionable clothes and all the latest gramophone records. She insisted I stay for supper and said I'd have to come again as I really should be thinking about starting to have more of a social life. You know what she's like.' Julia smiled. 'She even said she was married at my age and she wouldn't like to see me "left on the shelf".'

'Seems to be the favourite topic at the moment – marriage,' Charlie put in.

Julia shot him an enquiring look for she'd caught the sarcastic tone in his voice. Over the months, as she'd got to know him better, she'd decided there was something rather insincere about him. In her opinion his compliments were just a bit too flowery; he was often just too gushing, and there were still rumours at work about him but she'd said nothing to Cathie for her friend obviously adored him.

'Well, I'd better get off home. We've all got work in the morning,' he reminded them, reaching for his cap.

Cathie got to her feet. 'I'll see you out, Charlie.'

In the hallway he kissed her on the cheek, making no attempt to take her in his arms. 'I'll no doubt see you sometime tomorrow, Cathie.'

'Charlie, there's ... there's nothing wrong between us, is there? I mean...'

He bent and kissed her again but this time on the lips. 'Of course not, Cathie. Everything's just fine and dandy.'

She smiled happily up at him. 'I'm so glad, I really am. Thank you for such a wonderful day.'

'Next weekend we'll go to a dance on Saturday night and then, if the weather's still good, maybe we'll get the train up the coast to Southport,' he suggested.

'I'd love that. That's somewhere else I've never

been,' she replied as she saw him out. She stood on the step in the gathering dusk and watched him walk down the path. When he reached the gate he turned and blew her a kiss. He wasn't upset, she thought, he still loved her. She was glad now she'd heeded her mam's advice. They had plenty of time for all ... that, because she wanted nothing more than to marry him. She couldn't envisage a future without him.

They'd been busy for the early part of the week because the good weather continued and, as Julia had remarked, there seemed to be plenty of women who now realised they needed a wide-brimmed hat. Cathie had seen Charlie for a few minutes on Tuesday afternoon and they'd made plans for the weekend and he'd been his usual self, she'd thought.

'I hope this weather lasts, I've got a week's holiday coming up soon,' she reminded Julia on the Thursday, just before lunch.

'Have you thought about what you'll do?' Julia asked.

'I'm going to have a word with Charlie and see if there's any chance he can get the same week, then we'll be able to spend more time together – go to different places,' she confided.

Julia nodded although she knew that he'd only been with the company for four months and you didn't get holidays until the six months' probationary period was over. She checked her wristwatch. 'You go and get your lunch, Cathie, it's nearly twelve thirty. I have to go out in my lunch break today so I'll get a sandwich out somewhere.'

'You don't mind me going first?' Cathie enquired, hoping she might see Charlie.

'No, go on. I'll rearrange this display. I'm going to put the picture hats in a more prominent position. The time's obviously right for them – we'll sell more.'

Cathie left and she was soon engrossed in her task, until Mavis came across and interrupted her.

'Julia, do you have a minute?'

'Yes, what is it?' she enquired.

The girl looked embarrassed. 'It's ... it's a bit ... awkward, like. I wasn't going to say anything but ... but Dorothy said I should tell you.'

Julia looked bemused. 'Tell me what?'

Mavis lowered her voice. 'It's about Cathie.'

Julia's expression changed. 'What about her?'

Mavis twisted her hands together awkwardly. 'Not exactly Cathie, but that fellow of hers, Charlie Banks.'

Julia looked at her intently, beginning to feel uneasy. 'Charlie? What...?'

'I was coming down the back stairs this morning – I'd been up to the Welfare Office – and I saw him ... and he had his arm around that girl who works on the perfume counter. You know, the red-haired one who looks a bit "brassy".'

Julia felt her heart plummet as she thought of Cathie. 'Could it have just been ... accidental?'

Mavis shook her head. 'It didn't look very "accidental" to me – not from where I was standing.'

'Did he see you?' Julia enquired.

Mavis shrugged. 'I don't know but I ... I don't think so. Do you think Cathie should know? I mean, I don't want to upset her by telling tales,

196

but at the same time I don't want him to go making a fool of her.'

Julia nodded, agreeing with the girl's sentiments. 'Let me think about it, Mavis. It's a bit of a dilemma but ... but if anyone has to tell her it's got to be me.'

Mavis was very relieved. 'Thanks, Julia.'

As the girl went back to her department Julia frowned. The last thing she wanted was for Cathie to get hurt but should she tell her? Maybe there was really nothing in it but she didn't think so. Charlie Banks was just too ... glib, too fly by half. She really didn't trust him but how could she say that to Cathie? She would just have to try to think of something she could do or say to sort of ... warn her friend. But it wasn't going to be easy. She sighed. She'd tried, after the shock of that letter's discovery, to tell herself that not all men were like her father, but now she remembered her mother's words of warning again. Maybe she'd been right – you couldn't trust a single one of them as far as you could throw them.

Chapter Fifteen

Julia had found it impossible to broach the subject and so, to her shame, hadn't said anything. She just couldn't bring herself to see Cathie's world come crashing down – and what if her friend refused to believe her? She might even think that she was jealous and she certainly didn't want that.

197

Cathie and Charlie had gone dancing on Saturday night and then to Southport on the Sunday but when Cathie got home, looking flushed and tired, Julia felt it was really time to say something. 'You look a bit flustered. Didn't you have a good day?' she probed.

'I did. I loved Southport but it was very hot and crowded,' Cathie answered. They seemed to have spent the whole day walking, and she'd loved the shops in the Edwardian Arcades, but it had been exhausting. 'But ... but I'm a bit disappointed that Charlie won't get any time off while I'm on holiday.'

'So you asked him?'

Cathie sighed. He'd been rather abrupt about it when she'd mentioned the subject. 'He just said that it wouldn't be possible, he's not been working there long enough yet.'

'I did wonder about that when you first mentioned it to me,' Julia replied.

'Then he said that when he *is* entitled to some holidays, he'll probably have to take them in late autumn when there's no point going anywhere as usually the weather is awful. And then I reminded him that that's leading up to one of our busiest times, Christmas, and I wouldn't be able to get off.'

'What did he say to that?' Julia asked.

Cathie shrugged. 'Nothing; he just didn't answer.'

Julia sat down on the sofa beside her. 'So, what will you do with your time off? I'll be at work, it won't be much fun here on your own,' she reminded Cathie.

'I know – it won't be the same going to places by myself. So I've decided to go home and see Mam and the family. It's the perfect opportunity and I haven't seen them since I left. I've been saving up but I'll use the money for my fare instead.' She still had the money Violet Christian had given her but she'd never touched that. It was for emergencies when maybe she wouldn't have enough to get home if she needed to. She tried to sound more cheerful. 'I'm really looking forward to seeing everyone again.'

'You must be and I think it's a really good idea,' Julia felt very relieved: maybe this was just what Cathie needed, a break from routine and a break from Charlie. 'When will you go?'

'I'll go and book my ticket in my lunch break tomorrow and I'll leave on the Friday evening ferry and come back early on Sunday the following week.'

Julia nodded her agreement. That meant that Cathie wouldn't be available for two Sundays which might make Charlie Banks realise that she had other things to do and other people in her life apart from him. For the time being, maybe she didn't need to tell her about the brassy red-head from the perfume counter.

Cathie had written to Lizzie and booked her ticket and then, straight after work on the Friday, she went down to the Pier Head where the ferry was tied up. She was disappointed that Charlie hadn't protested about her going although he'd said he'd miss her and had promised to come to meet her on her return.

199

She settled herself in a seat in the public saloon, which thankfully wasn't too crowded, and tried to doze. It would be late when the ferry docked in Ramsey but her da was going to meet her and she was really looking forward to spending some time with her family. They'd kept her informed of their news but it wasn't the same as *being* there, she thought. She wondered if she'd see any change in them – it was two years since she'd seen them. Maybe Ramsey had changed too – perhaps there were now more shops and cinemas?

It was a calm and uneventful crossing – she even managed to get some sleep – and as the ferry tied up at the end of the Victoria Pier she realised that she really did feel glad to be home.

The pier was always illuminated at night but she was delighted to see both her da and Jacob waiting for her. She hugged them both happily.

Jacob took her case. 'You've certainly grown up, Cathie!' he remarked, grinning down at her.

'You look well, lass. Very smart, I might add,' Barney added.

Cathie smiled at them both, thinking her pale blue jacket and skirt looked a bit creased and crumpled from the journey but she was glad she'd worn the lightweight two-piece costume with a white blouse and a pale blue hat. 'It's great to be home again. It seems so long ago now since I last walked along this pier.'

'It *is* a long time ago, Cathie. We've missed you – especially Mam,' Jacob said.

'Aye, she wanted to come too but I told her to wait at home. It can get a bit rowdy in the Market Square on a Friday night when folk have been paid. And of course there are plenty of visitors – like you.' Barney smiled.

Cathie looked around as they headed towards home; yes the streets were still busy, but nothing compared to Liverpool at the weekend.

Collins Lane seemed even narrower and darker than she remembered but there was a light in the window of their cottage.

'Cathie, lass! Welcome home!' Lizzie greeted her.

Cathie hugged her, realising just how much she'd missed her mam. 'It's good to be home, Mam.' Her mother seemed to have aged, Cathie thought a little sadly as she put her arms round the familiar shoulders.

Lizzie stepped back. 'Let me look at you. My, you've grown up a lot, I can see that, and you look very smart. And with a suitcase full of clothes too!' she exclaimed as Jacob put the case on the floor.

Cathie smiled. 'I borrowed that from Julia. She's great. You'd like her, Mam.'

Lizzie busied herself making tea while Cathie took off her jacket and hat and looked around. Her younger siblings were in bed so it was quiet but Ella was still up and was regarding her with resentment and, she thought, envy. Nothing had changed much in the house, she mused as her da took his pipe from the mantel. Yes, it was small and far from well furnished but it was home. It was lovely to be back.

'I'm afraid we won't be seeing much of you, Cathie,' Jacob remarked as Lizzie handed him a mug of tea. 'We're away first thing in the morning – after the mackerel; we probably won't be back until Tuesday or Wednesday as this weather's set to hold.'

Cathie felt a little disappointed but she nodded her understanding. They always followed the shoals of fish, be they mackerel off the coast of Ireland at this time of year or the herring in October off the Scottish coast. They had a living to earn. 'Of course. I'm here until next Sunday, anyway.'

'At least we'll have a bit more room with the three of you away and we can have a good catch-up.' Lizzie smiled at Cathie as she handed her her tea.

'I'll enjoy that, Mam, and I'll be able to give you a hand with the chores.'

Lizzie shook her head. 'Not tomorrow you won't. You're on holiday – you deserve a bit of rest.'

'But, Mam, you know how busy you always are on Saturdays and you'll be up early if they're intending to catch the tide,' Cathie protested.

'Our Ella and Meggie can help, and Hal too,' Lizzie replied firmly. 'No, you do whatever takes your fancy tomorrow.'

'Oh, thanks for that, Mam!' Ella muttered.

Lizzie shot her an angry look and Cathie sipped her tea. She wanted to ask if the girls pulled their weight but she said nothing. She didn't want to start an argument the minute she'd got home.

'Is Jack not home yet?' she enquired, having noticed the absence of her eldest brother despite the fact that it was nearing midnight.

Barney frowned. 'He's courting. I know he's a grown man but he should be back by now. He knows we're off early tomorrow.'

Cathie's eyebrows rose and she looked

pointedly at her mother. This was news.

'He's taken up with Nancy Camaish; she works in Brown's Grocer's in Parliament Street. She lives in Glen Auldyn, so he's a fair walk back after seeing her home. They were going out somewhere after she'd finished work,' Lizzie informed Cathie.

Cathie made a mental note to ask her mam tomorrow if she approved of this Nancy Camaish, but Brown's was a high-class grocer's so she must at least be what Mam would term 'respectable'.

'Well, we're not staying up half the night waiting for him, everyone is tired, so we'll get off to bed now,' Lizzie pronounced as she collected the mugs and took them into the scullery to wash.

It would be strange to share a bed with her sisters again, she thought, used as she was not only to a bed of her own but a room of her own too. She kissed her father and brother goodnight – no doubt they'd have gone in the morning when she got up – and went quietly up the stairs followed by her sister.

'I don't know where you're going to put all those fancy clothes you've brought,' Ella hissed, trying not to wake Meggie.

'I've not brought that many,' Cathie whispered back.

'But I suppose you'll be dressing yourself up and parading around the town while I'll be stuck at home helping Mam – as usual,' came the bitter reply.

'I won't and I did offer to help Mam, Ella.'

'Oh, you always get the better deal, Cathie! Mam's favourite, and I suppose you think you're really someone special now? Miss High and Mighty from Liverpool with the great job in that fancy store!'

Cathie sighed heavily. 'Oh, for once, Ella, just shut up! I think nothing of the sort and I'm tired. I'm going to sleep.'

Ella glared at her angrily but then shrugged. At least she wouldn't be here for long.

Only Lizzie and Meggie were in the kitchen next morning.

'I've sent Ella on an errand. She's taken Hal with her but they won't be long,' Lizzie informed her.

Meggie stared at her, openly curious. She'd expected Cathie to look exactly the same as when she'd left but she didn't.

Cathie smiled at her sister. 'You've grown, Meggie.'

'So have you. Do you like Liverpool?'

Cathie nodded. 'It's very different to Ramsey, much, much bigger, but people are friendly and I live in a nice house and I like my job.'

'So, lass, have you decided what you'll do today?' Lizzie enquired.

'I thought I might take a stroll around the town, Mam, to see what's changed.'

'Not very much, I can tell you, but it's another beautiful day so you go and make the most of it.'

She was about to say she might take a walk along the promenade when Ella and Hal arrived back, Ella clutching a parcel.

'Goodness, Hal, what's Mam been feeding you!' Cathie greeted her brother, who seemed to have shot up in the time she'd been away. He obviously took after Da, she thought.

He laughed, looking a bit awkward.

Ella said nothing but was secretly very envious of the bright yellow and white dress her sister was wearing. It made her feel very drab and dowdy, which didn't improve her mood.

Cathie smiled tentatively at her sister; she was prepared to put Ella's remarks last night out of her mind for the sake of peace. She wanted to enjoy her time here and she wasn't going to let Ella spoil it.

Ella ignored the smile and turned to her mother. 'It's already very warm out, Mam, and the sea is like a sheet of glass.'

'Your da and the lads will be happy about that then. They have to put up with enough wind and rain.'

'What's she going to do with herself?' Ella asked her mother. It was very unfair that Cathie was to have a free day while she had to stay at home and help Lizzie.

'*She* has a name, Ella,' Lizzie reminded her.

'I'm going to have a stroll around town then I'll come back home and, despite what Mam says, I'll help out,' Cathie said firmly. She wasn't going to give her sister any opportunity to complain about her lot. 'Then, tomorrow, after church and lunch, we're all going to go to Mooragh Park and I'm going to treat everyone to ice cream from the place that sells refreshments.'

Lizzie tutted at such extravagance but both Hal and Meggie's eyes lit up with pleasure at the thought of the outing. There was a boating lake in the park with rowing boats for hire, and a children's playground, and ice cream was a real treat for them.

'And there might even be music from the bandstand; you'd like that, Mam, wouldn't you?' Cathie said, smiling. It was a rare occasion when her mother got time to sit in the park and listen to a band.

Lizzie smiled back at her. 'It would depend on the music but it would be ... restful to sit there for a while. It's not something your da enjoys though – brass bands.'

Ella said nothing as Cathie put on a hat that matched her dress and went out. Well, if her sister thought she was going to come back here and lord it over her, splashing out for treats like ice cream, she was in for a shock. In the time Cathie had been away *she'd* been the one Mam had relied upon. She was determined not to go back to being the overlooked little sister again.

As Cathie walked along the quay towards the Market Square she realised Ella had been right and she was grateful for the wide brim of her hat, which shielded her face. By lunchtime it would be very hot, much too hot to go wandering around the town. Those with leisure time would head for the beach and the pier and she noticed that there seemed to be plenty of visitors around too. As usual the square was crowded but she stopped to pass the time of day with people she knew and eventually found herself by the Fish Steps, wrinkling her nose at the smell.

'Good God! Cathie Kinrade! I hardly recognised you!'

She turned to find Nora Gelling standing staring at her. 'Hello, Nora.'

'You've done well for yourself, all done up like a proper lady.' Nora was openly envious.

Cathie smiled pleasantly. 'Not really, Nora, but I do enjoy living and working in Liverpool.'

Seeing that Cathie wasn't going to be snobby Nora became friendlier. 'What's it like, Cathie?'

'There are some really grand buildings and shops, Nora, but there's terrible poverty too. Far worse than anything we have here.'

'You got yourself a chap yet?' the girl asked.

Cathie nodded, thinking of Charlie. 'Yes. I met him at work. We've been courting for a few months now.'

Nora asked what kind of a job Charlie had and after Cathie had explained she grinned. 'Well, I expect you'll be heading up the aisle before long and then we won't be seeing you back here, will we?'

Cathie smiled. 'This will always be home, Nora – for all of us, no matter how far away we go,' she replied.

Nora nodded, thinking she'd like to have the opportunity to go somewhere else although there was little chance of that. 'Well, better get back to work before Mam starts complaining.'

'Give her my regards and it was nice to chat, Nora,' Cathie said as the girl turned away. Nora really wasn't so bad, she thought, as long as you didn't have to work beside her all day. She thought how very fortunate she'd been to get a job in such pleasant surroundings – she could have been going back to the stink of fish innards, like Nora, if things had turned out differently.

Nothing had changed very much, she concluded as she wandered up Parliament Street gazing into the shop windows. The fashions did seem a little dated to her now though – not quite as up to date as those she was used to seeing at work. As she came to the Plaza Cinema she wondered if she should treat Ella? They could go this evening; she'd seen the film they were showing but she wouldn't mind that and she doubted her sister had ever been to the cinema before. She really should make an effort to get on with Ella, she thought. What her sister had said about her being Mam's favourite wasn't true. Lizzie was scrupulously fair in her treatment of them all, but obviously her sister didn't see it like that. Ella clearly resented her. Her sister was jealous of what she, Cathie, had achieved, and part of her could understand, but maybe she could try to change that. She made up her mind to broach the subject of the outing to the cinema when she got home; after all, she was only home for a matter of days and it would give Mam a few hours' break too.

'I see they are showing a Fred Astaire film at the Plaza,' she said as she took off her hat an hour later.

Lizzie was busy pressing a dress of Meggie's and the room was like a furnace for she needed the heat from the range for the flat irons.

'I suppose you go to the cinema all the time,' Ella remarked cattily.

'Not all the time but I do go quite often. I wondered if we'd go this evening – you and me, to give Mam a bit of peace. You won't mind, Mam? It's a musical with Fred Astaire and Ginger

Rogers,' she added – it was quite suitable.

Ella looked taken aback. She'd often stood outside the building scrutinising the posters of the current film. She looked enquiringly at her mother.

Lizzie paused and wiped the beads of perspiration from her forehead with the back of her hand. 'I don't mind as long as you're not going to be out too late,' she replied, thinking she should have a word with Cathie about the amount of money she seemed intent on spending. She was glad, though, that Cathie wanted to treat her sister.

Ella nodded, excitement overcoming her suspicion. Obviously Cathie was doing very well for herself across in Liverpool. A thought popped into her mind; why shouldn't she go across too? Mam had let Cathie go at fifteen and look at how well she seemed to be doing. Maybe she'd better start to be more ... pleasant to her sister, she mused.

'Right then, that's settled,' Cathie said firmly and went on to tell her mother of her conversation with Nora Gelling. It made her think about Charlie – she wondered what he would be doing this Saturday evening while she and Ella were at the cinema. She had always gone out with him on Saturdays and she missed him. Still, she cheered herself with the thought that she'd be going back to him next weekend. That was something to look forward to.

The outing had gone quite well and Ella had been mesmerised by the music and costumes, Cathie thought as she helped her mam to set the table the evening before she was due to go back.

They were having a family meal and Nancy Camaish had been invited too, so she could meet Jack's sister.

'Now, I don't want any bickering this evening,' Lizzie instructed, looking pointedly at both Ella and Cathie, although she had to admit that in the past couple of days they'd seemed to get on much better. But you never knew how long that would last. 'I don't want Nancy going home wondering what kind of a family we are.'

'She won't, Mam,' Cathie said firmly before looking enquiringly at Ella. 'What's she like? Do you know her?'

'I've not spoken to her but I've seen her around the town,' Ella replied.

Before there could be any further conversation Barney, Jacob and Jack, accompanied by an attractive dark-haired girl, entered the kitchen.

Lizzie smiled at them all. 'Good, you're all just in time. Supper is ready and you're most welcome, Nancy.'

As they took their places at the table Jack smiled proudly as he introduced Nancy to Cathie. 'Nancy, this is my sister Cathie.'

Cathie too smiled as she took the girl's hand. 'Hello, Nancy, I'm happy to meet you.'

'Thanks, Cathie. Jack's told me all about the great job you have across in Liverpool.'

She seemed very pleasant, Cathie thought, and from the way she looked at Jack it was obvious that she was very fond of him. 'It is a great job and I really enjoy it, Nancy, but you work in a shop too, don't you?'

'I do, although it's nothing on the scale of

Lewis's. Still, I enjoy it. I like meeting people. You'll have to tell me all about the food hall; I'd be interested to hear about that.'

'Not until we've all eaten. There's nothing worse than a lukewarm cottage pie,' Lizzie interrupted, smiling. Cathie and Nancy Camaish did have quite a lot in common, she supposed.

Nancy complimented Lizzie on the meal and they all chatted amiably; even Ella seemed to be making an effort. Once the men got engrossed in the prices they would get for the recent catch, Lizzie turned to Cathie.

'Now, Cathie, tell us all about this young man you've been writing so much about in your letters. Charlie, is it?'

Cathie nodded and smiled at Nancy. 'Yes, Charlie Banks. He works in the stockroom and we ... we've been walking out for a good while now.'

'Is it serious then, Cathie?' Nancy asked.

Cathie nodded. 'Yes, I ... I think it is, Nancy. He's really special.'

Nancy glanced fondly at Jack. 'I know how that feels.'

'What kind of a family does he come from, Cathie?' Lizzie probed, feeling rather anxious that her daughter was obviously very taken with this young man. She hoped Cathie would be sensible about it and not be led astray.

'Very respectable, I believe, Mam. His father has a steady job on the railways so his mother doesn't need to work. I ... I've not met them yet, of course, but I'm sure I will in the near future.'

'Is he handsome?' Ella asked, curious.

Cathie nodded. 'He is. Everyone says he looks

like Clark Gable, but without the moustache.'

'Looks aren't everything, Cathie,' Lizzie put in.

'Oh, I know that, Mam, but he's ... nice. Well mannered, generous, funny, and he's ambitious too.'

'He sounds perfect,' Nancy said gently, smiling at Cathie.

She smiled back. 'Almost, and although I've loved being home, I've missed him.'

Nancy nodded. 'Of course you have, I ... I miss Jack when he's away.'

Ella was tired of this conversation. 'So, tell us about all the gorgeous hats and clothes they have in Lewis's. I'd love to see them for myself.'

Lizzie shot her an enquiring glance but Ella ignored it as Cathie began to describe the latest fashions.

Chapter Sixteen

The week had gone all too quickly, Cathie thought as she stood on the deck of the ferry. She'd enjoyed her visit, but she'd forgotten just how cramped it was with so many people living in such a small house in a very dark and narrow lane. She'd got used to the big rooms of the house in Everton Valley, their high ceilings, the long pathway to the gate and the wide thorough-fare beyond. After their trip to the cinema Ella had been far less prickly and argumentative and they'd got on much better than they used to, and when her da and her brothers had returned, looking fit and suntanned and very pleased with their catch, they'd been a happy, close-knit family once more. She'd enjoyed the supper last night and she liked Nancy Camaish. It was obvious that Jack loved her and she suspected they'd get married before long for Nancy had turned twenty-one. She'd jokingly asked Jacob if there was anyone special in his life but he'd just shrugged and replied 'no one in particular'; then he'd laughed and told her to stop probing for information. The good weather had lasted all week although her da had said it was due to change at the beginning of the new week and she'd prayed it would hold until she reached Liverpool. Yes, she *had* enjoyed her trip home but now she was looking forward to getting back, she thought, as she went to find a seat in the public saloon. She was eager to see Charlie again.

By the time they reached the Mersey Bar the sky had clouded and a stiff breeze had sprung up and Cathie was thankful that the journey was almost over for she was beginning to feel a little queasy. She was glad she had worn her jacket, she thought as they tied up at the Landing Stage and she prepared to join the queue at the gangway. She hoped it wouldn't rain, at least until they got on to the tram, otherwise her hat would be ruined, it being made of a light straw and decorated with marabou feathers.

As she disembarked she eagerly searched the crowds for Charlie's familiar face but to her acute disappointment there was no sign of him. He'd definitely promised to meet her – she'd told him which ferry she was getting and the time it would dock. Maybe he's just late, she thought, and put down her case and prepared to wait. Maybe he'd even forgotten, she thought desperately when the hands of the Liver clock reached the hour and she reluctantly picked up her case and made for the tram terminus. All the way home she told herself there was bound to be some simple explanation: maybe something had happened at home and he hadn't been able to get away, and there'd been no time to notify her? Perhaps he'd got the time of the ferry's arrival wrong and there wasn't another one due in until late evening? Maybe he'd got all the arrangements confused and was waiting at Julia's house for her? It was all so disturbing and upsetting and she began to feel a little irritated. Surely he couldn't have deliberately not turned up?

Her heart sank when she got home and found that Julia hadn't seen him, apart from a few times at work and then not to speak to. 'He was going to meet me off the ferry. He promised,' she said dejectedly, taking off her jacket and hat.

'There's bound to be a reason, Cathie,' Julia said briskly. 'Now, you must be parched, I'll put the kettle on.' She was trying to sound very matter-of-fact although inside she'd been dreading this moment. These last few days she'd been tormented by guilt. She'd told herself over and over that she should have told Cathie what Mavis had told her about Charlie Banks. Now it was too late. She was going to have to break the soul-destroying news to Cathie that Charlie Banks appeared to have dropped her and was now taking out another girl, Eva Morris, the girl Mavis had seen him with.

214

It was the talk of the store and she, Mavis and Dorothy were furious that he'd waited until Cathie was on holiday to carry on like this. She'd tried to convince herself that he'd go back to Cathie when she got home but, after such a betrayal, would she really be glad to see them together again? The answer to that was a definite 'no'!

Cathie was still feeling disappointed when Julia brought in the tea but was distracted by the expression on her friend's face. Something was up, but before she could enquire what was the matter, Julia spoke.

'Did you enjoy yourself?' Julia asked, pouring the tea.

Cathie nodded. 'I really did. It was great to see everyone and even Ella and I seemed to get along much better. And I met Jack's young lady too – Nancy Camaish.'

'Well, you said yourself Ella's older now,' Julia replied.

'So, I'm back now and it's work tomorrow. Has anything happened? What's the latest gossip?' Cathie asked.

Julia took a deep breath. Cathie had just provided the perfect opening for her. 'I'm afraid it's … it's not good news, Cathie. I blame myself, I should have told you before you left but I didn't want to spoil your trip home.'

'Tell me what?' Cathie asked, wondering what could possibly have happened. A terrible thought struck her. 'Oh, Julia, it's not my … job, is it? I do still have my job there?'

'Of course you have! You're the best assistant I've ever had. No … it's … Charlie.'

215

Cathie's hand went to her throat. 'Oh, Julia, Charlie hasn't been sacked, has he?'

Julia shook her head, fervently wishing he had. She took a deep breath. 'No, but he ... he ... is now apparently taking that Eva Morris from Perfumes out. They ... they've been seen together nearly every night and often at lunchtime too.'

Cathie's eyes widened and she shook her head in disbelief. No! It *couldn't* be true! Charlie loved her; he'd said so. He couldn't have taken up with someone else, just ... dropped her like a hot brick. 'But ... but, Julia, he loves *me!* He ... he couldn't do this to me.'

'Oh, Cathie, I'm so very, very sorry but it's true. Mavis saw them together even before you went on holiday. I'll never forgive myself for not warning you but ... but I just didn't know *how* to tell you!'

Cathie felt as though her heart had turned to stone. It was a painful lump in her chest, beating very slowly and oddly. Tears welled up in her eyes and slid down her cheeks. She loved him. She loved him so much but he ... he'd just cast her aside for someone else because she wasn't pre-pared to let him make love to her. He *hadn't* loved her at all – he'd just wanted to *use* her. It hurt, it hurt terribly. She collapsed in racking sobs.

Julia gathered her in her arms, tears stinging her own eyes. 'Oh, Cathie! I'm sorry, I really am!' She wondered if her friend had thought about what it would be like having to return to work where everyone knew that she'd been so publicly dumped. She doubted that Charlie Banks would

216

even have common decency enough to tell Cathie to her face that he was going out with someone else. He was just a pathetic, unprincipled coward, she thought bitterly, and she hoped that one day he'd be treated in the same way as he'd treated poor Cathie. Her mother, she recalled, had always said 'you reap what you sow'. She hoped that would apply to wretched Charlie Banks.

Cathie sobbed uncontrollably, feeling that her heart was broken, that nothing else mattered now. She couldn't even bear to think about what her life would be like from now on – without him – and the fact that he preferred that brassy Eva Morris to her made it all the worse.

'Cathie, let me bathe your eyes and then you should go to bed and try to sleep,' Julia urged. 'You'll have to go into work in the morning,' she ruefully reminded her friend.

'Oh, Julia, I ... I ... can't! How ... how can I? How can I see ... him ... with ... *her?*' Cathie sobbed.

'You won't have to. I doubt he'll show his face on our floor for a while,' Julia replied bitterly, thinking he would get the height of abuse from herself, Mavis and Dorothy if he did.

'And we never go to the stockroom now and you don't have to go to the canteen,' she added.

'Say I ... I'm ill...' Cathie pleaded. She just wanted to curl up and ... *die!*

Julia bit her lip. If she carried on crying like this then she'd be in no fit state to serve customers tomorrow. 'All right, I will, Cathie, if you'll let me bathe your face and try to sleep. Perhaps a day off to try ... try to accept what's happened will help, but you can't stay off indefinitely. You can't let

him treat you like this, Cathie. You just *can't!'*
This wasn't the time to urge Cathie to think of
her pride, self-respect and dignity; she was so
hurt that at this precise moment she had none of
those things. Maybe later, in the coming days and
weeks, her friend would try to hold up her head
again, but not now.

Cathie cried herself to sleep but it was a
restless, disturbed slumber and she woke with a
heavy heart, red swollen eyes and a feeling of
pure misery.

'I'm going to say you've developed a summer
cold and won't be in today. I'll manage; we're
never very busy on a Monday,' Julia said when
she took Cathie a cup of tea early that morning.
'Did you get any sleep?'

Cathie shook her head. 'Not much. Oh, Julia, I
wish... I almost wish now that I'd not come back
from the island, then I would never have known,
never felt ... like this!'

Sadly Julia nodded her understanding. 'But
look at it this way, Cathie. You'd not have been
happy if you'd stayed at home. I recall you telling
me how you hated working at the Fish Steps,
how hard it was to persuade your parents, then
how miserable your life was at the Johnstons –
remember all that, Cathie, and how much you
wanted a job at somewhere like Lewis's. Don't let
... *him* spoil your life – or your dreams.'

Cathie stared mutely at her. She knew Julia was
trying hard to comfort her but there was no one –
and nothing – that could give her solace now.
Charlie had betrayed her and it was as if her world
had come crashing down around her. Jacob had

once said dreams were like circles drawn in the sand and now she felt he'd been right. Hers had been washed away.

'I'll have to be leaving soon, but promise me you won't stay in bed all day crying?'

'I'll ... try, Julia,' Cathie replied.

Because of that promise she forced herself to get up at lunchtime. She washed and dressed and as she brushed her hair she thought how dreadful she looked. Her eyes were puffy and red, dull and expressionless, and her face was all blotchy. She made herself a cup of tea but she couldn't eat anything at all, she just felt sick and desolate.

She spent the afternoon curled up on the sofa and went over and over in her mind all the compliments he'd paid her, all the things he'd said: she really had believed he loved her. He hadn't meant a single word. He was probably saying the very same things to that Eva Morris – and she wondered now how many other girls he'd said them to before he met her?

When Julia arrived home Cathie tried to appear interested in what had happened in the store that day but it was hard to concentrate on anything other than how she felt. She toyed with the food on her plate, just pushing it around with her fork.

'Cathie, do try to eat something,' Julia urged, looking anxiously at her friend. She was certain Cathie hadn't eaten all day.

She put her fork down in despair. 'It just seems to stick in my throat.'

Julia knew it was useless to press her any further. She didn't say that Mrs Fleetwood-Hayes had come in that afternoon and that she'd told her about Charlie. The woman had looked sympathetic but had remarked that Cathie was young, she'd get over it and by the sound of it she was better off without him. She'd no doubt meet someone more worthy of her in the future. Julia was now wondering if Cathie should have another day off or if that would that only make things worse...

Somehow Cathie managed to get through the evening and the hours of darkness but when she got up next morning she didn't feel any better. She washed and dressed automatically, ate a slice of toast and accompanied Julia to work. How she was going to get through the day, be pleasant and helpful to customers she didn't know, and she dreaded even catching a glimpse of Charlie for she was certain she would just break down.

She received sympathetic looks from both Mavis and Dorothy but they didn't mention him and she was grateful for that. As the day wore on she found that she *could* be agreeable to customers but it was as if it was someone else who was smiling and indulging in small talk, the real Cathie just felt numb.

At the counter next to her, Julia thought she was coping quite well; her eyes were still a bit puffy and she was quieter than usual but Julia was now glad she hadn't suggested Cathie take another day off. She sincerely hoped that what Mrs Fleetwood-Hayes had said was true, that Cathie would get over it. But, she thought sadly, it might take some time.

Cathie went out at lunchtime although Julia suspected she wouldn't eat anything, just probably walk around in a daze. But at least the fresh air seemed to have put a bit of colour in her cheeks, Julia thought after Cathie got back, and, having handed the counter back to her, made her way to the canteen. As she approached the double doors, they opened: there was Charlie Banks himself. At least he looked very uncomfortable, she thought with grim satisfaction as he shuffled around, avoiding her eye.

'I'm glad I've got the opportunity to speak to you face to face,' she addressed him coldly. 'I presume you have no intention of trying to explain your ... change of affections to Cathie?'

Charlie had always felt that Julia Vickers didn't really like or trust him and now he knew he'd been right. He shrugged. 'What's to say?' he muttered.

Julia felt fury rising in her. 'I thought so. You're a spineless, heartless coward, Charlie Banks! You're the most pathetic excuse for a man I've ever met! But you listen to me: one day you'll be treated in the same way as you've treated Cathie and I wouldn't be surprised if it's not Eva Morris who'll be the one to do it – knowing the reputation she's got. But maybe you deserve each other! Just don't you dare show your face in our department and if you even try to speak to Cathie I'll ... I'll go straight to Personnel and report you for "improper conduct". Believe me, Miss Edgerton will take my word over yours!'

Charlie didn't speak but his face flushed with anger and humiliation as he pushed past her.

Julia squared her shoulders and went into the canteen feeling that she had at least stood up for Cathie.

When the day was over and the store closed Cathie felt relieved but utterly exhausted and drained.

'Well, you survived the day and I'm proud of you, Cathie,' Julia said as they made the journey home. She had said nothing to Cathie about seeing Charlie.

Cathie managed a weak smile. 'Thanks, but I feel so tired.'

'That's because you've not eaten and the strain of being friendly and helpful to customers has taken its toll. Perhaps you'll sleep well tonight.'

Cathie nodded. 'Do you think I'll feel any better tomorrow?'

'I don't know, Cathie, but I really do hope so.'

'At least I ... I didn't see him. I couldn't have stood that.'

'I've a feeling we won't be seeing him for quite a while. There are others working in the stockroom should we need things,' Julia reminded her.

'I just wish I didn't feel so terribly hurt. It ... it's like a real, physical pain.'

'I'd love to be able to do or say something, Cathie, to take it away. I feel so helpless but I was talking to Mrs Fleetwood-Hayes yesterday and she said that it won't last forever, you *will* get over it and that you'll meet someone who is "worthy" of you. I think we should listen to her – you know how much I respect and trust her judgement. She's usually right about things and she's older and wiser than either of us.'

Cathie didn't reply, thinking how she would feel having to face that astute lady again, knowing she knew about Charlie. But then suddenly she realised that perhaps it wouldn't be so bad – she'd had to face her work colleagues today and she'd coped. Maybe what the older woman had said was true? She hoped it was. She wanted to get over it; she didn't want to go on feeling like this forever. But she still felt her emotions had been stripped raw and it was far from easy to put real faith in what Mrs Fleetwood-Hayes said.

It was the end of the following week before she could honestly say she was feeling a little less miserable. In fact she was beginning to experience rising anger and bitterness at what Charlie had put her through when Julia nudged her and she looked up from arranging a display of ribbons and artificial flowers to see Charlie coming across the shop floor towards them, carrying a large cardboard box. She felt her heart plummet but she squared her shoulders. There was no way she was going to let him see that his appearance had surprised and upset her.

'I take it there was no one else available to bring that down to us?' Julia addressed him curtly.

He just nodded and avoided looking at either of them. 'Then put it down on the end of that counter,' Julia instructed briskly.

He did as he was bid but before he turned away Cathie spoke. Although her hands were shaking slightly her voice was steady and clear. 'And then I think you'd better get back to the stockroom, Charlie. Out of my sight – where you belong!'

They both saw the back of his neck redden as he strode away and Julia smiled at her friend. 'Good for you, Cathie! He asked for that, coming down here as though there was nothing wrong.'

Cathie smiled back. Facing him hadn't been as bad as she'd expected. She was going to be all right.

Chapter Seventeen

It seemed to Cathie that the aching desolation and the pain of rejection and humiliation had gone on for ever but now she realised that it had only been a matter of weeks – just over a month – and that these past few days she had begun to feel more like her usual self, especially as she had overcome the ordeal of facing him. Thoughts of him didn't make her cry any more. She could talk about him now where before she'd hardly been able to bring herself to utter his name. She'd at last been able to write to her mam and tell her how he'd treated her for Lizzie had been puzzled and a little worried when her letters had stopped arriving. She remembered Lizzie's advice not to rush into anything, not to make herself cheap, and also said that Cathie was still very young and marriage was a serious matter, a decision not to be taken lightly because it was for life; Cathie had promised that if or when Charlie mentioned marriage she would think carefully, and she was glad now that she had. But all that was over and maybe, given how he'd turned out, she was best rid of Charlie Banks. She was even looking forward to going out with Julia, Mavis and Dorothy at the weekend, she thought, something she hadn't done for a long time. She was beginning to regain her confidence, self-respect and pride.

She was aware that so far her friends had deliberately avoided mentioning Charlie but she and Julia had discussed their futures quite openly one evening.

'I'm beginning to wonder if my mother was right about men,' Julia had remarked. 'I certainly haven't met one yet who'd make me change my mind about my future.'

Cathie had nodded slowly. 'But don't you ever want to fall in love, get married and have children?' she'd asked, thinking that despite Charlie Banks, that's how she saw her future – some day – but definitely not for a long time yet.

Julia had sighed heavily. 'Perhaps ... but I was so dreadfully shocked about how my father behaved and then seeing the way Charlie Banks treated you ... I don't know. I've been wondering if choosing to be like Miss Edgerton would be the best thing for me?'

This had surprised Cathie. 'You mean you'd try for a very senior position?'

Julia had nodded. 'Something like a buyer. I think I'd enjoy that. Deciding what would sell best, instead of just selling hats someone else has chosen. I've certainly got experience in millinery. I might even have a word with Miss Edgerton to see what the prospects are. I don't want to just keep working on the sales floor all my life.'

Cathie had smiled. 'I always wanted to work in a shop, even when I was a little girl and ... and...' she had faltered, looking a little embarrassed.

'And what? Cathie, don't leave me in suspense!'

Julia had asked.

'Promise you won't laugh?'

'I promise!'

'Well, sometimes I even used to think it would be wonderful if I had a shop of my own – only something small, perhaps just selling groceries. But I knew it was an impossible dream.'

'There's nothing wrong in having dreams or ambitions, Cathie.'

'I know, but I'm happy enough selling hats, Julia, at least for the present, and picking up the threads of my … social life again,' she'd replied firmly and it was true. She was looking forward to the weekend.

Then yesterday Julia had imparted a piece of news that she had found strangely satisfying and to a degree comforting. Charlie and Eva were no longer walking out.

'Well, that "romance" didn't last long!' Julia went on gleefully once she'd delivered the glad tidings on her return from lunch. 'It's common knowledge on the ground floor that Eva has given him the brush-off. Oh, she's a bold one. She got a better offer from the new clerk in the accounts office, so I hear. He's got a decent job and obviously more money to spend on her.'

'How … how is he taking it?' Cathie had asked, wondering if Charlie now felt as upset as she had been.

Julia had shrugged. 'Oh, trying to put a brave face on it, saying he doesn't care, that it was nothing serious anyway. But I bet he's had his pride dented in a big way and it serves him right!'

Cathie had thought about it for a while. 'Julia,

you don't think...?'

'Cathie, if he comes crawling back and asks you to forgive him, don't believe a word he says,' Julia had urged vehemently.

'I won't. I'd never, ever be able to trust him again. If he was more than ten minutes late I'd get into a state thinking he wasn't going to turn up at all and ... and I won't be humiliated by him again either,' she'd replied firmly, surprised that she actually meant it. Oh, there had been a time when if he'd done just that she'd have gladly forgiven him but not now. She'd smiled at the older girl. 'I really do think that I'm getting over him.'

'Good. "Plenty more fish in the sea", so the saying goes,' Julia had replied, placing the wide-brimmed hat she'd chosen as the display centre-piece at the very front of the counter.

As the month of July drew to a close both girls were fully occupied with the autumn styles which would be in stock in a few weeks' time. The weather was sultry, bringing thunderstorms and airless nights: an unwelcome contrast to the pleasant warmth of June. It was a particularly oppressive Monday morning and they were studying the catalogue of designs the fashion buyer had sent down, appropriately marked with which hats had been ordered.

'I can't believe we're looking at designs for autumn and winter when it's so sticky! The air in the whole store seems so hot and heavy,' Cathie remarked.

'And these long-sleeved shop dresses don't exactly help,' Julia added, looking up to see Mrs

Fleetwood-Hayes approaching. Julia was a little puzzled; as far as she knew the Captain was still home and his wife usually curtailed her shopping trips while he was on shore leave. 'Good morning,' she greeted the woman pleasantly.

'Good morning, Julia! I fear we're in for another storm; the sky out there's looking very dark indeed. But perhaps it will clear the air – no doubt what we need,' she greeted them both. 'How are you, Cathie?'

'I'm feeling much more like myself now, thank you, madam,' Cathie replied, smiling.

'Good. Young hearts mend quickly and you'll meet someone else with more scruples who will treat you in the way you deserve to be treated. Now, I've called in to ask you to a little celebration the Captain and I will be holding for Eileen's sixteenth birthday. Her birthday isn't actually for three weeks but by then the Captain will have sailed so he suggested we bring the party forward. We're having a sort of small garden party in two weeks' time, on the Sunday afternoon at the house.' She beamed at them as she proffered her invitation.

'Oh, thank you,' Julia replied, quite surprised and rather excited at the prospect, for she had been cooped up for so long when her mother was alive. They'd certainly never been invited to any celebrations at the Fleetwood-Hayeses' in the past and had they been she doubted her mother would have gone. Now she wondered what on earth she could get the girl as a present. 'What time does it start?'

'Three o'clock. I hope there will be no sudden

downpours. There's nothing worse than a garden party that has to be moved indoors.'

Cathie didn't think the invitation included her; after all she wasn't related to the Fleetwood-Hayeses. 'I hope your daughter has a wonderful day,' she said sincerely.

Mrs Fleetwood-Hayes looked amused. 'I'm sure she will but you'll be able to judge for yourself, the invitation is for you both. You're to come as well, Cathie. It will take you out of yourself.'

Cathie was both surprised and delighted. Julia had described the house but it would be great to see it for herself. She might feel a bit overwhelmed in such company but at least Julia would be with her. 'Oh, thank you, madam. It's very kind of you.'

'Cathie, I realise there are formalities to be maintained whilst you are at work but I do hope you don't intend to call me "madam" in my own home? You are not a maidservant – you're a guest.'

Cathie felt herself blushing. 'No, of course not,' she said a little apprehensively.

'Good, then I'll see you both at three in two weeks' time.'

'Wasn't that kind of her to include me?' Cathie remarked once she'd gone.

Julia nodded. 'Now all we've got to do is decide what to wear: I expect it's going to be quite a "dressy" affair. And think of what we can buy for someone who has so much already.'

'Oh, I never thought of that,' Cathie replied with a note of dismay in her voice. 'Maybe if I try to think what someone of Ella's age would like and then look for a more expensive version?'

'Perhaps it might be better if we bought something from both of us – pooled our resources?'

'That's a great idea, Julia. We could afford something that would look better than two cheaper gifts,' Cathie added, already wondering what she could wear to something that was obviously going to be quite an occasion. She'd never been to a party before, let alone a 'garden party'.

The weather that Sunday morning was a little overcast but at least there were no great dark thunderheads looming overhead. Maybe later on the sun would break through, Cathie thought as she gave her yellow and white dress a final press. She'd bought two artificial flowers from their stock of trimmings – one white, one yellow – and had sewn them on to the ribbon band of her hat. It now looked much better, she thought, more fitting for a garden party, and she had white shoes and a white handbag.

They were both ready by two o'clock, Cathie in her yellow and white and Julia in pale pink and white, and they had wrapped the birthday present in tissue paper and tied some narrow red satin ribbon around it. After lengthy discussions they'd decided to buy a good handbag from Accessories, for, as Julia had remarked, if the girl didn't like it she could always change it. It had been Cathie's idea for she knew Ella would have been delighted to receive a handbag as a gift. It would have been Ella's first, of course, although she realised that Eileen Fleetwood-Hayes probably already had at least one.

As they walked down the wide tree-lined street Cathie gazed around at the houses. They were as large as Julia's, of a similar style but detached and in a much quieter residential area. And they were obviously better maintained. Alton Close turned out to be a cul-de-sac and each house had a neatly tended, flower-filled front garden and there were even a few cars parked outside some of the houses. It looked very grand and she wondered if it would be even more opulent inside. She began to feel a little apprehensive; she'd never mixed socially with the class of people who owned houses like this and she hoped she wouldn't disgrace herself.

Julia pressed the doorbell and the front door was opened by a slim, middle-aged man with sandy hair and blue eyes. It was obvious from his tanned complexion that he'd spent a great deal of time in warmer climates and although he was wearing a well-cut lounge suit rather than any kind of uniform, Cathie realised at once that this must be Captain Fleetwood-Hayes.

'Come in, Julia and...?' He looked questioningly at Cathie.

'This is Cathie Kinrade,' Julia informed him.

'Ah, yes! I'm very pleased to meet you,' he said pleasantly as he ushered them into the wide light hall. 'Elinor tells me you're from the Isle of Man? There are some tricky waters around the Calf of Man in the south of the island, I believe.'

Cathie smiled shyly at him. 'Yes, I've heard my father say so. But I come from Ramsey in the north.'

'It's a very pretty island. Reminds me of the Lake District. And don't you both look delightfully ... summery. Like two roses – one pink and one yellow. Now, I'll show you through to the garden – I'm on "door duty", at least until every-one has arrived.'

Cathie decided she liked him; he wasn't at all stiff or formal as she'd half expected him to be, being the captain of a ship large enough to cross the oceans. She also wondered what 'exotic' crea-ture he had brought home this time – she might even see it.

The Captain led them into a bright sunny room with French doors opening directly on to the garden, which was large and boasted a pond with a small fountain, flower beds that were a riot of colour, a sweep of lawn and a shaded area where a table covered with a white damask cloth was laid with a very appetising buffet. There were already about twenty people of all ages gathered there and Cathie was quite overawed by both the furnishings and the garden.

Both girls stood looking around. 'Not many familiar faces here, except for Monica and Eileen and the lady they're talking to. She's another dis-tant relative,' Julia muttered, feeling a little apprehensive herself.

Mrs Fleetwood-Hayes came towards them, smiling; she was wearing a lilac crêpe-de-Chine tea dress with a matching picture hat. 'Girls, you both look lovely! Now, come along with me, you must have something to drink and I'll introduce you. Julia, your cousin Evadne is over there talking to my girls but I don't think you know everyone?'

'No, I don't, Mrs Fleetwood-Hayes,' Julia re-plied as they followed their hostess across the lawn.

She turned round and fixed Julia with a stern

gaze. 'Gracious, Julia! I can't have you addressing me so formally; this is a party. "Cousin Elinor" is far more appropriate and it's who I am, after all,' she instructed firmly.

Julia wondered how she would cope calling her 'Cousin Elinor' but she had to admit that it was accurate.

They were both given a glass of champagne with instructions to sip it slowly or it would go straight to their heads, and introduced to the friends and relations of the host, hostess and their daughters. As the introductions continued, Cathie thought she'd never remember everyone's name or whether they were a relation or a friend.

'I hope you like this, it's from both myself and Cathie,' Julia said as she handed over the present.

Eileen Fleetwood-Hayes wasn't quite as tall as her sister or as slim but she had the same light brown hair, which waved naturally. 'Thank you both. It's really very smart and just the right colour,' she said when she'd opened the carefully wrapped parcel. She smiled. 'I always think cream goes with everything.'

Cathie decided that she rather liked the girl; she seemed more pleasant, less stand-offish than her elder sister.

Julia turned to speak to the older lady to whom she was also related and Eileen resumed her conversation with her sister and some friends, although she did try to include Cathie. After a while, feeling a little awkward, Cathie excused herself and moved away; she sat on a bench in the shade of a large hydrangea bush and sipped her drink. She'd never had champagne before, she thought, and she couldn't decide if she liked it or not, but it was pleasant to sit here with the tall crystal flute in her hand. It made her feel very grown up, even a little ... sophisticated.

'Do you mind if I join you? It's rather hot standing in the sun.'

She looked up to see a young man with reddish-gold hair and blue eyes looking down at her. He appeared to be both shy and, judging from the beads of perspiration on his forehead, feeling the heat. 'Please do,' she replied. 'It *is* very hot in the sun. I'm thankful for my hat.'

He nodded and wiped his forehead with a white handkerchief. 'I haven't seen you before: are you a friend of Eileen's?'

Cathie shook her head before taking another sip of her drink. He seemed pleasant enough. 'No, I'm a friend of Julia Vickers. We work together.'

'Oh, I see. I'm David Kendal, by the way. My mother was the Captain's sister, she died when I was very young. There's just Dad and me.'

'Oh, I'm so sorry. I'm Cathie Kinrade,' she replied.

David ran his finger around his collar. It really wasn't much cooler in the shade, he thought, yet she looked fresh and very pretty in that dress: the colour suited her. 'Whereabouts in Liverpool does your family live?' he asked conversationally.

'They don't. They live in Ramsey on the Isle of Man. I came here to work, although they weren't very happy about it at the time,' Cathie told him.

He glanced at her with admiration. It must have been quite a daunting thing to undertake, he thought. 'Have they got used to you being away?'

Cathie nodded. 'I went home earlier this year and they were delighted that I am happy, I have a good job and a comfortable home. I live with Julia and we get on really well.'

'I see... That's great,' he added, although he didn't want to pry into her life too closely, so he sipped his drink.

'What do you do?' Cathie asked to break the silence.

He smiled at her, glad that she seemed interested 'I'm supposed to be "learning the business from the bottom up" – my father's idea, not mine. So at present I'm a humble clerk in an accounts office.'

She smiled back. 'What would you really like to do?' she enquired. He was pleasant enough to talk to, quiet and unassuming.

'I'd really like to emulate the Captain, make a career at sea, but Father won't hear of it even though Uncle Benjamin has often spoken to him about it.' He became more animated. 'It's the adventurous side to it, you see, and the chance to travel and meet new and different people and the ... challenge of it too.'

Cathie nodded. 'I can understand that and I know how challenging it can be,' she replied, thinking of her father and brothers. Before he could answer she saw Julia approaching.

'Oh, there you are, Cathie. I've to tell you that we're to help ourselves from the buffet: Cousin Elinor's instructions. And I have to say I'm rather hungry and it all looks delicious.'

'I'm David Kendal, the Captain's nephew. I've heard Aunt Elinor talk of you,' he said, standing

235

up and extending his hand. He'd never met Julia before although he'd heard of her and knew she was a sort of cousin of Elinor.

'I know. It's nice to meet you at last, David,' Julia replied, smiling.

Cathie got to her feet and as they walked towards the rose-covered pergola the Captain joined them and engaged his nephew in conversation, so the girls dropped behind and Julia smiled archly at Cathie. 'David looked quite taken with you. I heard he's rather shy with girls, probably because he's no sisters and his mother died when he was little more than a toddler.'

'He told me that and did seem very nice, but really, Julia, we've only had one conversation! Anyway, I've no intention of getting ... involved with anyone for a long time. For the present I just want to enjoy myself.'

Julia laughed. 'And are you?'

Cathie smiled and nodded. 'It's a great party. I'm delighted to be here and you're right, that food looks like something you see in the food hall.'

'Which is where most of it probably came from,' Julia replied. Cathie was wise not to be looking for someone to replace Charlie Banks in her affections just yet but she thought her friend could do worse than David Kendal. However, she doubted Cathie would ever see him again.

Chapter Eighteen

Autumn had arrived with some force, Cathie thought as she battled against the wind that was buffeting her as she walked back towards work through Clayton Square. Even though she'd anchored her hat firmly with a large pin she still had to hold on to it. The Mary Ellens – as the flower sellers were known – were having a hard time keeping their displays from being blown over but the colours of the chrysanthemums and dahlias did brighten up a rather grey day, she mused. She barely thought of Charlie these days; she hardly ever saw him around the store and her life was busy and happy. She and Julia often went to the cinema after work and they both went dancing with Mavis and Dorothy, although Mavis now had a steady boyfriend and so didn't accompany them very often. She'd been down to C&A Modes in Church Street to look for a reasonably priced winter coat but hadn't seen anything she particularly liked and was debating whether or not to bother – perhaps she'd get another season out of the one she had although she really would have liked a change. Maybe she could smarten it up with a bit of velvet ribbon around the edge of the collar and cuffs? she thought.

She had her head bent against the wind and almost collided with a young man coming in the opposite direction. She started to apologise. 'Oh,

I'm terribly sorry–'

'It's Cathie, isn't it? Cathie Kinrade!' he interrupted.

She looked up and was taken aback; she'd not expected to see him again. 'Goodness! David Kendal!' The summer garden party seemed like a distant memory now, and it was a surprise to be reminded of it so unexpectedly.

'How are you?' he ventured, not wanting her to walk away. He'd thought about her a lot after the garden party, though he hadn't been able to envisage their paths crossing again. And here, literally, they had.

'I'm very well, thank you,' she replied, smiling. 'I'm just on my way back to Lewis's. I've been out in my lunch break although I didn't realise it was quite this windy,' she added, still hanging on to her hat.

'I'm on my way back to work too, I had a couple of errands to run.' Unused to holding long conversations with girls, he was frantically trying to think of something else to say to her. He didn't want her to walk away just yet.

Cathie vaguely remembered he'd said he was a clerk in an office but this was not the business area of the city; that was nearer to the Pier Head. 'Where do you work?' she asked thinking it would be Castle Street or Dale Street or Exchange Flags.

'Just across the square at Owen Owen's,' he informed her.

She looked surprised. It was another of Liverpool's large department stores although not quite as big as Lewis's. 'Oh, so you've not far to go then.'

'Neither have you.' He smiled, thinking that she

looked very attractive if rather windblown. He plucked up courage and made a determined effort. 'Cathie, I know we only spoke for a few minutes at the party but ... but I wonder if sometime we ... we could meet for lunch, seeing as we work so near to each other? I ... I'd like to see you again. Perhaps I could meet you in Lyons Tea Rooms or the Kardomah Café?'

Cathie looked unsure; she hadn't expected this.

'I really would like to get to know you better. As I said, we didn't have much time together at Aunt Elinor's,' he urged.

What harm would it do? She would insist she paid for herself; that way she'd be under no obligation to him. And he was a pleasant enough lad and it wasn't as if she intended to get involved with him, she thought. Slowly she nodded her agreement. 'I'd like that, David.'

Despite the chillness of the wind his cheeks reddened with pleasure. 'Then what about tomorrow? Say the Kardomah in Whitechapel at twelve thirty? Will that time be suitable? If not–'

She smiled. 'Twelve thirty is fine. I'll see you then. Now I really must go so Julia can go for her lunch,' she informed him, wondering if she'd done the right thing. Still, if she found him a struggle to get on with she needn't see him again.

Julia was very surprised when Cathie told her of the meeting and her lunch date the following day. 'Well, wasn't that a coincidence? I never expected you'd see him again.'

'Neither did I and I didn't know he worked at Owen Owen's either. It's a wonder I haven't bumped into him before now.'

'I didn't know that either. What does he do?' Julia asked.

Cathie frowned, trying to remember the brief conversation she'd had with him at the garden party. 'I remember him saying he was a clerk in an office but that what he really wanted was to be like Captain Fleetwood-Hayes but his father won't allow him to go away to sea.'

'If he's over twenty-one then his father can't stop him,' Julia remarked but then she thought that she'd been over twenty-one and her mother had effectively managed to stop her doing the things she'd wanted to do. Although she was coming to terms with her mother's death she realised that it had changed her. She was more self-reliant and she undoubtedly had a far better social life but she sometimes felt a little guilty that Maud's demise had in many ways made her feel able to view her future with more optimism.

'I don't know exactly how old he is but he's older than me. Still, I don't have to make a habit of going for lunch with him and I'm definitely not going to stop my outings with you and Dorothy,' Cathie replied firmly. 'We are still going to the Gaumont Cinema after work?'

Julia smiled and nodded. 'Of course. But you never know, Cathie, you might find you like having lunch with him.'

'We'll see,' Cathie said, wondering what tomorrow would bring.

The two girls arrived home later that evening after enjoying *Naughty Marietta,* starring Jeanette MacDonald and Nelson Eddy, at the Gaumont to find a letter from Cathie's mam had arrived with that day's post.

Julia sorted through the rest of the mail, which she announced was mainly bills, and went to put the kettle on. The room was chilly so Cathie stirred the embers of the fire and built it up with more coal. She didn't take off her jacket while she sat and read Lizzie's letter. It was always something she looked forward to, hearing about what was happening at home.

When Julia came in with the tea she was concerned to see that Cathie was frowning as she scanned the lines of her letter. 'What's the matter? Is there something wrong at home?'

Cathie looked up, still frowning. 'It's our Ella; she's got Mam half demented with her antics.'

'What's she done now?' Julia asked.

'Mam's never mentioned it before but now she says Ella's been going on and on at her to ask me if she can come to Liverpool and if can I get her a job. I knew that when she left school like me she refused to work at the Fish Steps but that the only job she could get was scrubbing floors and vegetables in the kitchen at the Commercial House Hotel. Apparently she hates it and Mam says she complains constantly and says it's not fair that I was allowed to come across and that I've got a good job and she hasn't.' Cathie put the letter aside. 'I just don't know what to do, Julia, what to write and say to Mam.' She paused and sighed heavily. 'In some ways I feel I *should* try to help Ella. I can see her point of view. After all I *have* got a good job so why should she have to scrub floors? But I really don't want to have to

241

take on the responsibility.'

'I thought you said you got on better when you were at home last?'

'We did but that was only for a week. She'd be here permanently. She's fifteen and if she decides she wants to do something I don't approve of – and I know Mam wouldn't either – how can I possibly stop her? But I don't want her to be upsetting Mam and if she harps on and on, she will. She'll make life a misery for everyone. But if I refuse ... I'll feel so *selfish*. And I suppose that as I've made a successful life for myself Da wouldn't object too much.'

Julia pursed her lips; she could see both sides of the argument. 'I'd think long and hard about it before you write back – it is your decision. I don't know her but as she's your sister, Cathie, she would be welcome to stay here. We have a spare room.'

Cathie nodded, grateful for the offer and knowing her friend was right. 'Thanks. I don't know if I can get her a job though. She obviously wants to work in Lewis's like me.'

'You could try. There are usually a few vacancies and with Christmas in the not too distant future she might be taken on. You've proved to be an excellent worker in all respects so I'm sure Miss Edgerton would try to find her something.' Julia could see that Cathie was troubled but she was sure she would make the right decision concerning Ella.

Cathie sighed again. She'd take Julia's advice and think hard but she felt very uneasy about it all. She really felt she was too young to take on the responsibility of her sometimes troublesome sister.

The problem of her sister remained at the fore-front of Cathie's mind and she still hadn't reached a decision as she made her way to the Kardomah Café at lunchtime the next day. When she arrived she was a little relieved to see that David Kendal was waiting for her at a table by the window. It was always busy at this time of the day and she hadn't wanted to have to sit on her own and wait.

He smiled and rose to greet her. 'I was lucky that I managed to get this table. Will we have a look at the menu?'

She took off her gloves and tucked them into the strap across her clutch bag. 'I usually only have a sandwich and a cup of tea and ... and David, I insist on paying for myself.'

He frowned, looking concerned. '*I* asked you to meet me, Cathie. I'd expected... I'd *like* to pay for your meal. It wouldn't be right for you to pay.'

Cathie smiled at him. He really was nice. 'Well, thank you, David, that's very kind of you. Now, here's a waitress so we'd better order before she goes off to serve someone else.'

When they'd given the girl their order David looked hopefully across at her. 'Have you been busy this morning?' he asked. It was all he could think of to say but it sounded so ... hopelessly boring.

'Not too bad although from next month on-wards it will get busier and busier with Christmas approaching. But I don't mind – I love Christmas,' she replied. Then a thought struck her: this year maybe Ella would be over.

'It's always a busy time but we usually spend it rather quietly,' he said, toying with his napkin.

'Do you not see the Captain and Mrs Fleetwood-Hayes over the holiday?'

'If he's home. If he is they hold a huge party on Christmas Eve but if not Aunt Elinor always invites us for tea on Christmas Day.'

'Will he be home this year?' Cathie enquired, thinking the Captain's long absences must make life rather strange for his family.

He beamed at her and for the first time began to relax. She was so easy to talk to. 'I think he will but I'm not entirely sure. I'll ask when I next see my aunt.'

'Heaven knows what he'll bring home this time.' Cathie laughed. 'You do know that that marmoset they had when they gave that party was in Lewis's Menagerie the following week?'

He laughed too. 'I do. She says the house would resemble a menagerie if it was left to him – it wouldn't be fit for human habitation.'

'Well, I have to admit it was a very endearing little thing although I wouldn't have wanted to hold it,' Cathie confided.

The waitress returned and Cathie poured the tea. 'I've forgotten which office you said you work in,' she confessed.

'When I first met you it was Accounts, now it's Wages and in the New Year I think it will be in the buying department,' he replied, slowly stirring his tea.

Cathie cut her toasted teacake in half. 'They do move you around a lot, David. I'm glad I've stayed in the same department but then I suppose it's not quite the same for me.'

He shrugged. 'I can see some people would find it a bit unsettling but as it's not really what I want to do it doesn't bother me a great deal.'

She thought it must be awful to have no interest or any enjoyment in your work but hadn't she been in a similar position? She'd hated gutting fish. 'So, you still would like to go to sea?'

He nodded. 'Maybe one day I'll achieve it, although it takes years and years to become a captain. Do you enjoy your job, Cathie?'

She smiled. 'I do.' Then she remembered Ella working at a job she hated. 'I do know what it's like, David, not to enjoy your work and now ... now I'm trying to decide whether or not to write home and tell my younger sister that she can come to Liverpool. I'd have to try to find her work. She's been pestering my mother about it for ages, apparently.'

'And have you come to a decision yet?'

She shook her head. 'You see she's only fifteen and I'd have to take responsibility for her. We have no relatives here.'

'That's very young,' he agreed. 'Do you mind me asking how ... how old you are, Cathie?'

She laughed. 'No, David. I'm seventeen. I'll be eighteen next March. How old are you?'

'Twenty-two,' he replied. 'Do you have any other sisters or brothers?'

As she poured them both another cup of tea Cathie told him a little about her family and he listened intently, occasionally asking a question.

At last she realised that she would have to get back. 'We'd better be going, David, or we'll both be late.'

He nodded reluctantly but swiftly attracted the waitress's attention, paid the bill and escorted her out into the street. The pavements were busy with shoppers and workers on their lunch breaks but they walked around the corner and into Church Street together. When they reached its junction with Parker Street, which led into Clayton Square, Cathie stopped. 'This is where our paths separate, David. It's quicker for me to go straight on but thank you, I've enjoyed lunch.'

People were pushing past them and he realised they couldn't stand there for much longer, they were causing a bit of an obstruction. 'Cathie, will you have lunch with me again?'

'I will, but not for another week or so, David, until I've sorted things out about Ella,' she replied. She had a lot to think about at the moment and she wasn't quite sure if she wanted to encourage him. She couldn't help being conscious that he was of a higher class than she was.

He smiled broadly, delighted she hadn't refused. At least she hadn't found him boring, he thought. 'How will I know when...?'

'Come into the store in your lunch break. If I'm not there, Julia will be, she'll pass a message on,' she replied, walking away but giving him a smile and a little wave. She had enjoyed his company, she thought as she walked back up Ranelagh Street, but now she had to concentrate on her decision regarding Ella.

She put off writing to Lizzie for as long as she possibly could, still not knowing what to do for the best, but she knew that the longer she waited, the more worried her mam would be. She just *had* to make a decision and *soon,* she told herself. All thoughts of David Kendal were pushed from her mind by her dilemma until she returned from lunch one day and Julia told her he'd been in and had been disappointed when she'd informed him that she still hadn't made up her mind about her sister.

'What did he say?' she asked, before Julia left.

'He said he'd call in again at the beginning of next week,' Julia called back to her.

She stared after her friend, knowing she just had to make up her mind today. She resolved to discuss it yet again with Julia that night.

'If I say I can't help, that I'm not prepared to take the responsibility, she'll blame me for the rest of her life and she'll probably cause an almighty fuss too and upset everyone. But if I agree...' Cathie didn't finish.

'I'm not trying to influence you at all, but you coped very well when you first came over even though you had to live with the Johnstons. At least if Ella comes she won't experience that and you'll be able to keep your eye on her. She'll probably find everything a bit overwhelming at first,' Julia reminded Cathie.

'I know. It's what'll happen when she gets used to everything and finds her feet that bothers me but perhaps she'll be fine, she'll be more ... grown up about things. I really might be worrying unnecessarily. Oh, I'll write and tell Mam to let her come. I just can't be that selfish, Julia.'

Julia smiled as she got to her feet. 'I'll go and fetch the writing pad before you change your mind.'

Cathie grinned back. 'I suppose if she gets completely out of hand I can always ask Da or Jacob to come across and take her back.'

'Oh, Cathie, honestly! I'm sure things won't get as bad as that. You and I rub along famously and I'm sure she'll settle in well. And it will be a relief for your mother not to have a sulking, resentful daughter around all the time. So now when David Kendal comes in looking for you you'll have no excuse not to go out to lunch with him again.'

When she'd written the letter Cathie did feel as though it was a weight off her mind. It would be the beginning of November next week and she would go and ask Miss Edgerton if there was any possibility of Ella being taken on even if it was just for the Christmas period. If she agreed and gave Ella a job and her sister proved satisfactory, they might keep her on; if not she'd at least by then have some experience so she could seek work somewhere else. Julia had suggested that she move into what had been Mrs Vickers's bedroom, which was larger than her present room, and she'd agreed. That would leave her room vacant for Ella: there was a double bed and plenty of wardrobe space for Ella's things, although she realised that, like herself when she'd first arrived, her sister probably wouldn't have much. Ella, again like herself, would have to contribute to the household budget but she did that at home. Cathie, now that she'd made the decision, had resolved to pay her sister's fare. Her parents might be stretched at the moment: Jack was getting married after Christmas and so her mam wasn't taking much money off him for he was saving to provide a home for Nancy; and now they'd be losing Ella's contribution too.

She had a reply from Lizzie by return post and included was a short note from Ella, thanking her and saying how delighted she was and that she'd take any job for Cathie wouldn't believe how awful it was spending each day on her knees scrubbing, her hands were a disgrace. Cathie wrote back, enclosing the money for Ella's fare and asking her mother to send her across on a Sunday ferry so she would be able to meet her. She was going to see Miss Edgerton after she'd been out to lunch today and would let them know how she got on.

As she walked to the Kardomah to meet David as she'd promised when he'd called into the store she remembered how excited she'd been when she'd first come over and got her job in Lewis's. She'd had no idea then how dull and miserable her life with the Johnstons would be. At least Ella wouldn't have to put up with that, she thought, and moving here just might be the making of her sister too. She realised that she was looking forward to telling David her news. He might be quiet and rather shy but she felt completely at ease with him... Suddenly she realised that he was exactly the opposite of Charlie Banks. Now she wondered what she had ever seen in such a glib, thoughtless, selfish and unprincipled lad. She knew instinctively that David would never treat her the way Charlie had, it wasn't in his nature.

Chapter Nineteen

It was a bitterly cold November Sunday afternoon; the sky was the colour of gun metal and the waters of the Mersey were turgid and dark as they lapped against the Landing Stage. As the afternoon progressed it would become even colder and darker, Cathie thought as she pulled the collar of her coat higher around her ears, trying to remember the rhyme her mam had taught her as a child. 'No morn, no noon, no night, no moon – November': it just about summed up the month accurately so far, she thought. It was possibly the most depressing time of the year; still, it would soon be Christmas and that was something to brighten up the short cold winter days. She shivered and stamped her feet, trying to restore some circulation, glad she had a warm coat, a hat, scarf and gloves. At least there was no wind, so Ella would have had a calm crossing, for the last days of October had been very windy and the ferries had often been delayed.

The Pier Head wasn't as busy as it had been the day she'd first arrived, owing mainly to the weather, but there was the usual traffic on the river. The ferries plied back and forth and a Blue Funnel Line ship was tied up at the Landing Stage in front of Cunard's *Laconia* with its attendant tugs, and then at last the much smaller Steam Packet ferry the *Lady of Man* docked. The passengers started to disembark and she moved closer to the top of the floating roadway, searching the crowd for her sister. At last she caught sight of her, a slim figure in an old-fashioned navy blue jacket and a slightly lighter blue hat carrying a rather battered Gladstone bag. She smiled to herself; Mam had obviously been to Quale's again to kit Ella out.

'Ella, you've arrived safely. Here, let me take your bag, you look a bit pale. Didn't you have a good crossing?' she greeted her sister.

Ella shook her head. 'Oh, it wasn't rough but the smell of engine oil seemed to be everywhere, it was horrible and it was too cold to go out on deck for some fresh air. I'll be all right now, though,' she replied as they walked towards the tram terminus. The jacket Mam had bought her wasn't very warm and she noted with envy that Cathie's red and black checked wool coat was much heavier and smarter, as was her red and black felt hat. Her sister had black gloves too, something she didn't have.

'You look frozen, Ella, but it will be a bit warmer on the tram and it doesn't take long to get to Everton Valley. Julia will have a good fire roaring up the chimney and some soup on the stove. You'll like Julia, even though she's older than we are – she's twenty-three – she's easy to get on with and very stylish too. She taught me a lot about colours and how to wear different styles.'

Ella thought twenty-three sounded really old and wondered why Julia Vickers wasn't married. Most girls of that age were. Still, she was looking forward to a warm room and some hot soup. Mam had given her a packet of sandwiches but because of the smell of oil she'd not felt like eating them. Now she realised she was hungry. 'Did you have any luck getting me an interview?' she asked. Oh, she did hope so. She was thankful that she'd left the drudgery of the Commercial House Hotel behind and wanted a better job so much.

'I did. You're to see Miss Edgerton tomorrow morning. Don't worry, she knows you've had no experience but neither did I. I'll tell you what to say and we can only hope you'll be taken on. They always employ more staff for Christmas so–'

'I won't mind what they offer me, Cathie, as long as it's *something*. Just look at the state of my hands with the carbolic and Jeyes fluid, I feel ashamed of them,' Ella interrupted, holding out a calloused, reddened hand with short broken nails.

'I see what you mean. Well, you can wear a pair of my gloves,' Cathie said firmly. 'And I'm sure there'll be something on the cosmetic counters to soften them. I'll have a look tomorrow,' she promised.

Ella nodded her thanks. Cathie was certainly doing well if she had more than one pair of gloves. Ella herself own a single pair but she intended to remedy that as soon as possible.

As the tram trundled towards Tithebarn Street Cathie informed her of the few house rules they had, what she would be expected to do and how much she would be asked to contribute to the household budget. She also explained how, if she got a job, she would have to work 'a week in hand'.

'Did Mam give you any money at all?' she asked.

Ella nodded. 'Seven shillings. She'd have liked to give me more but ... you know how things are. She was very grateful that you paid my fare, Cathie and ... so am I,' she added.

Cathie didn't reply, thinking that it looked as if her sister had indeed mellowed – in the old days Ella wouldn't have thanked her for anything. 'Well, I know Mam's always hard up but at least with the pair of us away and sending money home and Jack leaving after Christmas, things might be a bit easier for her.' She paused. 'You do know you will have to send money home, Ella?'

'But I won't be earning as much as you, Cathie, and I'll have expenses and my clothes are really terrible! I've already noticed that *everyone* seems to be better and more fashionably dressed than me,' Ella protested.

'Just you wait until we get further along Scotland Road, Ella, you'll soon change your mind about that,' Cathie replied grimly. Obviously her sister didn't want to send money home. Well, that was something Ella would just *have* to do but she wouldn't press the matter yet, she didn't want to start an argument the minute Ella got off the boat. Just let her get a job, then she'd remind her of her responsibilities to her family. 'I'll lend you something to wear tomorrow, Ella; we're about the same size now. Nothing of Julia's would fit you; she's much taller than both of us.'

Ella smiled at her; she'd been thinking about what she would wear and had come to the conclusion that nothing she owned was suitable. Oh, yes, things were indeed looking up, she thought happily as she gazed out of the window at the already darkening streets. She'd managed to escape the drudgery and restrictions of her life at home, and she was certain that from now on things were going to be far more exciting.

Ella was delighted to find that she would be living in what to her appeared a very large house and with all the modern conveniences of a bathroom, a well-equipped kitchen and hot water; she would even have a room to herself. She liked Julia instantly for she'd been welcomed with warmth and sincerity and as the evening wore on she began to realise that her sister seemed to have a wonderful life compared to what hers had been. Cathie could more or less please herself; she went to dances and the cinema and apparently had a boyfriend, although she'd said firmly that David was just a 'friend' she met for lunch. Her sister was far more confident, poised and grown up now.

Julia produced some Pond's cold cream which she instructed Ella to rub well into her poor hands at regular intervals. 'We'll soon have them looking much better,' she promised.

'Cathie's going to lend me a pair of gloves for tomorrow,' Ella informed the older girl after she'd thanked her.

Julia smiled. 'I'm afraid that only my hats and handbags will be of any use to you, Ella, but between us we'll have you looking "the bees knees", as my mother used to say.' Ella was very like her sister in looks, Julia thought: younger of course, but she seemed pleasant enough and she hoped the two girls would find they could get along better now.

'Well, at least she'll look better than I did when

I went for my interview,' Cathie remarked.

'Why don't you come into town with us in the morning, Ella?' Julia suggested. 'You don't know your way around yet and you wouldn't want to get lost. I know we start at eight although the store doesn't open until nine, but you could go and get a cup of tea or have a wander around, sort of get your bearings. Your interview is nine thirty, isn't it?' The girl would feel rather daunted having to make her own way into a city she was unfamiliar with, she thought.

Ella nodded eagerly. 'That's a great idea, Julia. I'll be nervous enough about the interview without having to find my own way there and I would probably get the wrong tram or get off at the wrong stop and then I'd work myself up into such a state...' she confided.

'That's settled then and I'm sure you'll be fine. Miss Edgerton is very nice, isn't she, Cathie?' Julia said, remembering how considerate the woman had been when she'd confided her ambition to become a buyer to her. It had been explained that at present there was no suitable vacancy – Miss Barton, the present buyer, was not due to retire for some years – but her ambition was admirable and of course she did have suitable experience in millinery – and would obtain more – and she would definitely be considered for the position when it became vacant.

'She is. Now, we'd better get your things unpacked, Ella, and then we'll sort out something for you to wear tomorrow,' Cathie instructed. The sooner her sister got a job the better; she wasn't sure how Ella would cope with her new life at first but the less spare time Ella had on her hands the happier she would feel. Still, although it was early days, it looked as if she would indeed settle in.

And so it proved. Next morning an obviously delighted Ella arrived in the millinery department to announce that she had been taken on as a junior assistant on Accessories on the ground floor and, totally unexpectedly, at a higher wage than she'd imagined. Now she realised just what a pittance she'd been paid in the Commercial House. She felt she looked very smart in Cathie's black and white checked jacket, a black skirt and a black felt hat trimmed with white and emerald green. Julia had lent her a black leather bag and Cathie a pair of black gloves to hide her work-roughened hands. With eyes filled with excitement she said she'd soon be able to buy some decent clothes of her own and that there would even be money to send home. At that Cathie felt relieved; one hurdle less, she thought. Of course Ella would find things very different here but she'd soon get used to the working routine of the store, the tram and bus routes, the city streets and all the shops, and she'd be able to help her sister and keep an eye on her. She could tell David that it appeared that she had made the right decision when she saw him next for lunch.

'I did wonder if you'd be too busy settling her in to see me,' David confided when they met.

Cathie smiled at him. 'Not at all. Ella is being kept very busy – Accessories is one of the more popular departments and at this time of year they

256

increase their stock with seasonal items at reasonable prices. She's got a lot to learn, but she seems to be enjoying it.'

'So, you've no regrets, Cathie?' David asked.

'Not yet at least,' she replied, sipping her tea.

'I spoke to my aunt about Christmas,' he informed her, 'and actually Uncle Benjamin will be home. They're due to dock two days before Christmas Eve, depending on the weather across the Bay of Biscay.' He smiled. 'Aunt Elinor said she isn't really too bothered if they're a day late as then she won't have him under her feet while she's in the midst of organising a party. You know what she's like – always speaks her mind.'

Cathie smiled at him. 'Oh, she does. I wonder what he'll bring home with him this time?'

David laughed as he shook his head. 'I dread to think. But ... but will you come with me to the party, Cathie?'

She was surprised. 'Me?'

He nodded earnestly. 'Yes. We're allowed to bring a friend or a partner and I'd like to escort you.' He sincerely hoped she'd agree for he felt it would be just the right opportunity to show that he was serious about her, that he had become very fond of her. In fact he hoped that after Christmas they could go out in the evenings too.

Cathie felt both pleased and flattered. 'I'd love to, David.'

'You'll enjoy it. There will be far more people there than at the garden party: friends, neighbours, relations. I'll be able to introduce you to my father.'

Cathie felt a little perturbed by that. She and

257

David did get on well and she liked him but being introduced to his father sounded a bit daunting. Well, she'd accepted now and she didn't want to let him down or hurt him. 'I presume Julia will be invited too?'

'Of course and, just between you and me, I think Aunt Elinor is going to invite a couple of chaps she thinks Julia might like. I heard her mention it to Cousin Monica,' he confided.

'Oh, Lord! She's not matchmaking now, is she?' Cathie cried in mock horror.

He laughed. 'It very much sounds like it.'

She leaned across the table towards him. 'David, do you think I should mention it to Julia? Sort of warn her? Julia does occasionally go out with chaps, you know, but she seems to be rather … cautious. They never seem to last for more than one date but that might be because she is rather more interested in her career at the moment. I know she would like to become a buyer.'

He frowned, wondering now whether he had been wise to mention it at all. 'You do what you think best, Cathie, after all you know Julia far better than I do.'

'I'll think about it,' she'd replied whilst wondering what, since both she and Julia had been invited to this party, she was going to do about Ella. The party was on Christmas Eve and she couldn't leave her sister alone on her first Christmas away from home.

Julia solved that dilemma for her that evening when she told her of her conversation with David. 'Don't worry about Ella; I'll take her along as my guest. That way she won't be left on her own and it might discourage Cousin Elinor from shoving her "eligible" young men at me!' Cathie had mentioned Cousin Elinor's matchmaking ambitions, to Julia's amusement.

'Just don't tell her yet or she'll get unbearably excited,' Cathie advised, thankful that Julia had both solved the problem of Ella and didn't seem at all upset about Mrs Fleetwood-Hayes's attempts at matchmaking. She'd simply laughed and said if she married at all it would be her own choice, not Elinor's.

The first argument came one evening in early December when Cathie and Julia were discussing the department's annual Christmas outing. Neither of them had gone the previous year but both were looking forward to this year's festive evening, which was a dance at the Locarno Ballroom. All the sales assistants from the first floor were going, some with husbands or boyfriends, others on their own, but, as Julia pointed out, they all worked together so no one would feel left out, and as it wasn't exclusively a Lewis's event, there would be plenty of other people there too. 'Will you ask David to go with you?' she asked Cathie.

'I don't know. I suppose they must have some sort of Christmas party or outing where he works too, but I expect he'll go with the office staff – he might feel a bit out of it with all our lot.'

'He might not. If he asks you to their Christmas do, will you go?'

Cathie thought about it as she rose to poke the fire. Outside a cold, blustery wind was rattling the window frames. 'I might. I'll have to wait and see if he asks me first,' she replied, thinking that if he didn't then she wouldn't mention him going with her to the Locarno.

Ella came into the room holding a damp collar. 'Is it all right if I put this on the fender to dry? I'll need it for tomorrow.'

Cathie nodded. 'We were just discussing our department's Christmas night out at the Locarno,' she informed her sister. 'I suppose the ground-floor staff have got something organised too?' she queried.

Ella nodded. 'Some of them are going to the theatre – the older ones – and some are off to a dance.' She paused. 'I was going to mention it to you, I … I've been asked to go to a dance at the Grafton next weekend. Eva Morris from Perfumes and some of the others from Cosmetics asked if I'd like to go with them.'

Cathie frowned both at the mention of Eva Morris and the prospect of Ella going to a dance without some sort of supervision – she was only fifteen. She shook her head. 'I'm sorry, Ella, but you're just too young to go to a place like that. And I doubt they'd let you in,' she added. You were supposed to be at least sixteen.

Ella pursed her lips and frowned. This was why she hadn't mentioned it before. 'You were only fifteen when you came here,' she reminded Cathie curtly. 'You could go out and enjoy yourself, so why can't I?'

'Yes, I was the same age as you but I didn't go out to dances or the cinema, Mrs Johnston didn't approve. I was nearly seventeen before I went to my first dance. At the time I thought Mrs Johnston was being old-fashioned and over-protective but now I can see her point. I was too young.'

Ella's attitude became mutinous. 'You just don't want me to have any fun or excitement, Cathie! There are two other girls the same age as me going. When we're all dressed up we can pass for being older than we are, Eva says.'

Cathie was losing patience. 'Oh yes, *she* would! She's a very fast piece is Eva Morris and everyone knows it! You're not going to the Grafton with the likes of *that* one, Ella, and that's the end of it!'

'I *am* going! You can't stop me!' Ella cried, her dark eyes full of anger and resentment.

'No you are not! I'm not being awkward or mean, I just don't want you to be classed as one of *her* friends. She really isn't a very nice person at all and I'm not going to have people talking about the fact that I'm happy for my sister to mix with the likes of her. I've got *my* reputation to think about too!'

Ella lost her temper. 'That's all you ever think about – yourself!'

'I don't!' Cathie protested hotly.

'You are just being spiteful, Cathie! You're not Mam! You can't order me around! I'm going!'

Cathie was now furious. This was exactly what she'd feared would happen. 'Oh, yes I can, Ella! I'm responsible for you, it's what Mam expects of me and she'd be horrified if she knew you wanted to go out with the likes of Eva Morris and her cronies. You're not going!'

'And I suppose you'll write and tell her? I was so looking forward to it! Oh, I hate you, Cathie!

I really hate you!' Ella cried before running from the room, slamming the door behind her.

'I wondered how long it would be before she started carrying on like this,' Cathie said dejectedly. 'I did do the right thing, Julia, didn't I? She's too young yet to be going around with the likes of that Eva and her fast friends. They certainly wouldn't be watching to see who she was with or how she was behaving. I couldn't let her go.'

Julia nodded sympathetically. 'You couldn't, Cathie. But she must be disappointed; I don't suppose she's ever been to a dance before?'

Cathie shook her head. 'No, she hasn't, and Da would be furious if he thought I'd let her go to a place like that at her age. Besides, she can't dance.'

Julia smiled. 'Neither could you.' She paused; she could see both sides of the argument and didn't want there to be any continued animosity between the sisters. 'Let me have a word with her.'

Cathie nodded gratefully. 'Go and see if you can talk some sense into her, because she's not going to listen to anything more I have to say,' she urged.

Ella was sitting on her bed crying when Julia went into the room. She sat down beside her.

'Ella, Cathie is only thinking of you and your reputation,' she began.

Ella turned a tear-stained face towards her. 'No, she's not! She's just thinking of herself! She's always been like that! She doesn't want me to have any ... fun!'

Julia sighed. 'Of course she does, she simply wants you to wait until you're a bit older and I

262

might add ... wiser. Eva Morris has got a terrible reputation for being "fast", Ella.' After both Charlie and the clerk from Accounts the girl had had a succession of short-lived 'romances'; it was rumoured that one fellow had even been married. 'There will be plenty of time for you to go to dances and parties; in fact you'll be going to a rather grand party very soon.' Cathie hadn't wanted to inform Ella of this earlier as she'd have got over-excited, but now it seemed the right moment.

That caught Ella's attention and she wiped her eyes with the back of her hand. 'What party?' she asked curiously.

'My cousin Elinor – Mrs Fleetwood-Hayes – is having a big party on Christmas Eve. Her husband the Captain will be home this year, you see, for a change. David has asked Cathie to go as his guest and as I'm also invited I'd like to take you as my guest.'

The disappointment at not being able to go to the Grafton Ballroom began to fade. Ella had heard all about the rather grand but formidable Mrs Fleetwood-Hayes as soon as she'd arrived. 'And you'd ... take me?'

Julia nodded. 'We'll have a great time. She has a big house; there will be dancing and wonderful food and her youngest daughter, Eileen, is only a bit older than you so there are bound to be people of your age there too. I'd forget about quarrelling with Cathie over Eva Morris, she's not worth it. Save your money, Ella, and buy a really lovely dress for the big party,' Julia advised, pleased that the girl now looked very enthusiastic.

'Oh, I will, Julia! I've never been to a party before!' Ella agreed happily.

'I doubt that any of us have ever been to a party such as this one is going to be. Now, come on back into the sitting room; it's cold in here. You can tell Cathie you're not bothered about going to the Grafton now and we can discuss what we're all going to wear,' Julia urged, hoping that she'd successfully poured oil on troubled waters. Cathie and Ella might look alike, but they had very different personalities, she thought.

Chapter Twenty

The argument was forgotten as Ella concentrated on looking for a dress for the party. She'd informed Eva that she wouldn't be going out with them as she wanted to save up for a special dress since she'd been invited to the Fleetwood-Hayeses' house on Christmas Eve. She'd felt a sense of satisfaction when the older girl had looked decidedly envious and had remarked rather cattily that she hadn't realised Ella mixed with such illustrious people as the Captain and his wife.

Cathie had decided that she wouldn't mention the incident to David, nor did she bring up the subject of the department's Christmas outing to the Locarno, and after he'd remarked that he didn't join his own office celebrations as he didn't drink a great deal and his knowledge of modern dances was negligible, she was thankful for the fact.

As the festive season approached they all became busier and Cathie was relieved that her sister seemed as enthralled as she had first been by the decorations and the lights and the grotto; what with that and excitement over the forthcoming party she seemed to have completely forgotten about their quarrel. She herself had bought a very smart cocktail dress in black taffeta and had purchased a slim diamanté necklace and earrings from Woolworth's which Julia said set it off perfectly without looking overdressed. The whole ensemble looked smart and sophisticated, Julia had enthused. Cathie had thought about wearing the magenta dress but had decided against it, although it had originally been a far more expensive dress than the black taffeta. She felt it was just a bit too bright for the occasion; she didn't want to outshine anyone else, particularly Monica or Eileen Fleetwood-Hayes. Julia had bought a royal blue taffeta dress and was going to wear a sapphire pendant and matching earrings which had belonged to her mother.

She wasn't exactly sure about Ella's choice though, she thought when her sister showed both herself and Julia her purchase, a couple of days before Christmas Eve.

'I've searched every shop in my lunch breaks but there was just so much choice that I found it hard to decide, but I finally settled on this,' Ella said happily as she drew it out of the layers of tissue paper. She'd never had so much money to spend on a dress in her life before for she'd scrimped on her lunches, some days she'd gone without having anything altogether, but she'd happily spent the time searching through the rails of dresses in C&A Modes, Blackler's and some of the other cheaper stores. When she'd tried this dress on she'd known it was just right and the colour was so ... festive.

'It's rather ... bright,' Cathie at last commented. It was vivid scarlet satin with a full skirt, no sleeves and both the front and back appeared to be cut in quite a low V. Far lower than anything she herself would have worn. Around the neckline and armholes it was trimmed with black satin ribbon and tiny black beads.

'I think the colour is just lovely and very festive considering it's a Christmas party. And I bought a pair of black and diamanté earrings and a necklace to wear with it. All I need now are a pair of shoes and a bag,' Ella informed them. 'I think I can manage the shoes but can I borrow your evening bag, Cathie?'

Cathie nodded. She'd bought a new one, but she was beginning to think that Ella's whole outfit was going to look rather 'flashy'.

'Ella, why don't you try everything on and then we can get a better idea of how it looks,' Julia urged, thinking like Cathie that Ella could possibly have chosen something a bit more tasteful.

'What do you think?' Cathie asked her friend when her sister had gone to put the dress on.

Julia frowned. 'What do *you* think?'

'It's not what I would have chosen. I don't want to upset her but ... but I think it looks rather cheap and flashy.'

'It's not only the colour – like you she does suit

bright colours – I think it's the material. It's too shiny. It might look better without that black edging. But she's young and it is her first special dress, Cathie, and she's saved very hard for it.'

'I know, so I'm not going to make any remarks, Julia,' Cathie promised.

When Ella appeared, looking highly delighted with herself, both girls smiled dutifully, although Cathie's heart sank. That neckline was far too low for a girl of Ella's age and the necklace and earrings only added to the illusion of cheapness. Oh, Ella had a lot to learn about fashion, she thought.

'Well, isn't it gorgeous?' Ella asked, twirling around to show the skirt to full advantage.

'It's certainly very eye-catching, Ella. And festive,' Cathie added.

Julia looked thoughtful. 'Do you think, Ella, that it would look much more ... elegant without that black trimming? I mean, your necklace and earrings do set it off perfectly but I think without the trimmings it would look more ... expensive,' she suggested.

Ella considered this. 'Do you really think so?'

'I do,' Julia replied firmly. 'What do you think, Cathie?'

'You know, I think you're right. It would definitely look like a more expensive dress without that black trimming. You've got black in your necklace and earrings and you'll have black shoes and a bag: I think that's enough black for someone your age, Ella.'

'I might spoil it by taking off the trimmings,' Ella said. She thought it looked lovely with the black velvet ribbon and beads, but maybe Julia was

267

right. She certainly didn't want her dress to be considered 'cheap'. Of course it certainly hadn't been expensive but she wanted it to look so.

'Oh, don't worry about that, Ella, I'll unpick it very carefully and once it's been pressed you won't know it ever had that ribbon trim on it,' Julia said confidently. There was nothing they could do about the neckline, she thought – she could well imagine Ella's reaction if she suggested that a little piece of black lace be inserted into the V at the front – but hopefully with the removal of the braid it would look better.

'Thanks, Julia. Oh, I'm really looking forward to wearing it. I'll feel so grown up! I've never had a dress like this before!' Ella said, her voice and eyes filled with excitement.

'You'll look as good as everyone else, Ella,' Julia replied, feeling she couldn't spoil the girl's excitement and anticipation.

'Yes, you will, Ella,' Cathie added, trying to sound confident but wondering just what the reaction of their hostess and her daughters would be to her sister's choice of attire. Ella would certainly stand out, that was for certain, but she just wished it wasn't for the wrong reasons.

David had insisted on calling to escort all three girls to his aunt's house on Christmas Eve. He arrived promptly at eight o'clock in his father's car, which he had borrowed for the occasion, after first dropping his father off in Alton Close. The fact that she would be travelling in a car for the first time added to Ella's excitement. Cathie had only ever been in a car once before and that had been to Mrs Vickers's funeral, which hadn't been a very happy occasion.

'Don't you all look ... wonderful,' David exclaimed a little bashfully as he escorted them down the path to the waiting vehicle, which was a Humber 12 saloon so there was plenty of room for them all. He'd not met Cathie's sister before and thought that although she was almost as attractive as Cathie, Ella's dress looked rather bright and a bit too old for her. Over her dress Julia wore a short evening cape which had belonged to her mother while both Cathie and Ella had decided that even though it was cold, as they were travelling in the luxury of a car and not on the tram, they would forgo covering their dresses with a coat.

'I feel as grand as the Queen,' Ella commented delightedly as the car moved off up Everton Valley.

Cathie smiled at David; she was feeling both excited and a little nervous. 'When the King and Queen visited Ramsey in nineteen twenty, Mam took us to see them, but as I was only two I really don't remember much about it. I think I recall a tall lady, dressed all in white with white fur on her collar and cuffs, but I expect that's because I've been told about her – and also that she had a marvellous hat and she carried a white umbrella. That was of course Queen Mary; I don't know what King George looked like at all.'

'Some people call it "Royal Ramsey",' Ella added, not wishing to appear ignorant of royal visits to her home town. 'Mam saw King Edward and Queen Alexandra when she was young and of course Prince Albert visited although Queen Victoria stayed on the boat. He took a walk through Ballure Glen and to the top of Lhergy Frissell where they built the Albert Tower in his honour, isn't that right, Cathie?'

'It is, Ella,' Cathie replied, thinking that her sister had parroted all that knowledge from her school history book.

'It all sounds very grand. Maybe I'll go over to see it for myself one day,' David mused aloud before becoming more thoughtful. 'It's said that the King isn't very well.'

Cathie was sympathetic. 'Oh, that's terrible. I do hope he gets better soon.'

'Everyone does, Cathie,' Julia said quietly while Ella thought that in fact King George really was very old. After all, Princess Elizabeth was nine and he was her grandfather; they'd never known any of their grandparents; they'd died before they were even born.

When they alighted in Alton Close the Fleet-wood-Hayeses' house was ablaze with lights and there seemed to be cars parked everywhere but David managed to find a space.

'It looks as if things are already in full swing,' he remarked as he escorted them towards the gate. 'And won't I be the envy of everyone, arriving with three lovely girls,' he added gallantly.

Julia laughed and both Cathie and Ella smiled, although both were apprehensive: Cathie about what she would find to say to David's father and Ella at the prospect of actually being entertained in a house like this and mixing with such people. However, she was excited too.

They were ushered into the hall by a serious-looking man dressed in formal evening attire and, after Julia had given him her cape, he directed them to the drawing room where he assured them their host and hostess would welcome them.

'Goodness, she's even hired a butler,' Julia whispered to Cathie. 'And I bet she's employed staff to wait on us,' she added.

All three were welcomed by the Captain and Mrs Fleetwood-Hayes, who was dressed in a long evening gown of black and gold brocade. Cathie noticed that her daughter Monica looked very elegant in a long evening gown of royal blue velvet with narrow shoulder straps and a fish-tail skirt. She also wore long white evening gloves and there was a diamanté clip in her hair. Eileen Fleetwood-Hayes's dress was of a more modest design with cape sleeves and a sweetheart neckline in peach organza over peach satin.

'Well, you all look wonderful!' their hostess remarked. 'And this must be your sister, Cathie?' she stated, taking in the close resemblance but privately thinking that the girl's choice of dress was rather unfortunate.

'Yes, this is Fenella, although everyone calls her Ella.'

Ella inwardly cringed. She loathed her full name. 'It's very ... nice to meet you and thank you for inviting me,' she answered a little hesitantly.

'You are very welcome, Ella. Are you enjoying living and working in Liverpool?'

'Oh, indeed I am,' Ella replied enthusiastically.

The older woman smiled at her. 'Then let me introduce you to some people of your age – they are mainly friends of Eileen's – and there are some people I'd like you to meet, Julia,' she added as she guided Ella towards the group around her younger daughter.

They were all served with champagne and Julia raised her eyebrows and smiled at Cathie. 'Well, I suppose I'll at least have to be pleasant to her protégés. She's certainly gone to a lot of trouble on every front.'

'She has indeed,' Cathie replied, thinking the champagne seemed to be flowing very freely. There would no doubt be a sumptuous buffet laid out somewhere and the Christmas decorations were nothing short of magnificent.

As their hostess made her way back towards them accompanied by two young men, Cathie sipped her drink and then smiled at Julia. 'Best of luck,' she mouthed.

'I think we'll leave you to Aunt Elinor and her "friends",' David said. 'Cathie, I'd like to introduce you to my father.'

Cathie nodded and followed him across the room. This was the moment she *hadn't* been looking forward to. Mr Kendal was talking amiably to the Captain but they both turned as David approached.

'Dad, I'd like you to meet Miss Kinrade – Cathie. We often have lunch together. I did mention it to you.'

Cathie smiled politely and took the hand that was extended to her. 'I'm very pleased to meet you, Mr Kendal,' she said, thinking that David bore a strong resemblance to his father although Mr Kendal's manner was more formal, less friendly somehow, or so it seemed to her.

'Yes, indeed he has mentioned you, Miss Kinrade. I'm pleased to meet you.'

'Is that your sister by any chance? The young lady in the scarlet dress?' the Captain enquired.

Cathie nodded, cringing. 'It is. She's only recently come to Liverpool. We're both Manx, you see,' she added for Mr Kendal's benefit, fervently wishing once again that Ella had bought something darker and more suitable.

Both David and Captain Fleetwood-Hayes asked her about the port of Ramsey and her home on the island but she noticed that David's father didn't join in the conversation; she was relieved when David suggested that they go and see how Julia was faring. She had the distinct impression that Mr Kendal didn't approve of his son's choice of partner for the evening and that made her feel uncomfortable.

'That must be Cousin Monica's young man,' David remarked as they made their way across the room.

Cathie looked interestedly at the young man in question. He was very tall and slim, had wavy light brown hair and looked rather nice. 'Is it serious, do you think?' she asked.

'Aunt Elinor would like to think so; apparently he's a very gifted artist. I've only met him once but he seems pleasant. Not a bit boastful about his talent or his growing success.'

Julia seemed to be getting on very well with the two young men, Cathie thought as her friend introduced them. David went with one of them to get more drinks and, a short while after they returned, the butler announced that the buffet would be served in the dining room.

'She really does put on a splendid spread,' Julia remarked, taking note of the huge joints of cooked beef, pork, ham and turkey and all the accompanying delicacies.

'She says the Captain would be mortified if she didn't,' David informed them. 'He's used to such fare. They only carry a dozen passengers, not being huge liners but mainly cargo ships, but they're all treated as if they're sailing first class with Cunard. And of course he's not always home for Christmas so it is a rather special occasion.'

'There'll be dancing after the buffet, so Mrs Fleetwood-Hayes told me,' one of their companions stated, looking meaningfully at Julia, who just smiled.

'I love dancing but will there be enough room?' Cathie wondered aloud, thinking the drawing room had been very crowded.

'Oh, plenty. There's another room beside the drawing room and of course not everyone will be dancing,' David remarked, feeling for the first time that he really should have taken some lessons. He didn't want to spoil Cathie's evening.

After the buffet they moved into what was termed the 'garden room' and Cathie realised that it was the room with the French doors that led out into the garden. It had been cleared of furniture and the carpet had been removed. Monica Fleetwood-Hayes was already selecting records from a pile that stood by the gramophone and it wasn't long before the young people were taking to the floor.

Julia was whisked away by the young man

called Gerald and she stood with David.

'I can sort of shuffle around, Cathie, if you wouldn't mind that or me treading on your toes,' he said rather apologetically.

She smiled at him. It really didn't matter, she thought. She was quite happy just to be here with him. 'Maybe we'll take a turn around the floor a bit later on, David. I don't mind, I'm content to be with you and watching,' she replied.

He smiled gratefully at her. 'Then should I fetch you a drink?'

She shook her head. 'Not just yet, thank you, David.'

Julia returned, looking flushed but smiling. 'Now, I suppose I'd better take a turn around the floor with you, Bertram. That's only fair, isn't it?'

Before he could reply their attention was diverted by a loud burst of laughter from the other side of the room and the sound of a breaking glass. Cathie frowned as she noticed Ella in the centre of a group of young men. She'd obviously stumbled or tripped over something but was laughing loudly, her cheeks flushed. One of the young men had his arm around her, obviously trying to steady her, while another was pushing the broken pieces of glass to one side with his foot. 'Oh, Lord! What's going on over there?' she said, feeling decidedly uneasy, for both Monica and Eileen Fleetwood-Hayes were obviously annoyed by Ella's behaviour and her heart sank as she caught sight of David's father's expression as he too took in the scene. He was positively glowering.

'I think we'd better go and see, Cathie,' Julia said firmly, steering her friend across the dance floor.

275

'Ella, how much have you had to drink?' Cathie demanded, taking in the fact that her sister looked very unsteady on her feet. Oh, she could kill her!

'Cathie, not ... not much. Jusht ... jusht a couple of glasses, it's del ... del ... lovely,' Ella slurred, giggling.

Julia glared at the young men. 'And I suppose you all think it's very entertaining!' she snapped.

Cathie had never felt so angry or humiliated in her life. 'Julia, help me get her out of here,' she hissed.

'Come along, Ella, I think it's time you were going home,' Julia urged, taking hold of Ella's arm while Cathie took the other; together they propelled Ella towards the door.

'I'll have to get her home, Julia. She's drunk! Oh, I could murder you, Ella, I really could!'

David approached them, looking concerned and accompanied by his father. 'Is she all right?'

'No, I'm afraid she isn't, David. She's had too much champagne and she's not used to drink of any kind. I'm sorry, I am really very sorry but ... but I'll have to take her home before she disgraces us all further.' And before the Captain or Mrs Fleetwood-Hayes sees her, she thought.

'Yes, I think you should do that, Miss Kinrade. Quite obviously neither of you should ever have been invited. You are clearly not the type of people who know how to conduct yourselves in polite society,' Mr Kendal snapped, glaring at David.

'I think that's rather uncalled for, Father!' David retorted angrily.

Cathie's humiliation deepened; although she

hated to admit it, David's father had a point. Neither she nor Ella had been brought up to mix with people like this, they were the daughters of a poor working-class fisherman, but she at least had tried to fit into what he had termed 'polite society'. She'd never felt so belittled in her life before and they would never be invited here again, she thought miserably. How was she to face their hostess next time she saw her? And what would David think of her, even though he had protested at his father's cutting remarks? 'It's all right, David. Don't worry, I'll get a taxi. I don't want to completely ruin everyone's evening.'

David was frowning, still very annoyed with his father. 'Cathie, you'll not get a taxi tonight and I can't let you go home alone – neither of you have coats and it's freezing out there. No, I'll drive you. I insist,' David said firmly.

'And I'll come too,' Julia added. 'I'm tired of those two young chaps vying with each other for my attention. It's just a game to them – neither one appears to have a brain in his head. And I wonder just who invited those young idiots who were plying Ella with drink? Quite obviously they don't know how to behave in "society" either!' she snapped, glaring at David's father. She too was furious at the way Cathie had been insulted.

Mr Kendal turned away and left them, his lips tightly pursed, his cheeks red with anger at what he considered Julia's downright impertinence.

Cathie was grateful for their support. Ella had made a real spectacle of herself – of them both – with that flashy dress and jewellery and then to crown it all by getting drunk. It was the most degrading thing a girl could do!

David went to find his aunt to inform her of their departure and Julia helped her to get Ella into the hall. 'Just wait until I get her home,' she hissed through clenched teeth to Julia.

'I'd wait until tomorrow morning if I were you. I doubt she'll remember much about this evening,' Julia advised. 'And no doubt she'll have a terrible hangover too.'

'I hope she does! It serves her right! What must David think of us? What kind of a family must he think we come from – although it's quite obvious what his father thinks.'

'Take no notice of that man! As David told him, it was completely uncalled for. It's not your fault,' Julia protested. 'She's been very silly but part of the blame lies with those lads who were encouraging her.'

'Oh, Julia, the whole evening has been a disaster! First of all that dress, then *this* and then ... *Mr Kendal!* I should have told her the dress wasn't suitable and I should have kept a close eye on her.'

'Cathie, you can't blame yourself.'

Cathie didn't reply as David appeared in the hall accompanied by his aunt. Her heart sank and she felt her cheeks burning with shame; was their hostess going to be as outraged and angry?

'Oh dear, too much champagne, I see,' she said, gazing at Ella's slumped figure. 'Well, I suppose she'll have learned a valuable lesson after she's slept it off. Now, I'm sorry that you are both leaving but I agree it's for the best. David will get you all safely home,' Mrs Fleetwood-Hayes said briskly, shepherding them towards the door. She could see Cathie was mortified and she felt sorry for her, but obviously her sister was a very different kettle of fish. Monica had already informed her that she thought the girl was rather loud and coarse and had wondered at the wisdom of her cousin Julia in bringing her.

With some difficulty they got Ella into the car and almost at once she fell asleep. That at least was something of a relief, Cathie thought as she sat beside David, silently fuming. Well, she would have quite a few things to say to her sister in the morning – hangover or not! Ella had effectively ruined the evening for herself, Julia and David.

Chapter Twenty-One

It was a very subdued and pale Ella who emerged on Christmas morning to find her sister and Julia busy preparing the lunch. She'd never felt so awful in her life before. Her head was pounding; her mouth felt as if she'd been chewing old socks and she felt decidedly queasy.

'I ... I won't be able to eat any ... lunch,' she said, her stomach turning over at the very thought of it.

'I don't wonder after the carry-on out of you last night!' Cathie snapped at her.

Ella sank down on a kitchen chair with a groan. 'I ... I don't remember ... much.'

'I don't wonder! You passed out as soon as we got you into the car. You were a disgrace, Ella! An

279

absolute *disgrace!* I've never been so ashamed or humiliated. I just don't know what everyone will think of us! What possessed you to drink so much champagne when you know you're not used to it?'

'It tasted so lovely, Cathie, and I just didn't think and then ... then I was really enjoying myself, everyone was so funny and we were all laughing ... and I think I tripped,' Ella said miserably.

'Yes, everyone was laughing, Ella, but they were laughing at *you*. I don't suppose you realised that, did you? Oh, they thought you were hilarious, the spectacle you were making of yourself!' Cathie fumed. 'I blame myself. I should never have let you wear that dreadful flashy dress and that awful jewellery – you looked like a Christmas tree! And I should have kept my eye on you, but I mistakenly thought you at least knew how to behave yourself in decent company,' she finished, wiping her hands on a tea towel which she then threw down in a fit of exasperation.

Ella looked hurt: she understood that she'd disgraced herself and she really did regret that but she hadn't thought her dress was flashy. 'Did you not like the dress?' she asked rather timidly.

'No I didn't! You've got a lot to learn about clothes, Ella, and about how to ... to conduct yourself, although I doubt either of us will ever be invited there again!'

'I'm sorry, Cathie, really I am. I didn't mean to behave like ... that,' Ella said contritely, realising that what her sister said was true and smarting from the knowledge that people had been openly laughing at her. Humiliation was swiftly added to everything else she was feeling.

Julia intervened now that Cathie had had her say and Ella was obviously sorry. 'I think that now we should put it all behind us. It *is* Christmas Day, after all, so let that be an end to ... hostilities. Ella's learned her lesson. Now I'll get you some water, Ella; you should drink plenty of it and you'll feel better. Then I suggest that you go and have a lie-down. If you can't face eating you can have some of the goose this evening when perhaps your appetite will have returned.'

Cathie didn't look very pleased. 'We haven't even opened our presents yet,' she muttered, thinking that in her opinion Ella had got off lightly for ruining Christmas.

'Well, we can do that now and Ella can open hers later,' Julia replied, trying to placate Cathie.

Cathie pursed her lips. A fine way to spend Christmas Day, she thought, but she realised that there wouldn't be much in the way of 'festive spirit' with Ella sitting there looking like a corpse.

Christmas Day passed quietly but with some degree of muted celebration as Cathie realised that her sister was indeed truly sorry for her behaviour. She was surprised, however, when on Boxing Day evening David Kendal arrived. Apart from Christmas Eve, he'd never called to the house before.

'David! This is a lovely surprise,' she greeted him, feeling immediately embarrassed, remembering their last meeting.

'I wondered how you ... all ... were? I know you were very ... upset the other evening,' he ventured.

'That's an understatement! You know I was livid, but she did have a terrible hangover and she is very sorry.' She sighed heavily. 'Really I suppose some of the blame lies with me. She'd never been to a party before, she was over-excited, she's young and she isn't used to drink. I should have kept a closer eye on her.'

'You can't blame yourself; she's old enough to make her own decisions. Part of the blame lies with those young fools who were plying her with champagne. I can tell you that after we left my aunt had quite a few words to say to them all, Eileen included – they were her friends; she'd invited them. Needless to say they won't be invited again. Cousin Eileen is sulking because Aunt Elinor was very forthright in her views on the type of people she expects her daughters to avoid mixing with.'

'How do you know all that?' Cathie asked.

'We went for tea yesterday afternoon,' he replied.

Cathie's heart sank. 'David ... I hope you won't think any the ... worse of me?'

'Of course not! You're very different to Ella and she ... she was just rather silly. And I want to apologise for my father. He should never have said such things and I told him so later that night. You're to forget everything he said.' There had in fact been quite a row, which had put a decided damper on the Christmas spirit until they'd gone for tea with the Captain and his wife, but he wasn't doing to tell Cathie that. He paused, searching for the right words. 'In fact I was wondering if in the New Year you would let me take you out one evening? We could go to the theatre, I'm sure you'd enjoy it.'

Cathie smiled at him. 'I'd like that,' she replied, thinking that even if his father didn't approve of her David obviously liked her enough not to be influenced by it and to have stood up for her.

Julia appeared in the doorway. 'Are you going to keep that poor young man standing in the cold hall all night, Cathie? Come on into the sitting room, David, it's much warmer.'

'Sorry, we were just talking,' Cathie replied, wondering if this was indeed the start of a closer relationship between them. She hoped it was.

They went to see a Noel Coward play *Tonight at 8.30* and Cathie enjoyed it very much. David had called for her in his father's car again and had brought her a box of Terry's All Gold chocolates and he'd purchased good seats in the dress circle. When he drove her home and stopped outside the house Cathie smiled at him and thanked him for a truly wonderful evening.

'It was such a change, David. I really enjoyed it. It was so amusing.'

'I'm glad you did. Will we go again?'

She nodded, pulling on her gloves.

'I ... I wanted to ask you out one evening long before this but ... but I just never seemed to be able to pluck up the courage,' he confided, looking a bit embarrassed.

She didn't laugh, realising that this confession hadn't been easy for him. 'Oh, David, you really are such a nice person and I won't bite! You should know that by now.'

He did laugh. 'And I'll tell you something else. I'm going to take lessons so I can take you dancing and not make a fool of us both.'

'You'd do that for me?'

He nodded enthusiastically and then reached out and took her hand. 'There's ... nothing I wouldn't do for you, Cathie.'

'I was worried that ... that after Christmas Eve you'd ... go off me. Not want to see me again. I realise that I'm not of your ... class,' she said quietly.

'I'd never do that! And I don't want to hear any more of this "class" thing! And ... and you can always confide in me, you know that,' he said earnestly – and he meant it. He hated to see her distressed or angry and she'd been both. He leaned across and kissed her gently on the cheek, feeling happiness rising in him.

She looked into his eyes; she'd not expected him to kiss her but she wasn't in the least upset or embarrassed, she felt happy. Very happy indeed. She stroked his cheek gently and smiled. 'Goodnight, David. I'll see you again very soon.'

'Oh, you will. I'll take you for lunch tomorrow. Goodnight, Cathie,' he said happily before getting out of the car to open the door for her. He felt as if he were walking on air.

As the bitterly cold days of January progressed Cathie saw quite a lot of David Kendal and they became closer, a fact noted by both Julia and her cousin Elinor Fleetwood-Hayes, who, when she had called into the store, had assured Cathie that the episode of Christmas Eve was to be put firmly behind them all and that David was a very sincere young man who could be trusted totally with her affections and that she should take no notice of anything Albert Kendal said; she'd always thought he was an out-and-out snob and now he'd proved it.

Much to Cathie's relief her sister seemed content to spend most of her evenings at home. She had agreed that Ella could go to the cinema with friends from work as long as she wasn't home late and that in April, when she was sixteen, she could start going to dances – after all, Ella had to have some fun in her life. She was continuing to enjoy her job and Cathie was confident she would be kept on. Julia was now teaching Ella to dance and Ella had confided that when she had saved up enough money for a dance dress she wanted Julia to accompany her and give her the benefit of her advice. She had no intention of repeating her mistake over the scarlet dress, which had been consigned to the bottom of the drawer in the base of the wardrobe.

As they all got off the tram opposite Lewis's on the morning of the twenty-first, muffled up against the bitterly cold wind, Julia was the first to notice the large black headlines of the newspapers the vendor standing on the corner was selling. She quickly bought a copy and they stood, as many other people were also doing, reading that King George had died at Sandringham the previous night.

'Oh, may he rest in peace! He was a good man,' Julia said quietly.

'He was,' Cathie added, wishing she had a clearer memory of him when he'd visited Ramsey all those years ago. He'd been seventy, of course, which was considered a good age.

'So, does that mean that the Prince of Wales is

now King Edward?' Ella enquired.

Julia nodded. 'It does, although he won't be crowned for a while.' She folded the newspaper. 'Come on, we'd better get into work: there will be so much to do, I'm sure. There's bound to be some sort of announcement about official mourning.'

All three girls felt saddened by the news and indeed later that morning the store was declared to be in mourning for the death of the King. Yards of black crêpe were issued to be used to drape across counter fronts and pictures of the late monarch were to be displayed prominently on each floor. An atmosphere of shock and sadness seemed to prevail and as Cathie went to meet David for lunch she saw many people in tears on the streets.

'Oh, David, isn't it sad?' she greeted him as he sat at their usual table in the Kardomah.

He nodded seriously. 'But he didn't suffer; the bulletin said he "died peacefully". There will be a state funeral, of course and then – later – a coronation.'

'It sort of makes everyone feel ... unsettled,' she mused.

David looked grave. 'These are "unsettling" times, Cathie. There could be civil war in Spain, Herr Hitler is growing more and more powerful and treating the Jews abominably, Mussolini's intent on carving out an empire for Italy and there's trouble between Japan and China. We need a strong, stable monarchy.'

'Do you think King Edward will provide that?' Cathie asked. Of course she'd listened to the news on the wireless but she didn't take very much interest in what was going on in the world or in politics.

'We can only hope so,' he replied, stirring his tea.

'I suppose your place has all the trappings of mourning too?'

He nodded. 'We all have to show our respect.'

'Then I don't think we should go out ... socialising until the funeral is over, do you? It wouldn't seem right.'

David agreed but looked a little disappointed.

'But there is nothing to stop you from coming to visit. We could play cards or listen to the wireless and of course still meet for lunch,' Cathie added.

'Julia won't mind?' David asked, relieved that he wouldn't have to stop seeing her in the evenings.

'No, she's busy teaching Ella to dance, although I think we should call a halt to that for the next few weeks.'

Seven days later on a very dark and miserable Tuesday morning the gun carriage bearing the body of the 'Sailor' King was pulled through the silent but crowded streets of London by 124 naval ratings. From Westminster to Paddington Station people stood, some openly weeping, in the cold January air. The girls listened to the BBC broadcast on the wireless at home for it was a day of national mourning. They heard the grave, reverential voice of the commentator inform them that the King was to be taken to Windsor to be buried.

'I think it was very ... respectful of King

Edward and his brothers to keep an overnight vigil in the abbey,' Julia remarked.

'And isn't it brave of Princess Elizabeth to accompany Queen Mary to Windsor by train? She's only nine,' Cathie added. All this information had been broadcast, as had the fact that the widowed Queen – heavily swathed and veiled in black – had followed her husband's funeral procession in a carriage while her sons had walked behind the gun carriage.

Ella had surreptitiously wiped away a tear when the commentator had said that when the procession passed the home of the Duke and Duchess of York in Piccadilly, the small figure of Princess Margaret Rose was seen in an upstairs window and that the child had curtsied deeply as a tribute to her grandfather.

When the broadcast was over, Julia switched off the wireless. 'I think that was all very ... moving,' she said.

Cathie got to her feet. 'So do I. I'll put the kettle on; I think we could all do with a cup of tea.'

'What happens now?' Ella asked for none of them had ever experienced an event like this before.

'I suppose everyone tries to get on with their lives as normal. We'll be back in work tomorrow,' Julia replied.

Ella nodded. 'I bet things will be rather quiet though.'

'It's always a quiet time of the year. The sales are over, the weather is still cold and people won't be thinking of spring just yet.'

Cathie came in with the tea. 'I'll be glad when we

can start to look forward to the better weather; it seems to have been a very long and miserable winter.'

Julia tried to lighten the mood. 'We've got the new spring styles to look forward to, your eighteenth birthday, Cathie and then Ella's sixteenth and hopefully this year will prove to be a good one after all. We'll have a coronation to look forward to, don't forget,' she reminded them.

Ella brightened up at her words. 'Yes, and after my birthday I'll be able to go to dances and I might even meet someone ... special.'

Cathie frowned at that; then she remembered that she'd only been sixteen when she'd met Charlie Banks. She hoped her sister would have more sense than she'd had then. But she too brightened up. She had David now and she realised that she'd become increasingly fond of him, very fond indeed. Not in the same way she'd experienced with Charlie but in a deeper, more serious way. She knew she could always depend on David but she still worried that she wasn't good enough for him. She glanced across at Julia; she'd be twenty-four this year, she thought, and many people considered that to be an age when a girl had been 'left on the shelf'. She wondered if there would ever be anyone special in her friend's life. Oh, Julia said she was really only serious about her career but she wondered what would happen if Mr Right came along? Would Julia change her mind? Perhaps this year he would, she mused. None of them knew what the months ahead held for them but she felt quietly confident that it would prove to be a good year;

after all, they were entering a new era, they now had a new king. And he was forty-one and wasn't married – yet.

Chapter Twenty-Two

Ella's first dance had proved to be a resounding success, Cathie thought to herself with some satisfaction as she got ready to go out that summer evening. By the time her birthday had arrived Ella was a proficient dancer and Julia had gone with her sister to choose the outfit she'd been saving hard for. She had been delighted with Ella's choice of a lemon crêpe-de-Chine dress with cap sleeves, a square neckline and a full skirt that was artfully draped into a sash at the waist. Julia had lent Ella an evening bag and some rather nice silver ear-rings and a necklace and she had looked lovely. So different and far more elegant than she'd looked on Christmas Eve.

When Ella had returned home she had confided delightedly that she'd been asked up for every single dance and that one lad had asked to walk her to the tram. She'd refused him as she wouldn't abandon the friends she'd gone with and, besides, she didn't want to give the impression that she was 'fast'. But Ella had said she intended to go again to Blair Hall and indeed she had and she'd become very friendly with Eddie Mercer, the lad she'd met that first time. Of course they'd not met him yet – her sister always met him outside the dance hall – but Ella had told them all about him. Cathie hoped to meet him soon: her sister seemed very taken with him and she wanted to ascertain that he was 'suitable' for she still felt responsible for Ella.

She put the finishing touch to her make-up and tweaked a curl into place and got up from the dressing table. She hoped she looked elegant for she was accompanying David to an engagement party – that of Monica Fleetwood-Hayes and Walter Lennox – and she knew that Mr Kendal would be there.

Although David called regularly to their house she had never been taken to his home, but that was understandable. Her dress of pale blue cotton, sprigged with tiny white flowers, wasn't new but she felt it was appropriate for a summer's evening. Julia too had been invited, of course, but there had been no mention of Ella. She knew her sister wasn't upset by that fact. Ella wanted only to forget her last visit and anyway she was going out dancing with Eddie Mercer, which she thought a much more attractive alternative.

Julia looked cool and smart in her pale apple-green dress and they both carried light jackets for they would be travelling on the tram. Cathie had refused David's offer of transport, saying that he shouldn't abandon his father and that the evenings were light until much later now.

'Is Mrs Fleetwood-Hayes quite happy with Monica's choice of future husband?' Cathie asked as the tram moved along County Road on its way to Aintree.

'Delighted, I believe. She's very fond of Walter

291

and he comes from a good family. His parents, brother and an aunt will be there tonight. Cousin Elinor says he's a quiet, steady, reliable young man,' Julia replied.

'A bit like David then,' Cathie mused aloud.

Julia smiled. 'Yes, I suppose so. You really do like David, don't you, Cathie? Do you think you're in love with him?'

Cathie thought about it. 'I think I am, Julia. Oh, it's not the same as ... Charlie Banks. I was just young and very naïve then with a head full of romantic nonsense. I got to know David slowly and it's a different feeling. It sort of has more ... depth,' she tried to explain.

Julia nodded, thinking of Ella and Eddie Mercer; she hoped Ella wouldn't get hurt the way Cathie had, but Cathie had got over it and had found love with a much nicer person.

'What about you, Julia?' Cathie probed.

Julia smiled. 'Oh, I know I'm twenty-four but I don't intend to settle for someone I don't love for the sake of a ring on my finger and the title "Mrs" – just to satisfy social convention, or Cousin Elinor for that matter.' She laughed. 'And I've still got my sights set on becoming a buyer, don't forget.'

Cathie laughed too. 'Then let's hope she hasn't got any more young men lined up for you this evening. Did you say Walter Lennox has a brother?' she asked mischievously.

Julia raised her eyes to the ceiling. 'Oh, stop it, Cathie! You're getting as bad as she is!'

To Cathie's relief there was no hired butler or staff and there didn't seem to be as many people at this gathering, but she was still pleased when

David quickly made his way to her side.

'You look lovely, Cathie.' He smiled, taking her arm and guiding her towards the French doors, which were wide open, allowing the perfumes of the flowers in the garden to drift into the room. He'd been thinking about their future a great deal lately and he'd decided that this was the perfect occasion to broach the subject. He was also determined not to let his father insult her again.

Julia had greeted her cousin Elinor amiably and was being steered to congratulate Monica and her new fiancé.

'Shouldn't we go and offer our congratulations too?' Cathie asked David.

'We've plenty of time to do that; let's wait until everyone's stopped fussing around the happy couple. Let's go out into the garden; it will be quieter there and ... and there's something I ... I want to say,' David said hesitantly.

There were a few people in the garden but he led her past them towards the rose-covered pergola underneath which a bench had been set. Dusk was just beginning to fall and here the perfume of the roses permeated the air with a heavy sweetness. It was the perfect place, he thought – romantic – although he was feeling very nervous.

'It's lovely out here, so ... peaceful,' Cathie said, feeling a little apprehensive herself. 'What did you want to say?'

David took her hand. 'Cathie, we ... we've been seeing each other for quite a while now and ... and you must know how I feel about you.'

'I think ... I know you're very ... fond of me, David,' Cathie said quietly, her heart beginning to beat more rapidly.

'I ... I'm more than that. I ... I love you. I know there will never be anyone else for me. You are kind, sincere, loyal, thoughtful and beautiful.'

She shook her head although she felt very flattered. 'Oh, I'm not "beautiful"!'

'You are to me, Cathie. You are the most beautiful girl I've ever met.' He paused, summoning up every ounce of courage. 'We ... we do get on well together and ... and I'd hate to lose you...'

'You're not going to lose me.'

'Then ... then will you marry me? I mean ... not right away. I want to do things properly, but I thought that this was just the right occasion to ask you to become ... engaged to me?'

Cathie smiled at him, feeling joy welling up in her, yet something was holding her back from agreeing immediately. 'I do love you, David, but ... but we mustn't steal their moment of glory; it wouldn't be right. And you see ... I promised Mam once that I'd think long and hard about marriage. It's ... forever and I'm only eighteen. I'll need my parents' permission...'

'Of course, Cathie! I did say "not right away" and it's sensible to think hard about it, but–'

'But I *do* love you,' she interrupted, not wanting to hurt or disappoint him.

'Then that's all that matters! I won't press you, I promise,' David replied, gathering her into his arms.

She was oblivious to the other people in the garden as she clung to him and kissed him. She did love him, she felt so happy, so secure, so ... cherished in his arms, but she'd promised her mother and she wanted to be sure about her decision.

At length he drew away from her, the love he felt shining in his eyes. 'I think we'd better go inside before someone comes looking for us,' he said reluctantly.

She nodded. 'We should congratulate your cousin and her fiancé. I don't want anyone to think I've no manners,' she confided, thinking of their hostess and of his father. But she could hardly wait to write to Lizzie and tell her of his proposal.

As they approached the newly engaged couple Cathie noted that Walter Lennox's mother and aunt looked very alike, so alike in fact that they were almost identical, and both were dressed in black velvet with jet beadwork embellishments. Walter's father was a tall, grey-haired and rather forbidding-looking man but his brother, who was obviously younger, looked sociable and quite handsome. It was also obvious that Walter adored his fiancée.

'Any plans for the wedding?' David asked his cousin, who looked flushed and happy and delighted to be the centre of attention.

Monica raised finely arched eyebrows and laughed. 'Oh, David! *Everyone* has been asking that. We really haven't thought that far ahead yet and you know Mother, she'll want it to be a huge, grand affair which takes time to organise.'

'I suppose you will have to make sure that your father will be home – to give you away,' Cathie added a little shyly. She was rather in awe of Miss Fleetwood-Hayes, whom she thought very, very sophisticated and confident, although she was about the same age as herself.

'Yes, I'd already thought about that, but of course if by some chance he couldn't be there Mother's brother would give me away. Uncle Thomas: he's over there with his wife, Aunt Leila.'

Cathie glanced across the room but thought Monica's reasoning sounded a bit ... heartless.

David took her arm and guided her away as an older couple approached to speak to the pair.

'I know I'd definitely wait until my father was home,' she whispered to David. 'He'd be terribly hurt not to be able to give me away and I'm sure the Captain would be too.'

He smiled at her. 'I'm looking forward to meeting him, Cathie, and your mother, but now let's go and talk to *my* father; I fear we've been rather neglecting him and I've been assured he's on his best behaviour.'

Mr Kendal shook Cathie's hand politely. He was aware that his son spent a lot of time with the girl, which he found annoying, and he was wondering what kind of relationship there was between them. Nothing serious, he hoped. She was pretty enough but he knew very little about her, except that she worked as a sales assistant in Lewis's – apparently in the millinery department. And that her sister appeared to him to be common and quite charmless.

'They seem very happy,' David remarked, looking in the direction of Monica and Walter.

'Yes, and both your aunt and uncle approve of him,' his father replied succinctly.

'His mother and aunt are very alike,' Cathie remarked, feeling she had to try to contribute to the conversation. Mr Kendal seemed to be making an effort to be polite.

'That's because they are twins,' Mr Kendal replied flatly. 'Do you have any other sisters, Cathie?'

She nodded. 'I have another sister and three brothers.'

'Do they live with your parents – apart from ... your sister who is here in Liverpool?' He refrained from saying 'the girl in the appalling dress who got drunk last Christmas'.

'My eldest brother's married, but the rest live at home. Hal – Henry – is the youngest, then Meggie – Margaret. Both Jack and Jacob work with my father,' Cathie informed him, very relieved that he was showing some interest in her family. She wondered if David had confided that he was going to propose to her.

'I see, and what does your father do?'

'He's a fisherman, Mr Kendal, as are my brothers. They work on a boat out of Ramsey, but they don't own it. You see there isn't a great deal of work on the island...'

He was taken aback. He'd not known that she was the daughter of a *fisherman*, one so humble he didn't even own his boat. Obviously there wouldn't be much in the way of opportunities for a working-class man and his sons, particularly if they were poorly educated. He looked pointedly at his son, the colour rising in his cheeks. He was furious that David had taken up with a girl like this – pretty and polite though she was. He'd expected more of his son; he had high expectations of David and he'd not been making sure that he was being trained in all aspects of the business for him to end up with a girl like Cathie Kinrade.

'You mean he's a *trawlerman?*'

'He is. As I said there isn't a lot of ... choice,' Cathie replied, feeling her spirits plummet at the horror in his voice.

'Which is why presumably you came to Liverpool,' he stated bluntly.

Cathie just nodded. You couldn't fail to notice his expression as he looked at David or the note of disgust in his voice and it hurt her. She wasn't ashamed of her father or her brothers – she was proud of them; they worked hard. 'It ... it's a tough and often dangerous life. It's not a big boat and they go as far as the south coast of Ireland and up to the coast of Scotland in all weathers and sometimes ... sometimes a boat is ... lost,' she replied firmly.

'I think they must have a great deal of courage to endure such conditions,' David said seriously. He'd known what her father and brothers did for a living but hadn't mentioned it, for he had no intention of letting that come between himself and Cathie and his tone left his father in no doubt that he was becoming increasingly annoyed.

'Indeed,' Mr Kendal replied curtly. 'If you will excuse me, I should go and speak to Elinor's brother and his wife.'

Cathie looked up at David and shook her head. 'I know he ... he doesn't like me. He thinks I'm beneath you...'

'He doesn't *know* you, Cathie, but when he does he'll change his mind.'

She shook her head. 'He won't. That much was very clear. He doesn't think I'm good enough.'

'Don't let him upset you! Of course you're "good enough". More than good enough.'

She felt tears pricking her eyes. 'No, I'm not, David. I'm the daughter of a poor Manx "trawlerman"!'

David's anger at his father's conduct was increasing. 'Oh, he *has* upset you! I'm sorry. We all work for a living – no one works without being paid, just solely because they enjoy it. And I certainly don't enjoy my job but I keep at it because it's what he expects of me, but in the matter of whom I should love and marry I certainly have no intention of letting him dictate to me. It's my choice and I intend to tell him so!'

'I don't want to cause trouble between you, David. It will only make him think even more badly of me.'

'You won't cause trouble, Cathie. I've made up my mind and I don't intend to change it. I'm of legal age and I don't need his consent. Now, let's not let this spoil the evening. Let's have some champagne and go and talk to Julia,' he urged, taking her arm.

She smiled ruefully at him. For her Albert Kendal had indeed spoilt the evening.

Julia had noticed that she was subdued and when they left to return home she asked her why.

'It all started so well, Julia. He ... he proposed,' she confided.

Julia was very surprised. 'Did he? What did you say? Did you turn him down? Is that why you're upset?'

'No! I told him I'd think about it. I was going to

299

write to Mam and tell her, see what her reaction would be, but I told him I did love him and I do. But then...' She told Julia of the conversation with his father and of how it had made her feel.

'But you're not going to let that stop or influence you, are you? He's a snob because the family has money; you know Cousin Elinor thinks so too. She tolerates him and his attitudes because he was married to the Captain's sister, but she doesn't think it right that he won't let David choose his own career.'

Cathie bit her lip. 'David was adamant that he's not going to influence him but I don't want to cause trouble.'

'Good for David! Take no notice of him, Cathie. Put everything he said out of your mind. All that matters is that David loves you and wants to marry you. It doesn't matter where you come from or what your father does for a living. He loves *you* – that's all that matters,' Julia said firmly.

Cathie sighed. Julia was right but she knew she couldn't put out of her mind the fact that his father totally disapproved of her and her family.

Neither David nor his father said a great deal on the journey home but David was determined that before they retired for the night he was going to inform his father that he had proposed to Cathie. It was a conversation he wasn't looking forward to but one that had to be held, whatever the outcome, although he hoped there would be no permanent rift between them.

'There is something I would like to say and I'd sooner get it off my chest now,' he stated, pouring himself a small whiskey from the cut-glass decanter on the sideboard.

Albert Kendal stared hard at his son. 'Really? Then you'd better pour me a glass too. I'm obviously going to need it.'

David did so and handed him the glass before taking a sip of his own drink. 'I think you should know that I've asked Cathie to marry me and she has agreed, although she needs her parents' consent and it will not be in the immediate future.' He took another deep swig and waited apprehensively.

'Then you are a damned fool! It is obvious the type of family and background she comes from and I don't consider that to be at all suitable! You can do much better than that. I *expected* you to do better. We... You have a certain position to maintain and do you really think a girl like that will prove to be an asset as a wife?' Albert Kendal's tone was cold but there was no mistaking the anger in it.

David had expected such remarks. 'Yes, I do think Cathie will be "an asset as a wife", as you put it, Father, although being an "asset" is secondary to being someone I love and who loves me. Someone who is kind, honest, thoughtful, loyal and hard-working. If you could only put aside your preconceptions regarding class and Society and get to know her, I'm sure you will find out that she will make a perfect wife and daughter-in-law.'

'Never! I will never accept that girl as part of this family. You are a great disappointment to me, David.'

David stood his ground, his cheeks flushed with anger and hurt. 'I suppose I am. However, I've agreed to put aside my hopes of a career at sea to work with you in the business, despite the fact that I do not enjoy it, because it was your wish, but I will not let you dictate whom I should marry. I love Cathie and I will marry her and I don't need your consent. I'm of age!'

Albert Kendal drained his whiskey and slammed the glass down on the top of the sideboard. 'Do as you please but when it all goes wrong – as it will do – don't come looking for sympathy or understanding! And don't expect me to attend the wedding or accept her as a daughter-in-law. She will never be that to me. I also have no wish to set eyes on her again, so do not even contemplate bringing her here or mention her to me again! The matter is closed. Goodnight!'

David didn't reply; he just stared bleakly as his father left the room, slamming the door behind him. Well, now he knew exactly where he stood. From now on there would be tension between them; his father might even attempt to come between Cathie and himself. He finished his drink. He would never allow that to happen. He was determined to marry Cathie. It was his life and he intended to make his own decisions and if his father refused to even get to know Cathie, well, then that was his loss.

Chapter Twenty-Three

Cathie wrote a long letter to her mother explaining how she felt about David Kendal and the fact that he wanted them to get engaged and be married at some time in the future and then waited a little apprehensively for Lizzie to reply. She was aware that quite often it was her father who helped Lizzie with the letters and she thought that in this instance it would be useful as she would learn of Barney's views on the matter too. She was therefore surprised by the contents of her mother's letter when it duly arrived but she was more astonished by Ella's reaction to it.

All three girls had had their supper but were still sitting around the table in the dining room, which was bathed in the last rays of the evening sun streaming in through the window.

'What does she say?' Julia asked, seeing that Cathie was looking a bit puzzled but not in a worried sort of way.

'She's a bit ... non-committal,' Cathie replied.

'What's that supposed to mean? Is she happy about you and David or not?' Ella demanded.

'She says that seeing as both you and I, Ella, are apparently courting seriously, she'd like to come over to meet these fellows before she gives us any advice but obviously she can't spare the time away from the family, so – and this is the really surprising thing – Jacob is coming across just for two days at the weekend.'

Julia grinned. 'To meet the two "suitors" and then to go home and give her his opinion of them before you both get her blessing – or not. Well, at least it will be nice for you both to see your brother again,' she added.

'He needn't be wasting money coming across on *my* behalf'.' Ella said sharply, frowning at her sister. She hadn't deemed her romance to be serious at all. Of course Cathie had asked her quite a few questions about Eddie, which she'd mainly shrugged off, but she'd not even considered bringing him to meet her sister or Julia.

'Why not?' Cathie asked.

'Because I'm not seeing Eddie Mercer again, that's why!' Ella stated flatly, annoyed that Cathie had taken it upon herself to inform their mother independently of her romantic affairs without mentioning it.

Both Julia and Cathie stared at her, taken aback.

'What happened?' Cathie demanded.

Ella shrugged. 'I sort of ... went off him. I got bored with him; he could be very ... childish.'

'But I thought...? Oh, honestly, Ella, you might have told me before I wrote to Mam!'

'I wasn't aware that everything I do has to be reported straight back to Mam. You had no right to go telling her my business, Cathie!'

Cathie was stung by her sister's words. 'Ella, I honestly thought you and Eddie were serious *and* it wouldn't hurt you to write to Mam more often than you do. You'd been seeing Eddie for a while and you were always going on about him and how wonderful he was, so I assumed–'

'Well, you assumed wrong! I wasn't "serious" about him!' Ella snapped.

'Was he upset, Ella?' Julia enquired, thinking Ella had been a bit callous. As Cathie had said it wasn't all that long ago that Eddie Mercer had appeared to be the love of Ella's life.

Again Ella shrugged. 'I don't know, he didn't seem to be, and anyway I don't really care. I've got a new boyfriend now. I've only been out with him once so far but I'm seeing him again. I met him on the tram coming home from the Gaumont Cinema. The tram was packed and he gave me his seat which I thought was really charming.'

Cathie and Julia exchanged glances: Julia thinking it wasn't the wisest thing to do to accept invitations from strangers on a tram, and Cathie thinking that Ella hadn't wasted any time after dropping Eddie and that she hoped her sister wasn't going to turn out to be what was known as 'fast'.

'I see. Well, I know David will be delighted to meet Jacob and *I'm* delighted that he's coming across. I haven't seen him since I was home last,' Cathie replied.

Ella got up and collected the dishes in preparation to taking them into the kitchen. 'You two were always as thick as thieves, but don't expect me to stay in on Saturday night to entertain him. I'm meeting Frank.'

Cathie sighed as she left the room. 'She's always resented the fact that Jacob and I are close, but I *will* be glad to see him.'

'So will I. I'm looking forward to meeting him,' Julia added.

Cathie smiled. 'I'm sure you'll like him. Now, Ella will have to share my bedroom so Jacob can have hers and I don't suppose that will please her either.'

'Well, he can't be expected to sleep on the sofa, that wouldn't be very hospitable at all, so she'll just have to put up with it. It will only be for a couple of nights,' Julia said firmly. 'Does your mother say exactly when he will be arriving and when he's going back?' she asked.

'He's coming over on the Friday-evening boat but she doesn't expect us to meet him as it will be quite late and she's a bit worried about us being out. He'll find his own way here. And he's going back on the Sunday-afternoon ferry,' Cathie informed her, scanning the lines of Lizzie's letter. 'But I'd like to go to meet him.'

Julia looked thoughtful. 'We could both go — safety in numbers,' she suggested.

Cathie nodded. 'I don't suppose Ella will want to bother coming, but I'd feel a bit happier if you were with me – rather than going alone.'

'You'll have to let David know,' Julia reminded her.

'I'll tell him tomorrow at lunchtime and I think it would be best if David came here on Saturday evening. That way it would be more ... informal, a bit more relaxed.'

Julia nodded her agreement. 'Ask him for supper. I'll get something from the food hall on Friday.'

Cathie smiled at her. 'Yes, let's make it a bit of a special evening for everyone. Except Ella, of course, as she's going out with the new chap, this

Frank. Just what Jacob will make of that I don't know,' she added tersely.

It was a mild summer evening as the two girls stood at the top of the floating roadway waiting for the passengers to disembark from the *Peveril*. There were still many people out and about taking advantage of the weather and the lighter evenings but now dusk was rapidly falling and the pale light of the rising moon was reflected in the dark waters of the river.

It wasn't long before Cathie spotted the tall figure of her brother making his way through the crowd and she began to wave.

'Jacob! Jacob, over here!' she cried.

He grinned but then looked a little perturbed. 'Cathie! I thought Mam told you I'd make my own way. She didn't want you to be out this late.'

'I couldn't not come to meet you so I brought Julia with me. Oh, it really is great to see you!'

Julia was surprised by Jacob Kinrade. He wasn't what she had expected at all. Somehow she'd thought he would resemble Cathie and Ella but he didn't, he was well over six feet tall with fair hair and blue eyes, their colour intensified by his tanned complexion, and as she smiled up at him she felt instantly attracted to him, a feeling she'd never experienced before.

Cathie introduced them. 'Jacob, this is Julia, my best friend.'

Jacob smiled as he shook her hand, thinking she was a very pretty girl, older than both his sisters of course, probably even a few years older than himself. She had a lovely smile. 'It's nice to meet you at last, Julia, we hear so much about you in Cathie's letters.'

'Only good things, I hope,' Julia replied, laughing.

'Of course, and Mam's very grateful that you took Ella in. Where is Ella, by the way? Is it too late for her to be out?'

'No, but...' As they walked towards the tram terminus Cathie explained that unbeknown to them Ella had dropped poor Eddie Mercer and was now seeing someone called 'Frank' but that they didn't know his surname or anything else about him.

Jacob frowned. 'Where did she meet this Frank? She is behaving herself, Cathie, isn't she?'

'Of course she is,' Cathie replied as they boarded the tram, paid the fare and settled on to a seat.

'Ella is still very young so I suppose we should make allowances; she'll probably have quite a few boyfriends before she settles down,' Julia added, noting that Ella's behaviour at last Christmas's party clearly hadn't been reported to her family by Cathie.

'Cathie didn't have a string of boyfriends,' Jacob replied seriously. 'And that's the reason why I've come across. Mam wants another ... opinion of David Kendal.'

'We assumed that, Jacob, but let's talk about it when we get home,' Cathie urged, not wanting to discuss the matter on a crowded tram.

Jacob was quite surprised by the size of the house his sisters lived in; he knew from Cathie's letters that it was much larger than their cottage but he'd not expected it to be quite so big and so comfortably furnished. He knew part of it was rented out but obviously Julia's parents had left her quite well off.

Ella had waited up for their return and she greeted her brother affectionately. 'I wanted to see you tonight because we're all in work tomorrow.'

'So I understand, Ella,' he replied as Julia indicated he should sit down and make himself at home.

'So, what are you going to do with yourself all day?' Ella asked.

'Oh, give him chance to catch his breath, Ella. We've only just got home,' Cathie instructed. 'Go and put the kettle on, please,' she added.

'She's right. All three of us will be out at work tomorrow. I'm afraid you're going to be left to your own devices, Jacob.' Julia smiled at him.

He smiled back; his liking for Julia was growing – she was such a pleasant, friendly girl. 'Oh, I won't mind that, Julia. I'll take a good look around the city and the docks. I've not been to Liverpool before so I'm sure there is plenty to see and do.'

'You could meet up with us for lunch?' Cathie suggested, before remembering that she and Julia never took their breaks at the same time and she doubted Ella would want to spend hers with Jacob, she'd be trotting around the shops no doubt looking for some new accessory to wear that evening.

'No, don't be worrying about me or changing your routine. I'll be fine,' Jacob insisted.

'Well, we've invited David for supper tomorrow evening,' Cathie informed him.

'I'm afraid there will just be the four of us as

Ella's going out,' Julia added.

'What are you saying about me?' Ella queried as she entered with the tea tray.

'Only that you're going out tomorrow evening with Frank,' Cathie replied.

'Frank who?' Jacob asked, taking the cup that Julia handed him and scrutinising his younger sister more closely.

'Miller, if you must know,' Ella replied. 'And before you ask, I met him on the tram. He gave up his seat so I wouldn't have to stand all the way home.'

'Isn't that what any decent lad would do?' Jacob stated flatly. 'And where is he taking you?'

Ella raised her eyes to the ceiling impatiently. 'Honestly, you sound just like Da! We're going to a dance at Blair Hall – satisfied?'

Jacob frowned. This sounded like the Ella he knew and he wondered how she and Cathie got on these days. 'So, I don't suppose it's much use me meeting him then?'

'Not really. I know that Mam sent you across to ... "vet" David and Eddie, but of course Cathie didn't tell you that I'd finished with him–'

'I didn't *know!*' Cathie interrupted.

Ella ignored her. 'So you can tell her that I'm seeing someone else and I don't know if it's serious or not – yet,' she instructed her brother.

'Ella, Mam worries about you both but particularly you since you're younger than Cathie,' Jacob said seriously.

'Well she needn't, Jacob. I'm fine. I'm enjoying myself. I've got a good job which I like and you have to agree that I've got a lovely home.'

He nodded and smiled at Julia. 'You have indeed. You're both very fortunate in having such a good friend who's happy to share her home with you.'

Julia decided it was time for a change of subject. 'I hope you've got a good pair of comfortable boots, Jacob, if you're going to take in all the sights of the city tomorrow? You can get the overhead railway; it runs the whole length of the docks and gives you a good view of all the shipping. Then there are the ferries too – it's only tuppence for the fare and you can go to either Egremont, Seacombe, Woodside or even New Brighton.'

'He'll be worn out if he does all that tomorrow,' Cathie remarked, smiling.

'I'm used to being out for days on the boat in all weathers, don't forget. I think I'll manage a walk around Liverpool.' He grinned at his sister. 'And I might even come in to see what kind of a place it is you work in.'

'We're on the first floor but it's all ladies' fashions,' Cathie said, thinking he'd feel out of place surrounded by hats and dresses and costumes and coats.

'But if you take the lift to the top floor there's a menagerie up there. It might be more interesting than ladies' hats,' Julia added.

'I heard that but I didn't quite believe it,' Jacob replied, amused.

Julia laughed. 'Oh, it's very true, I assure you, and a great many of the "exhibits" have been donated by my cousin Elinor.'

'I've heard about her too. Isn't David related to her?' he asked Cathie.

She nodded. 'She's his aunt.'

'I see. And ... you've met his father?' Jacob probed. Cathie had mentioned this fact briefly in her letter and Lizzie had asked him to try to find out more about the family her daughter was contemplating becoming part of.

Cathie frowned but nodded. 'I have, but only twice and ... and...'

'And what?' Jacob urged.

'He doesn't like me; he doesn't think I'm good enough for David.'

Julia spoke before Jacob had time to comment. 'I've told her to take no notice. Mr Kendal is a bit of a snob and quite ... dictatorial. David really wants a career at sea but his father won't hear of it.'

Jacob thought about this. At least David Kendal appeared to have some choices, which was more than he'd had. 'Being at sea isn't all it's cracked up to be, believe me. But what does his father want him to do?'

'What he's doing now, learning the business,' Cathie informed her brother. 'But ... but David said while he's prepared to stick at that he'll not let his father tell him whom he can or can't marry.' She paused, frowning. 'I think there has actually been a row over it, something I really didn't want to happen.'

Jacob nodded. At least he sounded as though he had a mind and a will of his own. He was looking forward to meeting David Kendal and hopefully to having a good chat to him about Cathie.

'Well, even if there has been it's not your fault, Cathie, so don't let it worry you,' Julia said, getting to her feet. 'And I think it's time we all went to bed. We've to be up early tomorrow. I hope you'll be comfortable, Jacob, and we'll try not to disturb you in the morning.'

He too got to his feet. 'I doubt you will, Julia. It will be a rare treat for me to have a lie-in. Thank you for putting me up and so comfortably.'

Julia smiled at him. 'It's just a pity you're not staying longer, Jacob, but while you are here please do treat this as home.' She meant it; he seemed to fit in well here, she thought. He didn't appear awkward or uncomfortable but maybe it was because she had taken such a liking to him. He was Cathie's brother and came from a family that she knew was honest and trustworthy so there was no need for her to worry. She was just sorry his visit would be so short.

'I'm looking forward to tomorrow. It should prove to be a very interesting day,' Jacob replied. He really only had one full day to spend in Liverpool before returning on Sunday, but he wondered if there might be time for him to spend some time with Julia before he boarded the ferry. He'd certainly like to get to know her better.

Chapter Twenty-Four

Jacob had spent a busy day taking in all the city sights. He'd taken a trip on the overhead railway, as they'd suggested, and marvelled at the number and size of the ships in the docks, the varieties of cargo being loaded and unloaded and the large brick warehouses where these goods were stored. Liverpool was the second port of the Empire and he knew those ships travelled the oceans of the world. He'd taken a trip on the ferry to Egremont and from the deck of the *Royal Daffodil* he'd viewed the panorama of both the Liverpool and Birkenhead waterfronts and the shipbuilding yards of Cammell Laird. Then he'd gone to Lewis's intent on seeing where his sisters worked and viewing the menagerie. He'd been astounded by the sheer size of the store and of the choice of goods on sale. Cathie hadn't exaggerated, he'd thought, and both his sisters and Julia looked very neat and professional in their working dresses. Before he'd gone up to the top floor he'd visited the menswear department and realised that he'd never be able to afford to shop in a place like this.

He was back in the house in Everton Valley before they arrived home and had a pot of tea waiting for them on their return.

'Oh, Jacob, how thoughtful of you! We've been really busy this afternoon,' Julia thanked him.

'He never does that at home!' Ella remarked tartly, taking off her hat.

'That's because Mam is always there to do it,' Cathie reminded her, not wanting his effort to be belittled in any way.

Ella pulled a face and shrugged. 'Well, I'm going to have a bath and then get ready to go out.'

'I'll make you a sandwich. I don't suppose you had anything at lunchtime?' Cathie offered.

'I did. I went to the canteen as I knew you were all eating later,' Ella informed her before she disappeared in the direction of Cathie's bedroom.

'Right then, when we've had this tea, Cathie and I will make a start on supper. Jacob, you just sit here and have a rest and read the newspaper. I bought a copy of the *Echo*. It's the late edition so it will have all the football results – that's if you are interested?' Julia handed him the paper.

'I'm not really, Julia, but I'll be fascinated to read what's been going on in this busy city.'

Julia laughed. 'Thank goodness for someone who doesn't view football as something of a religion – there're too many in this city who do that,' she informed him as she and Cathie went to prepare the meal.

Jacob flicked through the paper, taking more interest in the shipping report than the sports pages. He'd got washed and changed earlier, knowing the girls would need the use of the bathroom when they got home. It was a novelty for him to have hot running water so shaving had been something of a treat.

He thought Ella looked very smart as she came into the living room to say goodbye and told him that she'd not be late back.

'Do Cathie and Julia tell you to be in by a specific time?' he queried.

'No. Just as long as it's not after midnight,' she replied, thinking he was rather old-fashioned in his outlook, which she put down to him living in a small place like Ramsey.

Both Cathie and Julia had changed too and he thought that Julia looked particularly attractive in a pale blue cotton dress printed with darker blue flowers. It suited her and made her look younger,

315

he thought.

'I thought you'd like a drink before supper, so I bought some on the way home for you and David,' Julia said, handing him a glass of pale ale.

'That was very thoughtful of you,' he replied, taking the glass from her.

'David doesn't drink a great deal but he does sometimes like a glass with a meal,' Cathie informed him.

Jacob nodded approvingly. At least that was one vice David Kendal didn't seem to have: a fondness for drink.

David arrived a few minutes before half past seven looking a little apprehensive and bearing a box of chocolates, which he duly handed to Julia as she was officially the hostess.

'David, this is my brother Jacob,' Cathie introduced him.

Jacob got to his feet and shook the hand that was extended to him. His first impression was of a rather shy young man with reddish-gold hair who was a little shorter than he was but dressed in a suit that was far more expensive and fashionable than his clothes were. 'I'm pleased to meet you, David. Cathie's told us a lot about you.'

David smiled, thinking he was quite different in looks to Cathie but he seemed amiable enough. 'And I'm pleased to meet you too, Jacob. It's not often I get to talk to someone who spends most of his life at sea – apart from my uncle of course. Captain Fleetwood-Hayes.'

Jacob nodded. 'Well, you can't really compare me or my experiences with those of the captain of an ocean-going ship.'

Now that the introductions had been made Julia thought it best if they all went into the dining room and ushered the two young men in while she and Cathie went to put out the meal. 'Give them a bit of time to get to know each other – alone,' she said to Cathie.

'Oh, I hope they get on well,' Cathie replied, looking a little anxious.

'Stop worrying and take that joint of cooked ham out of the food press,' Julia instructed as she busied herself with the vegetables.

Jacob toyed with his napkin, something they didn't use at home, and wondered how to begin. He certainly didn't want to sound as if he was interrogating David. 'So, you and Cathie have been courting for a while?'

David nodded. 'We have and I can assure you and your parents that I love her and will take care of her. I can offer her a good life, Jacob. We've sort of discussed it and if she doesn't want to, she'll not have to work after we're married. In fact she'll want for nothing, I'll make sure of that.'

Jacob grinned. He didn't really think there was much more to say. David seemed very decent and clearly cared for his sister. He wouldn't prolong the agony any more. 'You've answered everything that I was asked to find out. I'd have preferred it had Mam come herself but obviously she couldn't spare the time, so I got the job.'

David smiled back. 'It's only right that she knows what kind of a person Cathie's promised to become engaged to.'

Jacob became serious. 'I'm sure Mam and Da will be happy about it, but Cathie has mentioned that she doesn't think your father approves.'

David sat up straighter and a determined look crossed his face. 'He doesn't but you can leave my father to me, Jacob. I don't need his permission; he barely knows Cathie and refuses to try to *get* to know her. He seems determined to persist in this attitude but that's his loss...' He shrugged.

'I see. But won't you have to live with him after you're married?'

'No. I always intended to have my own home one day,' David replied firmly. 'What about you, Jacob? Is there a girl in your life?' he asked to move off the subject of his father.

'Not yet, but maybe one day,' Jacob replied thoughtfully.

'You're fortunate to be able to follow your chosen career. I work with my father but I suppose Cathie has told you that it's not what I want? I'd like a career at sea.'

'She has but I didn't exactly "choose" it, David, and it's a hard life – it can be very dangerous. The sea's a treacherous taskmistress – but I suppose your uncle has told you that?'

'He has. He's been through some terrible storms in his time and he fought at Jutland in the Great War which I'm assured was an horrific experience. He was fortunate to come through it alive and un-injured.'

'And it hasn't put you off?' Jacob queried, thinking of some of the terrible conditions he too had experienced.

'Not at all.' David paused. 'I haven't mentioned it to Cathie yet, but I'm actually thinking of joining the Royal Naval Reserve. It means I won't need to give up my job – yet. I look on it as my duty; things are not looking very good on the other side of the Channel.'

Jacob's expression became serious. 'Do you think there could be another war? I've heard people talking about it. Some are saying it's inevitable.'

'I hope there won't be but if Herr Hitler keeps up his aggression and goes on increasing his forces, who knows? He's already marched his army into the Rhineland in defiance of all the treaties made at the end of the last war.'

Jacob nodded. He tried to keep abreast of events taking place beyond the island and had already decided that should there be another war he'd join the Royal Navy. 'And things don't look good in Spain either,' he mused aloud.

'This sounds like a very serious and gloomy conversation,' Julia announced as she and Cathie brought in the supper.

'We were just discussing what's going on in Europe,' Jacob replied.

'But now we'll change the subject,' David put in. 'What time is your ferry tomorrow, Jacob?'

'One o'clock, so I'll have some time to spend with Cathie and hopefully Ella before I have to go back.'

'If we get up early enough we could go for a stroll in Stanley Park. They've a boating lake and some magnificent glasshouses full of exotic plants,' Julia suggested.

'I doubt you'll get Ella up that early on a Sunday,' Cathie commented. 'But maybe we'll find out a bit more about her latest boyfriend – this

Frank Miller – that you can relay back to Mam, Jacob,' she added.

Her brother nodded. 'That'd make a nice change for me. We've a beautiful park in Ramsey – no glasshouses though – but I seldom get the chance to go there,' Jacob informed them, looking hopefully at Julia.

'That's settled then. We'll leave Ella to her own devices if she doesn't want to join us,' Julia said firmly.

Cathie turned to David. 'Would you like to come too? We could meet you there,' she asked, thinking that it was further for him to travel from Aintree than it was for them.

'I'd like that, Cathie. It seems a shame for Jacob not to get every bit of enjoyment out of his brief visit.'

Cathie smiled at him. 'And you do seem to be getting on well.'

'Oh, we are indeed, Cathie,' Jacob replied, thinking he'd be quite happy to go home and put his parents' minds at ease about David Kendal and Cathie. He'd decided he liked David Kendal. He wasn't too sure what he would tell them about Ella though, but, as Julia had said, Ella was very young so perhaps they should make allowances for her.

'Then we'll meet you at the gates at ten o'clock,' Cathie said happily, relieved that David and her brother seemed to really like each other.

It was a warm, sunny morning and David was waiting for them as they alighted from the tram. As Cathie had suspected Ella had declined to accompany them, saying she was tired and was looking forward to a lie-in, but that she would be up and ready to go with them to the Pier Head when Jacob left for the ferry home.

'I brought a bag of crusts to feed the ducks,' Julia informed Jacob as he fell into step beside her.

'Good idea!' he remarked, thinking how he'd been looking forward to this morning's outing.

'There are quite a few people taking advantage of the weather,' Cathie mused as they strolled towards the lake where two or three boats were moving slowly over the water.

'Should we hire a boat, Cathie? Would you enjoy that?' David suggested, thinking that not only did he want to spend a few moments alone with her but he was sure that Jacob would like time with Julia for they'd seemed to have become very friendly the previous evening.

Cathie laughed. 'As long as you don't catch a crab and soak us both to the skin!'

'I used to row for my school so I'm not that bad!' David protested with mock indignation as he took her arm and they walked away in the direction of the hire hut.

'They're very happy together and she deserves someone as caring as David,' Julia remarked, breaking a crust of bread into crumbs and scattering them on the water at the edge of the lake, immediately attracting a crowd of ducks, geese and a couple of swans.

Jacob nodded. 'I'll be able to reassure Mam that Cathie's future looks settled. I'm not sure about Ella though.'

'She'll be all right. It's only natural that your

parents worry when both Cathie and Ella are far from home.'

'What about you, Julia? Who worries about you?' Jacob asked gently.

She smiled at him. 'Oh, I'm so old and staid that I suppose people think I can take care of myself.'

'You're neither "old" nor "staid". In fact I think you are by far the nicest girl I've ever met. I really mean that.'

Julia felt herself beginning to blush. 'Thank you, Jacob.' She cast the last of the crumbs into the water and looked up at him. She had felt an instant attraction towards him the moment she met him, and that attraction had only deepened as they chatted over supper last evening. He was thoughtful, considerate and sensible and she knew, she just *knew* that she could trust her future to him. She was certain in her mind that he wouldn't let her down the way her mother had been. Well, she'd decided to grasp the nettle for it was important to her to tell him how she felt. 'I'm also the type of girl who doesn't believe in beating around the bush and ... and I like you too, Jacob. I like you a lot. I did from the first minute I met you and ... and that's something that hasn't happened before.' For a brief instant she wondered had she been too forward but it was done now and he would either say he felt the same or he'd just ... go home.

He felt a rush of pleasure course through him. 'And I like you, Julia, a great deal. I ... I'm not much of a letter writer but ... well, would you consider coming over to the island to visit one day? We could get to know each other better then.'

Julia nodded, delighted he'd suggested it. 'I've got a week's holiday next month, I could come over then. I won't impose on your parents; there must be a boarding house I can stay in?'

He smiled happily. 'There are plenty of them. I'm afraid there wouldn't be much room at our house – you can barely swing a cat in the cottage.'

Julia laughed. 'That's settled then and ... and I'll look forward to it.'

Jacob hesitantly reached for her hand. 'Will we walk around the lake and then go and meet Cathie? David's quite a good oarsman, which I didn't expect.'

Julia nodded and squeezed his hand. It was incredibly sudden but she felt absolutely sure that she'd at last met the man she would love for the rest of her life and all thoughts of a career as a buyer disappeared. It no longer seemed important.

Cathie had sat back in the small boat and had trailed her hand in the water as David expertly rowed them towards the little island in the centre of the lake. 'Julia and Jacob seem to have hit it off very well,' she mused aloud.

David smiled at her. 'They have but I'm not surprised. Your brother's very easy to get on with and so is Julia.' He paused. 'Jacob assures me that I'll come up to the mark where your parents are concerned so ... so shall we go for the ring soon?'

Cathie nodded slowly, smiling happily at him. 'Yes, I'll be so happy to marry you and yes I ... I'd like to go for the ring, David.' She felt sure now that she was doing the right thing.

'I suppose we should have some sort of celebration,' he suggested.

'Oh, but nothing elaborate,' she protested, thinking of his father's attitude towards her. She didn't want announcements in the paper or a party like Monica Fleetwood-Hayes had had.

'What if you and I and Julia and Ella went for a meal in a hotel? Say next Sunday at lunchtime? Of course Father won't attend; in fact I've no intention of even asking him.'

Cathie frowned. 'Won't your aunt be upset that we've not invited her?' she asked.

'If we ask her then we've got to ask Monica and Walter and Eileen. No, I think just the four of us. Although it is a pity that Jacob will have gone back.'

'It is but it's not possible for him to stay on, he's needed on the boat. So, just the four of us will be perfect,' Cathie agreed, thinking that when she was married she would be related to Captain and Mrs Fleetwood-Hayes and their daughters and of course Julia too. It was truly amazing how things had turned out. She looked over to where Julia and her brother were walking back towards the landing jetty. She was so glad now that Mam had sent Jacob across.

Chapter Twenty-Five

They had decided to go for the ring on Thursday lunch-time; David was waiting for her at the staff entrance of Lewis's. Although Cathie had passed the jeweller's shop many times and had sometimes gazed into the window she had never expected to walk through the doors of somewhere as grand as Boodles in Lord Street and she had felt rather overawed. They had been courteously shown to seats in a little booth and she had been quite surprised when David had asked for a tray of rings to be brought for their inspection. When the assistant had returned she had been stunned by the size and brilliance of the stones, not even daring to think how much these rings cost. She had finally chosen one that was quite plain, two diamonds set on a twist, which she thought was rather unusual. The stones were not as large or as ostentatious as some of the others for she knew she wouldn't feel comfortable wearing a very showy ring.

'If we had more time I'd take you to one of the hotels for a celebratory drink,' David remarked as they'd left the shop, the ring in its velvet covered box safe and secure in her handbag.

She didn't know exactly how much it had cost for David had accompanied the assistant to the till to pay for it and she certainly had no intention of asking him. She smiled up at him, feeling wonderfully happy. 'That would have been lovely, David, but sadly we have to get back to work. Still, we have our celebration on Sunday to look forward to,' she'd added.

Both her sister and Julia had greatly admired the ring and as they sat at a table in the dining room of the Stork Hotel on Sunday, the light from the chandelier caught the stones and made them look even more brilliant, Cathie thought. She felt very proud and so very, very happy.

'So, I suppose you'll be making some plans now,' Ella stated, thinking how Cathie seemed to have done well for herself: David Kendal obviously wasn't short of money even though he did only work in Owen Owen's, not the way he was treating them all to lunch. And that ring must have cost a pretty penny.

Cathie smiled at her and then David. 'I suppose we'd better start thinking of the future now.'

'Oh, I've been doing that for a while. But of course the wedding itself will be entirely your domain; it is your special day, Cathie,' David replied.

'And yours too!' she reminded him with a smile.

'Will you go home or will you get married here?' Ella asked bluntly, thinking of the expense should the entire family have to come across for the occasion – not to mention her parents' possible disapproval of her own lifestyle if they witnessed it. But if Cathie went home she would incur some expense herself for fares and a suitable outfit and would need time to save up. She always spent what she had left over each week, usually on make-up or clothes.

'I really haven't had time to think about it yet, Ella,' Cathie replied.

'And do you think Frank Miller will still be around for the occasion?' Julia asked, smiling at Ella with mischief in her eyes.

Ella laughed. 'I don't know. It depends on how far in the future the wedding is.' She became serious. 'I hope when you visit you're not going to go telling Mam that I'm always gadding about.'

'Of course not! You should know me better than that by now, Ella. But I am looking forward to my visit to the island,' Julia added.

Cathie smiled at her. She was delighted that Julia was going across to see Jacob and to meet her family. 'Have you had a reply from that place you wrote to?' She knew it was one of those large houses on the Mooragh Promenade, which made her think of Violet Christian's home further down the promenade. How long ago it seemed now since the day she and Jacob had pulled the young woman from the sea and taken her home to Claremont.

Julia nodded. 'Yes. This Mrs Crowe seems very friendly and helpful.'

'How long are you staying, Julia?' David asked. He was looking forward to the time when he himself would meet Cathie's family.

'Six days. Of course Jacob won't be able to take all that time off, but I will see him when he's not at sea and Mrs Crowe said in her letter that there are plenty of things I can do to occupy myself.'

'You can travel all over the island either by bus or train because you'll have seen everything of any interest in Ramsey in one day, not that I've ever been all over the island. I've never even been to Douglas,' Ella added.

'Have you never been to the far south, Ella?' David asked, thinking it strange that on an island so small she hadn't seen much of it; she hadn't even been to its capital.

'Neither of us have,' Cathie replied. 'And we've relations down there too; Mam comes originally from Port Erin, but there was never the time or the money to go visiting when we were growing up.'

He smiled at her. 'Well, the very first time we go over together I'll hire a car and I'll drive you over every mile of it, Cathie,' he promised.

Julia smiled at them both. They were so very happy, she thought. She herself was eagerly awaiting the day when she would see Jacob again. She'd written a short note to let him know when she would be arriving and he'd replied to say he'd do everything he could to meet her. If not, he would make sure his mother did.

Ella raised an eyebrow at the thought of David's suggestion. She could just hear the likes of Nora Gelling now: 'Would you just look at that! Cathie Kinrade from Collins Lane being driven around in a car! Hasn't she come up in the world?' Oh, indeed there would be talk. But she didn't envy her sister at all. She had no intention of settling down – she was enjoying herself far too much.

Cathie was both concerned and a little alarmed when, after Julia had departed for Ramsey for her holiday, Ella announced that she had yet another new boyfriend.

328

'What was the matter with that Frank Miller?' she asked her sister as they sat having a cup of tea after supper.

'He was mean – with money,' Ella stated flatly.

'I don't suppose he earned very much, Ella, and you really can't expect lads to spend everything they have on you,' she reminded her sister gently.

'He hardly spent anything, Cathie!' Ella protested. 'I paid for myself wherever we went and there was never even a hint of him buying me sweets if we went to the cinema.' She frowned. 'And he never offered to see me home in case he had to pay my fare. I can't stand meanness!'

Cathie sighed. 'So, I suppose you're now "fancy-free"?'

Ella's mood lightened. 'No, I've met someone else. He's older and he pays me the nicest compliments and he's very generous. In fact he insists on paying for everything.'

'Where did you meet this one? And just how old is he?' Cathie asked. She wasn't too sure about Ella going out with someone older.

'He's in his twenties. I'd guess he's twenty-two or -three, perhaps even a bit older.'

Cathie frowned. That was quite an age gap, she thought. 'That's a good bit older, Ella.'

Ella shrugged. 'I don't think age matters that much.'

Cathie thought about that. 'If he's that old perhaps he's looking for someone to ... settle down with,' she suggested, thinking that maybe this young man might be a good influence on her sister.

'Oh, I don't think so, Cathie. He told me he

likes enjoying himself and that there's plenty of time in the future to look at life more seriously and I agree with him,' Ella replied flippantly.

'So, where did you meet him?'

'Strangely enough, at work,' Ella replied, refilling her cup from the pot that sat on the stand on a side table.

'Work! What ... what's his name?' Cathie asked, beginning to feel uneasy.

Ella smiled at her. 'Charlie.'

Cathie drew in her breath sharply. 'Not ... not Charlie Banks from the stockroom?'

Ella nodded.

Cathie was horrified. 'Oh, Ella! He only means one thing when he talks about "enjoying himself", and he's "generous" because he expects something in return – I should know! Don't you remember? He ... he was the one I thought loved me and then he just dumped me when I said no to his ... advances!'

Ella frowned. She really had forgotten that her sister had once been out with Charlie 'I ... I'd forgotten that, Cathie and I didn't know that was why but he's different with me,' Ella persisted. She really did like Charlie Banks; he made her feel so much more grown up and she had no intention of giving him up.

'At the moment, Ella, but it won't last, believe me! He has no respect for the girls he takes out. Oh, I wish you'd not got involved with the likes of him, I really do! Give him up before you get hurt!'

'Well, *I* won't get hurt and I am "involved", Cathie, so there's an end to it. And I'm not going to start fighting with you over it. I'll go out with whom I please.'

Cathie bit her lip. All she could do was pray that Ella had sense enough not to give in to his demands or that her sister would tire of him and quickly. In that instant she really wished Julia was not away, at least she might have been able to help her persuade Ella that Charlie Banks wasn't at all trustworthy; in fact there was only one word for him: a cad.

Julia was enjoying her holiday. It made a change being away and she got on very well with Jacob's family, she thought as she and Lizzie stood in the late-afternoon sunshine at the narrow entrance to Ramsey harbour, waiting for the first of the fishing boats to arrive back. She'd been to most of the places of interest on the island, as suggested by both Mrs Crowe and Jacob's mother, and the weather had been perfect.

'It's a good job you decided to wear that hat, Julia, the sun is still strong,' Lizzie remarked as they both leaned against the wall, looking out over the glass-like surface of the sea to where the faint outline of the Scottish mountains and the coast of Cumberland could be seen in the distance.

Julia nodded, smiling at the older woman. 'I couldn't have asked for more glorious weather. Do you think there will be time for Jacob and me to go for a stroll around the lake in Mooragh Park later on?'

Lizzie nodded. She'd taken a liking to Julia, she was just as Cathie had described her and she hoped Jacob wouldn't let the distance between the island and the mainland become an obstacle to what she hoped was the beginning of a serious romance. 'Of course. It doesn't get dark until late these evenings so I'd make the most of it.'

Julia sighed. 'I just wish I could stay longer, Mrs Kinrade.'

'So do I but will you be over again ... soon, do you think? You'd be very welcome, Julia.'

Julia smiled at her. 'Oh, I hope so. I've really enjoyed myself and it is such a beautiful place!'

Lizzie laughed. 'You wouldn't think so in the depths of winter when the mist covers the hills and mountains and chills you to the bone or the rain is lashing down driven on by a howling gale and the sea comes crashing over the harbour wall!'

'I suppose it is different then,' Julia agreed as she squinted into the bright sunlight reflecting off the sea. 'Am I seeing things or is that a boat?' she asked, pointing to what looked like a dark speck on the horizon.

Lizzie shaded her eyes with a hand. 'You're right, lass. It's the first of the nickies and the rest won't be far behind.'

Lizzie was right for soon other boats could be seen heading for the harbour with the accompanying gulls wheeling and diving around them, their raucous, strident cries heralding the return. Julia felt a wave of joy fill her. Jacob would soon be home and after supper they would spend a pleasant evening together in the park. What would it be like to live here with him? she wondered. It was so very different to her world in Liverpool but it was a world she was sure she would happily embrace if he asked her to.

Cathie went to meet Julia off the ferry on the Sunday and she thought that her friend looked well, and content too. The sun had bleached Julia's hair to an even lighter shade and she had acquired a healthy glow to her skin and a dusting of freckles across the bridge of her nose.

'I thoroughly enjoyed myself, so much so that I really didn't want to come home,' Julia greeted Cathie. 'Why on earth did you ever want to come to Liverpool? It's a beautiful little island; it has everything. Gorgeous beaches, pretty glens and rivers, hills and mountains, quaint towns and villages and the people are so friendly. It's so quiet and peaceful compared to this city.'

Cathie laughed. 'It is all that, but there's very little work, Julia. Well, there wasn't for the likes of me and you have to admit that you just can't compare the shops.'

Julia linked her arm through Cathie's as they walked to the tram stop. 'Big fancy shops are not the be-all and end-all of everything! In fact I don't think I even ventured into a single shop at all.'

'What did you do?' Cathie asked.

'I did what Ella suggested. I travelled on the bus and the train. Your mother was kind enough to give me all the information I needed. I liked her, Cathie, and Meggie and Hal. I only saw your father a couple of times and he seemed a bit ... shy?'

Again Cathie laughed. 'Not exactly "shy", Julia, more reserved. Da doesn't say much. Did you meet Jack and Nancy?'

'I did. I got on very well with Nancy; she seems

a sensible girl. Your mother's obviously fond of her.'

'And what about Jacob? Did you get to see much of each other?'

Julia nodded happily. She and Jacob had spent as much time together as possible. They had grown very close in that short time, and she'd hated to leave him, something she'd told him with great sincerity on the previous evening. He'd promised to come to Liverpool as soon as he possibly could, even if it was only for a day or two, for he'd admitted he was in love with her and would miss her. 'Yes, we saw each other lots, even though he did have to go out with the boat. And he's promised to come over to see me ... us soon.'

'Then he really must like you, Julia.'

'I ... hope so. Because I know now that he's the only one for me, Cathie. I love him and I'll never love anyone else.'

Cathie nodded, delighted; she had a feeling her brother felt the same way.

'I ... I went and watched the girls at the Fish Steps, Cathie, and I can honestly see why you hated it.'

'You can understand now why Ella refused to even consider it although she found scrubbing floors almost as bad.'

'How is Ella? Is she still seeing Frank?' Julia asked as they settled themselves on a seat on the tram and the driver hauled the trolley from one end of the vehicle to the other in preparation for departure.

Cathie frowned. 'No. She said he was really mean, never paid for anything and she hated that.'

'Oh, I see. Well, I have to agree with her.'

'I did point out that he might not have had much money to spend on her but ... she's got someone new.'

Julia laughed. 'That didn't take long! She certainly doesn't waste much time, but then she *is* a pretty girl.'

Cathie sighed heavily.

'You don't look very happy?' Julia wondered aloud.

'I'm not and neither will you be. She ... she's seeing Charlie Banks.'

Julia's eyes widened in surprise. 'Charlie Banks! From ... from Lewis's? The same Charlie Banks who...? But he's years older than her!'

Cathie nodded. 'I know. I tried to warn her, I asked her to give him up, but she wouldn't listen. Oh, I wished you'd been there to back me up.'

'And has she been out with him since...?' Julia was shocked at Ella's callousness towards her sister. Ella must have known how heartbroken Cathie had been over the way Charlie had treated her but maybe she'd forgotten that fact.

'She has. Oh, Julia, I just hope she'll tire of him soon, the way she seems to have done with every other lad she's been out with.'

Julia nodded her assent. Ella's flighty nature might prove to be an asset in this instance.

'I worry about her, Julia, I really do. I'm not going to mention to David that Ella has yet *another* new boyfriend. I dread to imagine what he'll think of us.'

'It's no reflection on you, Cathie, you mustn't think like that. Having met the rest of your

335

family, I am beginning to wonder if Ella really is the black sheep.'

'God knows what will become of her, Julia. I'm starting to feel it might be best if she goes home.'

'And how on earth will you make her do that, Cathie? She'd refuse point blank and if you wrote and explained everything to your parents, well...'

'I know. Da would be furious and Mam ... Mam would be very upset,' Cathie replied gloomily.

'She would. She's a very hard-working, caring and good-living woman, Cathie. Ella wouldn't make life easy for any of them if she went back. And what kind of a job would she get?'

'Then all we can do is hope she behaves herself and meets someone more ... suitable.'

Julia stared out of the window at the rows and rows of back-to-back, dilapidated old terraced houses that ran off Scotland Road. She felt upset that Cathie should have to bear the responsibility and worry of her increasingly wayward sister. Maybe when Jacob came over next he might be able to talk some sense into Ella. Try to make her understand that if she carried on in this way she would get a reputation and then no decent lad would want to marry her. Ella's behaviour would affect them all to some degree – she'd have to do everything in her power to make the girl see sense and she felt certain she would have Jacob's support in this.

Cathie sighed, sensing this news had affected Julia. 'It wasn't exactly the homecoming you were expecting, was it?'

Julia smiled. 'No, but I'm sure we'll cope. Now, tell me what's been happening. Have you and

David made any plans?' she asked to change the subject and Cathie informed her that Mrs Fleetwood-Hayes had congratulated her when she'd called into the store during the week Julia had been away.

'At least she was happy about our engagement. She admired the ring,' Cathie informed her.

'Did she mention Mr Kendal?' Julia enquired.

Cathie shook her head. 'I think she was being diplomatic.'

'She probably was,' Julia replied firmly. 'Well, I have to say I will be glad to get home and have a cup of tea. The stuff on the ferry tasted rather ... odd. I suppose you do get something decent in first class though.'

Cathie laughed. 'I don't think we'll ever get to find out, Julia,' she replied, thankful that her friend was back.

Chapter Twenty-Six

To Julia's great disappointment – and Cathie's too – Jacob wasn't able to visit them until the beginning of December. During the late summer and autumn months, he, with his father and brother and many other fishermen from Ramsey and Peel, had sailed to the increasingly tempestuous waters off the coast of Scotland, for that year the shoals of herrings had been more sizeable than usual. It was exhausting work – each time they hauled in their catch they had to either make for a port on the mainland to sell it, or sail home and then return yet again to the waters off the Mull of Galloway. But it was an opportunity that couldn't be passed up.

'The weather up there must have been awful. I hate to think of him out in the rain, wind and the cold,' Julia had confided anxiously.

'So do I, but they've done it for years, back as far as my great-grandfather's day. And he *is* coming across next week. If the crossing's rough at least it won't bother him,' Cathie replied. 'Do you want to go to meet him on your own? I don't want to be playing gooseberry.' She smiled. She knew how much Julia was looking forward to Jacob's visit and so was she. It was a bright spot in their increasingly tense household. Despite Julia having warned Ella about Charlie Banks her sister hadn't tired of him – in fact she seemed to be as besotted as Cathie herself had once been. Ella had been seeing him for months and the relationship between herself and Ella was now definitely strained. Cathie had become increasingly angry and resentful at the situation, feeling that Charlie Banks must find the whole thing amusing – he had to be fully aware that she was Ella's sister, even if Ella hadn't chosen to tell him so. 'Kinrade' was not a common name in the city and they resembled each other closely. She wondered if he derived some kind of perverse enjoyment from the fact that he had her sister so mesmerised.

'If you don't mind, Cathie, I'd like to go alone,' Julia replied. 'It's ages since I've seen him. If it's all right with you, I'll tell him about Ella and ... *him* before we get home.'

Cathie nodded. 'I don't want to ruin his visit, Julia, but I ... I do feel he should know about that, and about how things are between Ella and me because of it.'

'Of course he should. It's not right that you have to carry the responsibility for Ella's behaviour alone. He's bound to notice the coolness between you. It is a shame that he can't stay until Christmas though,' she added.

'I know but it can't be helped. Ella and I might not be on speaking terms at all by then. She's not going to take kindly to him lecturing her and she'll blame me. She always does.'

Julia had sighed. 'I hope not. It's for her own good.'

'I doubt she'll see it like that. I know she thinks that because I'm engaged to David and we're planning a spring wedding I should concentrate on that and keep my nose out of her affairs.'

Julia hadn't replied but she had prayed that the relationship between Ella and Charlie Banks hadn't developed into just that – an 'affair'. Ella was only sixteen. Oh, how silly and stubborn the girl was!

She was really looking forward to seeing Jacob again, she thought as she stood shivering in the bitingly cold wind that was sweeping across the Pier Head that Sunday afternoon. It was high tide and the waters of the river were the colour of steel and the waves, driven by the wind, crashed against the Landing Stage sending plumes of cold spray high into the air. She dreaded to think of what the crossing would have been like out in the open sea, even though Cathie had assured her that it wouldn't worry Jacob, and the ferry was indeed late.

At last she saw him amongst the weary and grey-faced passengers who were disembarking with obvious and profound relief. His shoulders were hunched against the wind and his cap pulled well down over his forehead as he made his way towards her. She hastened the last few steps and, heedless of convention, flung her arms around him. 'Oh, I'm so glad to see you! Are you all right? The weather is awful! Was it very bad?'

He hugged her tightly, thinking that even with the wind blowing her hair across her face she looked incredibly beautiful. 'I can't say I'm sorry to be off that boat, Julia, love, although I've been through much worse. Mind you, I did feel so sorry for the other folk. Most were sick, others were frightened at being thrown around so much and some – I think they were remembering the *Ellan Vannin* – were even terrified that we wouldn't make Liverpool at all. But we're all here safe and sound.' He kissed her on the forehead, thinking how much he was looking forward to spending some time with her. He'd missed her so much.

'Thank God! Now, let's get home before it starts to sleet or even snow!' Julia urged as he took her arm and they hurried towards the line of waiting trams.

'The strength of the wind should keep it at bay,' he assured her.

'Well, it won't be much warmer on here,' she added as they boarded the tram, 'but at least we'll be out of the weather.'

When they'd paid the fare and were settled Julia glanced out of the window at the already darkening streets and wondered how to broach the subject of Ella.

'I suppose you've read in the newspapers about the King and this American woman?' Jacob asked, for he could sense there was something she was anxious about and presumed it must be the shocking news which seemed to be the main topic of conversation. It was a cause of concern and anxiety everywhere, causing unprecedented friction between the King, the Prime Minister Mr Baldwin and his ministers, and of course the Church – to say nothing of the ordinary citizens of the entire Empire, the Isle of Man included. Although the island was not part of the United Kingdom of Great Britain Edward VIII was their king since they were still part of the Empire.

Julia nodded. 'This Mrs Simpson? It really is a ... *disgrace*, Jacob. I mean, even though he's been having an affair with her – which is shocking enough – why would he want to marry her at all? She's been divorced once and in the process of getting divorced again. What's wrong with the woman that she can't stay married, or even faithful for that matter?'

Jacob frowned; he agreed entirely. Marriage meant for life but obviously not to the scandalous Mrs Simpson. He didn't want to add to Julia's worries by saying that with war in Spain, the increasing aggression of Germany and Italy and even rioting with fascists in the East End of London, now was not a good time for the King to cause a political crisis throughout the Empire. And

341

for the life of him he couldn't see what someone as dashing, charismatic and wealthy as King Edward saw in Wallis Simpson. He thought she was far from attractive: she was plain and thin to the point of gauntness, although she did have a certain brash style, he'd give her that. 'I suppose she's just the type of woman who can't settle down, although I read that she declares she loves him. I've also read that it's a crown she really wants. Oh, I suppose they'll have to sort it out sooner or later.'

Julia nodded her agreement. 'Mrs Simpson isn't the only one who doesn't seem to be able to settle down or stop causing trouble, Jacob,' she said quietly, glancing around. The tram was far from crowded for few people had ventured out on that cold, miserable December afternoon.

He looked at her intently. 'Ella?'

'Yes.' She proceeded to tell him of Ella's involvement with Charlie Banks and of how he'd treated Cathie. She went on to leave him in no doubt about what type of person she considered Charlie Banks to be and the fact that he was much older and more experienced than Ella. 'Both Cathie and I are really worried about her, Jacob, and of course it's all far from pleasant for Cathie. I really think it's taking some of the joy out of her wedding plans and that's just not right.'

Jacob looked grim; he'd known little about all this. 'I think it's about time someone gave Ella a good talking-to, before she manages to ruin her life and upset everyone else's into the bargain.'

'I know but neither Cathie nor I want it to spoil your visit. Oh, I've been looking forward to it so much for it seems so long since I saw you last.'

He smiled at her and took her hand and squeezed it. 'It *is* a long time and I've missed you. I've no intention of letting Ella spoil things, either for us or for Cathie and her wedding plans. Does David know any of this?'

Julia shook her head. 'No. At least I don't think so.'

'Well, there'll be no screaming arguments or tantrums – just a few home truths and hard facts that Ella will just have to face,' he promised.

Julia felt relieved; she'd been right to hope that he would take measures to resolve what was becoming a very unpleasant and unsettling situation.

It wasn't until the following evening that Jacob found an opportunity to speak to his younger sister alone. Julia and Cathie were in the kitchen preparing the supper and Ella had brought him a glass of beer as he sat in the sitting room reading a newspaper, which was full of the ever-deepening constitutional crisis. He laid it aside as Ella sat down opposite him.

'It's a scandal, nothing less. A woman like her with no shred of ... decency or shame thinking she can carry on like that and then become queen by *marrying* our king,' Ella remarked, having noticed the headlines.

'Isn't that rather like a pot calling the kettle black, Ella?' Jacob replied seriously.

Ella frowned. 'What's that supposed to mean?'

'Granted the situation is hardly the same but, well, the way you are carrying on is getting out of hand. It's not how you were brought up and you don't seem to be giving much thought to either your own reputation or Cathie's position by insisting on continuing this "romance" with someone who is too old for you and totally unsuitable into the bargain, from what I've heard.'

Ella's cheeks flushed with anger. 'So, both Cathie and Julia have been telling tales about Charlie and making him out to be something he's not. Yes, he is older than me but he ... he's not as bad as they think he is and I really like him.'

'They are both worried about you.'

'Well, they needn't be! I can look after myself. I've no intention of giving Charlie up just because *they* think I should!' Ella retorted defiantly.

'Then you're a fool, Ella, if you can't see what kind of man he is! He's only interested in one thing and it's not leading you up the aisle and promising to love and cherish you forever or provide a home for you. You *are* behaving yourself?' he asked pointedly.

'Oh, for heaven's sake, Jacob! Of course I am!' Ella cried angrily, her cheeks burning now. He was treating her like a silly child and she resented it deeply but she couldn't hide the sudden flash of guilt that momentarily crossed her face.

Jacob saw it and his resolve deepened; things had obviously gone much further than he'd anticipated. He hadn't wanted it to come to this but he now knew he was going to have to be very hard on her. 'Stop lying, Ella! You forget I know you too well. You are a stupid little fool to forget everything Mam tried to instil in you and let him ... use you!'

'He isn't *using* me!' she shot back, a little too vehemently.

'Really? Well, it's got to stop! So, I'm going to

344

ask you for the last time to think not only of yourself and your future but also of Cathie and your family's reputation. Give him up, Ella, *now* – before he totally ruins your life.'

Ella pursed her lips tightly together and shook her head. She wasn't going to be browbeaten – doubtless her sister and Julia had put him up to it. It was her life and they weren't going to tell her how to live it.

Frowning, Jacob got to his feet, thrusting his clenched fists deep into the pockets of his trousers. 'Then there's nothing else for it Ella, you'll have to go home.'

She jumped to her feet, anger and resentment flooding through her, her dark eyes full of determination as she faced her brother. 'No! I won't go! I won't and you can't make me, Jacob Kinrade!' she cried.

Jacob shook his head. 'No, *I* can't make you Ella, but Da can and he will when I tell him what's been going on. He'll come across to fetch you and as you're only sixteen there is absolutely nothing you can do about it. He'll take you back home.'

Ella was shaking with anger. 'Then ... I ... I'll just run away!'

'Where to, for God's sake? We live on an island, Ella, and there's only one way off it. No, he'll take you back to Ramsey, back to some ... supervision and no doubt back to scrubbing floors or gutting fish. Is that what you really want? Is this Charlie Banks worth all that?'

Ella sat down suddenly. She hadn't expected this but she knew everything he said about the island was true. If she were dragged off home in disgrace she doubted she'd get over the doorstep to go out to enjoy herself for a very long time and the thought of having to return to such menial, poorly paid jobs was utterly abhorrent. How humiliating it would all be. Was Charlie worth all that? 'You ... you wouldn't do that to me, Jacob?' she pleaded.

'I'm sorry but I would, Ella. You're letting this Charlie Banks make a fool of both you and Cathie. And you seem to be letting him take advantage of your age and inexperience with no thought at all for your feelings or your self-respect. I can't let it go on; I won't let him ruin your future, Ella. You're my sister and I care what happens to you – even if you don't. The choice is entirely yours: give him up or go home in disgrace.'

Ella's anger had drained away and she began to cry quietly. She knew she had no choice, she was beaten, but in her heart of hearts she also knew that what he said was true. She'd been a fool to give in to Charlie and sometimes lately she'd even begun to suspect that he really didn't mean it when he said he loved her and that he'd stand by her. She knew he'd had a string of girls in the past even though he swore none of them could compare with her, and if she was utterly truthful she resented that fact. She had begun to be perturbed, even disturbed by it. She didn't want to settle down and get married, not for some time, but she felt that she couldn't really trust everything Charlie said and the doubts had begun to niggle away at her, even though she'd tried to ignore them. She liked him a great deal, sometimes she thought she really did love him, especially when she lay in his arms afterwards... But she hadn't really thought about what lay in the future, she'd been enjoying life too much. Now, though ... now she could see all the fun, the freedom and the joy of life disappearing and probably for a long time to come if she didn't give him up. Reluctantly she made her decision. No, he wasn't worth the kind of life she would have to endure if she went home.

Slowly she nodded. 'All right, Jacob. I ... I'll tell him it's all over between us when I see him tomorrow,' she agreed quietly.

Jacob felt sorry for her but he was also very relieved. She'd get over it; she was still very young and he hoped that she would find someone more suitable who would truly love and respect her, just as Cathie had done. He went and put his arm around her shoulders. 'You won't regret it, Ella, believe me. I know you don't think so right now but you will in time. You have a good life here, a nice home, a job you enjoy with money to spend on yourself, friends, and you deserve someone better. You'll meet him soon.'

She managed a weak smile as she nodded. Again he was right; she'd have none of those things if she had to go home.

'So, now that we've got that ... unpleasantness over, can things all get back to normal? No more friction between you and Cathie?'

She nodded again, although she wouldn't forget the part her sister had played in this matter, she thought bitterly. Cathie always seemed to come off best and it rankled.

Jacob smiled down at her. 'And I can enjoy the rest of my visit? For I'll be honest with you, Ella, I hadn't been looking forward to that … discussion.'

She knew he meant it for he'd always been considerate of other people's feelings. 'Julia's very lucky, Jacob,' she said a little wistfully.

'No, I'm the lucky one, Ella. I never thought I'd meet someone like her.'

All thoughts of Charlie Banks momentarily forgotten, Ella looked at him quizzically. 'Will you ask her to marry you? After all, neither of you are getting any younger.'

Jacob laughed. 'We're not in our dotage yet, but you'll have to wait and see, Ella!' he replied, although he had every intention of doing just that before he returned home.

True to her word Ella had prepared what she would say to Charlie when she met him next evening but she wasn't looking forward to it and still felt resentful about having to give him up. They were supposed to be going to the cinema but she didn't intend to sit through the whole evening before dropping her bombshell and she had no idea how he would react, so it was best to just get it over and done with, she thought grimly.

Before they reached the building she stopped and stepped into a shop doorway.

'What's the matter, Ella?' he asked, puzzled by this move.

She took a deep breath. 'I've got something to say to you, Charlie, and I think it's best I say it now.'

He frowned. 'What? What's so important that it can't wait until later? We'll miss the beginning.'

Ella felt she couldn't look him squarely in the

eye. 'I ... I've decided that I don't want to see you any more in future. It ... it's over between us, Charlie. I really mean it.'

He was very taken aback. 'In God's name, why? What's brought this on, Ella? Why this sudden decision?' He began to get annoyed. 'I thought you loved me? You swore you did often enough!'

She shook her head. Oh, this wasn't easy. 'I only thought I loved you. I ... I've changed my mind. I ... I know now that I ... don't.'

His eyes narrowed and he tried to hide his feelings. 'Have you taken up with someone else?'

'No! No, I haven't!' Ella replied determinedly. 'I'm not the kind of girl who would two-time you, you should know that, Charlie!'

He stared hard at her. 'Should I?' he snapped. Then he began to nod slowly. 'Oh, I see now. This is all to do with your sister.'

'No, it's not! It's my decision. I don't want to see you again. I'm sorry.'

He was certain she was lying. Oh, she'd been easy enough to seduce for in a lot of ways she was very naïve and trusting but he didn't believe this was her decision. Ella liked enjoying herself; someone had put her up to this, most likely Cathie or Julia Vickers or both of them. He shrugged nonchalantly although he felt angry, bitter and humiliated. 'I don't believe you're sorry at all, Ella. You couldn't care less; all you're interested in is yourself and having a good time. But suit yourself. There're plenty more girls like you around! Easy! Cheap! Because that's what you are, Ella Kinrade!'

She watched him stride away, her cheeks burning with shame and tears stinging her eyes. She hadn't expected that! He hadn't even *tried* to make her change her mind, hadn't pleaded with her or said he loved her, just ... walked away. And how could he have called her such things – 'cheap' and 'easy'. So Cathie and Julia were right, she thought miserably as she stepped into the street and prepared to make her way home. It didn't make her feel any better though.

Chapter Twenty-Seven

1937

Last Christmas hadn't been very festive at all, Cathie thought as she pulled the curtains across the windows in the sitting room to shut out the sound of the February gale hurling hail against the panes of glass. The storm, which had started during last night, was at last showing signs of abating but they'd all been cold and wet when they'd arrived home from work. She shivered for although the fire was banked high the room still felt chilly.

The day after Jacob had returned home the whole country had been greatly shocked by the abdication of King Edward. No one had expected such a drastic conclusion to the crisis and everyone had been stunned, for no monarch had abdicated for centuries. She had felt close to tears when on that Friday evening they'd heard his speech to the nation and the world on the wireless.

She could still recall his sad and weary tone as he'd announced: 'I have found it impossible to carry the heavy burden of responsibility and to discharge my duties as king as I would wish to do without the help and support of the woman I love... God bless you all. God save the King.' The following day he'd left the country as everyone tried to come to terms with the fact that they suddenly now had a new King and Queen, George VI and his wife Elizabeth, the former Duke and Duchess of York.

She poked the fire vigorously, remembering how no one had really had the heart to put much effort into making the Christmas of 1936 very festive and jolly. There had been no lavish party given by Mrs Fleetwood-Hayes, for the Captain had been away, although David and his father had been invited for a meal as usual. Oh, she and Julia had put up the tree and the decorations and they'd bought and wrapped the gifts and prepared the food, but Julia was missing Jacob, and worrying about him too, and Ella was still subdued after ending her romance with Charlie Banks. So far she hadn't found anyone else although she did go out with her friends from work much more. Cathie herself seemed to have been swamped by plans for her wedding; it was to be in early May, which, as she'd confided to David, was a better time than either March or April to make the crossing to the island, for she had decided to go home to be married.

She sat back on her heels and stared into the leaping flames. There was still the unpleasant fact that David's father would not be attending the

351

ceremony but David had assured her he wasn't going to let that upset either of them or their plans. She sighed; it seemed doubly difficult to organise the ceremony and the small reception from a distance, but she, Julia and Ella had agreed that they would at least get their dresses here in Liverpool, plus a matching bridesmaid's dress for Meggie. Now she was faced with deciding on the guest list, which seemed to be growing for David had informed her that his uncle would be home and that both he and his aunt and their daughters, plus Monica Fleetwood-Hayes's fiancé, were all expecting to make the journey to the island to support him, seeing as his father wouldn't be there.

'Have you not made a start on that list yet?' Julia asked as she came into the room, a magazine in one hand and a cup of tea in the other.

Cathie got to her feet. 'I was just about to. I was also thinking that it's harder to organise things from over here.'

Julia nodded her agreement. 'I saw something in this magazine that I think would be nice for our headdresses, you having said you don't want us to wear hats.'

Cathie smiled at her. 'Ramsey would never get over it. Cathie Kinrade and her sisters all sporting picture hats; that in addition to the presence of Captain and Mrs Fleetwood-Hayes and their elegant daughters!'

Julia laughed. 'We'll still cause something of a stir, I'm sure.'

'I never intended it all to be so ... fancy, Julia. I just wanted something quiet but ... stylish.'

'I know,' Julia replied, leafing through the magazine to find the page displaying the bandeau head-dresses decorated with artificial flowers that had caught her attention. She knew that when she got married Jacob certainly wouldn't want any fuss. She'd never felt so happy in her entire life as when on the night before he'd left he'd asked her to marry him. She could remember every word clearly and she smiled to herself at the memory.

They'd been sitting in this very room, side by side on the sofa. Both Cathie and Ella had tactfully gone to bed.

'Why does the time fly by so quickly when you're here, Jacob?' she'd mused for he was going back in the morning.

He'd taken her hand. 'And seem to drag when we're apart?' He'd paused. 'But I hope it won't always be like this, Julia. My life is sort of ... empty when I'm not with you. It's as if there is something missing, something vital that's not there. I ... I've not much in the way of ... material things to offer you. I haven't got what you could call a decent a job so I'll never have much money and I can't offer you a home like this ... but ... but you know I love you and want you always at my side, where I can ... cherish you for the rest of our lives. Will you ... marry me?'

She'd been ecstatically happy. 'Yes! Oh, yes, Jacob! I really don't care what kind of a job you have or what kind of a house we'll live in. I love you! That's all I care about: being with you and knowing that you love me,' she'd replied as he'd taken her in his arms.

'I'll have to save hard now, Julia, so we can't plan anything definite just yet,' he'd said when they'd at last drawn apart. She was quite prepared to wait, she'd told him, and they had a lot of decisions to make about their future, such as where they would get married and where they would live and of course all the financial aspects. It was enough to know that one day they would be together – for always.

'What do you think of these?' she asked, coming out of her reverie and passing the magazine to Cathie.

'Yes, they could look quite stylish without being too over the top. Ella, what do you think?' Cathie asked her sister, who had joined them and was sitting on the rug in front of the fire.

'I think it's very hard to think about pastel colours and light fabrics when it's as cold and miserable as this! I hate winter!' Ella held her hands out to the blaze. 'I'm only just getting warm after the soaking we got coming home,' she added.

The two older girls exchanged glances. Something beside the weather was troubling Ella, Cathie thought.

'I know, but is it just the cold or are you upset about something else, Ella?' Julia asked quietly.

Ella shrugged. 'I wouldn't say I'm "upset" but I heard today that Charlie has left Lewis's. He went two weeks ago apparently.'

'Oh,' Julia replied for the want of something better. She had in fact heard that news herself from Miss Turnbull, who was the head of Ladieswear and a close friend of Avril Edgerton. Charlie Banks hadn't been liked by the more senior ladies at Lewis's; they considered him a bit too 'fly' and not very reliable at all.

'I suppose he's found a better position?' Cathie queried, although she was quite relieved at this piece of news.

'I suppose he has but I do think that Australia is a long way to go to find it,' Ella replied bluntly.

Cathie was taken aback. 'Australia!'

'So, he's emigrating then. He must think the opportunities are better out there,' Julia remarked rather cuttingly. Maybe he'd outworn his welcome with the girls in Liverpool, she thought.

'Are his family all going too?' Cathie enquired, remembering that Charlie's father had a steady job on the railway. To move the entire family to the other side of the world would be a huge step.

Again Ella shrugged. 'I don't know, I don't think so but I don't really care. He's not a part of my life now.'

'Well, what do you think of these for our headdresses?' Julia asked, passing Ella the magazine to steer the subject away from Charlie Banks.

Ella studied the photograph and nodded. 'Yes, I think they'd be perfect, providing we can get the colours to match our dresses.'

'If not we could make them ourselves. We stock artificial flowers in all colours and they wouldn't be hard to attach to the fabric of the headband,' Julia mused aloud. 'Oh, who on earth is that at this time of night?' she finished sharply as the sound of the doorbell echoed through the hallway.

'Maybe Mr Hardcastle has forgotten his key – again,' Cathie remarked, getting to her feet.

Julia too got up. 'No, I'll go, Cathie, because if it is him I'm going to have to remind him that this is the third time in as many weeks and it's a bit annoying for us to keep having to let him in.'

When she returned Julia had a telegram in her hand. 'It's for you, Cathie,' she said, looking anxious. No one liked receiving telegrams, especially this late in the evening; people still associated them with the terrible casualties of the Great War.

Cathie also looked concerned as she ripped open the envelope, hoping everything was all right at home. She scanned the three words of the message and then gasped aloud in horror.

'Cathie! What is it? What's wrong?' Ella cried, having watched the colour drain from her sister's face.

'It ... it's from Mam. All it says is *"Girl Violet* missing",' she read aloud, tears brimming in her eyes.

Julia looked in confusion from Cathie to Ella. 'Cathie, who is this "Girl Violet"?'

Cathie shook her head in disbelief. 'It's not *who,* Julia. It ... it's the name of the boat Da and Jack and ... Jacob work on.'

Julia's hand went to her throat, remembering the recent storm. Even though she'd seen the boat a few times when she'd stayed in Ramsey the name of it hadn't registered with her but now... 'Oh, God! Jacob!'

'Cathie, is that all it says?' Ella asked. She looked shaken, tears sparkling on her dark lashes.

Cathie nodded. There was a lump in her throat and she felt she couldn't speak. Oh, her poor da and her brothers – she knew only too well how dangerous were the waters around the island, especially in the force nine gale that had been blowing since last night.

356

'What can we do? There must be *something* – *someone* who will have more information!' Julia cried. Her heart was beating like a lump of lead in her chest. She couldn't bear to think about what had happened to that boat and ... Jacob.

'It ... it might be days, Julia, before there's any news,' Cathie at last managed to reply.

Julia shook her head. 'Oh, dear Lord, no! We'll go out of our minds with worry!'

'Mam! What about Mam? How must she be feeling, Cathie? She's on her own with Meggie and Hal. Should one of us go over?' Ella reminded her stricken sister.

Lizzie would indeed be frantic, but: 'Nancy,' Cathie remembered. 'Nancy will be with her – Jack will have been out with Da.' She was trying to think clearly for she could see that both Julia and her sister were struggling with the shock. She had to do something *positive*. She was trying to recall what people in Ramsey had done in the past when disaster struck. 'The Coastguard! I'll go to the phone box and ring them. We have to try to find out more.'

'Let me go?' Julia begged.

'No, you stay with Ella. Maybe they'll know something, or can contact ... someone who can let us know.'

Julia nodded; she too was trying to be logical. 'How will they let us know, Cathie? We haven't got a phone and you can't stand in the street in this weather waiting for them to call the public phone box.'

Cathie bit her lip, knowing Julia was right. Her thoughts were racing. 'When I've spoken to them

I'll ring David. They have a phone, they can take a message and–'

'Give them David's number, Cathie, before you phone him,' Julia interrupted. 'He'll understand that it really is an emergency,' she urged as her friend ran from the room.

It was so hard to think straight, Cathie thought as she sped down the road to the phone box without a coat or jacket, heedless of the cold and the rain, but she was sure that neither David nor his father would object to her giving the Coastguard their number. This was indeed a terrible emergency. They couldn't just sit and wait for news.

Julia and Ella sat holding each other's hands for mutual comfort; both with tears of shock and grief sliding down their cheeks. Ella's mind was full of her father and brothers and her poor distraught mother. Both she and Cathie had known of instances of boats going missing in the past but they had been much younger then and those tragedies had never touched them so closely. When at last Cathie returned they both turned imploring gazes towards her.

'David is going to drive here. He insisted on coming but ... but he's going to contact the Coastguard again first,' Cathie gasped, panting from her exertions. 'When I spoke to them they didn't seem to know ... anything, or maybe they felt they couldn't give me any information ... yet. They were polite but asked me a lot of questions,' she informed them, sinking down on the sofa, shivering with cold and distress. Oh, she could depend on David so much; he always knew what to do and always considered her feelings. He'd tried to calm her, promising he would get as much information as he possibly could from them before he drove here.

Julia got to her feet a little unsteadily. 'I'll put the kettle on. Cathie, you're shivering with cold and ... and we've all had a shock.'

They all had a cup of hot sweet tea and Cathie felt that the time was dragging unbearably slowly as she watched the fingers of the clock crawl towards nine o'clock. She wished David would arrive soon; she prayed he would have something to tell them ... *anything!*

Ella sat huddled in an armchair frequently brushing away the tears on her cheeks, but Julia felt she couldn't sit still at all, so she paced the room, her hands clasped tightly together to stop them shaking, thinking back to that night her mother had died: although she tried to push away the memories, the feeling of being disconnected from reality by the shock of a disaster was very similar.

David looked cold and worried, Cathie thought as she opened the door to him, but he instantly took her in his arms and held her tightly.

'Oh, Cathie! I'm so sorry. It's terrible and I just had to come and try to help you bear it.'

'I don't know what to think, David. It's such a shock and I'm trying not to ... fear the worst but...'

He kissed her forehead gently. 'I know it must be so hard for you but I do have some news. When I first spoke to them I emphasised how desperately worried we all are. They promised to make further enquiries and ring me back. They seemed to take a while, which is why I've been so long, but it's not much that will help, I'm afraid,' he said apologetically, wishing he could tell her that everything was fine, that the *Girl Violet* had made it safely back to port.

Julia stopped her pacing as he entered. 'David! Did they know... Had they heard anything yet?'

David eased Cathie down on to the sofa and sat beside her, his arm around her shoulders. 'They were very co-operative and very concerned. They'd contacted the Manx Coastguards, who'd had a report in of a fishing boat in distress off the Calf of Man earlier in the day, then another report that the lifeboats from Port Erin and Port St Mary had been launched after seeing distress flares go up.'

'They'd be the nearest,' Cathie said quietly, trying to reassure Julia.

Julia swallowed hard, her heart beating rapidly. 'Did they... Was there...?'

David held Cathie more tightly, wishing the news was better. 'A further report stated that there was no sign of the *Girl Violet* but there was a lot of ... wreckage. The Port Erin boat picked up two survivors while the other boat searched on, but they found no others, I'm afraid.'

Cathie cried out, clinging to him. 'That boat had a crew of five, David, and none of them could swim! Did they say...?'

David hadn't known that and he shook his head. 'I'm so sorry, Cathie, they said just two had been picked up – they were found clinging to pieces of wreckage – but as yet they've released no names. They promised to make further enquiries and inform me. The weather conditions were atrocious at the time and apparently the currents around there are strong and dangerous.'

'And there are rocks ... lots of rocks,' Cathie added. 'How soon, David, before they know?' she asked, desperately thinking not only of her father and brothers but also Captain Samuel Quirk and Tom Kermeen who was younger than Jacob. How soon would they know who had survived and who ... who had been lost? The waiting wasn't over yet; the agony would go on and for some families it would for years.

'Probably they'll know by mid-morning. I said I'd wait in for the call. I won't go into work tomorrow and I'll come straight here to tell you,' David replied, wishing he had more definite news to give them but knowing that whatever the outcome there would be grieving families in Ramsey tomorrow.

'We can't all stay off,' Julia stated flatly, desperately trying to cling on to the hope that Jacob might be one of the survivors.

'I ... I don't think I could stand staying at home just ... waiting. I think I'll be able to manage better if I go to work,' Ella informed them.

Julia nodded. 'I'll go in too although I don't know how I'm going to have the patience to cope with customers who are only interested in such trivial things as ... flaming hats!'

David smiled sadly at her. 'It's very brave of you both, and sensible too.'

Cathie nodded her agreement, knowing she would have to endure the worst hours of her life waiting for David to arrive with news, but she had to remain here. At least she would have him to support her, she thought thankfully, whatever the outcome of this tragedy. But she wondered how her mam and Meggie and Hal were coping, and her sister-in-law, Nancy. She and Jack had only been married a year – poor Nancy Kinrade was too young to become a widow. Even though her mam had been married far longer and had faced the constant worry of the dangers of her husband's occupation, she knew her mother would be just as devastated and her heart went out to her family waiting on the island.

None of them had slept much but Julia and Ella, both quiet and preoccupied, had gone to work and Cathie waited, trying to fill the hours by cleaning – anything that would help to pass the time. All thoughts and plans for her wedding had been forgotten but as she vigorously polished the top of the dining table she tried to concentrate on what she could do: how she could help her mother if ... if the news David brought was the worst it could possibly be. That both her brothers and her father were... No, she told herself firmly! I won't even *think* it! She renewed her efforts until her shoulders began to ache but she prayed that when David arrived the tidings wouldn't all be bad and that he'd help her get through it.

Julia had been to see Miss Edgerton before she went down to her own department, to explain what had happened, and then she'd forced herself to concentrate on work, trying to blot out of her mind the image of Jacob struggling in the cold, raging, treacherous waters of the Irish Sea.

362

She hadn't known that Jacob couldn't swim and it had tormented her all night to think that they'd all taken their lives in their hands each time they'd set sail. Why hadn't he ever learned? she'd asked herself over and over through the long dark hours when sleep had evaded her. Surely he could have made time – they'd lived so close to the sea, it might have made the difference between life and death. She was surreptitiously dabbing at her eyes with her handkerchief when she saw her cousin Elinor approaching.

'Julia, I wondered if you would be in this morning. I heard the news. Albert Kendal phoned me last night after David had spoken to the Coastguard. Is there any more news?'

Julia shook her head. 'No, Cousin Elinor. We don't know just who has survived, but three almost definitely haven't. David's hoping to find out later this morning. Cathie's stayed at home to wait for him.'

Mrs Fleetwood-Hayes nodded sympathetically. 'It's not an easy life, Julia, being the wife or daughter of a seafarer, no matter what size the ship. I've had almost thirty years of it and I know how fond Cathie is of her family. She must be distraught, and her poor mother too.'

Julia was fighting hard to keep the tears at bay. 'She is ... and so am I. You see, Cousin Elinor, before Christmas last year Jacob asked me to marry him and I agreed. I love him.'

'Oh, Julia! Oh, my dear child, I'm so sorry. I didn't know.' She reached and took Julia's hand. 'Try to be brave, dear. It may not all be ... bad news.'

Julia struggled to speak. 'I ... I ... hope not but you see ... he ... he couldn't even swim! None of them could. So, what chance...?'

Mrs Fleetwood-Hayes nodded, looking very concerned. 'Shall I tell you something, my dear? It may help. The Captain can't swim either – just never learned – and he survived having his ship blown apart from under him at Jutland.'

Julia bit her lip; she hadn't known that. She nodded slowly. 'I ... I'll try to be brave.'

'There is always hope, Julia. Cling on to that belief; never give up hope even for a minute.'

Julia felt a little reassured by her words: if the Captain had survived the carnage of that terrible naval battle and the freezing cold waters of the North Sea then maybe, just maybe there was hope that Jacob had too. She wouldn't be able to get home quick enough after work, she thought.

Chapter Twenty-Eight

Cathie had gone to the window at least half a dozen times that morning, praying to see David walking up the path, but now it was nearing midday and she felt sick with fear and anxiety, wondering why he was so late.

When at last she heard the doorbell she flew into the hall, her heart pounding. 'Oh, David, what's happening?' she pleaded as she opened the door.

David wished with all his heart that he had only good news to tell her; she was so young to have to endure a tragedy like this. He took her in his arms. 'There is good news ... and bad, Cathie.'

Her dark eyes as she gazed up at him were filled with fear mixed with hope. 'What?'

'Jack and Jacob were the two survivors but ... but sadly Captain Quirk, Tom Kermeen and ... and your father are feared ... drowned.'

The brief spark of relief she'd felt on hearing that her brothers were safe died at his last words. Her poor da was ... dead. He'd gone from them – forever. Another life the sea had taken. She leaned against his shoulder as sobs tore through her; she'd never see him again, never hear his voice; she'd never help him out of his oilskins or pull off his sea boots. Her lovely da would never come home safely from sea again.

'Oh, Cathie, I'm so very sorry. And so very sorry that I never had the chance to meet him. But at least Jacob and Jack were saved. Try to find some comfort in that,' David tried to console her. He hated to see her so dreadfully upset.

Gently, he led her into the sitting room and eased her down on to the sofa and held her until at last she became calmer.

'Oh, poor, poor Mam!' she said at last, thinking of how devastated Lizzie must be.

'Your mother will have Nancy to comfort her and they'll both be relieved that at least your brothers have survived.'

Cathie nodded. After all the hours of waiting and hoping it wasn't all bad news, she thought. She couldn't begin to imagine what her brothers had gone through. 'Are Jacob and Jack all right?'

David nodded. 'There was an ambulance waiting in Port Erin and they took them to hospital. They were both suffering from exposure and shock, cuts and bruises, and Jack has a broken leg too.'

'And ... there was no ... sign...?'

David shook his head. 'No, I'm afraid not, Cathie darling.'

She dashed away her tears. There would not even be a grave that her poor mam could visit.

'Do you have any brandy?' David asked, thinking they would both benefit from a small tot.

She nodded. 'There's a half-bottle in the cupboard of the sideboard. Julia keeps it for medicinal purposes,' she replied, then: 'Oh, David! We'll have to get word to Julia and Ella,' remembering how worried they both were.

'One thing at a time, Cathie,' David urged, pouring two small measures into the glasses he'd also found in the cupboard.

The liquid burned her throat and she coughed.

'Sip it,' he advised gently.

As the brandy warmed her she felt a little calmer. She had to try to think clearly about just what she would do now. 'I think I'll have to go home, David. To make sure everyone is ... coping.'

He nodded. 'I think we should both go, Cathie. There must be something I can do to help and I can't let you face that journey alone.'

'Thank you, David. I ... I didn't want to go on my own.'

'I've been giving a lot of thought to things lately – our future, I mean – but this ... tragedy has made me come to a decision. You're not in any fit state just yet for us to discuss it fully, but maybe when you get home...'

'I can't think about anything at the moment, David, except relief about Jack and Jacob and ... sadness about Da.'

'You need time, Cathie, but just be assured that I've got everything in hand. There's nothing for you to be anxious about.'

'Ella and Julia?' she reminded him.

'At first I thought I'd go into the store to tell them both the news, I know Julia would be so relieved, but then ... well, it wouldn't be right for Ella to learn about your father while she is at work, Cathie.'

She could see the sense in this. 'So what will we do?'

'I know it seems very hard but I think we should wait until they both get home. I'll stay, of course; I won't leave you to face that alone.'

She sighed heavily; she was torn between the emotions of relief and grief but very thankful that she could rely on him for comfort, security and the strength to face the days ahead.

Cathie was much calmer when at last her sister and Julia arrived home. David had assured her that he'd make all the arrangements for the trip back to the island and would let her mother know.

As the two girls entered the room Julia instantly noted Cathie's red, puffy eyes and knew that there had been bad news. 'Oh, David!' she cried, stricken, looking at him desperately for information.

'Jacob is safe, Julia. He and Jack were the two survivors,' he answered and saw relief flood her eyes. He turned to Ella. 'Your father...' Sadly he shook his head.

Ella broke down. All day she'd had this horrible feeling that a terrible tragedy was about to overtake her and now it had... Her da was dead.

'Oh, Ella, I'm so sorry!' Julia cried. 'I only met him once but I liked him and ... and I know what it's like to lose a parent suddenly.' Yet as she went to comfort the girl, she couldn't help the sense of sheer relief that filled her knowing Jacob was alive.

When Julia had calmed Ella down a little she suggested that she make them all some food for she was certain that neither Cathie nor David had eaten all day. 'I know you might not feel like it but you have to eat,' she urged.

Cathie and Ella both just toyed with the meal but David at least ate well.

'Cathie feels that she should go home to see her mother and brothers, so I've agreed to make all the arrangements,' David informed her.

Julia nodded. 'I think Ella should go too but I wish we could all go.'

David regarded her seriously. 'I've told Cathie I'll go with her, so I'll accompany them both.'

Ella said nothing. She didn't feel as though she could face the family's grief and loss: it was all too much to cope with and she wasn't strong enough. But she couldn't say so. Cathie would never understand.

'I'll write to Jacob and to your mother, Cathie,' Julia promised. She was disappointed that she couldn't accompany them as well for she desperately wanted to see Jacob, but it wouldn't be fair on the poor woman if they all descended at this terrible time.

In the two days that followed Julia tried hard to bring some form of normality back into their lives. Neither Cathie or Ella had gone to work the following day but she had and the others had both returned the day after that, Ella saying that she had to do something to keep her occupied, it was awful staying at home brooding, and Julia had agreed. She had written a long letter to Jacob and one of heartfelt condolence to Lizzie. David, too, had returned to work but he had visited each evening and informed them that the ferry was booked for them for Saturday and that he had also booked accommodation for himself with Mrs Crowe, as suggested by Julia.

'I should feel stronger by then, David, more able to help Mam through all this,' Cathie had confided. She had already told him not to send a telegram to Lizzie – it would only panic her more; she'd write and let her know of their impending arrival.

On Friday evening, David came round to go over the arrangements with Cathie for their journey the next day. Ella was listening only listlessly to what he was saying – she hadn't been feeling well these last few days but it was only to be expected, she thought, after what had happened – and she jumped in shock when the doorbell rang.

Getting up from her chair, Julia went to answer the door and suddenly all their thoughts were diverted as they heard her cry out in surprised delight. Two minutes later she pulled a decidedly weary Jacob into the room.

Cathie rose and cried out in relief. 'Jacob! Oh, Jacob! We ... we were going across tomorrow!' she sobbed as she hugged him.

'I know but ... but I *had* to come, Cathie,' he replied with a sad smile. He turned to Julia and put his arm around her shoulders and kissed her. 'I *had* to see you, Julia. There was no mention of you coming over in your letter to Mam and I couldn't wait.'

Tears of pure joy were sliding down Julia's cheeks but she was smiling. 'I didn't want to put more stress on your mother by coming too, but I'm so glad to see you. I can't tell you how ... how happy I am! Oh, sit down, let me get you a drink, have you had anything to eat?' She was so delighted and relieved to see him that the questions tumbled over each other. Jacob hugged Ella and then shook hands with David, before taking off his cap and sitting down. He hadn't fully recovered physically from his ordeal and it had taken a degree of mental strength to make the crossing – his mam had begged him not to go – but he'd been determined. All he'd thought about these past few days had been Julia and how lucky both he and Jack had been.

'It was extremely brave of you to set foot on a ship again and so soon,' David said sincerely as Julia fussed over Jacob.

'I have to admit it wasn't ... easy,' Jacob admitted. He was still trying to come to terms with the loss of his father and his two shipmates in such terrible circumstances. 'A bit like getting back on a horse after you've fallen off but far worse.'

'How is Mam?' Cathie ventured.

'She's still dazed and shocked but she's ... coping. All the neighbours have rallied round and Nancy has been a Godsend to her. She stayed with Mam all the time until ... until they got the news and she's there every day to help.'

'And Jack?' Ella asked.

'He'll be in plaster for about six weeks but the leg will mend.' He smiled as Julia handed him a hastily made sandwich and a glass containing the last of the brandy. 'Mam told me to ask you not to go over just yet, Cathie. She'd sooner you both waited until the memorial service.'

Cathie bit her lip and tears again pricked her eyes as she thought of her father. There could be no funeral but at least there would be something to mark his passing and that of young Tom Kermeen and Captain Samuel Quirke.

'Will that be a problem, David?' Jacob asked.

'No. I'll cancel the tickets. Do you know if Mrs Crowe has a telephone? If so I'll phone her and explain; if not a telegram will have to suffice. I won't be cancelling, just postponing, and under the circumstances I'm sure she'll understand. When is the service to be, Jacob?'

'Most likely in a couple of weeks,' Jacob replied. The time lapse was in case by some very remote chance any bodies were washed up. They seldom were; the currents were very strong.

'How long can you stay, Jacob?' Julia asked him. She never wanted to let him out of her sight again and as she'd made him the sandwiches a plan had begun to form in her mind.

'I said I'd go back in a few days. It's hard for Jack to get around and ... and there're other things to be done.' On the journey over he had thought, with something akin to despair, about the future. He'd have to talk to Julia about it for it concerned her too.

'Well, you need a good rest now,' Julia assured him. 'Ella won't mind sharing with Cathie.'

Ella nodded her assent and David rose, feeling it was time he left.

'I'll go and let you all get some rest,' he said and Cathie went into the hall with him to show him out. 'I'll see to everything, Cathie, don't worry. Just get some rest yourself,' he advised as he kissed her goodnight.

After Cathie and Ella had gone to bed Julia urged Jacob to do the same but he shook his head.

'There's something I want to talk to you about first, Julia.'

She sat beside him and laid her head on his shoulder as he put his arm around her. 'Are you really all right? Was it ... terrifying?' she asked gently.

'I'll get over it,' he replied but she felt the shudder that ran through him. 'But ... but I'll not forget it – ever. We ... we'd battled for hours as the wind and the seas rose and we'd made it almost to the Calf. The skipper was making for Port Erin, the nearest shelter, but the currents caught us and there was nothing we could do.' He was filled again with the feelings of dread and helplessness he'd experienced when his father had yelled to him over the noise of the wind and the sea that they were drifting towards the rocks in the narrow channel that separated the tiny island from the main island's southern coast. 'Jack managed to get two of the flares off but the others were damp and it was so dark and cold … we were all soaked through and then…' Again he shuddered involuntarily as the memories flooded back. 'I looked up and saw that wall of water towering above us … I was paralysed with terror as it came crashing down. Then … then there was just confusion! I went under but I remember struggling to the surface, fighting for my breath, thrashing about and finding something to hold on to. I didn't know what it was. I didn't care! I didn't know what had happened to the boat or to the others. All I could do was just hang on but it was so cold, I was so cold, Julia. I knew I had to stay awake. I don't know how long it was before I saw the lights and heard the shouts and was hauled into the lifeboat. I didn't even know they'd pulled Jack out too until we reached port.'

Julia was clasping his hand tightly for he was trembling. She tried to imagine the sheer horror he'd experienced but it was beyond her. 'Oh, Jacob, you were so lucky.'

He nodded. 'I know and so was Jack. The others … weren't. When I think about it I can understand that both the skipper and Da were not young men, maybe they were injured and didn't have the strength, but Tom … he was younger than me.'

'Try not to think about it, Jacob. It was just … fate. No one can control the weather.'

'I try not to but it affects the future, Julia, our future. I don't know when or if I'll get a job on another boat…'

Julia pulled away from him and gently stroked a lock of hair from his forehead. 'I don't want you to work on a boat again, Jacob! I just can't bear the thought of waiting and wondering every time you go out, if ... you might not come back,' she pleaded.

He stared at her, frowning. 'But what else can I do?'

'I've been thinking that I'd like to open a guest house. That perhaps it's something we could do together? You could see to the maintenance side of things and I'd see to the guests. We could make a living out of it, I know we could! I'll give up my job but I have the rents from this house to compensate and I'll rent out this floor too if I have to. I've a little money my mother left me as well, and some savings. I don't want you risking your life ever again. I just couldn't bear it, Jacob! I just couldn't stand the thought of ... losing you!'

Jacob stared at her in astonishment. 'You ... you'd be prepared to do that for me?'

'I'd do *anything* for you! I love you, I couldn't face a future without you and I couldn't go through all the worry each time you went to sea. We'll make it work – that Mrs Crowe seems to. We'll have a good life together, Jacob.'

He gathered her in his arms unable to speak as his emotions overwhelmed him. He hadn't wanted to admit to himself that he never wanted to go back to fishing, the thought terrified him, but he'd assumed he had no choice and would just have to overcome his fear. He'd not expected that she would offer him a new way of making a living, one with no risk to his life, and one that would earn as much if not more than his share of the catch had ever yielded. He was good with his hands, he enjoyed repairing and making things, and there would be heavy tasks too that he could undertake. Thanks to her, he'd not face ending his days as his poor father had done and for that he'd be eternally grateful. She was right; they *would* have a good life together and now he could discuss their future with optimism.

Chapter Twenty-Nine

Julia had decided that after supper on Saturday evening would be a good time to divulge the plans she and Jacob had made the previous night so as to give Cathie and David some time to discuss them before Jacob had to return home.

Throughout the meal she had noted that Ella had just toyed with her food so she wasn't really surprised when the girl excused herself, saying she didn't feel very well and that she was going to have an early night.

Cathie looked concerned as her sister left the room but Julia tried to reassure her.

'I think she's taking it very hard, Cathie. She hasn't said much but she's had a tough couple of months. She'll get over it all, given time.'

'I suppose she will. I suppose we all will – in time,' Cathie replied with a sigh.

'Jacob and I stayed up quite late last night, discussing the future and making plans,' Julia began tentatively as she folded her napkin.

'Yes?' David asked curiously.

Julia smiled at him. 'Jacob and I are going to get married very quietly, after a decent interval, of course, and then we're going to open a guest house in Ramsey. That Mrs Crowe seems to do very well and I don't want Jacob risking his life at sea again. We'll run it together.'

Cathie looked at her in amazement. 'How will you afford it?'

'I have some savings as well as a little money my mother left me, the rents from the two floors above and ... I might have to rent out this floor too, so that's why we wanted to discuss everything with you. It might affect you, Cathie, and of course Ella.'

Cathie nodded slowly, trying to take all this in, and David looked pleased. It fitted in very well with everything he had planned himself, although he hadn't yet discussed his ideas with Cathie. But now seemed the right time – Julia had presented him with an opportunity he couldn't miss.

'No, I don't think it will affect us, Julia; you see I have plans too, although I intended to discuss them with Cathie before sharing them like this.' He turned to Cathie. 'You'll still want to get married at home?'

She nodded, wondering what he had in mind and why he hadn't mentioned it to her.

'And then we'll stay on the island too – permanently. It's my intention to open a small department store. A very small one compared to Lewis's or Owen Owen's. To sell ladies', men's and children's clothes and some soft furnishings: towels, bedding, maybe curtains. From what I've gleaned from both Cathie and Ella in the past there's a need for such a store in Ramsey. I'm qualified and experienced enough to undertake the ordering, the accountancy and the administration. And it will provide jobs in the town too.' He hadn't given up entirely on his desire to go to sea, despite recent events, but he'd take up sailing as a hobby, as a substitute.

There was silence as they all stared at him in complete astonishment until Cathie broke the silence.

'But, David, how can we possibly afford to do that?' she cried, thinking of the huge amount of money that would have to be invested in such an undertaking. It was a good idea, there was definitely a call for it, and she'd be happy to go home and to work beside him – she'd once secretly dreamed of a shop of her own – but the immensity of the enterprise stunned her.

David reached across the table and took her hand, smiling. 'Don't worry about that, Cathie. I, too, have money my mother left me.'

'But ... but, David, it will cost hundreds! No, not hundreds ... *thousands!*' Cathie interrupted, looking horrified. Of course she'd realised that he was quite well off by her standards – hence his father's disapproval of her – but surely he didn't have such an enormous amount at his disposal?

Jacob was staring incredulously at David, wondering if he had gone mad, but Julia was smiling.

'I know but, Cathie, I do *have* "thousands". I know I can comfortably raise the amount we'll need,' he replied quietly with no trace of pride or boastfulness in his voice.

Cathie was even more stunned. She just

couldn't take this in. 'How? Your job? You … work with your … father,' she stammered, unable to take this in.

'I do, Cathie, but my father is part *owner* of Owen Owen's and although it's not as big as Lewis's it's a very profitable business. I should know, I've spent my working life there – learning every aspect of it. I have the shares in the company my mother left me, which are considerable, and I'll have no trouble selling them. I also have an inheritance from her too which has been invested and which has increased over the years. No doubt in time I'll inherit my father's share of the business too although I hope that won't be for many years to come.'

Cathie shook her head in disbelief, unable to speak. She hadn't known all this! She'd thought his father was just a senior manager of some kind who had some family money; she'd never realised that he part-*owned* the store. Oh, no wonder Albert Kendal didn't approve of her or her background.

'You didn't know, Cathie, did you?' Julia said gently.

Cathie shook her head.

'So you never realised David didn't just *work* at Owen Owen's? Why didn't you say something to enlighten her, David?' Julia asked, thinking that perhaps she should have said something after Cousin Elinor had informed her of the fact.

David smiled ruefully. 'Maybe I should have but … I didn't want to risk losing you, Cathie. I thought if you knew, it might put you off me. Remember you once thought this "class" thing would come between us? I couldn't risk that. I'm sorry but you see we *can* afford to open a store in Ramsey and we *will*. I'm financially independent of my father,' David added firmly. 'And we will be able to employ Ella and Nancy – they both have experience – and in time Meggie and even Hal.' He turned to Jacob. 'If Jack doesn't want to go to sea again there will be work for him too and it goes without saying that your mother will want for nothing.'

Jacob nodded slowly, trying to digest the astounding fact that his future brother-in-law was in reality a wealthy man, something he was just as surprised as Cathie to learn. David Kendal seemed to have none of the supreme self-confidence, bordering on arrogance, of the few wealthy men he'd encountered. 'I'd not expect you to take on the support of the whole family, David. Julia and I will give Mam a decent home and look after her,' he said.

'Of course we will. The cottage is quaint but it hasn't got many modern amenities,' Julia added. 'That of course is if she'd be happy to live with us – she might prefer her independence,' she added.

'We'll ask her – when the time is right,' Jacob agreed.

'So you will be able to rent out this whole house, Julia,' David reminded her.

Julia nodded happily. Their futures seemed to have been resolved and very satisfactorily. She was delighted with the fact that Cathie would be living on the island too. 'I will and hopefully I'll find tenants as decent and reliable as those I already have.'

'I'd think about putting it all into the hands of an agent, Julia. After all, it won't be easy for you to keep your eye on things when you're not living here in Liverpool. I know you'll have to pay a percentage but I think it will be worth it for peace of mind,' David suggested.

Both Julia and Jacob could see the sense in this.

Cathie had remained silent during all this but she'd been thinking. Both David and Julia's plans would benefit everyone hugely but there was one thing that was troubling her: her sister. 'What about Ella? Suppose she doesn't want to go home, doesn't want to work for David? She likes her job and her life here and the freedom she enjoys; she's no responsibilities so she might refuse.'

Julia frowned, as did Jacob; neither of them had thought a great deal about how Ella would react to their plans.

'But she'd be excellent with her personality and experience!' David protested. 'She could have her own department, and earn a good wage too.'

'That would be a big step-up for her. It certainly would give her some standing with the girls she went to school with,' Julia added.

'And surely she wouldn't have to sacrifice any of her freedom?' David put in, eager as they all were to allay Cathie's doubts.

'She might well benefit from a bit less freedom until she's older and has more sense, particularly where lads are concerned,' Jacob voiced his thoughts aloud.

'Oh, Jacob, don't for heaven's sake say that to her!' Julia cried in mock horror, which lightened the mood. She smiled. 'Leave Ella to me. I'll talk to her and point out all the benefits she'll have.'

Cathie nodded. 'I think that we're all going to be very busy in the coming months, which might be the best thing for all of us.'

David smiled at her, thankful that she had expressed no real doubts at all about his venture. 'We will. When we go over next, I'll have to start to look for suitable premises and suppliers and no doubt find a solicitor and–'

'An advocate as we call them,' Jacob informed him.

'And we'll have to look for premises too,' Julia reminded him, thinking of Mrs Crowe's Edwardian villa on the Mooragh Promenade. Something like that would be perfect, close to the beach and park and with spectacular views of the sea and coastline.

Cathie sighed. 'My head is swimming with all these plans!'

David nodded; he could see she was tired and probably mentally exhausted too. She'd had a lot to come to terms with this evening. 'Then perhaps it would be a good idea if we all slept on them.'

Julia got to her feet. 'A good idea, David. Now, Cathie and I will clear away these dishes while you and Jacob go into the sitting room to talk.'

David shook his head. 'I think I'd better be going. Jacob and I can "talk" tomorrow.'

Jacob stood up. 'There'll be plenty to discuss, David, and there'll also be plenty for me to tell Mam about when I get home. Knowing that Cathie and Ella and you and David will all be coming to the island to live might help cheer her up, and I'll have a talk to Jack too,' he promised.

He would certainly be going home with much better news than he had dared to hope for on his journey across, he thought. It might help to blunt the edge of their grief and the financial anxiety about all their futures.

Next morning Julia told Cathie that she would go and have a talk to Ella, who as yet hadn't made an appearance, although it was past ten o'clock.

'I'll explain everything, tell her about her part in it all and then give her time to ... take it all in. I think it's best coming from me, Cathie, rather than you or Jacob. She's less likely to feel she's being manoeuvred into anything if I tell her.'

Cathie nodded her agreement. 'If she doesn't want to go home she'd think it's just a ploy on our part to get her to agree to go back. But don't be surprised if she refuses point blank,' she added.

'Oh, I'm sure she won't,' Julia replied confidently, leaving Jacob and Cathie in the sitting room.

Ella was actually up and dressed and was sitting at the dressing table, brushing her hair. Julia thought she looked rather pale and there were dark circles under her eyes.

'Did you sleep well? We thought we'd let you lie in,' she greeted Ella, sitting down on the bottom of the bed.

Ella turned towards her. 'I ... I didn't sleep very well at all, in fact.'

'Oh dear, but I have some news that should make you feel more cheerful.' Julia smiled at her and then outlined all the plans they had for going home and the businesses they would start and of

Ella's intended position as head of her own department in what would be Kendal's department store – the first of its kind in Ramsey. 'It's a great opportunity for you, Ella, especially at your age, to have your own department. It's your experience and personality that impressed David. I suppose like Cathie you didn't know that his father is part-owner of Owen Owen's and that David can more than afford to fund this enterprise. Just imagine how people will look up to you, Ella, especially those you went to school with. You will be the very successful and elegant Miss Fenella Kinrade, sister-in-law of the owner and – I might add – quite a catch for some young man.'

Ella stared at her blankly, which wasn't the reaction Julia had been expecting. She wondered if Cathie had been right. 'Ella? Don't you like the idea?'

'It ... it's a great idea, Julia, and I'd love to have a department of my own, but ... but I ... I can't go home!' Ella replied with a sob in her voice.

'Why not?' Julia asked, confused. What on earth was the problem if Ella agreed it was a good idea? To her consternation Ella broke down in tears. 'Oh, Ella! What's the matter? Why can't you go home? Is it because of your poor father?'

Ella's distress increased but she shook her head. 'No!' she managed to get out.

Julia stood up and put her arms around her. She'd not seen the girl as distraught as this before and if her distress was not for her father then ... what? 'Ella, please try to calm down and tell me what's wrong? I can't help you if I don't know what is upsetting you so much,' she said gently.

Ella clung to her tightly. 'Oh, Julia! I can't go home ... but I can't stay either! I don't know what to do! I never thought...! I ... I'm ... expecting a baby!'

Julia was so shocked that for a few seconds she couldn't speak. Ella was only sixteen! She was distracted for a moment by the thought that Cathie would be just as horrified by this news and would no doubt blame herself for not being harder on her sister, but then her practical side came to the fore. 'Oh, Ella, you poor thing! Are you sure?'

Ella nodded. 'I ... I've missed my "curse" for two months now but then with all the worry and grief over Da I ... forgot, until last night when I felt so ... sick and then ... then ... I remembered. Oh, what am I going to do, Julia?' she pleaded.

'Is it Charlie's?' Julia asked.

Again Ella nodded.

Julia felt fury rising in her. Typical! By now Charlie Banks was on his way to a new life on the other side of the world, leaving Ella to face this on her own with not a thought or a care about the poor girl or his child! Venomously she hoped he never reached Australia or if he did that he would find that his prospects of work had evaporated into thin air. She hoped he never had a day's luck in his miserable life again. 'Oh, Ella, this couldn't have happened at a worse time for everyone. You know you're going to have to tell Cathie and Jacob? You can't hide it from them. And then we'll have to try to think what will be ... best.'

'How can I tell them? They already think I'm a fool! A stupid, silly, good-for-nothing young girl ...

and this ... this will make it worse,' Ella sobbed. She wished she were dead. She had no future now. Charlie had gone. All the wonderful plans Cathie and David had, offering her a lifestyle and position she would indeed have enjoyed and been proud of, would come to nothing and there would be no eligible young men queuing up for her hand – not now, not ever.

'That's just not true, Ella. They both care about you. We... we'll tell them together. Come on, dry your eyes and try to calm down and we'll go through and get it over with,' Julia urged, although she wasn't looking forward to their reactions. Ella had let everyone down but most of all herself. She had no idea what would happen to the girl now.

Chapter Thirty

As Julia led Ella into the sitting room Cathie took one look at her sister and leaped to her feet. 'Ella! Julia! What's the matter? You haven't had a row, have you?'

Julia shook her head. 'No, there's been no row, Cathie, but Ella's terribly upset, as you can see.'

'She's refusing to come with us, isn't she?' Cathie stated flatly. She wasn't surprised.

Julia looked sympathetically at her friend. 'Yes, but not for the reasons you think. She's something to tell you.' She nodded at Ella to encourage her but the girl dissolved into tears again.

'Julia, what's wrong with her? What's going on?'

Jacob demanded, mystified by Ella's obvious distress.

Reluctantly Julia realised she was going to have to break the dreadful news herself. 'I think we'd all better sit down. You're not going to like this – either of you – but you *have* to know and I must say that I'm ... shocked and upset myself. She's just told me that she is ... expecting a child.'

Cathie's eyes widened in horror and her hand went to her throat. 'Oh, my God! Oh, Ella, no! You can't be!'

Anger flooded Jacob's face. 'Ella, you bloody little fool! Whose is it? That bloke Charlie's?'

Ella's sobs increased and she couldn't speak so again it was left to Julia to reply. 'Yes, it's his. The same Charlie Banks who is now on his way to a new life in Australia so there is no hope whatsoever of him marrying her – even if that had been acceptable, which it isn't. So you can see now why she doesn't want to go home,' Julia replied calmly but with a note of bitterness in her voice.

'Too right, she's *not* going home! How can she in that ... state? She's disgraced us all!' Jacob turned to his sister in fury. 'This will break Mam's heart completely, Ella! Hasn't she suffered enough having just lost Da without now ... now you proving to be a little trollop? Everything she held dear, her husband, her reputation as a responsible and caring mother, a good-living woman – all gone! This will destroy her! How could you do this, Ella? How could you do this to us *all*? I never thought I'd say this, but I'm thankful now that Da didn't live to see your disgrace!'

Cathie too had begun to cry quietly as she

thought of her mother. Jacob was right: this could prove to be the last straw for Lizzie, and if Ella went home none of them would ever be able to hold their heads up in the town again. It would tarnish Barney's memory and it wouldn't bode well for either David's business or Julia and Jacob's either. They would all be tainted with the stigma of Ella and her bastard child. And what on earth was David going to think now? She dreaded his reaction. But what was to become of her sister? She dabbed at her eyes and tried to think more clearly.

'Ella, I'm ... utterly horrified! You *have* been a stupid little fool but ... but it's done. Jacob is right; you can't go home and disgrace everyone. But we have to try to think of what will become of you now,' she said.

'You'll have to give up your job, in time, of course,' Julia said to Ella, who was still weeping quietly.

'So how will she manage?' Jacob demanded, still fuming at his sister's conduct. 'She'll have no money at all and we can't just leave her to starve.'

'And if you rent these rooms out, Julia, where will she go?' Cathie added.

Jacob stood up and began to pace the floor. 'It's all such a mess! She can't stay and she can't go home.'

'There's a Home for Fallen Women here in Liverpool, in Gambier Terrace,' Julia informed them both. 'But they wouldn't keep her after she's had the child.' She looked pityingly at Ella. 'I ... I suppose she could stay here. I couldn't see her without a roof over her head.'

'But what would she do then? How will she manage? We can't be expected to support her, we'll need every penny. Jack has no job at present so he and Nancy'll have nothing to spare and it's just not right that we expect David to help out. It's going to be hard enough for him at first to get his business up and running.'

Cathie stood up and crossed to her sister, guilt that she hadn't been stricter with Ella now adding to her emotions. It was utterly abhorrent to her that Ella was carrying Charlie Banks's child and she was furious with her but Ella was still her sister. 'Ella, we'll just have to think of something. Try to stop crying, it ... it's not good for you.'

'Why don't you go and have a lie-down, Ella, and try to calm down,' Julia suggested, fearing Cathie was right.

When Ella had left the room Jacob sat down again. 'This has really thrown our plans into chaos. You're going to have to tell David, Cathie.'

'I know and I ... I'm dreading it. His father doesn't think I'm good enough for him as it is, he's refused to come to the wedding, and now with ... this he'll be even more convinced that David is making a dreadful mistake.'

'Cathie, Albert Kendal doesn't have to know. Oh, David will be as shocked as we all are, but it won't affect how he feels about you, I'm sure of that. You can't be held responsible for what Ella's done,' Julia said firmly.

'Oh, I hope not,' Cathie replied earnestly.

'But what *are* we going to do about her?' Jacob reiterated.

Cathie shook her head. She could see no way

out of this dilemma without either her mother being badly hurt and humiliated in the society she'd been part of for so long, or Ella being left to fend for herself, utterly abandoned by everyone.

'I don't know but I'm going to talk to someone who might just be able to find an answer,' Julia stated. 'Cousin Elinor. She's the most sensible and practical woman I know.'

'Oh, Julia, what will she think of us? She might be so shocked and scandalised that—'

'She *will* be shocked, Cathie, but she might also have an answer,' Julia replied firmly.

Jacob looked doubtful. 'I'm not at all sure that airing the family's dirty linen in public is the best thing to do.'

'She *is* family, Jacob. Don't forget that she'll be Cathie's aunt and your relation too when we're married,' Julia reminded them both.

Jacob nodded. 'Then let's hope she can think of something, because for the life of me I can't.'

Julia found her cousin in the middle of writing a letter to her husband but thankfully it appeared that both the Fleetwood-Hayes girls were out. 'I'm so sorry to disturb you, but you see there is no one else I ... we can turn to for advice.'

Mrs Fleetwood-Hayes indicated that she should sit down as she put aside her half-finished letter. There was obviously something wrong and she wondered what it was. 'I can finish that later. It doesn't have to be posted to the shipping agents until tomorrow. I'll make some tea and then you can tell me what's the matter.'

Julia carefully informed her of Jacob's arrival and of all the plans that had been made for the two weddings and the two businesses that were to be set up, but when she reached the point where she had to explain Ella's predicament she hesitated.

'Everything sounds perfectly splendid, Julia, so what's the fly in the ointment?'

Julia sighed. 'It's Ella, I'm afraid.'

'Doesn't she want to go home? Is she proving difficult?'

'She can't go home because ... and this is ... delicate – it's going to shock you, Cousin Elinor – I'm afraid Ella's expecting a child.'

The older woman's eyes widened and then she frowned. 'Good God! That *is* a shock! Why, she's little more than a child herself! Who's the father?'

'Charlie Banks from Lewis's.'

'That young fellow from the stockroom? The one who treated Cathie so badly years ago?'

Julia nodded and sipped her tea, relieved that she'd got the worst part over and done with.

'Well, he'll have to marry her. He won't be the first or the last who'll have to face up to his responsibilities and do the decent thing by a girl,' Mrs Fleetwood-Hayes stated firmly.

'He's on his way to Australia so there's not much chance of that. He's emigrated,' Julia informed her curtly.

Mrs Fleetwood-Hayes frowned. 'I see. So, what will she do?'

'Cathie and Jacob are adamant she can't go home. It would utterly devastate their poor mother and destroy her reputation and that of the entire family. Ramsey is a small town.'

'And it would do your business prospects no good either,' Mrs Fleetwood-Hayes remarked succinctly.

'Yet how can we leave her to fend for herself in Liverpool? She'll be seventeen, an unmarried mother with an illegitimate child, no job, no money ... nothing. I couldn't see her without a roof over her head and I'm willing to let her stay in the house, although I did intend to rent out those rooms, but how on earth will she be able to afford to eat and heat the place in winter? How will she live? We're all at our wits' end to know what to do, Cousin Elinor!'

The older woman sighed heavily. 'She's put you in a terrible situation, Julia, to say nothing of her own future. Oh, the silly, silly girl to let a man like that ruin her life!'

'Can you think of any solution?'

'I'll have to think about it hard. At this present moment I can't see a way out. But there's one thing you must *not* let her do, Julia, and that's to become so desperate that she ends up going to one of those back-street abortionists. Those women are little more than out-and-out murderers, and they charge for it! They could end up killing her. Bad as the situation is, it's not worth risking her life. There has been enough tragedy in that family already.'

Julia was horrified; she'd not even thought about that. 'Oh, we'd never, never let her do that! It's a crime and ... and you're right, she could even die!'

'Then let me think about it. I'll try to find some way around it. I'll come to see you all tomorrow

evening, if that's convenient? I can't promise anything though.'

'Thank you. Just ... just having someone else's
advice will be a help. We've not as much experience of life as you have, I'm afraid.'

'Oh, I've plenty of that. Now, finish your tea
and then go back home and tell Cathie and her
brother that I'll do my best to think of a solution.'

As Julia left she felt a faint hope that the situation
could be resolved – just sharing the burden with
Mrs Fleetwood-Hayes seemed to help. However,
she couldn't help but wonder how David had
taken the news.

It was Jacob who opened the door to David and
from the expression on his face David could tell
something was wrong.

'Are Cathie and Julia all right?' he queried.

Jacob nodded as he took David's overcoat and
hat. 'Cathie's inside but Julia has gone to see your
Aunt Elinor. We have a problem – with Ella.'

David was perplexed but said nothing. He could
see Cathie was upset; he immediately went and sat
beside her and took her hand. 'What's wrong?' he
asked gently. They'd all been in much better spirits
the previous evening.

'Oh, David! I am so *ashamed!*'

David glanced enquiringly at Jacob.

'We are all mortified, David. Ella ... Ella's preg-
nant,' Jacob stated bluntly.

David didn't speak; he was trying to digest this
shocking news.

'So, apart from everything else, we're in a
quandary. She can't go home and disgrace us all

in the eyes of the whole community and we can't see how she can stay here and try to fend for herself and a child with no means and no job,' Jacob informed him.

David nodded, understanding now why Cathie said she was so ashamed. 'I can see the problem but, Cathie, it's not your fault. There's no reason why you should be ashamed.'

'She's my sister, David. It ... it reflects on me – on us all – and I feel guilty that I didn't supervise her more closely.'

'That's nonsense, Cathie. You did your best.'

'I just wish I'd been able to come across sooner than December, then at least I might have been able to put a stop to the affair before she ended up in this ... condition,' Jacob added.

'There's no sense in either of you blaming yourselves, that won't help anyone. Ella made her own decisions, even if they were the wrong ones,' David stated seriously.

'So that's why Julia has gone to see your aunt, to see if she can possibly think of a solution. Julia did intend to rent out these rooms but now she says she won't. We can't see Ella without some kind of a home,' Jacob informed him.

David nodded solemnly. 'Well, let's hope Aunt Elinor can think of something.'

'As far as I can see, David, there's no possibility that Ella can go home. It would ... destroy Mam and everyone else and it wouldn't be good for our businesses either,' Cathie added.

David squeezed her hand. 'Don't worry, Cathie. I'm sure that between us all we'll be able to sort something out.' His words were reassuring but like everyone else he could see it wasn't going to be easy. If Elinor Fleetwood-Hayes couldn't come up with something he didn't see what they'd do.

Chapter Thirty-One

They were all subdued and preoccupied the following day and at suppertime neither Cathie nor Ella felt like eating much: Ella because she felt too ill due to what she now realised was morning sickness, the worry of what was going to become of her and despair that such a golden future had to be sacrificed; and Cathie because of the strain of being pleasant and helpful to customers all day when she was racked with anxiety, which had resulted in a blinding headache. Julia and Jacob too were anxiously awaiting the arrival of Julia's cousin and David. They were all hoping against hope that she had come up with some feasible idea for Ella's future which would not jeopardise their own plans.

'Cathie, once you've finished eating what you can, take some aspirins, they might help. And, Ella, you really should try to eat something. I'm sure you will feel better if you do,' Julia urged.

'I couldn't, Julia. I really would be sick,' Ella replied miserably.

Julia sighed. She felt sorry for them both. 'All right then, why don't you go and sit in the other room, at least it's more comfortable in there,' she suggested.

Cathie got to her feet. 'I'll help you clear away. It might take my mind off things,' she said wearily.

'I doubt it; we're all nervous wrecks, and it's horrible!' Julia declared, giving Jacob a sympathetic look, knowing he was as tense as everyone else.

They'd done the washing up between them and joined Ella and Jacob in the sitting room. Jacob was trying to concentrate on the newspaper and Ella was hunched up in an armchair looking very young and very unhappy. Cathie leaned her aching head against the back of the sofa and closed her eyes whilst Julia, unable to sit still, made herself useful by building up the fire and then sweeping and tidying the hearth.

'I see the coronation is to be held on the twelfth of May,' Jacob remarked, mainly to break the oppressive silence.

'That should give people something to look forward to, instead of all the doom and gloom that seems to constitute the news these days,' Julia replied, thinking that until this matter that loomed over them all had been resolved, she for one couldn't think about things like celebrations and street parties.

Fifteen minutes later, to everyone's relief, the doorbell at last sounded and Julia rushed to greet David and, hopefully, his aunt. After taking their coats she ushered them both into the room where three very anxious faces were turned towards them.

'Do sit down, Cousin Elinor. This is Jacob, Cathie and Ella's brother and my future husband,' Julia introduced him.

He'd already risen when the woman had

entered the room but now he extended his hand. 'I am very pleased to meet you, Mrs Fleetwood-Hayes.'

'And I you. Congratulations, Jacob, you're getting a fine girl so mind you take care of her,' she replied, smiling.

David sat beside Cathie, taking her hand and noting the signs of weariness and anxiety in her eyes.

'So, here we all are. I suppose it's been a very fraught twenty-four hours for you all but I actually think I might have an idea ... a plan that might work,' Elinor Fleetwood-Hayes announced. 'Although I have to say it's not been easy and I've had to think it through thoroughly,' she added.

All eyes were fixed on her. 'Tell us, please?' Julia pleaded.

'Right. Ella, you will not have to go home, you will stay but...' She paused and looked seriously at Ella who was white-faced and drawn. 'But your life will change drastically. You are going to have to grow up rather quickly, I'm afraid, and take on some heavy responsibilities. I know you are very young but, well, that can't be helped.'

Ella nodded slowly but didn't speak, wondering just what Mrs Fleetwood-Hayes was going to suggest but thankful that it wasn't that she should go home.

'So how...?' Julia pressed.

'Ella will stay not as "Miss Kinrade" but as *"Mrs Kinrade"*, a young widow whose husband was tragically lost at sea. He was amongst the crew of a Manx fishing boat, a fact anyone can easily check out. She can buy a wedding ring and when the time comes she can register the child's birth with the fictitious name of a father and they will print the word "deceased" beside it. There will be no awkward questions regarding either a marriage or death certificate as she is Manx. I'm sure it's been done many times before and the child will not have to bear the stigma of illegitimacy all its life. It will mean that you can go and start your businesses and there will be no hint of scandal. Of course, Ella, your poor mother will have to be told at some stage – after all, the child will be her grandson or -daughter – but maybe not until after you have had the baby. The pain of your father's death may have lessened a little by then, and perhaps in time she may want to come to see you ... both. I know I would.'

Both Julia and Jacob nodded.

'But how on earth will she manage after she's had to give up work at Lewis's?' Julia asked.

Her cousin now turned to her. 'Julia, you have three bedrooms on this floor and a dining room, a kitchen and a bathroom, as well as this sitting room?'

'Yes,' Julia replied.

'Ella will only need one large room for herself and the child and I suggest you convert the dining room. If you are agreeable, Julia, Ella can then rent out the bedrooms, which should provide her with an income. Not a very large one, of course, but all the same enough to manage on.' She focused again on Ella. 'In fact, Ella, you will effectively become a young but respectable landlady. Your lodgers, if that's what you wish to call them, will of course be able to share the facilities of the kitchen,

397

bathroom and this room with you, and you will be here to keep an eye on everything for Julia and so save her the expense of employing a letting agent.'

At last Julia nodded. 'That would be useful and I can see that it could work, but what about the existing tenants?'

'What about them?' her cousin demanded.

'They know that Ella already lives here.'

'So? Does that really matter? They are, you've remarked in the past, quiet people who keep themselves to themselves. I can't see them gossiping to all and sundry about Ella.'

'But I'm going to have to explain that Ella is staying when I inform them that both Cathie and I are leaving,' Julia persisted.

'Tell them as little as possible,' Mrs Fleetwood-Hayes advised. 'But make sure they know that after you've gone it will be Ella who will be collecting their rents on your behalf and that arrangements will be made for her to forward them on to you.' She paused. 'So, what do you all think?'

'I think it could work,' Julia replied slowly.

'But how do you feel about using the tragic circumstances of your father's death like this? It's the one thing I was most concerned about,' Elinor Fleetwood-Hayes asked of both Jacob and Cathie.

'I think that at least perhaps something ... useful could come from it,' Jacob replied.

'And I'm sure Da wouldn't mind. It's better than having Mam suffer the humiliation and disgrace,' Cathie added, feeling very relieved. At last her headache had started to lift.

'As Julia and Jacob are going to take a loss financially from the rent of these rooms, I think it only fair that I help out too,' David said firmly.

'David, you will already be helping to support the family by setting up a business on the island,' Jacob reminded him. 'I think that's enough.'

David gave him a wry smile. 'We'll discuss it later.'

'Then it all depends on you, Ella. Are you going to be mature and responsible enough to carry it off?' Mrs Fleetwood-Hayes asked.

Ella nodded. 'I think so.'

'Then I suggest that you make some tea, Julia, while I have a quiet talk to Ella and you can all discuss your future plans. We'll go into the dining room. Come along, Ella,' she instructed, getting to her feet.

She and Ella sat themselves at one end of the dining table. Elinor couldn't help feeling very sorry for the forlorn young girl whose hopes and dreams for her future had been crushed by her own foolish actions. She considered her words carefully. 'So, Ella, are you quite willing to go along with all this? I know it isn't how you envisaged your future and you're going to have to make sacrifices, but we all of us have to in life. I realise that it will be hard for you to give up a job you enjoy, the pleasures of going out and socialising and of having money to spend on yourself, but it can't be helped. Now you can no longer think solely of yourself and what you wish to do. You're responsible for another life – your child's – and you will be bringing it up on your own. At times it will be hard and worrying, but at least he or she will not have to carry the shame of being born out of wedlock. It's a stigma that blights lives, my dear, believe me.'

As Ella listened closely, the fear, anxiety and despair, which had been her constant companions for days, began to drain away. She *had* only been thinking of herself – her enjoyment of life, her future, her shame – but Mrs Fleetwood-Hayes's words reminded her that she had someone more important to worry about now: her baby. She felt creeping through her a sense of wonder that she was carrying a new life. And it was a precious one. Instinctively she placed a hand on her stomach. She would put Charlie Banks out of her mind completely; she was well shot of him. This was *her* child and she would love it and care for it to the best of her ability. She had often helped and played with Meggie and Hal when she'd been younger, so she had some experience of babies and toddlers; she'd cope.

'I can only say thank you for your help. I feel so much better and now it's actually begun to sink in that ... that I'll be a mother. I will truly try to behave like one – a good one.'

'You might find that very hard, Ella. You will have to spend long hours here in this house with little or no company of people your own age. And you will have to learn to manage on what income you have,' David's aunt reminded her gently.

'I know but I'll do it. Mam taught us girls how to be thrifty and how to run a household. And I won't mind being at home all day. I'll have my baby to care for and my lodgers will be here in the evenings,' she replied. Yes, her life would change but she'd manage. She was already beginning to think of herself as 'Mrs Kinrade' – mother, widow and landlady – and it was all thanks to this woman. And maybe, as Mrs Fleetwood-Hayes had mentioned, her mam might want to come across to see her and her grandchild some time in the future. That helped too.

The older woman nodded. 'I think you're being very sensible, Ella, and of course you realise that you can always rely on me for help and advice, should you need it.'

'That's very kind of you, Mrs Fleetwood-Hayes,' Ella replied, her gratitude evident in her tone.

Elinor smiled at her. 'You know both you and Cathie are going to have to get used to calling me "Aunt Elinor" as David does.'

Ella managed to smile back, albeit a little wryly. 'I don't know whether I could get used to that.'

Elinor got to her feet. 'Come along, Ella, Julia should have that tea ready by now and I have to say it's much warmer in the sitting room than it is in here. We'll have to do something to remedy that before you move into this room.'

Cathie saw instantly that Ella looked far better, less pale, drawn and worried, and she felt re-lieved. Obviously whatever David's aunt had said had had the desired effect on her sister.

'Are you feeling better now?' she asked as she handed Ella a cup of tea.

Ella nodded, sipping the brew.

'She's quite happy now about how she'll face the future,' Elinor answered for her.

'Despite Jacob's protests, I've decided that I will make her an allowance for ... extras,' David informed her. He turned to Ella. 'After all, before all this, I envisaged you would be working for us and therefore we would have been paying you a wage. Will you be happy with that, Ella?'

'I'd be more than happy, David, thank you,' Ella replied.

Elinor Fleetwood-Hayes smiled at them all. 'Then I think everything will work out satisfactorily for everyone. And I will expect invitations to both weddings and to the grand opening of Kendal's department store. The Captain might even be home and we could bring you something "exotic" in case you want to open a menagerie in it, David – à la Lewis's,' she added.

'Oh, I don't think so, Aunt!' David replied, smiling, and for the first time since the loss of the *Girl Violet* everyone laughed.

Epilogue

On a very warm and sunny May afternoon, the day before the Coronation, David, Cathie and Julia boarded the ferry *Mona's Isle* at the Landing Stage. The city was bedecked with flags and streamers as people got ready for the celebrations next day and even the ferry was sporting red, white and blue bunting.

'It really is a shame to miss it all,' David remarked as he helped Cathie aboard.

'Oh, there's bound to be celebrations on the island too,' Cathie reminded him as they made their way through the main saloon towards the stairs which led down to the first-class lounge and dining room. He'd insisted that they travelled in style; it wouldn't do for the proprietors of Ramsey's first department store and a 'superior' guest house to arrive in any other way, he'd said laughingly.

'Not that we're going to have much time to be indulging in any celebrations,' Cathie reminded Julia. Jacob had already viewed two houses which he thought suitable but obviously wanted Julia to see them too and then agree on the one they would rent. They had decided to rent first to see how the business went and then hopefully in time they'd purchase the property. Jacob had also learned that the Saddle Building, in a prime position at the bottom of Parliament Street facing the old courthouse, was to become vacant and thought it would be the perfect premises for David.

'Well, I think it is all really exciting.' Julia laughed. She was looking forward to seeing Jacob again for she'd missed him so much.

'And Ella was quite looking forward to the celebrations too,' Cathie said happily. Her sister had left Lewis's before her pregnancy became obvious and seemed content that her first lodger would be moving in next week. Ella had indeed matured and had confided that as she would now be shopping locally there'd be little chance of her bumping into any of her former work colleagues, many of whom lived in different parts of the city anyway. She now wore a wedding ring and referred to herself as 'Mrs Kinrade' and was far more self-confident. Both the Hardcastles and the Butlers seemed to have taken the news that Ella would be replacing Julia as their landlady very well. When Mr Hardcastle had encountered Ella in the hall he'd gone so far as to greet her with a smile and a wink and had said that he for one was quite happy to have such an attractive young 'widow' as his landlady. Ella had been relieved and had whole-heartedly joined in helping to organise the preparations for the street party, which occasion would see Everton Valley closed off to traffic. Cathie felt much happier now that her sister seemed to have settled down and was also thankful that 'Aunt Elinor', as she must now call Mrs Fleetwood-Hayes, had promised that when Ella's time was near she would keep an eye on her to make sure everything went as smoothly as possible.

'Oh, this is all very elegant and comfortable,' Julia remarked, looking around as she settled herself into an upholstered armchair.

'And I have booked a table for us in the restaurant,' David informed her.

Cathie laughed. 'It's a good job the weather is so calm otherwise I doubt we'd feel like eating at all.' She became serious. 'There is one thing I have made up my mind to do when we get home and that's to go and see Violet Christian. I'll never forget that it was due to her kindness that I now have ... everything I ever wished for and more.'

'Then I think I should go with you, Cathie, to add my thanks,' David said.

Cathie smiled at him. 'We could benefit from her custom and that of her friends in the department store too.' She delved into her handbag and brought out two folded one-pound notes, now rather creased and grubby. 'She sent me these for an "emergency" and I kept them. I like to think they brought me luck but now I'll return them.' She placed her hand gently over David's. 'I have all the "luck" I need now.'

Julia smiled at them both, thinking that in a few hours they would all be together again. They had decided to have a double wedding at the end of July to give them time to organise the occasion and find a larger house. She, Cathie and David would stay with Mrs Crowe initially and Lizzie, with Meggie and Hal, would move into the new house with them after the wedding. Jack and Nancy were happy to take over the cottage in Collins Lane for they'd been living with Nancy's parents since they'd got married. Now they would have a place of their own and Jack had agreed to accept a job working for David for, like Jacob, he had no desire to return to fishing.

'The very first time I made the crossing to Liverpool I came down here and looked through the doors into the dining room,' Cathie informed David. 'I'd never seen anything as ... grand before. I never thought that one day I'd be travelling home in such style.'

He smiled at her. 'You're happy to be going home, aren't you?'

She nodded. 'Yes. I once told Nora Gelling that no matter how far we go, Ramsey and the island would always be home.'

'Home is where the heart is, Cathie. I know it is for me. My heart is with Jacob,' Julia said quietly.

'And me too; my heart will always be with you, Cathie,' David added before the mood and the quietness of the lounge was shattered by the three blasts of the ferry's steam whistle as the *Mona's Isle* pulled away from the Landing Stage and set out for the tiny island in the middle of the Irish Sea that would be home to them all.

The publishers hope that this book has given you enjoyable reading. Large Print Books are especially designed to be as easy to see and hold as possible. If you wish a complete list of our books please ask at your local library or write directly to:

Magna Large Print Books
Magna House, Long Preston,
Skipton, North Yorkshire.
BD23 4ND

This Large Print Book for the partially sighted, who cannot read normal print, is published under the auspices of

THE ULVERSCROFT FOUNDATION